FINDING
EDWARD

FINDING
EDWARD

a novel by

SHEILA MURRAY

Cormorant Books

We acknowledge financial support for our publishing activities:
the Government of Canada, through the Canada Book Fund and The Canada
Council for the Arts; the Government of Ontario, through the Ontario Arts Council,
Ontario Creates, and the Ontario Book Publishing Tax Credit. We acknowledge
additional funding provided by the Government of Ontario and the Ontario
Arts Council to address the adverse effects of the novel coronavirus pandemic.

Please see the Permissions page at the end of this book for information on
copyrighted material that has been reproduced, with permission, in this volume.

LIBRARY AND ARCHIVES CANADA CATALOGUING IN PUBLICATION

Title: Finding Edward / a novel by Sheila Murray.
Names: Murray, Sheila (Documentary filmmaker), author.
Identifiers: Canadiana (print) 20220207496 | Canadiana (ebook) 20220207526 |
ISBN 9781770866263 (softcover) | ISBN 9781770866270 (HTML)
Classification: LCC PS8626.U77825 F56 2022 | DDC C813/.6–dc23

United States Library of Congress Control Number: 2021938489

Cover photo and design: Angel Guerra, Archetype
Interior design: Tannice Goddard, tannicegdesigns.ca
Printer: Houghton Boston

Printed using paper from a responsible and sustainable resource,
including a mix of virgin fibres and recycled materials.
Printed and bound in Canada.

CORMORANT BOOKS INC.
260 SPADINA AVENUE, SUITE 502, TORONTO, ON M5T 2E4
www.cormorantbooks.com

For Joshua, Peter and Somae.

ONE

❧

THE NIGHT HIS MOTHER DIED, she said, "I'm glad you come to me early this evening, darlin'. You're a good boy, Cyril." He said nothing. Didn't remind her he often left his friends to come home early, that he always carried the family cellphone so he could be reached if needed. His mother's illness was unpredictable. Although the attacks were infrequent, the babies, his brother and sister, were too small to help her. It had been two years already since the babies' father died, and Cyril's father had been gone for so long he was almost forgotten. There was no one.

Her breathing woke him. The constricted suck of breath she'd made before. Worse this time. He sat beside her and fanned the hot air hanging heavy and moist over her head. His sister cried into her pillow, and his baby brother stroked her hair in imitation of Cyril with their mommy. After fifteen minutes, Cyril sent his brother to fetch a neighbour with a car to take them to the hospital. He made himself watch the fear in his mother's eyes as, desperate, she stared into his. He felt himself freeze in the August heat. The hospital was nearly an hour away.

His mother's breathing lasted for less than twenty minutes. It was noisiest just as the road turned toward Brown's Town. Then it stopped. Right at the silk cotton tree, with its enormous crown and ancient tendrils of strangling ficus vine dropping fifty feet from its branches. Just as the sky lightened with another morning. Their neighbour stopped the car. "For respect," he said. "I'll leave you with her for a little while."

THE FUNERAL WAS NOISY WITH tears and singing. The pastor said the right things because he'd known Cyril's mother for all of her forty-one years. She'd gone to that church just about every Sunday of her life. The wake lasted until four in the morning. Even the old ladies stayed with it. His mother was beautiful in a pink coffin with satin and lace for her pillow. Cyril felt singularly alone, his grief stained by anger at the tragedy of his mother's death and the dollar difference between those Jamaicans who could afford their medicines and those who could not. The ground he stood on had become unsteady, saturated with sadness.

It was a very different funeral from the formal Anglican observance that had served his mother's employer — whose house she'd cleaned for ten years — his adopted grandpa, Nelson. That had been four years earlier. Cyril, in a borrowed black suit, had sat rigid on a wooden pew, immersed in heartbreak and loss. Afterward, at the reception, he'd been unable to speak when Nelson's friends asked him how he'd manage without Nelson's tutorship, his mentorship. Cyril called it love.

But as his mother rested in the splendour she'd saved a lifetime for, her friends squeezed the speech from him, plied him with love and faith, gave him their very best counsel come straight from Jesus. They held up their church-sister's son, took their share of his pain.

After the funeral, the babies went to live with his mother's sister in Philadelphia. Families were expandable. Sisters, grand-mothers, aunties, and uncles looked after kids whose parents spent years working at seasonal jobs abroad, coming home in the winter. Or, having left for good, produced more family that expanded around the globe. Jamaicans were travellers. Many of the educated poured into the brain drain of doctors and lawyers and engineers who travelled to English-speaking countries, mak-ing new lives, creating middle-class English and American and Canadian children who would visit their extended families back in Jamaica for Christmas holidays at the beach and stay in homes where hibiscus bushes were strung with tinsel and holiday poin-settia grew vigorous and tall in people's gardens.

Cyril's immediate family was tiny: his mother's sister, Vi, was his only real aunt. But there were many cousins whose blood relationships were muddled and whose catch-all titles were uncle or aunty. Canada-Uncle Junior was one of these.

"Two more small ones won't make much difference," said his Aunty Vi as she embraced Keesha and Daren. "But, Cyril, you must go to Junior in Canada. When your mommy was still with us, she wanted you close. But here is not your future. Foreign's where you're going to find it."

The goodbyes and promises followed. Small gifts and requests. The excited jostle of neighbours and the tears of his brother and sister. His college friends, the boys, pledged to meet up when they finished their studies. Cyril had become the enviable one whose life was suddenly thrown wide open, though his friends' parents watched with some concern.

He'd paid the bills, the electricity and the water and the costs left over from the funeral, after the executor lawyer had released Nelson's legacy, intended for Cyril's graduation from college. The lawyer had said the money could come to him now, given the circumstances. Cyril gathered the courage to leave his home and the people there who made up his family. He did it immersed in a grief that made him compliant with other people's wishes.

Cyril left home because his mother was gone and his father had only ever been absent. He left because he had so badly failed to keep his mother safe. Had not challenged the illusory pride that had stopped her from asking other good folk for help. The cost of a prescription was a small thing beside the value of her life. She'd thought her God would keep her safe. Cyril had failed to understand the peril she'd brought upon her herself. He had neglected to protect his mother even though he'd been aware of her naïve belief.

Because other people said he should, Cyril used a part of Nelson's gift to buy an airplane ticket. He took two suitcases from the giveaways that Nelson's family had provided – one small, one large. He bought black shoes and black socks for Foreign, and a wallet to safeguard the precious plastic cards that would prove to the world that he was who he claimed to be. A new dark-blue passport contained the coveted Canadian visa, granted because of Junior's assurance to Canada that Cyril would not become a burden.

His mother's friend drove him to the airport. In addition to his two suitcases, Cyril had a small carry-on bag with Nelson's address book inside. He wore a dark-blue blazer that had belonged to Nelson. It was a little too big; he walked with a stiff, straight back so his shoulders filled it. He forced a confident stride as he approached the check-in desk.

"How long are you going to be away?"

His mouth was sticky and dry, and he licked at his lips to wet them. "At least ..." He sucked moisture to his tongue. "It will be at least a year," he said, watching the clerk's face to see if the open-ended nature of his travel shocked her as it did him. She smiled and handed him back his passport. His excitement overcame his trepidation. He was to be travelling as Nelson's friends did. As his father had. Easy as the drive from Kingston to Negril. He'd have real wings to fly across the sea.

His mother's friend watched him as he walked through the glass doors where only passengers were allowed. "Walk good," she called. "Send us an email when you get there." When Cyril turned to look back, stopped in a long line to pass through security, she'd already gone.

Cyril had never left his country before, had never been on a plane. When the engines roared and the huge thing began to hurtle down the runway, the old lady strapped in the seat beside him cried, "Jesus is taking the wheels," and Cyril's thrill spilled into laughter. He was flying into his future.

Face to the window, he saw below him the green miles of his mountains and the extraordinary turquoise sparkle of his sea, the big hotels of Montego Bay that were so quickly far away, distant ships on the water, and then, incredibly, the way clouds looked from the inside and then from high above.

When the captain announced they were thirty thousand feet above the ground, Cyril saw his mother moving through the brilliant blue sky: her thin and faded pink cotton nightgown, hairnet a cap on her head, knees curled in toward her chest, not quite fetal but deep asleep and unaware of her rush through the heavens. Her vulnerability startled him. He wiped his fingers over his eyes to push back tears. He was not surprised to see her there. He'd been waiting for her. "You are able to see through the creases in the universe," Nelson had once said. "You are four-eyed, but I promise you, Cyril, you are not destined to become an Obeah Man. Your ability is your own personal blessing, not for exploitation." His sight arrived without invitation and heightened his vision with a gauzy, bright light that changed what he saw. How he saw. When it happened, he stilled his mind and allowed himself to see what was revealed. It was his mother's gift; she'd had second sight too. "Don't tell your teachers, Cyril," she'd warned him. "It will trouble them. I have seen the spirits of the living and the dead all my life, and they are my friends." But the spirits hadn't warned him of the things that mattered most: the loss of Grandpa Nelson and then his mother. He had never missed his father, but he missed his mother in every step of each day.

"How about you, sir?" The woman's voice pulled his attention from the window. "What would you like to drink?" He didn't know. But on seeing a drink can he recognized near the front of her trolley, he said, "I'll have a Coke, please." He felt a surge of anxiety because he had never before been served by a white woman and he didn't know how much a drink would cost up here in the sky. All of the serving people were white. But there were lots of Black passengers, Cyril reminded himself. All being served by the same people. He was flying on an Air Canada airplane to Toronto. A place where most of the people would be white. All he had to do was figure out how white people in a white country behaved and comport himself appropriately.

"Pretzels or cookie?"

"Cookie, please." He lowered his tray as the man in the seat on the aisle had done. The old lady fiddled with hers, and he helped. The trays anchored the both of them safely to their seats, along with their seatbelts. The waitress leaned across the man in the aisle seat with Cyril's Coke. The lady, who had first refused a drink, now followed Cyril's lead, understanding that it was included in the enormous price of the ticket. He smiled at her, and she nodded back. *Could be my granny,* he thought, but his adopted Grandpa Nelson had been much younger than she when he died.

Nelson was gone, and all of the kindness and patience that he'd given to Cyril was lost with him. But Cyril knew what Nelson expected of him now. To be a successful person in all the ways that mattered, which meant that Cyril should be kind in turn to the people he was going to meet, who would make up his new life.

"Where you going, baby?" asked the old lady in a thin, respectful voice that made him think of church.

"To Toronto like you."

"I know that, darlin', but why you going? I'm going to my daughter. She lives in Scarborough. You know it?"

"No."

"I have been a house cleaner all my life, but now I'm going to be a grandmother living in Canada with my grandbabies. I prayed for this a long time."

"I had an adopted Grandpa Nelson. My mom cleaned his house, but he looked after me."

"That's not right," she said, voice suddenly sharp. "An employer is not your child's keeper."

"I didn't live with him. But I spent a lot of time there from six years old, like with a grandpa. He was a university professor. He taught me things."

"White man or Black man?"

"Black man."

"What tings he teach you?"

"Fast cars. Nature and wild things. Magic stories. Poetry. Philosophy. Then grown-up things."

"Ladies?"

"No."

Cyril laughed as she kissed her teeth.

"*Chupse!* Young men should know about ladies. Learn it in school. How old are you?"

"Twenty. My mommy taught me how to behave with women."

"I can see that," said the old lady.

Nelson had a cancer that had grown, insidious, for a very long time. With its diagnosis, he'd finally learned the source of the pain in his shoulder and the exhaustion that had begun to haunt him. He was gone inside a month. Cyril was with him in the last days, as much as Nelson's family allowed. The drugs captured Nelson's mind almost immediately, and he rarely knew who Cyril was. He'd died with Cyril's school fees paid for the current term. A small legacy was earmarked for university fees, contingent upon Cyril's graduation from Brown's Town Community College, where Cyril had been studying for only four months. With Nelson's passing, Cyril's mother had lost her reliable and generous client, and Cyril had to find work. Nam's Hardware, mirroring Nelson's generosity, increased Cyril's hours by hiring him as part-time counter help. Since then, his progress at college had been protracted – one course at a time – and he'd fallen behind.

"They're both passed over now," he told the old lady, who sucked loudly at her Coke through her straw.

Cyril longed for the company of spirits to travel with him. He turned back to the window. His mother and Nelson were gone, along with the sea and the world below, hidden by a blanket of cloud.

The plane began to shake and jolt like an old car on a bad road, turning Cyril's excitement into a churn of apprehension. Would the plane fall from the sky? Blow up in a mighty ball of fire?

When the seatbelt signs dinged on and they announced everyone should return to their seats, his anxiety fixed on the nausea that pressed at the back of his throat. He assured himself that there was a sick bag in his seat pocket, though his embarrassment would be unbearable. He squeezed his eyes closed and pretended that he was in a car on the bumpy road to Sturge Town.

TWO

THE ROAD TO STURGE TOWN was so narrow that when two cars met, one of them had to find a place to pull to the side, a patch of ground where bush was cleared to make a path through the hedgerow that led to a gate or to a field of yams or cabbages. It was a road used mostly by farmers and mules or foraging goats, though a few of the people who lived in the big houses rode in dignity over the potholes in four-wheel drives. Taxis came from as far away as Ocho Rios, carrying people from hospital visits or on urgent family matters. On market days, taxis travelled from Brown's Town, packed with people and bulging bags. At the worst potholes, the passengers had to get out and walk, unfolding and untangling limbs and grumbling because the difficulties of the day weren't over. The children, who'd been squeezed into the smallest corners, celebrated their liberation by running ahead and waiting for the taxi. No matter where they came from or to whom they belonged, the cars all travelled slowly.

Year-round, the sun dropped below the western horizon at about the same time of day. Night came at six o'clock, but after lunch, people greeted each other with, "Good evening." The hours were too short to talk about an afternoon. Birds rushed to complete their business before the swift close of the Caribbean day.

On Saturday evenings, Cyril walked the hour and a half to Brown's Town from Sturge Town. It was easy on nights when the moon came up big and bright and lit the road with the conviction of sunshine. Harder when the sky turned black and took everything along with it, hiding the bush that lined the way, the potholes, the bends in the road. The dark took the tall trees that were his landmarks, the way he measured how far he'd come, how far yet to go.

Cyril had taught himself to find his way by holding on to the night. With eyes closed, he walked in the centre, where the road held fewer obstacles, feet feeling for stones and craters under the thick soles of his shoes. He closed his eyes to the black night so that a banana leaf suddenly twisting tall in the breeze would not frighten him with the shape it made, like a tall person hiding behind the bush. If his eyes were open, they'd be caught by a scud of cloud less dark than the night behind it, and he, seeing movement in a brush of light, might imagine that something watched him from the top of the hill because the dark took with it any context to the landscape. If he opened his eyes, he was grabbed by childhood terrors, saw bad men and duppies in shadows. So, with eyes closed, he'd feel his way step by step, walking not at all slowly; if his shoulder or elbow or thigh brushed the shrub and branches at the side of the road, he'd take a few steps back toward the centre and keep on walking in the night thick with the racket of tree frogs and cicadas.

On Saturday nights, he met his friends at Raymond's, a big, white, burglar-barred house high over Brown's Town. Cyril's friends were unlike him, neither church people nor market people. They were younger, though certainly more sophisticated. It had taken Cyril longer to get through college. There'd been times when he hadn't gone at all. Not because he didn't want to but because he was needed at home to care for the babies or had to work at Nam's Hardware. In college, they were encouraged to plan for a life that did not include poverty for themselves or for Jamaica's future generations.

RAYMOND HAD A COMPUTER THAT made the world seem so small, so accessible, with a million jobs, easy credit, and cheap airfares. The boys drank Red Stripe or soda, talked travel and politics, and wondered where they'd see each other in five years. Cyril walked back through the town on those nights full of rice 'n' peas and inspiration. Past the men slamming dominoes, shouting their wins or keening their losses. Past the market people gathered on corners, laughing and talking or sitting back sleepy at the end of the night. There was always music from a flatbed of speakers at the foot of the market building and from the jukeboxes and stereos in the jerk and curry restaurants. There were clubs on Top Road with girls and dancing, but he and his friends didn't go there.

The walk home was easy, Cyril's energy charged with his friends' enthusiasms. Each of them was different. Cyril and Raymond were in pre-tertiary studies with more choices to come, and he could see possibilities. He wanted to finish his studies in Kingston.

"The University of the West Indies?" his mother asked. "Where we going to find the money?"

"I've got the money coming from Grandpa Nelson when I graduate from college. And I'll get one of the UWI scholarships, Mommy," he said. "Don't worry about me."

The little ones listened to Cyril. They called him CeeCee and flew to him when he came home from school. From the front door of the little house, they bolted down the four concrete steps, ran past the royal palm, the avocado pear, the ackee, and raced the two hundred feet to the road until they slammed to a stop at his legs, leaving the house small behind them with its tin roof and fringe of gingerbread trim under the eaves.

The house had two rooms. One for living, which included the kitchen. One for sleeping. He'd built himself some privacy at the back. Moved the potted plants to the front porch, walled in the back porch with some corrugated aluminum, and put his bed there along with a small table. They had a telephone. Digicel. It had made a huge difference to their lives. Soon after starting college, Cyril had won the coveted three-hours-a-week job in the college library. That, in addition to his hours at Nam's Hardware, made for enough extra money to top up the phone.

GRANDPA NELSON HAD PAID FOR the family's medical prescriptions. After he passed, Cyril's mother made sure the children saw the doctor when they were sick, but she stopped seeing him herself when the babies' father died. She couldn't afford the medications he prescribed. She and her church ladies put their faith in the healing power of pure homemade coconut oil. That and prayer, she said, would keep her safe.

Her favourite place at home was in the corner of the room on what they called the comfy chair, though the springs were loose. But it looked good, with its embroidered antimacassar and armrests that she'd tacked to the upholstery. She'd pull the stitches in order to free them for washing at Christmas and Easter. Cyril had taught the little kids to call those the "Jesus Holidays."

His mother balked sometimes at his irreverence, but she loved his commitment to her family. She loved his calm, his tidiness, his quiet sense of fun. She watched him from her chair as though she breathed him in and out. The children played on the floor. He worked at the table. She, the luminary of her church-ladies needlework circle, made pretty doilies with crochet needles. When she was too tired, she rested with her head back and mouth half-open.

AFTER HIS MOTHER DIED AND before the house was emptied, Cyril looked for evidence of himself among the things she'd kept in her dresser. A foot or so above it, he'd created a square display of the doilies she made: cartwheels and starbursts, daisies in yellows and pinks, brilliant blooms of red hibiscus, all pinned tight to the wooden wall with thumbtacks. The only other picture in the house was of a young Jesus gazing wistfully toward heaven. In the bottom drawer of his mother's dresser were exercise books filled with his own tidy handwriting along with a handful of unframed certificates and prizes for spelling and composition. His birth certificate was there too, along with those of his brother and sister. The largest of the three wooden boxes on top of her dresser held the sailor photograph of his father, their wedding picture, and two large buttons. Things he had once told his mother he didn't want to see again.

The air in the house was heavy and hot. Cyril closed the drawers and put the important things into a big envelope, then walked outside into a warm night redolent with tropical spice, alive with the clamour of cicadas and tree frogs. He sat on the fallen trunk of an old guava tree and opened his hand. In his palm were his father's two big, white buttons decorated with a black ship's anchor. He was stopped by indecision. His first inclination was to throw them from the doorstep, hard. Out behind the croton and into the bush beyond where only goats ventured. But he couldn't do it. He wanted to bury them in the red earth at his feet, twist them deep into the ground with the heel of his shoe, but his hand maintained its cradle, fingers curved upward, keeping the buttons safe. A familiar brightness flowed in from the dark, blurred his sight and muffled his ears to the garden sounds. He strained to hear through a taut skein of air. He saw his father, a man he'd no recollection of at all, sitting in a place he'd never seen that was reminiscent of images from television and Christmas cards. His father sat in what must be a pub in a cold land where inside was hot — noisy with men and a television set up high on the wall and a football game turned to full volume. All of the men sat facing it, talked at it and to each other without taking their eyes from the ball that flew back and forth across the pitch as the players chased it hard and fast.

His father had a red face and muted blue eyes. He was thin and pale, and Cyril imagined him as noisy as the rest of them, though his voice was thick and smooth, and his accent, the Northern English sound of it, camouflaged what he was saying; the words were unfamiliar. "She's dead," said Cyril, demanding his father's attention. "She dead two weeks now. Mi on mi own." His father stopped talking and looked down into his beer. Cyril saw the thin fingers around the glass, the big watch hanging loose on his wrist, his mouth closed and tight. Then the television screamed, "He scores!" The men erupted into cheers and shouts, his father with them, and the vision was gone.

Cyril was not going to England where his father lived. "You might have cousins there, baby," his aunt had said, "but how you going to find them?" Instead, he was going to Canada where the toys and cookies and cool clothes came from. For a number of years, his Canada-Uncle Junior had sent a shipping barrel of gifts to his sister's house next door to Cyril's. When their neighbours brought the barrel home, bouncing it into their yard on the back of a truck, there had always been something for Cyril, sent from Junior's wife. Until he got too big for toys – and she left Junior for a man she said was her best friend. Cyril had always hoped for books, but they never came.

He did have lots of books, of course, all of which came from Grandpa Nelson. In the bedroom that Cyril had built into the porch at the back of the house, there were two shelves full of them. Following an afternoon of lessons with Grandpa Nelson, Cyril would leave with a book in a black plastic scandal bag, along with a jar of guava jam or a package of cream cheese and crackers for the babies. His mother said, "God shares his blessings." Cyril never did answer, but always thought, *Not God. These bounties are Grandpa's.*

Cyril had loved Nelson, and, in turn, Nelson had loved the boy who listened to him with such avidity, who rewarded his mentorship by learning his lessons so well. In Nelson, Cyril had found a longed-for surrogate father who encouraged his uncommon nature and gave him the confidence to be different from the other boys. Nelson had been a good daddy. Cyril need never miss his factual, gone-forever English father.

What Cyril knew about Nelson Johnson was that he'd been born in Jamaica but lived many of his sixty-nine years outside of the country. He'd studied in England and become a senior lecturer in London, where he taught at University College for nearly twenty years. When the job offer came from the University of the West Indies, he took it because he'd been teaching a Third World Studies class for six of those years and wanted to "put my money where my mouth is." He had no children, though there had been two wives. Nelson Johnson made bad choices when it came to women. By the time he met Cyril, he'd been single for more than fourteen years.

Cyril's mother started working for Mr. Nelson Johnson when Cyril was six. Cyril had called him Mr. Johnson for a number of weeks until Mr. Johnson said for Cyril's mother to leave the boy in his care for two days while she went to Kingston for a funeral. She'd been desperate, her usual caregivers all away to the same wake and their children already filling the rooms and beds in that community. Mr. Johnson said, "Leave him with me. We good friends already, yes, Cyril?" And Cyril nodded because, while Cyril's mother cleaned, the two of them talked about many things. Lizards and snails and duppies. John Crow's occupation of scavenging carcasses. The universe. And the speed of a car versus that of the brightly painted market handcarts that the young men rode recklessly down the sloping roads in town. Mr. Johnson read him stories from books filled with colourful drawings and marvellous characters who had great adventures and learned their lessons well.

By the time Cyril's mother came back from Kingston, Mr. Johnson had become Grandpa Nelson and would remain so. Nelson was so much better than his regular teachers; the time spent in his living room beat being at school any day, and not just because Cyril was the only student.

"Let us sit up straight at our desks."

"Yes, Grandpa Nelson," and he'd square his books and line up his pens. Stiffen his back.

"Are you ready to apply yourself to some good work today, Cyril?"

"Yes, Grandpa."

"What have you studied in preparation?"

"I have my running writing in these two pages." Proud as punch because the writing looked good and the page was still crisp and clean, not smudged at all. But especially because the words he'd written were good, strong words. Nelson had him copy lines from a poetry anthology. These were the words, he told Cyril, that his university students learned.

> Art thou pale for weariness
> Of climbing heaven and gazing on the earth,
> Wandering companionless
> Among the stars that have a different birth,
> And ever changing, like a joyless eye
> That finds no object worth its constancy?

Cyril was eight when he first copied the words. When he was nine, they visited the poem again. And every year after that until Cyril knew that poem, and others, as well as he knew his way home from Grandpa Nelson's. Each year, he understood the poems better and cherished them more. Since his first encounter with "The Moon," he'd seen her always as the best duppy ever. A lonely ghost up in the sky.

They'd begun with the poets and their poetry, people and their callings. Moved on to books, how words looked on paper and the shape of type. Capital letters. White space on a page. Margins and titles. What an anthology represented, and why they chose to use the *Oxford Book of English Verse*. The children teased him: "Sissy Cyril. Teacher's pet. Books in his bag. Brain too big for his head."

For them, Cyril's lighter skin, the everlasting evidence of his absent father, underscored his difference.

"Never mind them," said Nelson. "They are not on your path.

What you learn makes you strong and happy. Tell them that their teasing doesn't hurt you."

And it didn't hurt, didn't matter. Cyril loved the time he spent with Grandpa Nelson and the lessons he learned in the big living room with fresh flowers in a bowl, books and magazines on all the tables. Cyril sat in his primary school classroom and listened to the teacher recite her lessons and, despite his boredom, applied Nelson's advice: "Where does your mind take you when she talks? Write it down. If she inspires a thought, make a note. There is always something to learn, Cyril."

When the children teased, Cyril learned to say, "I do what I choose, and I choose to learn." The children mimicked him, their tongues making the shapes of plums in their mouths. Playing with the words and the unfamiliar English accent that shaped the expressions he learned from Nelson – "I Dooo Wot I Choooz" – and dancing around him on the red dirt road to his house on top of the hill. They'd stopped teasing by the time he reached ten because Cyril could always be counted on to solve things. He knew how to help work backward out of a problem and pass the test. Could charm a parent. Knew the names of all the birds. He'd been different for so long that they came around to accepting him; his rarely ruffled calm, his apparent independence. The funny way he talked. He spoke English as easily as patois and was unembarrassed. By the time he was eleven, they called him "Teacher Cyril" and relied on his help with their homework.

Nelson told his friends that he encouraged and tutored a bright and determined boy who was older than his years. Not a brilliant boy, but one whose curiosity, whose spirit of inquiry, would lead him to a good life. Who loved words even though his mother read only the Bible and had never been further than Kingston, just sixty miles away on the other side of the island.

A simple, good woman who was in awe of her son. Nelson told his friends that he'd look after Cyril and make sure that he got in to university and out of poverty. When Cyril was twelve, Nelson got him a place at York Castle, the best high school in their parish, high on a hill above Brown's Town. Cyril was rarely bored after that.

Every few weeks, Nelson threw his famous Sunday Afternoon Party. While he mixed up the rum punch, ladies from the Little Queen restaurant cooked curry goat and jerk chicken along with rice 'n' peas, festival breads, callaloo, and plantains. Nelson pulled the furniture from the centre of the living room and pushed the tables to the walls. Cyril's job was to pile and tidy the papers, stack the books so they could be found the next day, pick hibiscus from the garden, and place a single blossom on each of the many small glass saucers that were scattered about the room.

Lunch put everyone in a fine mood. "Fit for conversation," said Nelson. They settled in the living room, where the doors were open to the garden. Cyril pulled a footstool up to the side of the couch and listened as the adults talked politics, crime, and more politics. Then theatre, and a Kingston actor who had embarked on a successful Broadway career. They talked about education because two or three of them were professors at the university.

When Nelson flirted with the women, he was a younger version of himself. His friends said he had a sexy smile, and he definitely used it a lot at his parties. He wore an expensive cologne and would let Cyril have just a drop or two for himself. Cyril served the drinks, another of his jobs. Not on a tray; he wasn't old enough. But he could carry a glass in each hand and learned how to make a little bow as he handed it over, just a quick dip of his shoulders, as Grandpa did. "This young man will be prime minister one day," Nelson said, "then he'll teach the World Bank and the International Monetary Fund some overdue and very necessary lessons." Despite how silly that sounded, and regardless of his own embarrassment, Cyril was always proud to be there.

At fourteen, Cyril was allowed to stay past the conversation and into the reggae. Nelson was smooth on the floor, smiled his straight white teeth at the women who'd begged him up to dance. Cyril liked the way that looked and learned it for himself, to slide the floor like Nelson. He never could quite bring himself to join the dancers, though. He never found the courage.

TWO YEARS BEFORE HIS DIAGNOSIS, Grandpa Nelson had said that he wanted to see the whole of the country one last time before his beloved nineteen-year-old car died. For two summers, he and Cyril criss-crossed the island. Threaded the corkscrew turns into the Blue Mountains and down through the coffee plantations. Across the flatlands on arrow-straight roads through acres of sugar cane and bananas. They saw the manatees at Black River and watched the man-o'-war birds soar the sky above the still lagoons at Alligator Pond. Nelson looked on while Cyril paddled the rocky pools and waterfalls at YS Falls and Dunn's River. They ate tourist food in Montego Bay and roasted yams from roadside BBQs in Hectors River. Walked the white sand beaches in Negril and climbed the rugged coastline at Port Antonio. They drove the narrow, winding road that ran though the dense bush of Cockpit Country and explored the caves along the north coast. The last summer, they drove all the way up to Accompong, the hidden mountain village founded by runaway slaves, the Maroons.

Cyril sat beside his grandpa, thrilled to travel, delighting in Nelson's refusal to meet the traffic around him on its terms.

Cars slid by them with only inches to spare, wailing horns punctuated by shouts from the drivers: "Get off the road, daddy! Park your car! You driving to your funeral?"

"He'll be there before me! Drive like a fool," said Nelson. Cyril drummed his feet on the floor in delighted celebration. Grandpa Nelson was his hero.

TWO SPIRITS WATCHED OVER CYRIL who had lost so much. His mother's veiled his eyes with flowers so that he would always see the natural beauty around him. Nelson's showed him what lay beyond the beauty and pressed him to stay curious, stay fair, and never, ever generalize.

The captain announced that they had started their descent and said the temperature in Toronto would be minus five. Cyril could not imagine how air that cold would feel.

THREE

IN TORONTO, CYRIL FOUND A crowded household near the top of a brick and concrete stack of apartments. Mount Dennis was a name that he'd heard in Jamaica. A destination for lots of people from home. But it was nothing like the television Canada that had informed his imaginings. It was a grey, flat place, holding close to streets as smooth and busy as highways that ran for miles: Jane and Weston, Black Creek and Eglinton. It was November. An early snow had left dark muck in the roadside gutters, and the wind stung tears into his eyes. The snow was a disappointment. He'd expected the Christmas-card kind. The cousin who picked him up at the airport ushered him into the dark lobby of the apartment building and showed him which floor button to push. He'd once been on an elevator, but only to the fifth floor. He didn't tell his cousin that he'd never before been as high as eight.

His Canada-Uncle Junior was a noisy man. "Voice too big for him body," his family teased. A short, loud, bombastic man. There was no real family here for Cyril. Just people who filled the living room with shrieks of laughter or shouts of complaint.

Who hugged him because he'd lost his mommy but couldn't always remember his name. They called themselves the Juniors — related or not. The young ones stopped long enough to check his clothes, his hair, his gear — he had so little — and found him odd, dull, and impoverished. They rushed out to enjoy their lives and left him stranded inside the four walls, his bedding and belongings hidden behind the blue-checked couch where he slept.

Canada-Uncle Junior took longer to deliver his dismissal. "I knew your benefactor," he said, "Nelson Johnson. It's a good thing he did, leaving you the money for school. I did a stint at the University of the West Indies myself. Johnson taught history, I think?"

"Yes, sir. English literature, but European history was always an interest, and he taught that, too, when he was younger."

"You have a similar character, similar speech. His refinements," said Junior, whose amused expression implied that he shared the view of many others who had found Nelson's manner odd, affected.

"Nevertheless," said Junior, "Johnson was a good man, and your mother was an angel. You're welcome to stay until you find your feet." With that he turned, entered his study, and closed the door behind him.

Cyril was on his own. For the very first time. Because even after Nelson died — who had been so much more a father to Cyril than the red-faced man in the wedding photograph his mother had kept hidden in a drawer — despite Cyril's grief and the constant need for money, he had always had his mother. His new life was strange and cold: the first time he left his building to walk on the Canadian sidewalk was an adventure; the second time made him as lonely as he'd ever been.

On his third day in Mount Dennis, Cyril left the apartment ready to explore. He found himself on an endless sidewalk alongside an endless road where the few shops were shuttered and shabby. He got as far as Jane Park Plaza, where the stuff in the stores wasn't so different from home, though there was a lot more of it: five styles of pyjamas, not just one or two. But it was nothing like the shiny glass-and-chrome promise of the airport where he'd landed. He'd thought all of Canada would be like that.

The Juniors laughed and called him "Freshy." That plaza's a shithole, they said. Go to Yorkdale Mall. He didn't dare. The tattered bus map they gave him was an alarming tangle of roads and numbers. He was very afraid of getting lost. Besides, he didn't have money to spare, so he stayed inside. It was quiet during the day when people had gone to work or to school. "Commerce and education," announced Uncle Junior. "That's what we're here for." He ran a busy courier company and spent evenings in front of his computer strategizing his stock market trades.

During the week, Cyril woke before them, unmade his bed, and restored the couch to its public role. He sat reading, steadfast, hugged tight into the shelter of its corner cushions while the Juniors came from their beds or their showers and hurried through the noisy kitchen where the television blared news and weather, traffic and jokes into the morning's beginning. By 8:30 a.m. everyone was gone and silence filled the rooms, settling heavily around him, weighted further by the drab, off-white walls and cold winter light filtered through cloud cover and sheer curtains. A regular run of airplanes skimmed the tops of the apartment towers in front of his on their descent to the airport that had seemed so far away, but which he now thought might be close enough to walk to.

He walked. After the Juniors left in the mornings and again in the evenings, unless all of them were out. One day, from a late start on an unusually mild morning, he headed south, following a downhill drift that was flanked by houses and small apartment buildings. He crossed a busy highway and came to a small patch of beach where Lake Ontario spread out in front of him. To the east was the CN Tower, closer than he'd seen it before but still a good distance off.

Cyril shivered inside the big black wrap of a coat that he'd bought second-hand. He pulled at the toggles, tightening the waist and pulling the lip of the hood down over his forehead. He'd tried the coat on for one of Junior's visitors, who dealt in used clothes and had searched it out for Cyril.

"Looks good, man," Junior's friend had said as Cyril stood in front of him.

"Not too big?" said Cyril, glimpsing his forehead's creased concern as he twisted to see himself in the mirror above the dresser.

"No, no. That's how they are, man. They gotta be large, gotta big job to do." He laughed and poked a finger at the puffy, quilted sleeves. "Also good for if you fall on the ice, got a lot of padding," and he laughed again.

"How do you fall on ice?" Cyril didn't understand.

"Think like climbing from the sea on rock covered in the slippery stuff? You know, when you can't keep your foot from sliding?"

"Yes."

"That's it, Cyril my man, that's slipping on ice. But it's on the sidewalk, where you do your everyday travelling. You won't see it, comes sneaking up to surprise you."

"Okay." Cyril pulled at the zipper, shrugged out of the coat, and put it beside him on a chair.

"I'll look out some boots for you too. With big treads to give you a grip on that ice."

Cyril was grateful for the coat now. And the boots. As he walked back to Windermere, the cold slapped at his face. At the streetcar stop, he put himself in behind the glass to cut the wind.

As he rode home, the lake stayed in his head. He couldn't imagine how big this country Canada must be. On maps, his little Jamaica sat like a peanut in the sea beside Cuba and Haiti and the Dominican. Puny alongside those two islands. And how far was it across Canada to the other side? He hadn't thought of that before, and now it seemed an urgent question. When the bus passed the library at the corner of Weston and Eglinton – where he had passed many times before – it was easy to get off at the next stop and double back. Cyril understood libraries. How the books were shelved. What the librarian was paid to do. It would be the same as home. He had a right to be in this public place and saw straightaway that it was a welcoming one because the people who sat around the big table, reading newspapers and magazines, one of them sleeping, were the close-to-the-bone types he'd seen about in the neighbourhood.

Cyril walked to the shelves as though he belonged and knew what he was looking for. But the Mount Dennis library was enormous, with a massive collection. As he passed Canadian History on his way to the atlases, something urged his attention, and when he looked about it was through a fine, bright film that suggested an importance he could not at first identify. Then he understood that this was what school would be like, that his future would come with books, and surely that was why he was here. It was a premonition, a half-formed glimpse of what could be, where light shone from the white spines of books in a place he hadn't yet seen but was as close as tomorrow or the next day.

Cyril found a world atlas, the biggest he'd ever seen, and sat with it at the nearest table. Canada was awesome. Huge oceans on three sides with the fame-and-fortune promise of the U.S. down below. He ran his finger over the pages and stopped at Lake Ontario, where he had stood just an hour before. He traced the scale of the page with his thumb and forefinger, measured the lake from its Canadian side to its American shore. His peanut country, only 234 kilometres long and 80 kilometres wide, would float inside it — that's how crazy big the lake was. How could a person ever know a place as large as Canada, which he now saw was vast? An impossible challenge. As he registered the size of the country that could hold multitudes of Jamaicas and all of the place names he had never heard before, never seen on television or in movies, all those unknown and unknowable places, he wanted to go home and sleep — which he did, once the Juniors had gone to bed and the living room was dark and empty.

The routine came fast; in the evenings, after dinner, when the Juniors collected in front of the television or absented themselves with computers to the other rooms, Cyril left the building. His regular destinations were, variously, the library, Weston, or a convenience store at an intersection about a mile and a half away. He walked to pump his blood, to move his arms and legs fast. Boots stamped the concrete, breath steamed in clouds from his mouth — a phenomenon he continued to find highly novel. He covered his head with a toque like the few other people he passed. Black faces framed by wool scarves or fur and hats and hoods. It was not just Jamaicans who lived here but English- or French-speaking West Africans and Spanish-speaking Blacks from South America. Cyril had thought that Canada would be mostly white.

His sight had been lost again since that glimpse in the library.

He wanted his mother and Nelson close and to see his brother and sister. But his gift was sucked up and swallowed into the white noise that saturated the apartment. The hiss and hum of the refrigerator and the central heating. The steady buzz of traffic outside and the hundred urban sounds that cluttered the landscape. A single new, unidentifiable sound had caught his attention early on. He'd asked the Juniors what it was: A train whistle! Don't you know that? He hadn't. He had never before heard a train, which seemed a haunting, romantic sound.

After dinner, when he'd made his way through a big stack of dishes, he dressed for cold and took his time looping through the neighbourhood. The convenience store was where he'd say "Good evening" and hand over a few dollars in return for chips or peanuts or chocolate or the Jamaican newspaper if it was in. The Korean man who ran the store was always friendly, asked how he was, to which Cyril always replied, "Not so bad, thanks." And then they might have a conversation about the weather or the Canadian news. But if the daughter was there, she barely registered him and only ever said "No problem" when he thanked her for change.

One Wednesday evening, there was a young Black man behind the counter whom he hadn't seen before. The new guy was good-looking, wore a cool dark sport jacket. He didn't look like he belonged in Mount Dennis. Cyril bought a chocolate bar and a three-day-old Jamaican *Sunday Gleaner*.

"You checking news from home?" the guy asked as he gave back change.

"Yes," said Cyril. "Try to stay in touch. Where are you from?"

"Born here, man. My mom too. And hers."

"I've been here nearly two weeks," said Cyril.

"What's your accent, man? You don't sound Jamaican."

"Everybody tells me that."

"So? What then?"

Cyril hesitated. He wanted to keep talking, but some people thought his relationship with Nelson was weird.

"It's my adopted grandpa, back home in Jamaica. He was a professor, taught in England and at the University of the West Indies. Old-school formal? He was always telling me to use my English. You know, 'Speak good!'"

"Hey, my parents were into that too. Grammar was a big deal. My mom's also a prof. English literature."

"So was my grandpa. He was a historian, but he taught some English too. He loved poetry," Cyril said.

"So does my mom."

"Did you ever have to recite the stuff?"

"Wow. Yeah. That was my party piece. They'd clean up after dinner, and then I'd have to stand up and deliver the lines to their friends."

"Me too," said Cyril.

"I told them no more once I got to be nine."

"I never said no," said Cyril. "I was kind of sad when he stopped asking. I guess I got too big to be cute."

"How do you like it here in Mount Dennis?"

"I'm just staying with family friends till I figure out what I'm going to do."

"I'm only here for six days," the guy said. "I spell Mr. Lee's daughter off when I'm around. I've known them both since I was a kid. He wants her to do well in school, so he's okay to pay me while she does homework — so long as it's just once in a while. But I'm really here to visit my grandma. She's in bed by eight, so this works for all of us. I live downtown. Have you been yet?"

"No," said Cyril.

"It's a totally different experience, man. You have to check it out." He grimaced. "There are people born up here who've never been down. Saddest excuse for exclusion."

Cyril didn't know what he meant, though the thought of being so close to the heart of the city and never going was incomprehensible. He just needed money and courage.

"Thanks, man." He paid for the paper and said, "I come by here every night. Evening constitutional." He laughed, accentuating the phrase with a plummy English accent. "I'll see you tomorrow?"

"Sure, I'm here until Monday. What's your name, man?"

"Cyril."

"I'm Evan. See you later."

The Juniors had warned him never to run, but he did. All the way home in the dark with random lines of poetry in Nelson's voice racing through his head. He was still smiling when he stepped into the elevator.

EVAN WAS NOT AN EASY guy to know. Sometimes he was so busy with his computer that he barely looked up when Cyril arrived. On those nights, Cyril paid his money and told Evan that he had to get home. He envied Evan's nonchalance. Even so, Cyril felt connected in a way he didn't with the Juniors. He figured it was the poetry thing.

On his last night, Evan was full of talk. "I love staying with my grandmother," he said, "we're real close, and it makes the whole family happy, which always pays off for me. But I'm glad to get out of here." He swept his arm dismissively to indicate the little store, the long, empty roads, the apartment blocks — what he clearly considered to be the dreariness of it all. "The job's shit money, but I can study when it's quiet." He motioned to the pile of schoolbooks behind the counter and gave his laptop an affectionate pat. "If you have one of these, you can work anywhere."

"I want to go to university too," said Cyril. "I'm trying to figure out how to get there."

"I've got one more year of journalism to go. I'll graduate next year, then I might do a master's somewhere," said Evan.

"I got good marks in school back home," said Cyril. "I was at community college. But then I came here."

"Do it, then," Evan said. "Go to school. Don't waste your talents."

Cyril heard the words as endorsement. "Yeah, man. You're right," he said. Evan's acknowledgement of his potential somehow made it real.

Cyril forced the question, screwed his courage to ask, "Can I call you if I do?"

"Sure. Why not? Here's a number to reach me," said Evan and handed Cyril a business card that read *Junior Journalist*.

"Welcome to Canada, Cyril." He laughed and reached for his ringing phone. "My girlfriend," he said, winking, "Ms. Penelope P. She's missing me."

Cyril walked home, grinning into his winter clouds of breath. He was living in Toronto. He had a friend. Now he had to make plans. He rediscovered the aspirations and motivations he'd put aside for grieving. He had Grandpa Nelson's telephone book, had asked for it after the funeral. They'd given it to him along with Nelson's suitcases and the old set of encyclopedias that Cyril had so often been encouraged to use. His aunt kept that now, for the little ones.

"You'll always find someone to help you among my friends," Nelson had said. "When you're ready to travel, I'll make some calls for you."

During the day, at the Mount Dennis apartment, Cyril swallowed his shyness and made himself telephone the people whose names he'd heard so often from Nelson.

He spoke to supportive, welcoming people who wanted to know: Was Nelson's a peaceful passing? Had there been any family with him? Was Cyril settled at school yet? When he got there, he had to study hard. They chatted happily about their grandchildren and inquired about the state of things at home in Jamaica. He didn't find a family to claim him. They were busy people whose lives were already full. They didn't hear the loneliness in his voice. They wished him luck.

FOUR

CYRIL WAS WAITING. HE HAD phoned the school and spent lots of time on hold. The papers had finally come in the mail. After days of fussing with the application, he had sent it back completed and signed. A student needed a computer, and Cyril did not have money to buy one. His evening strolls were shorter now. He spent more time at the library with their computers. His visits to the corner store had become occasional, to satisfy chocolate cravings or at the end of a week in hopes of the *Gleaner's* appearance. Despite its digital availability, the look and feel of the paper conjured smells, sound, and feeling that electronic type could not.

The girl at the store looked up and smiled, a thing she generally did not do.

"Hey," she said. "It's Cyril, right?"

It was the first time she had paid him attention.

"Question for you. I'm going away for school," she said. "It's a placement, for the winter term. I won't be here at night anymore, and my dad can't work more than eleven straight hours, his back won't take it." She looked at him as though she questioned his comprehension skills and said, "He's got a back condition."

"I'm sorry."

"Evan says you might take this job on? Here in the store. You're going to school, right?"

"About to start orientation. Soon as I get the acceptance."

"You don't know yet?"

"I'm pretty sure."

"Well, either way, I guess. If you want it, Evan already told my dad you're cool. It's minimum wage. That's non-negotiable, and you have to be here by six and stay open till eleven. Sometimes Dad has to go somewhere during the day, then he needs you to help out."

"That's okay. So long as I'm not in school."

"He knows who you are. He likes you."

"I don't know when my classes are yet."

"You have to do those hours. That's the job. Where are you going to school?"

"Ryerson University. Downtown. It's going to take more than an hour to get back here from there."

She rolled her eyes. "I know how long it takes, I'm at the University of Toronto. Anyway, you'll figure it out. And don't tell my dad this, but I'm not planning to work here in the summer, so you'll get to stay as long as you want."

Cyril turned briefly to look at the door then pushed his hands deep into his pockets and nodded.

"Don't let my dad down," she said. "He needs help."

ON HIS WAY HOME, CYRIL rehearsed his job announcement to the Juniors. Not a great job, but one that would accommodate his university schedule, he hoped, and he could do his homework sitting right there, at the counter, the way Evan and the daughter did. They were an attractive precedent. Successful students. The Juniors would tease him, but he'd finally have money to slow the steady draw on Nelson's legacy.

The apartment was unusually quiet for mid-evening. Empty except for a cousin's boyfriend who stood in the kitchen with a beer in his hand. They fought a lot, that couple, and it must have happened again because the guy was clearly pissed off and glowered at Cyril. Cyril nodded hello and walked around him to the fridge to get a soda. He was an unpleasant man, quick to take out his frustrations on others, as he did with Cyril's cousin. Cyril knew the guy was watching him as he walked with his drink to the couch and picked up a couple of library books that were tucked in behind on top of his suitcase.

"You think you're better than us? Your troubles are bigger than ours?" The guy walked into the living room and stood in front of him. Tilted his face up to take a long swig from his upturned can then squeezed the shape from it. The sound of that, the crackle of aluminum, brought Cyril fully alert.

"Maybe your problem is you just sit in here all day or take your long walks. Who's got time to walk? Are you sorry for yourself? We all have our issues, man. Don't make no difference to the fact that you got to work. So you got some inheritance money, well, that's good for you, but the rest of us have to work."

He looked like he could spit. Cyril sat still and waited because he didn't want it to get any worse. He had never been hit.

"You some kind of pussy, man? Are you a fucking faggot?"

The front door opened, and two of the Juniors burst in, laughing at something they'd seen outside, but stopping when they saw the trouble in the room and the heat of the boyfriend's anger. He pushed past them and left through the still open door. Slammed it closed behind him.

"I don't know what happened," said Cyril.

"Forget it," said one of the women. "He goes off. Anger issues. She should drop him before he really fucks her up. But she's still all in love." She spun out *luuuve*. "Nothing to do with you. Be careful round him, though." She threw Cyril a sideways glance and carried on to the refrigerator.

Cyril watched them make a plate of salsa and chips as they talked about a friend whose party was tomorrow night. And if they had ever thought to ask him to join them, they'd already forgotten. Cyril pretended to read, but his mind buzzed as fast as his heart raced. He had been at the Juniors' for six weeks, and it was already five weeks too long. As he left the apartment to walk, they grunted goodbye, took his place on the couch, and turned the TV on.

It was the tread of his feet, the smack to the pavement, the rhythm, the sway, the swing of his arms. That was how he walked it off, the buzzing in his head, the mounting distress that was anger or fear or a mash of both. And then only the looping refrain that moved along with him, repeating: so cruel, unfair, shit. It diminished to loneliness, and that was a simple, manageable emotion, an absence, not an urgent presence. Cyril kept his head down and watched the toes of his boots rise and fall and slap; rise, fall, slap. By the time he made his second turn of the nine long blocks that took him beyond the convenience store, behind the apartment blocks, and along the fence that separated the railroad tracks from the road, by the time he made that second turn, he was ready to make a decision. His own decision. About what was to happen next.

In the No Frills supermarket was a bulletin board with neighbourhood notices. Cyril had looked them over a number of times. Childminders, house cleaners, and temporary jobs. Stuff for sale: a TV set, a motor scooter, kids' toys. Rooms to rent, one that charged just a little more a week than he was asked to give Uncle Junior. He wrote down the number and made his way to the only pay phone he knew of. It was often in use, though not right now. He had rarely seen a pay phone in Jamaica, where most everyone had a cellphone. Before Digicel arrived on the island, most of the people in his village had had no phones at all.

The lady who answered asked a lot of questions, and when she learned that his only job was part-time in the convenience store, she said that she would be hanging up.

"But I can give you money at the start of the week," said Cyril, which calmed her.

"You talk good," she said. "Where you from?"

"Jamaica."

"Come by and see me. But I'm not deciding yet."

He made his way back down to the library and found the little street running off Weston — a short run to the fence in front of the railroad tracks. It was the fourth one in. A little house flanked by others like it, but not quite the same. It was one storey high with a small window above the main floor, just under the roof, and framed by shutters. Below that was a plastic awning that ran the length of the porch. The yard had a white picket fence, like those in English picture books, but this one, and the house too, was a shabby, grubby white: the plastic blooms of flowers on tall green stalks in a box under the window reminded him of Jamaica. The scale of the house, of the street, pulled him in. Small enough to navigate, to understand, to maybe feel at home. He opened the gate, one hinge tied with a coat hanger, and walked to the door. It opened before he touched the bell. "Come in," the woman said. They stood together in the hallway between a rack of coats and a gold-framed mirror in which he could see himself.

She was a dark-skinned middle-aged lady. She asked again for his history and the source of his income. For his future plans. Why he was here in her neighbourhood. Satisfied, she led him down stairs that were lit by a motion detector and into the basement of the house.

A real bed. The room smelled musty, like a place under the ground, which it was. There was a toilet that she said no one else would use. A shower stall and a sink. Luxury bonuses, the lady explained. He would not find these amenities for this price anywhere else in the neighbourhood. The room was small — the other half of the basement was hers and full of boxes. He would utilize the nearby laundromat. The microwave and kettle were his to use along with a tiny fridge — which meant less time in her kitchen. He would share the big fridge upstairs for overflow storage, and he might use the stove if he really needed it. He would use her kitchen either before or after she was finished cooking. A further list of rules — the breaking of which would result in immediate eviction and loss of deposit — he dismissed as irrelevant: no girls, no drugs, no weapons, no parties, no pets, no mess, no late-night noise, no loud music — especially rap. The lady was adamant, and Cyril was smug. None of those applied. He said, "Don't worry about me, Miss Beale. I'm quiet. I just got here, so I don't have friends. I'm focused on my university studies. That's it."

She took his money and gave him a key. "Ten dollars if you lose it and I have to make another." Then she asked about his parents, and he answered that his mother was dead. For the first time, she softened: "Your mommy? But you're so young." Cyril looked back at her and shrugged, played his bottom lip between his teeth. Then she was back to skeptical. "Okay. We'll see what happens. Remember to leave the kitchen exactly as you find it." He heard the door lock behind her — the door to the kitchen — and the pad of her thick slippers weighted by heavy feet as she crossed the floor above him. Then the sound of the radio, which leaked through the floorboards and heat vents until the furnace fired and the motor noise of the fan blowing hot air into the room covered it up.

A real bed. She'd left clean sheets for him, which she pointed out were also a bonus because if she allowed him to stay, he would have to buy his own. Cyril shook the sheets over the mattress and tucked them under the way he'd done at home. The way he couldn't on his couch at the Juniors'. This move. This immediate, urgent middle-of-the-month move would cost him two hundred dollars because he had already paid Uncle Junior and had now given the lady money. The deposit she wanted was okay: it was savings, he'd get it back, and not so long from now. It was all temporary. This place under her house with its two small windows and the door to her kitchen and another to the back of the house. He opened the back door, quietly, to look. Five steps led up to a square of yard. Grass and plants, a real garden probably, though he couldn't really tell in the dark. Another motion detector light revealed empty planters for flowers on either side of the steps. He walked back down and closed and locked the door. This was his way in and out, she'd said. The door that went with the key. A narrow path ran along the side of the house and out to the street.

Cyril sat on the bed, now covered with a purple quilt. The rest of the room included a chair, a small table, a bookshelf with a Bible and some women's magazines. A wardrobe and a dresser stained with water rings. His mother would never have tolerated that. Their house always had doilies for coasters, most of them crocheted. But it was his. It would take five minutes to pack his suitcase at the Juniors: take it out from behind the couch, close the toilet bag that had never been unpacked, remove his good jacket and pants from the hanger in the cupboard.

Uncle Junior was definitely pissed because he said, "You should give proper notice of your intentions." Cyril said, "Sorry, sir" and looked over Junior's shoulder to the photograph of a Junior wedding on the wall. All of the family gathered, dressed up and smiling. The sun shone prettily on them, the trees behind were green, the grass was green, and there were pink and red roses in the flower bed. Junior looked grand in the photograph. Smiling, warm as that summer day, all benevolent generosity.

"You have got to toughen up," said Junior. "This country is hard. The people are hard — they are not on your side. Stay out of trouble. Work. And signal your intentions, you hear? Because when people give you respect, you give it back." Then Junior looked as though even he had heard enough of his own voice, walked away to his study, and closed the door.

On the first night in his basement room, Cyril lay on his bed in the dense quiet with only intermittent sounds from the furnace. He woke in the night to the shaking house and the rumble of a train travelling just a few metres from the room where he was no longer sleeping. It seemed as though it would never end, and then suddenly it did. Cyril listened to the faraway trail of the whistle until it too was gone, and the distance between him and the train lulled him back to sleep.

At home in Jamaica, from his bed in their house — up on the hillside, above the road that ran through the valley — he would listen to the passage of big trucks making their way to dark early-morning deliveries. The valley slopes amplified their sound and broadcast it over long distances so the engine noise would fill the minutes and grow increasingly close till it passed, then run on for a long time before it was gone. Like the train, he realized with pleasure. He hadn't paid much attention to trains till now. He'd seen them in pictures and movies and television all his life, played with toy trains as a kid, but never seen a real one, never looked for one all these past weeks. Perhaps because they ran behind the big fence, so there had been no place to stand and watch them. Though he'd had glimpses of trains that pulled a few tall green carriages, carrying people back and forth to their work downtown. But they hadn't held any place in his imagination. Now he lived beside the track, and the size and the rumbling weight and the running length of them was awesome. He would look for a real train.

Shortly before morning, Cyril dreamed that a brown-and-yellow finch flew out from a hibiscus bush and into his hand. A baby bird. He opened his palm to help it fly, but it steadied there, tiny bones covered with the softest feathers. Clinging tight to his outstretched forefinger, claws pinpricks to his skin, staying even when he dared to stroke its back with his fingertip. His mother whispered, "Take courage, baby."

FIVE

AN OLD LADY WITH A bright orange woollen hat perched on top of her head and what looked like brown floppy earflaps dangling below stood in the front lobby of the library. She was large and assertive. "This is my bench," she said to a lady who wanted to sit down. "I need to have it for myself. You are not invited." She was loud, and Cyril was embarrassed for her because people turned to look. But it didn't last. She settled herself and her big, blue bag on the bench inside the door and began to empty the bag of its contents. When she found what she was looking for, a smaller, bright pink bag, she placed it in her lap. Cyril watched as she pulled out pale yellow thread and began to crochet – he could tell from the way her hands moved – which surprised and intrigued him because that was exactly what his mother had done under the single electric light at their house. Back home. When she was alive.

The lady was talking to herself. A muttered monologue, though she now and then looked up to the wall as though someone there were talking back. He saw all of this from where he stood in front of the librarian's desk, waiting for her to finish speaking to a small, pale man who struggled to understand English. Eventually, as the man walked away, she said, "Can I help you?"

"Sorry. All the computer terminals are in use, so I can't do a search. I am looking for good histories of Caribbean immigrants to Canada."

She looked up from her computer screen. "You're looking for Black history? History of Black immigrants? Because we have a whole section for that."

Although she was no longer looking at him, Cyril smiled at the librarian. "Thank you." Nelson said history was learning from those who had been before. If it could teach political leaders and royalty, it could teach Cyril. So long as he looked in the right places.

Cyril chose *The Caribbean Diaspora*, a book thick enough to start with. He walked through the lobby, past the big lady with her crocheting, and was about to open the front door when she looked up and said, straight at him, "What you doing here? Are you skipping school?"

Cyril was immediately indignant — he really didn't look that young — though that was silly, he thought, because look at her. But she'd smiled, and her voice was cheerful and intelligent.

"What are you making?" he asked.

"Little things for the church to sell."

"Like doilies?"

"What do you know about doilies?"

"My mom used to make them."

"Are you a Trinny?"

"Jamaican."

"So is your mother over there and you are here?" Cyril nodded again because that was the easiest way to answer.

"That's the way it is," she said. "Look at these," and she pulled a handful of crotched pieces from the bag. "See what I do?"

"They're very pretty."

"My eyes aren't as good as they were, but I've done this for so long I can feel my way through the patterns."

"Awesome."

"I haven't seen you before." She was demanding. Silence was not an option.

"I just moved here. Waiting to start university."

"You're doing research?"

"The history of Caribbean immigration here in this country."

"I am half-Ojibwe, and I can tell you about racism if that's what you need to know."

"Ojibwe is Indian?" Cyril had never talked to an Indigenous person before.

She nodded. "My mother married out, so sadly I am without status."

"What does 'status' mean?"

"Indian rights. Passed down from the male side."

"Okay?" He studied her white face, looking for Ojibwe. Her button eyes and tight, thin lips were like so many other white faces, though her skin shaded grey around her cheeks and across her forehead. At the outside corner of her left eye was a large, crepey mole. She looked white.

"My father worked hard, and then he died. There's lots more that I could say, but I won't."

She unscrewed the cap from the one-point-five-litre water bottle jammed between her hip and bag and held it up to drink.

The orange wool hat was now on top of her blue bag. On her head was a threadbare brown cloth cap with earflaps that were almost long enough to tie under her neck. It was, he thought, an aviator's hat, the sort he'd seen in children's cartoons — only those were fur-lined and leather. Her earflaps were cloth, old and worn. Her hair, under her flaps, was long and a surprisingly deep black, no grey, though her face looked at least as old as sixty.

"You must work very hard at the university," she said, stuffing the bottle back down at her side. "What's your name?"

"Cyril."

"Cyril! I've heard of you. And you probably know that my name is Pat." Neither of them moved to shake hands.

"Hi," said Cyril.

"I've got something to show you, Cyril. It is a secret kept safe by Mr. Addo, but he shares it with me. A history of racism that you can see for yourself."

"Thanks," said Cyril as he zipped up his coat and pulled his gloves from his pocket. He was hungry, and she was obviously crazy because he had no idea who she or her Mr. Addo were. But Pat kept talking.

"Mr. Addo has several things on view that I, unfortunately, cannot touch. They are very fragile and extremely valuable." She lowered her voice to a whisper. "They were appraised for at least a million dollars. But they're secret, so no one will ever buy them. If you come with me, we can examine them ourselves because you're a visiting fellow at the university and I have a PhD in physics."

"Yes. Sure," said Cyril. "But I have to go now, so we'll do that next time." Pat didn't object. As he left, she went back to muttering, raised her face to the opposite wall, and, without a doubt, addressed her words to that. Cyril soon forgot about Pat's ramblings, but he didn't forget her — physicist was a cool aspiration. So much more ambitious than the crazy ladies whom his mother's church people cared for.

A few days later, Cyril saw Pat on Weston Road, bag hanging from her arm, wrapped in her big coat but wearing a different wool hat, a blue and orange thing, aviator earflaps dangling below, water bottle peeking from her bag. She held out one hand for change while the other tossed crumbs to at least a dozen scavenging pigeons. When she saw him, she screamed, "Hello Cyril!" and waved, scattering the birds. He hurried closer because she was really yelling and swinging her mad windmill arm, and people were looking.

"Come in here," she said, pointing to the door of the storefront church behind her. "This is what I told you about. This is where the treasures are kept that you very definitely need to see." The pigeons that had flown off began to gather again. "It's gone," she said to the birds and shook out the paper bag that she had in her pocket, then dropped it to the ground, where it blew into the road. A couple of pigeons made a half-hearted hop behind it. "The Aviators don't know when to stop eating," she said. "Come," she commanded.

Cyril followed her into the church without too much reluctance, as he really did want to know what it looked like inside. It was larger than he'd expected. The walls were black and gold. A plush red carpet ran the length of the floor. Pat walked, somewhat lopsided, water bottle hugged under her arm. She led him straight to the back, where she stopped in front of a small but impressive chrome-framed glass display case.

She was out of breath from the short walk but managed a dramatic whisper: "Look, Cyril. Now you see!" Inside it were a couple of children's things. Old, because the little suitcase was made of cardboard, and the doll was dressed in an old-fashioned sailor's uniform with the anchor design on its buttons. The sailor's cap had fallen from its head and dangled by a single thread against its chin. The suitcase, baby-boy blue like the sailor's suit, was scraped through to brown cardboard in a strip along its side. Leaning upright at the back of the case were two books, one of them black, about a foot square, the word PHOTOGRAPHS in gold on its cover. The other was larger, with a brown cover that might be leather and a title he couldn't quite read. In front of the suitcase were a number of cream-coloured envelopes, handwritten in blue ink. One had an opened letter alongside. To the right was an incongruous but very pretty fan arrangement of crocheted and embroidered doilies. Cyril smiled with the pleasure of recognition.

Pat sidled toward him. "See here," she said, pointing to the sailor doll, "how his hat has been knocked off. Someone goes in here at night and interferes. It's happened to me too. But this is a boy without a mother!" She leaned in closer, peering at the open letter. "She gave him away, and where did he go? Back to Jamaica?" Her voice lowered to a growled mutter; she sounded like a different person. "Or is he dead? Perhaps you know him?"

As Cyril tried to read the letter through the glass, she quickly slid the door open and reached in to pick up the envelopes as well as the letter. That was something she probably shouldn't do, thought Cyril. Pat rearranged the doilies, spreading them out in the space freed up by the letters. "You see how pretty these are? They're as good as mine."

"They are," he said and reached in to stroke the sheen of red silk on the embroidered hibiscus.

"Read the letters. You know this lady?" she asked again, waving the handwritten page in front of him.

The paper was so thin it could be torn just by folding. It didn't seem right to read a letter that had been placed safely behind glass. But he wanted to. What he felt from the letter, beyond its fragility, was an insistent pull to know.

"I lost my glasses yesterday," said Pat. "Read it to me."

"See this date?" Cyril said, though she obviously couldn't. "It's from nineteen-twenty-two. That's a lot of years before my time." As he stood, holding the letter in the dim light of the room that really did command respect, standing in front of the luxurious display case and breathing the building's stuffy air with its familiar smell of furniture polish — he knew. Pat waited for him to read. But he already knew that there was a boy whose mother really did leave him, who had been left all alone.

October 1922

Dear Maggie,

I'm desperate now. I've tried all the people you said, and none of them will help. The baby is sickly and cries too much. The landlady wants me to leave, and I don't know where to go. I have to do something. I can't care for the baby anymore. His dark skin makes me long for his father, but he will never come, and even if he did, they would never leave us in peace. Oh, Maggie, what shall I do? I feel we would both be better off dead.

Davina

"Read the rest," said Pat as she opened another envelope and began to pull out the letter.

"Patricia," called out a loud bark of a voice that made both of them jump. A small, very dark man with silver hair and a formal black suit marched quickly toward them. Pat gave the envelopes to Cyril and smiled a greeting. "Ah! Mr. Addo," she said. "You've arrived. I'd like you to meet my friend Cyril, who is a senior fellow at the university school of foreign affairs. He's from Jamaica. Cyril, this is Mr. Addo, who is the guardian of this church."

"You shouldn't be in my case," said Mr. Addo.

"I did wonder about that, sir," said Cyril.

Mr. Addo's eyes glared through his wire-rimmed glasses. "You can't just take what you want," he said to Pat.

"My friend Cyril is going to solve this mystery."

Mr. Addo puffed out a short, loud sigh and crossed his arms. To keep his anger in, Cyril thought.

"We don't get along," said Pat to Cyril. She was dismissive then and would not look at Mr. Addo again. "We have never been friends. The Aviators and the Felines rely on me in this cold weather. They starve without my help. He wants me to let them die."

"I spent ten minutes cleaning up the cat food cans and the rest of your mess yesterday," said Mr. Addo. "You have got to give me a break. Go feed some other feral creatures at some other poor soul's place."

In an instant, Pat was angry and aggressive. She poured out vitriol about men and sexual abuse, incest and beatings, and the toxic state of the building in which they stood that made everyone sick. As she made for the door, she shouted, "You touch me again and I'll call the police." And she was gone.

Mr. Addo sighed and said, "I wish she would. Never come back. But Pat is an unlucky penny. And the Lord loves her too. How'd you hook up with her, anyway?"

"At the library."

"You're a reader? You interested in the history? Our history? Because I have to confess that the only folk who've looked into my display case without me telling them they should are you and Pat. And I can't say I have any idea what she really sees when she looks."

"Sorry."

"You can read the rest. Go ahead. I collected these things and put them out for people to puzzle over. But they don't. You are welcome to do so. They came in the suitcase," he said.

Mr. Addo folded his arms again and stood solidly by while Cyril read through the two remaining letters.

January 1923

Maggie,

I've done what I had to do. He's gone to someone who will look after him. He'll have to work hard as he grows, but he'll be safe. I've cried for six straight days. My milk stopped coming over a week ago, so I couldn't even feed him anymore. I don't know if it was the right thing. But it was all I could do. I can't protect him with his dark skin, and he would ruin me.

Please forgive me, Maggie. God forgive me.

Davina

Cyril looked up quickly to Mr. Addo, who nodded and looked pointedly at the remaining envelope.

November 1925

Maggie,

I had to see my boy. When I brought him back from my visit in April they told me never to come again, but I had to see him. He wasn't there. They said he became very sickly and passed away. They say he was buried in a pauper's grave at the churchyard and there is no marker for him. I dream of him every night. I miss him so very, terribly much. My sweet baby Edward. I am so ashamed of what I've done.

Davina

"Look at the photo album," said Mr. Addo as Cyril handed back the letters. "Not a lot of pictures, but what's there is good."

Cyril frowned and held out his hand for the book. His fingertips tingled as he struggled to understand the significance of what he had just read. He opened the album. The pictures were small, an unfamiliar black and white, fixed to the black paper pages with grey stick-on corners. On the first page was a young woman with wavy light-coloured hair pinned back by a barrette. Then empty pages: he could see where the little corners that held the photographs had been peeled away and the darker squares on the faded paper where the photos had been. A few pages in was a picture of the same woman in a long formal dress beside an older man. It must have been a wedding or funeral or some other important social occasion. Toward the end, at the bottom right of the page, was a picture of a little boy. He was probably about two years old, younger than Cyril's sister, Keesha. Seated with his plump baby legs dangling from a straight-backed wooden chair. A little dark-skinned boy in a white shirt. A small, square, black-and-white photograph with a scalloped white edge.

Cyril leaned forward, held the book closer. Felt a heartbeat's skip of excitement as he read the child's eyes. It was an old image, but he could see how alone the child was. Who had cared enough to take the picture? His mother before she'd left him? He breathed deep, waited again for the sense of knowing – the prickle of recognition — to feel his way in. "Edward?" Cyril said. "And the woman is his mother?"

Mr. Addo nodded. "There's another one at the back."

Cyril leafed through the empty pages to the inside back. It was a formal sepia-coloured photograph, a little bigger than the others — a studio portrait. It was loose, not pocketed to the page. Cyril held it up. A Black man, maybe late twenties. Dressed in a suit and tie. Handsome, intense, and self-assured, who challenged the viewer to judge him.

"His father?"

"Could be."

Cyril put the photograph down, tried to make sense of his agitation. What did the doilies have to do with all of this? His mother's doing? Was she watching out for him? He looked at the small squares and rounds of pale cream fabric, at the scarlet and white hibiscus lined up inside the case. Wished for the heat of a Jamaican sun and his mother's smile. He barely knew his brother and sister, the difference in age so significant. The few weeks that he'd been away already felt like a year.

"There's one last thing," said Mr. Addo. "Most important, because it continues the story — and begins the mystery." He picked up the leather-bound book leaning upright at the back of the case. He put it into Cyril's hands. It was bigger than the photo album with the word RECORD engraved on its cover.

"And don't ask me how these things were put together, because the place I found them didn't know. They told me they all came in the same box. From a house that was cleared out long ago, but the box was forgotten. Now, that book of records is another story. It came from a professor of our church whose research looks into children's workhouses. One day, when I was doing some sorting through, I put these things together — the suitcase and its contents and the book of records. I believe that the Lord gave me this knowledge. He works in mysterious ways."

Cyril turned the book over in his hand. It was surprisingly heavy. The back cover and the last few pages were warped and foxed.

"Look where I've put the ribbon," Mr. Addo said.

Cyril opened the book carefully. The page was a list of names under the heading CHILDREN IN PLACEMENT: DECEMBER 1928.

He read quickly through and stopped at a name toward the end of the list.

"Edward Davina," he read. "Is this him?"

"It must be," said Mr. Addo.

"He would have been six," said Cyril. "After they said he died?"

"Yes."

"Can we find out for sure?"

"It's possible. His name must show up somewhere on the city records. There should be something to say he passed away. I've been meaning to get there and look, but I never find the time."

"I'd like to know," Cyril said and closed the book as carefully as he'd opened it.

CYRIL WALKED HOME WITH THE puffy softness of his parka hood pulled over his head and tight to his cheeks. It was colder with the sun gone and the night dropped in as though someone had pulled the blind while he was in the church. Mr. Addo had patted him on the shoulder when he left and said, "God is always ready to see you. Come back on Sunday when we're all here."

It was good to talk to someone, and just now it didn't matter so much who they were so long as they saw him and wanted conversation. Cyril was hungry for that, for something beyond the careless, dismissive chatter of the Juniors, which he did not miss. He wanted to know people his own age, make real friends whose lives fit with his. But, in the meantime, he would make it up from bits and pieces – the people who acknowledged his existence. So far that was Evan. Mr. Lee and his daughter. Pat. And Mr. Addo, Elder of the Precious Eternal Life Church.

Edward was as alive for Cyril as any of them. His connection to the child whose parents had left him – *My parents abandoned me too*, Cyril thought, *they have forced me to this uncertain place where I don't know how I belong, just like Edward. And the little boy is half of this and half of that, like I am half-and-half.* The glimpse he'd had of Edward was as welcome as a close friend.

As he walked home, Cyril ached with the enormous distance that was between him and his mother. As though she were sitting just inside her front door on the wooden chair with her eyes on the path that ran from the road to the house. But she was not looking for her son – she was waiting for her husband. Because she had given away the boy who'd come between them, who had forced her husband from their home. She had tossed Cyril up to manage on his own, and how he survived didn't matter to her near as much as the possibility that he, her exotic, charming, pale prince of a man, would come home to her.

Cyril was startled and stopped by the twist in his gut. He stood on the sidewalk, waiting for the pain to ease. He didn't quite bend to it but pressed his gloved hand there, on top of the parka, to fend off the next squeeze. It didn't come. "She's dead," Cyril said out loud, a muttered voice from the back of his throat, like Pat's. "She's dead and never would have left me anyhow. But my daddy did." Cyril said that too, then started to walk again.

He knew how Edward must have felt. But he might have survived aloneness. The children's home had certainly lied to his mother. Nelson's counsel was at his ear: *Think it through twice,* he urged. Determine their agenda. The meaning of their intent. They didn't care about the mother or the son. They had a job to do. And he, Cyril, Canadian newcomer, lonely boy, was taking up the responsibility for uncovering Edward's truth.

When he got to the library, he found a *History of Children's Aid Societies* with a reference taken from a newspaper in the early 1920s:

> For the truly unfortunate there are few options. Young mothers must give up their children, too often into the hands of charlatans and criminals who use the children for financial gain. Sometimes the very young babies are sold into the arms of childless couples. These are the lucky ones. Other less desirable children, those from questionable backgrounds, are sold into labour. Our reporter has discovered that the unluckiest, sometimes those with deformities, become subject to medical research. That there are children hidden away in the darkest labyrinths of our hospitals and psychiatric wards is truly a vile secret. Humane sentiment should insist on preventing these cruelties with the care and protection of such children.

Edward was not lost forever, Cyril knew, as he turned onto his street, glancing briefly at the stony faces of a young couple carrying shopping and a woman who was not so old but leaned heavily on a walker. Edward had already made introductions for Cyril, to a crazy lady and to Mr. Addo. Edward himself, if still alive, would be older than Mr. Addo. Edward's life had met Cyril's with the force of collision.

THAT NIGHT, CYRIL DREAMED OF Brown's Town, of shopping for ripe papaya as he walked alongside the fence that enclosed the market, stepping around pools of water because the rain had only recently stopped. The air was sweet, the sun warm on his face. It was Christmas, and gospel carols played loud on the distorting speakers attached to the wooden wagon with CDs for sale: "Jingle Bells," "Silent Night."

Headed toward him on the concrete verge was a tall white man carrying a brown baby. As he passed Cyril on the narrow path, squeezing so close that his shoulder brushed Cyril's arm, the man dropped the baby, and only because he was right there, touching, did Cyril catch it before it hit the ground. It lay in his arms and looked up at him, wide-eyed with complete trust. All instinct, Cyril made his arms a cradle. Felt the baby's weight settle into them, stretched his palms across its back, secured it against his chest. The baby didn't smile or cry; it was undisturbed. The man was gone into the market, and the baby was Cyril's. Then Cyril woke to his cold room and the dim streetlight through the basement window. In the distance, a long way off, was the sound of a train that had already passed.

SIX

EDWARD IS NOT A BABY. He knows trains like he knows boots and mitts. He knows train tracks and how they shine hot in the sun and can burn if you touch. When it rains, you can slip, and they also shine when they're wet. He has crawled over them, knows how hard they are and that he could never ever lift one even if it was not stuck to the ground with the big pegs that he's watched the men hammer and bang. If he falls, he must not hit his head on one like the boy who doesn't work with them anymore. Also, if the train is coming, the rails will tremble, and then he must run fast and hide behind the big wooden boxes that are locked with padlocks.

When there is no one around, no men in uniforms, he and the other boys scramble under the high wire fence, the same places where the dogs and sometimes hobos crawl. Boys like ants swarming to find their food, he thinks, and imagines himself as small as that, an ant, and the pieces of coal they search for are treasure for the home nest, though the black dust is greasy and smells, and the sacks they carry are quickly too heavy if there is a good amount on the ground.

Here's where the trains slow down, and here's where the trains are loaded, and here's where what they carry sometimes spills — not lots, but enough for working boys who drag their sacks across the ground and back under the fence, and if they have mitts their hands are not too cut and grazed and scraped by all their efforts. Boots and mitts are for hard work with coal and wood, the two jobs that Edward works at, even though he is so small and the other boys are bigger. Their legs move faster, they can carry more. But all the sacks are precious to Mister, who collects them on the other side of the fence, easy for him like they've got feathers inside, and piles them on his wagon, and when the wagon is full the boys walk home. Back to the house where wages are paid out in food and drink and sometimes something sweet. At night they are a pile of sleeping boys, close-cuddled for extra warmth and comfort even though they have their separate places. And Edward knows who to sleep next to and who not. Those are the days as they go by, followed by nights that roll into days. Some days for coal, some for wood, and when he is old enough then his days will be at the garment factories, and his real work will begin. But now he is a small boy, one of the smallest and one who has got to jab back with his fists when he's pushed. He knows how to do that. Sometimes they laugh at him when he fights, but not always.

Trains travel through. They go a long way, further than he knows about. Further even than the end of the town, which a man once told him was just one town in a country of many towns. But Edward doesn't know what a country is. He knows only the road to the tracks and the road to the lumber yard and how to get home on his own if they leave him behind. It's really all he needs to know. That and mitts and boots, which he sometimes has — and then it is easier. He knows, too, the pleasure of water with soap and climbing into the dark bath when it's his turn, made even blacker by him, pulled from his hair, from under his nails that never come clean, same as his feet and hands. But the skin on his chest and belly, arms and legs, does turn clean, and for a number of hours it is pinky-brown like a nut and feels smooth and new like the skin of a baby mouse until the next day when he goes to work.

A woman smells of soap and food and safety. In the warmth and dark that follow the bath, he conjures the full pleasure of memory because he knows she came for him: "To take you out. You went to the park and looked at the swans. She bought you ice cream. Like a princess in her bonnet and carrying a basket with a picnic for you. You held her hand, and she was so proud ..." His mother looked like the nurse who comes to the home, who tells the story. Why would that be if he really remembers her? Another part of him thinks she died giving birth to him. Because she would never have let him go. He settles on that thought because the warm place he's found is dark but not safe. He will not cry.

EDWARD SHAKES THE SLEEP FROM his head. Lifts a hand to pat his face, large palm making slapping contact with his bony cheek, and paddles his slipper-clad feet against the floor. His body is numb from sitting. The damned chair swallows him; he can't fight the drift into sleep's unconsciousness. He must make himself move about, despite the immediate aches and pains that burn across his back. His eyes are wet, but these aren't tears, just the leaky waking of an old man.

He's lived with some sort of pain his entire life, from when he can first remember. He looks up on the south wall, where his view is framed by a small square window seven feet up, searches the sky for evidence as to time of day, the weather, fair or foul.

The window faces the side of the much smaller building next door. He doesn't see it anymore, though in the early days — five years ago, when he was younger — he climbed onto a chair to see what was outside. Sometimes, he lit a cigarette, blowing the smoke out of the window. He was never an addict; cigarettes were for relaxation and pleasure. Some relaxation: balanced on a chair that dipped in the middle, constantly wobbling to maintain his balance. Stretching upwards toward the light like some potted plant. This room and its up-on-the-wall window is his reward for a Lifetime of Hard Work.

But windows cost money; they don't come free in housing like his in big, expensive cities like Toronto. He is lucky to have light. Grateful, is what he tells the other guys, the ones nearer the front of the building who can look out onto the street. Doesn't need to see what's there anyway, he gets enough of it when he goes out to do his rounds.

He won't be making his rounds today. He hurts too much. And there's no money in his wallet. No cheque to cash. It's a day late. Tomorrow's Saturday. That's the week finished with. He has to make do with a couple of cans of kidney beans that came in the box from the food bank, where he wishes never to go again. Except that he does, every month or two. He should be able to take care of himself; he never needed this sort of help before. But he goes back because starvation is a pathetic end. A sad full stop that would bury all his past successes at survival. It's all people would remember.

SEVEN

THE ACCEPTANCE LETTER FROM RYERSON University arrived, with instructions to set up his student email account. Cyril took it to the library. His preferred computer was free, and he logged into his new student email. The inbox filled with a barrage of messages delivering invitations and proposals, credit card offers, deals on fashion; the emails opened the door to an overwhelming paradise of consumer delights. *Rubbish*, grumbled Nelson as Cyril's finger hovered over easy passage to the cellphone he wanted to purchase. Listening to the voice, Cyril stopped himself and instead gathered his wits for a first trip to the centre of Toronto and the school that was going to launch him into a successful career and the life that came with it.

Cyril took two buses and then transferred to an eastbound streetcar to get to Ryerson. He did not take the subway, not yet, as he wanted to see the city. He was a man on the move, and he behaved as though he'd done it all before. People shouldn't think him unsophisticated. If he was surprised by all the new things he'd see, he wouldn't show it; he'd refrain from raising his eyebrows and staring. Would not blink if something he'd never before imagined displayed itself in front of him. The trip into the city took a lot of his concentration, especially the street-car. He dropped his paper transfer just as the trolley arrived but managed to catch it in an updraft on the street. He retrieved it just before the doors closed. As Cyril squeezed into a standing space between two middle-aged men, the sun cut free from the clouds, transforming the day, shining winter brilliance over the buildings and glass storefronts, people, cars, and bicycles. Every-thing glowed and sparkled. The city was radiant.

The streetcar rolled on, and he saw all around him and through the windows the variety of eyes and noses and hair. He heard several languages. The faces were fascinating. In Brown's Town, just about everyone was dark, descended mostly from West Africa. Some few were lighter, brown-skinned as he was. There were two Chinese families, and he could count the whites on the fingers of one hand.

Cyril read the street signs, listened for his stop, and wondered whether what he felt, the battle of butterflies in his stomach, the pull of tension across his shoulders and squeezing into his forearms, was more anxiety than excitement. Or was it the other way around? He stepped off at last, swept along by a crowd of kids who pushed to the exit. Looking up, he saw an awesome tumult of colour and the moving, flashing images broadcast from the tiers of billboards surrounding Dundas Square. People packed the sidewalk. The expanse of concrete with the big stage at the back must mean free music. Something new every day, the signs informed him. But the school was what he needed. Ryerson. And though the streams of kids in all their fabulous variety were a surprise, the size of the building whose doors he stepped through with artfully feigned confidence, the escalators jammed full – all of it overwhelming – he did not show disquiet.

Good lad. He heard Nelson's voice. He walked, a little less purposefully than he'd intended, toward the admissions office.

The students were lined up on either side of him, long rows of chairs on both sides of the room. The man he needed to see was in an office just around the corner from the waiting room. The pink slip of paper Cyril had pulled from a device and now held in his sweaty palm was number ninety-two. He sat, opened a book, and tried to concentrate but read the same line seven times before finally giving up. The arms on the clock at the back of the room moved slowly.

Most of the other students were playing on their devices. One guy dipped his head to music that no one else could hear, every now and then letting out a squeak. Cyril's hands rested on the arms of his chair. Next to him was a white girl. On his other side a brown South Asian girl whose hands, fingernails painted blue, were wrapped around her phone, texting like crazy. Her hands, he guessed, were thirty percent darker than his. And on his other side, the girl was maybe thirty percent lighter. He moved his gaze in a line from his hands to the texting fingers and across to the forearm of the white girl, bag on her lap, leaning back with her eyes closed. Back to his own hands, the brown in the middle. The room was full of brownish kids, a few very dark, mixed in with the whites. If you spun them all together, they'd blend to a colour much like his. He had never considered these distinctions before. They were not subtle variations. They were right there on people's faces: their brown or dark or white faces. A boy with a shaved head had a red face like Cyril's father in his English pub.

There was a story that Cyril wanted to hear directly from his dad — and it was strange to attach the word *dad* to his thoughts. What he wanted to know was: How do you father a child and then move five thousand miles away? If his dad were here, would his life be different? Would his dad take him to the places that he wanted to see — Niagara Falls, the Rocky Mountains? Would his dad hold him in a bear hug and tell him that everything's going to be okay, that there's a future for him in this university, in this city? Cyril kept his eyes on the blended brown of his hands, his legacy, his father's genetic contribution.

Before he had a chance to ponder his situation more, the process kicked in. His number was called. He approached the clerk, who was the model of efficiency. He signed away his money and was given a card with his photograph and student number, his class schedule, and a school calendar. In the bookstore, he bought a student transit pass and put it at the front of his wallet. He wanted to tell someone, anyone, that he'd arrived. But the students all around him were so sophisticated. They were all with their friends.

But Grandpa Nelson would be smiling, fist-bump proud — calling for rounds of ginger beer and extra fries. Cyril straightened his shoulders and held his head upright. The other students were mostly younger than him. Some spoke unfamiliar languages. Despite that, he chose to be encouraged because he had, on this day, made the final selection of his classes.

Outside of Ryerson was another foreign place. Not like Weston, which he had assumed was properly Toronto, despite Evan having told him that it was certainly not. But he'd thought that the rest of Toronto just meant bigger stores with more things. Cleaner streets and brighter lights. Better cars, people moving faster.

It was so much more than that. He walked south toward the CN Tower, which he had seen a number of times before from a distant view. All around him were the financial towers, the corporate headquarters housing the economic engine that made Canada a first-world country. Looking up made him increasingly breathless as the soaring city leaned over him from so high above. It seemed the mix of air below contained something more than oxygen – something that could suffocate him – and it made him almost claustrophobic as he looked up at the towers against the sky. He had seen the pictures but could never have imagined that walking down the street would feel like this.

All of the glamorous TV images that played behind the broadcast news readers, in entertainment stories, and in the movies. Downtown was all of those – added quickly to his mind's inventory – and something else that ran taut over the surface of the places and people and the things for sale. The city hummed with electricity. He did not think it was just the novelty of it – the first-time intensity of seeing how very different things were here. He was certain he would experience this sensation every time he walked this way. It was something else that connected them all, the people who moved around him, jogging along the sidewalks, walking, fit and trim, fur-framed painted faces, men and women, groomed and sleek with little dogs on leashes or luxurious carriages transporting children and babies. In Brown's Town, babies travelled in the crooks of arms or, once they were big enough, on their own two feet.

Cyril could almost touch it, the energy that bound them, that they possessed so easily. It was a force that bypassed others, the few whose collectivity of non-belonging was so painfully obvious. This new awareness snagged at his spirit, skimmed a micro-thin sheen of hazard over all the shiny surfaces, made the energy an exclusionary force.

He'd chosen to explore Front Street, walking west. It was long, but not so long as Eglinton. He might go further, as far as the big park – the large square of green on the map. He wanted to see more of the lake and imagined crossing the city along the shoreline.

For a while, he walked behind a young Black man and his two brown daughters, slowing his pace to match theirs. Both of the girls had long ponytails that swung free from their winter caps as they skipped and bobbed. They were eating red lollipops. Their father steered the smaller one, hand to her shoulder, when people approached. He didn't need to, she was aware and capable, but her father maintained the instinctual gesture to teach and protect. On his right, the older girl, whose range of movement was wider, crossed in front of them or fell a step or two behind before trotting on. The ties that bound them were as palpable as the connections among all the other sleek people moving quickly inside their invisible energy lines.

As Cyril began to cross Spadina Avenue, he was stopped by a Black girl who wouldn't let him pass. She didn't hesitate. Stood in front of him, all smiles, and said, "Hey, brother, I got something you need to know." He shook his head at her. She unnerved him, with her bright blue jacket and tall, striped woollen hat that he guessed held dreads piled inside on top of her head. "Brother, I got something to share," she said. "What are you doing for Black History Month?" He shook his head again, but she pushed her brochure at him, and he saw that he had to take it. He did and said, "I don't have any change."

"Doesn't matter. I've got a lot of these to put out, you get yours for free."

"What exactly is Black History Month?" He read the line of text at the top of the booklet.

"The celebration of who we are, my friend. But turns out the celebration has a message that's talking dirty under its breath. 'Bout how we're bad and need fixing. You know what I'm saying?"

"No."

"You're new here?"

"Uh-huh."

"I was born here. I'll tell you how it is. You ask the little kids — white *and* Black — what Black History Month is, and they'll tell you it means that Black folk are bad and this month is about changing up the story for four weeks till the old tale comes round again and is told with disappointing regularity for the rest of the year. And then we're back to normal, which is to say Black folk are pathologically disposed to failure."

"I never heard of that."

"Then you were never listening."

She wasn't fair, and *she* wasn't listening. "But I don't even know what it is. Where I'm from, all my history is Black history."

"Which is?"

"Jamaica."

"Your history is white colonization underpinned by slavery. Don't kid yourself."

"We've been independent since 1962, and if you haven't lived there then you shouldn't judge."

"Independent from the IMF? The World Bank? The multinationals? The Chinese? Tell me who runs your country?"

"Black men and women."

"Wrong. It's money. Like everywhere else, but worse, my friend, because yours is a poor country, and the people stay poor. The wealthy plant their money to grow outside of the country, tell me that isn't so?"

Cyril wanted to walk away from this girl who wouldn't stop lecturing. Who hovered in front of him, immovable except when he moved, then mirror-stepped with him. He shook his head then and smiled. "Okay, you win. You're right. About lots of it. But there are other things too. Like a real functioning democracy."

"Hey. He's listening!" She was smiling too. A beautiful, full-on grin that made him want to stay and watch it, watch her.

"I can be intense," she said.

"You're passionate."

"I am." She touched his arm. "Sorry."

Cyril wanted to ask her name. To see what shape she had under her big coat. To know whether he was right about the dreads in her hat. But he was stopped by the shyness that always shut him down when he wanted to talk to a girl. He could listen and empathize, but he couldn't flirt, didn't know how to do that in downtown Toronto on a street busy with people who walked around them, heading for lunch, back to work, to meetings. He was hungry for contact, and she was right there. He thought her smile was for him, and he was sure he was right about that. But it was just a smile.

"It's the end of my shift anyway."

"Shift?"

"Yeah, I've got a class in twenty minutes. Can't be late for organic chemistry." She grinned.

"Chemistry. Wow."

"Med school coming right up. Just gotta get the marks in." Then she picked up her bag. "Nice to meet you, Mr. Jamaica. Are you living here or just visiting?"

"Moved here."

"Good luck. Don't let them kid you about how we all have the same opportunities 'cause we don't."

She must have seen the disappointment on his face. "If you want to meet people, come out to Moon Moves, over in Parkdale, near Gladstone. Saturday nights."

She hoisted her bulging knapsack effortlessly onto her back and walked away. Seemed like her feet had springs as she moved fast through the crowd of people. He watched her tall hat bounce far down the street. Slowed by the drag of missed opportunity, his walk suddenly seemed too long, his destination too far. He was hungry. But there was nothing familiar in the restaurants around him, and he was certain he couldn't afford them. He moved on, followed where she'd gone though he didn't see her again.

He found a restaurant on the corner that was full of students. He could sit in there and look like he belonged. They wouldn't have much money, either, so it was likely that his eight dollars could buy him something decent. The push of students, the heat in the restaurant, and the noise reverberating from the tiles, the walls, and the steel counters relaxed him. They were mostly Asian. They looked good. He was conscious of his oversize coat and pulled at the zipper because he was starting to sweat in the heat. When it was his turn, he ordered a small fries and a burger, found a place at the window, and ate fast, greedy for the grease and the salt, then slowed as his stomach acknowledged that more food was coming. He was anonymous in the din with the crush of young people eating the same food. No one knew that he was alone.

Outside, piled around the lamppost on the corner, were bags, a blanket, and a handwritten cardboard sign with only the word *please* visible. A dog bowl. No one around, but they were for sure coming back. There were some apples in a box that looked pretty good.

Two weeks before, Pat had waved him down on Weston Road to tell him that it was her birthday. Would he buy her brunch? He hadn't had an immediate reason to say no. The diner was small and narrow with unevenly spaced red plastic bench seats. The owners knew Pat and nodded when she entered. They weren't so friendly, but she wasn't banned as he knew she'd been from other places. There were a few kids his age, but no one he recognized. Pat put her big bag and giant water bottle onto the bench first, then squeezed herself in, belly pressed against the little table. Cyril sat on the skinny side.

"I had an operation," she announced, excited by her birthday and the anticipation of breakfast.

"When?"

"My ovaries were dreadfully diseased, so they took them out. That surgeon is exceptionally skilled, so it wasn't too bad, and when I got home the Felines cared for me." Her voice softened. He had never before heard her speak so earnestly. "Billy and Zigzag came over to my place. They helped me to stand up from my bed and held me by my elbows so that I wouldn't fall. They made me walk around and around and around my room for three days." Her tone became almost reverent. "Billy had to cancel his commercial work for the whole week. He's very, very busy, you see him on the television all the time." Pride made her eyes shine, and her cheeks were puffed from smiling. "I'm fine now," she said, squirming with delight as two plates of the all-day breakfast of fried bacon and eggs arrived. Pat scooped the yolks out with her toast and made small grunts and moans of pleasure as she ate. She'd asked for extra bacon, which she wrapped in a napkin and put into her purse.

"Can I grab that stool?" This restaurant was nothing like that Weston diner. Cyril nodded as two kids sat down at the window beside him. They were downtown types with piercings, spiky hair, and peculiar clothes.

The sky had turned the same familiar grey that it had been, intermittently, for three days. In Mount Dennis, he'd watched seagulls drift down through a thin fog of sky that hid the sun. He hadn't known that he would see those beautiful birds, and so far from a sea or ocean. There were no gulls here, among the steel and glass, skyscrapers and cranes, and another helicopter — he'd seen five already that day. The sun was a diffuse pale candy yellow behind a screen of cloud. That was a Canadian winter sun. And he was surprised at how pleased he was to know that. It was something he could have talked to Nelson about. A water-colour sun in its northern sky. The girl with the hat and the smiling eyes that made him want to see her again. Despite her accusation, he'd say to Nelson. Never mind her politics, he'd say. He finished his burger and fries and rubbed at his fingers with a napkin.

EIGHT

CYRIL PHONED EVAN AT THE end of his first full day at school, though it would be several weeks before they met downtown. Evan was always busy. But his growing interest in writing a feature article on the first-year experience of foreign students in Canada changed his priorities. He'd been told by his prof that he could sell a piece like that, but he was going to have to write it on spec. He'd have to prove himself. Evan and Cyril established a short-term routine, meeting around the corner from the magazine where Evan was an intern. Cyril always made the call, and Evan generally found a time that suited Cyril's schedule. Not evenings, though. Evan reserved any spare evening time for his girlfriend, Ms. Penelope P.

Cyril's visits with Evan were rare enough to bring excitement. They validated him. When he found himself tucked into a corner of a hallway — hiding like a sad sack, Nelson would say, eating the lunch he'd brought from home, looking at all the kids who had friends and lists of things to do — he'd try on Evan's confidence like a costume. He hoped someone would look at him and not through him.

Once, as a kid, when things were really bad, he'd spent a week of lunch breaks hidden in the school janitor's cupboard. Sometimes this new thing, this university with so many possibilities but all out of reach, made him feel lonelier than that time at school in Sturge Town. Because he wasn't a kid anymore. All he really had was Edward, his rationale for being alone, for hanging out in libraries, for eating lunch with his head down and a book on his lap.

A lot changed when Randall found him; a page turned, and he discovered his story might actually have a happy ending. Randall was a designated university mentor and had picked him out from the school's meet-up wall. He'd seen right away that Cyril was new to Toronto, and he recognized the Bob Marley reference on the front of Cyril's bag. He stood over Cyril, all of his six-plus feet, and said, "I am your student guide." Pointing at the bag, he added, "Sent by Bob and all people like him. Tell me how you're doing?"

"Okay. Yeah, fine."

"Right, I can see that. Come with me. You had lunch yet?"

For the first time, Cyril wasn't alone in the cafeteria. Randall knew so many people, from United Black Students and School of Performance members to students in his Poli Sci and Sociology classes; he knew the editors of *The Eyeopener*. And then there were the people he played music with, went to concerts with. He was Bredren and Bro, Dude and Randall-Radical. Everybody's friend.

CYRIL PACKAGED UP HIS TORONTO experiences in pretty language with colour commentary, ready to entertain Evan, who generally sat at a window table of a Queen Street West coffee shop with an open laptop and a pile of books. The coffee shop was alien culture to Cyril. It was filled with people of different ages, though most were young — under thirty — and nearly all were white. With glossy haircuts, fashionable clothes and eye-glasses, casually sipping expensive drinks and operating expensive phones. Evan was often the only Black person, and he didn't look so dark as he sat with his cappuccino, talking, quiet and friendly, into the telephone microphone hung under his chin. He looked like an actor in a film, not a student. Glasses with designer frames, short dark curls, striped scarf. His smile had star quality, such that Cyril often glanced around to see if people took a second look to see if he was a celebrity.

When Cyril sat across from Evan, he was so far from Brown's Town that he couldn't even conjure the feel of Spicy Nice with its crowds of uniformed school kids squeezed into vinyl padded booths, eating patties, shedding pastry crumbs, and drinking Ting through straws. He'd never had a cup of coffee in Brown's Town, though it grew in the fields all around. Coffee went overseas or sold for crazy prices in the tourist supermarkets.

"How's school, dude?" was usually how Evan opened conversations with Cyril. Like Grandpa Nelson, Evan waited to hear it properly: his social experiences, the details of his courses, and how he felt about his professors. What he had learned.

He told Evan that he preferred his own company to that of most of the people at school, whose preoccupations meant little to him: the status of their relationships, money, smartphones, sex, music videos, clothes, shoes, hair. Facebook. Most of them seemed very young. They were. He was the older guy, and he wore his age older than his years when he was with them. He understood why they weren't interested in him. He told Evan about the three third-year guys who had befriended him in the third week, Randall, Leon, and Paul, who had taken him up like a token elder. That they were funny and silly and smart and knew their way around the campus. They introduced him around to people and made him welcome.

What he didn't tell Evan was that, despite their friendship, they didn't really get him – they didn't need to. And if he tried to be like them, he invariably got it wrong, which they found particularly amusing. But they were usually around to meet for lunch three days of the week, and they always found a place at the table for him. Cyril didn't tell Evan how good it felt to be walking into the cafeteria beside Randall. Evan would never understand the shame of loneliness.

He did not tell Evan about his loneliness and self-doubt. About his constant sorrow and the undermining fear that he'd made a mistake in coming to Toronto to further his education. He should have stayed at home, where he was wanted and needed. But his sessions with Evan helped; in them, Cyril was important. That he avoided the truth – the parts that hurt – was perhaps unfair, but he needed to appear successful.

The opening paragraph of a brief biographical assignment for his English composition course revealed some truths he hadn't known about himself.

> I am an independent man. My allegiances are to my family, whether far away, dead, or estranged. I refuse to define myself as an outsider, though that is what I feel. I work hard, and deserve to be included if I so choose. As a rule, I don't make that choice. I don't want to belong to any group that declares itself better or badder than any other. I don't want to belong to a woman because I don't want the accident of fatherhood. I do want to be successful in my career and to help my brother and sister grow up.

He read it over ten times before he handed it in — and almost didn't. He worried. Did it sound arrogant? Did he think himself above others? His mother would be dismayed. Grandpa Nelson would ask him to clarify. He fussed over the words. Worried about using *badder*. Finally knew it was right. He had watched the other students make their lifestyle choices and understood well the ones who struggled and failed. He saw how cliques diminished those who didn't belong. How they created their own worlds, were self-supporting, self-regarding. "Self-aggrandizing," Nelson would have said. He wanted to write that, too, but thought it would sound pretentious. He'd never used the word *estranged* before. Had his father gone to college? Did he have many friends? In his waking dreams, Cyril only pictured him on his own – even when he was in a crowd, he stood apart. Was he like his father?

The assignments were handed back on a Friday. The note on his read, *You are a very good writer*. His mark was an A. Reading this, a warm blush stroked Cyril's cheeks, but he kept the smile from his face. He glanced up at the teacher, who wasn't looking at him. He had worked hard, and it was worth it. The kids around him burst into chatter as they checked their marks, slid back on their chairs, and talked to their friends — this was a very small percentage of their total marks, would not affect their course grade. This mark didn't really count for much. But it did to Cyril.

THE ROOM IN MOUNT DENNIS had become a home now that Cyril's sphere had widened. From the very first time he'd returned from downtown, the walk to his little street beside the tracks had relaxed his tensions. Up until then, the basement had been a stranger's place. A room where a newcomer put his head down to sleep, sheltered from everything outside that threatened to overwhelm. Because he felt so very inadequate when he couldn't try something new, when he couldn't make himself talk to a stranger. He didn't know how to relax at the café on the Mount Dennis corner where the college guys hung out. He wanted to. Then he went back to his street, to the room downstairs, a hiding place, with the radio tuned to music he liked to listen to.

So much of what he knew about Toronto, about North America, he'd learned from television. When he'd seen his first squirrel on a tree below the Juniors' apartment, he'd recognized it immediately. Some part of his rigorously informed self had expected it. He was ready for racoons. And foxes and coyotes, because those also lived in urban spaces. He knew he'd see wealth alongside poverty. But he hadn't learned the language of social interaction, which seemed cleverly coded to the advantage all of the groups and cliques and ethnicities that did not include him.

He was glad to return to his house, to open his own door. His landlady was upstairs and called out when she heard him, "I got some mail for you." This was an out-of-the-ordinary thing, so he stepped into the kitchen. Miss Beale was holding court with a couple of friends, a man and a woman, who nodded when he walked in. She handed him the envelopes. One was from Ryerson, the other from his brother and sister, a crayoned name and address with a picture of Cyril next to the CN Tower sketched on the back.

"What is it, your birthday?"

"Last week already."

"When you get to my age, you try to forget them." She laughed, turning to her friends.

The man glanced at him and launched back into the conversation that Cyril had interrupted. "Like I said, you can't take everyone, even if you want to, because that's putting all of us in peril. Because they'll work for less. That's what I'm saying. Sure, they need some help, but government's got to do that for them."

"Not with my taxes," the woman said.

Cyril lifted his hand, a gesture seen only by his landlady, who mirrored his goodbye. As he walked down the stairs, she said, "I pray to God to keep us safe because this country takes up these people faster than is good. They should stay in their own part of the world." A chorus of agreement filled the kitchen as Cyril closed his basement door to the argument that people should be kept out. He'd only known the argument about trying to get the good ones to stay. The brain drain hurt Jamaica — except for the remittance money sent from abroad. If he knew those people upstairs, he'd go back and tell them that they were probably getting the good ones. Like him: smart, educated, with ambition. But then he was not so sure that's who he was. He did not have a good job, and that's the first thing they'd ask. An approaching train cancelled out their voices. It was not really so loud, but it could stifle his thoughts if he let it. He welcomed the sound of the train in his room. Was glad of it. Would one day ride on it and see where it took him.

Uncle Junior had given him a map of Toronto on the day he'd arrived in Mount Dennis. He'd put it on top of Cyril's suitcase, along with printouts of job centre addresses. Cyril had kept it safe since then. The young Juniors had laughed when they saw him with it and said that he should get a smartphone with maps and GPS that showed where he was and plotted his route so he couldn't get lost. Both Cyril and Uncle Junior defended that paper map — for context, they said, to read the topography and get a sense of spatial distance. "You can't get that on a phone," said Uncle Junior, though he had GPS in his car and several apps on his smartphone. Cyril didn't respond to the phone criticism. He'd hadn't seen a map app until that moment, when one of the guys pushed it under his nose, pointing at the glowing blue dot that was, he said, where they were. But when Cyril held out his hand to see for himself, the guy put the phone back in his pocket.

Cyril's map had become a sort of diary, in the way that he and Nelson had used their map to mark off the roads they took in the summers they toured Jamaica. Nelson had made journal pages to go with it and marked the map with dates to match his entries. The map kept the memory for them, presented the cues. The river where they'd watched the goats crossing. The village with the old lady who sold them the best roasted breadfruit they'd ever tasted. Nelson christened her Queen of the Barbecue. By the time they got home, the map was used up, a tangle of lines marked in red and purple and small numbers written meticulously so as not to obliterate the names of the places they'd never been.

In his journal, Nelson had listed the distances travelled and the condition of the roads. He made notes on the conversations they'd had, the two of them in the car and with the people they met along the way. But he didn't list the places they passed through. That information was on the map. Nelson put them both away to keep them safe. Cyril had not been able to find them after Nelson died.

Cyril pulled his map from the outside pocket of his suitcase. Standing on the bed with a new box of pushpins, he pressed the first into the top left corner of the map, then moved over to pull the right corner up and twisted in the second pin. It took strength. The wall was hard, concrete, with the slightest feel of damp – though it might not be damp, just cold – as he smoothed the paper with his fingers, careful not to smudge the penciled lines that traced previous walks. He held his palm to the wall alongside his map, felt the winter outside and then the movement of the train beyond the fence. This one didn't shake the house, but he could feel its progress on the wall.

Once he was finished, he turned his desk lamp to light the map then traced the roads he'd travelled. Along Eglinton for miles. South on Jane, then Windermere, to where he'd stood on the shoreline. He guessed how much of the lake he'd seen from there. Then, with his yellow pencil, he traced the short distance from the university buildings at Yonge and Dundas south to Front, then west on King as far as Roncesvalles. At the Spadina intersection, he made a thick brown exclamation point, a little bigger than he'd intended, for Black History Girl, whose memory he curled up with at night. At the top of the first virgin page in the notebook he'd bought in the school's bookstore, he started the list of his travel dates. A yellow pushpin on the map showed where he stood now. His house with the plastic awning and picket fence on the little street that ended at the tracks. And then he added a second for the convenience store, already marked with a red asterisk, where he'd met Evan, his friend, where Cyril now worked. He stepped down from the bed and wrote in his book:

> The start of my new life in Canada begins in my basement room from whence I take a bus then subway and streetcar and arrive by foot at my new school: Ryerson University.

Cyril looked again at the map, at what was yet to be discovered. It was immense, the reach of the city in all directions. His tiny little piece of it in coloured lines. He stood back on the bed and pushed a blue pin to the storefront church on Weston Road where Pat had introduced him to Mr. Addo, the display case with the letters, and the little lost boy, Edward.

CYRIL WAS IN BED WATCHING his desk take shape in the first dim light of the winter morning. He had homework to do, but the bedclothes held him warm and sleepy. He heard a car door slam, an engine start, next door's dog barking, and the loud voice of the man who talked to himself while he sat smoking on his porch across the road. These sounds were familiar in a way that was still layered with strange.

When Edward walked into the room, that was stranger still. Cyril's head snapped sideways at the sound of shoes on his linoleum floor. A small boy with an old face. Bleary-eyed and confused. Cyril smelled him. That made him real. Sour from the stale sweat of hard physical work. Edward looked at him with resignation, not surprise. He looked as though he took whatever was handed to him. The layer of dust on his nutmeg skin made it a dull beige. Cyril wanted to speak, but his throat was paralyzed. If he sat up, he could have touched Edward's sleeve. But he could not move. Then Edward was gone.

NINE

EDWARD IS DRESSED IN TROUSERS too tight, seams strained and split in the crotch. Four layers of clothing on top. Each a hand-me-down from one of the other children. He has a jacket that he snatched from a reject pile with a mess of stitching on the back where the sewer was struck suddenly ill. The reject pile is for recycling. The clothes will be picked apart, the pieces resewn. Nothing is wasted. Nothing given away.

Edward is small for nine. He's learned how to slip into shadows. He can hear conversation through closed doors. He's sharp and nervous; his stomach hurts a lot of the time. He works hard because it is easier than being screamed at, pushed about.

He is always hungry. Most hungry after he's eaten because there is never enough food. Every few weeks, the inspector comes to the house, and Edward wears the clothes from the closet upstairs. They are scrubbed clean, all of the children in and out of the same dirty water. Dressed and set to wait in a room with exercise books and pencils and a big blackboard with letters that only two of them can read. Edward can do his sums. Count past a hundred. Subtract and add. A bundle of thirty-five shirts. Take away ten for number 235 Spadina. Deliver twenty to 45 Augusta. Collect the fabric in two big bundles from Bathurst Street and take it back to the shop, a house on Denison with three floors of sewing machines and a tiny room downstairs called the office. His feet are sore and swollen by the end of the day. Though they started all right in the morning.

ALWAYS HUNGRY IS SOMETHING HE'LL never forget, thinks Edward. If he doesn't eat, he'll starve. And if he starves to death, that's all anyone will remember about him. Does it matter what anyone thinks? It shouldn't. But even so. He pulls himself from his bed and shuffles from his room, locking the door behind him. Travels down the dark hallway, feeling the wall on his right with his fingertips, triggering the motion detector lights. He turns in to the bathroom at the end of the hall. Washes himself with a shower hose and a facecloth. He doesn't need to shave anymore, can feel the stubble, but it doesn't grow longer, and anyway, he can't see it on his face. White hair disappears into the lines that surround his chin. That's a bonus. No need to shave!

The food bank is open until 5:00 p.m. What people who have to work should do he doesn't know. This annoys him. The thoughtlessness of it. But then he remembers the sweet ladies who worry about the size of the boxes and how he'll get them home and forgives the Powers That Be for their mistakes.

TEN

THERE WERE TWO CHAIRS ON either side of a small, square table in the hallway waiting area. The display rack across from them held magazines and brochures. More stuff about careers, which Cyril had learned were the staple products of this school. He was waiting to see how he would connect to his. His history teacher's office was just around the corner, and these were his office hours. Cyril had thought hard about making the connection, asking for something that required attention from this man who taught so many of them. A youngish white man, straight brown hair cut close with a little curl on the top at the front. Thick-rimmed glasses — he had two pairs, one dark purple, one black. He always wore jeans, and he was invariably cheerful. The kids had found their seats on the first day and mostly didn't change after that. Cyril sat in the fourth row from the front. It was the women who talked in class. Only one man, charged with blustering confidence, challenged the colonial slant to which he claimed the teacher was predisposed. Even after five weeks, the prof always responded with respect.

This man knew how to make a story come alive so that

when they unpacked the material from the week's reading, the characters triumphed or suffered, strategized or struggled, and, whether they lost or won, ultimately contributed to great events that affected many others: important change that was recorded in history. Nelson's counsel stayed with Cyril: "Follow where your mind takes you." That was Cyril's focus now, learning history through real people. How their convictions had changed the world. Though what they learned in class was too often the vision of one man. And they were often white men. Like the prof said, men and women and children all around the world had their own billions of histories, but the ones who made it into the books were most likely to be what one of the students called "pale, stale, and male."

Cyril had arrived at office hours on the previous Tuesday only to walk away again before he even sat in the chair, concerned that his interest would seem pretentious. His inquiry had nothing to do with the history that this teacher taught. Cyril had spent the rest of the week nursing disappointment; he'd found a need in himself that wanted feeding, and he couldn't do it without help. So he was back, and his turn was next. In his bag was the photograph of Edward's father. Its formality seemed to make it the most hopeful clue. Mr. Addo had agreed to loan it. But only temporarily. Cyril pretended to focus on his textbook, but he was really only waiting for the door to open and the kid inside to leave so that he could go in. When it did, Cyril stood too quickly, and his book slid from his lap to the floor. He bent to stuff it back into his bag.

It was the first time he had been in a teacher's office at this university. The man sat back in his chair and smiled. "You sit on the left, a few rows up?" Cyril nodded. The teacher looked at the sheet in his hand. "Cyril?"

"Yes, sir."

"No need to call me sir. John is fine."

Cyril kept silent because where he came from a teacher's first name was his own private business. Had nothing to do with his students.

"So, how's it going?"

"I'm okay, thanks."

"Marks are good. You're a foreign student. Jamaica. Have you studied Canadian history before?"

"No, this is the first time. I like it."

"I guess you do."

Now was the time for Cyril to ask his question, but the phone rang, and the teacher answered. Which was okay because Cyril needed to find himself in this office. Settle into the role of student engaging his teacher. It was Nelson he found as he looked about the room: *The man is paid to help you learn, Cyril, and the money you give to the school pays his salary.*

The bookshelves beside Cyril were filled with history, mostly Canadian, books that lined up the country by province and issues and the relationships of people to the land and the North and the First Nations. Conquests and battles. The church and the state and Québec. Many of them had inaccessible titles. There was so much he didn't know.

"Thanks for calling," the teacher said, putting down the phone. "Sorry, Cyril. Go ahead, please."

"I'm interested in pursuing some research about something I found," said Cyril. "Just a small thing, but I want to know more. It's from the 1920s. Here in Toronto. It's history, and I thought you would know what I should do."

"Tell me more."

Cyril described the contents of the display case in the church and the letters that told of a boy given into care who then disappeared.

"But there's a book," said Cyril, "that shows him alive two years after that. So he didn't die."

"You're a historian, then," said the teacher, who, to Cyril's relief, seemed to approve of his interest. "A little detective work will be fun." He named a number of research resources, and Cyril wrote the names down: the relevant libraries, the archives. The newspaper collections.

"You could start here, with the photograph of this man who might be Edward's dad." The professor picked it up and checked the back. "It's *Varsity*, see this stamp on the back? That's a University of Toronto student newspaper. They must have something on him. I'd start there." He set the photograph on his desk. "If this had a connection to our course material on post-Confederation Canadian history, I could give you some sort of credit. I'm sorry I can't. But keep me posted anyway, please. I'm interested."

"I will. Thanks very much."

As Cyril was readying his things to leave, the prof pulled a book from the shelf behind him and gave it to Cyril. "I have this, *Blacks in Canada*, a little background for you. Bring it back, please. I'm writing you down here, see, in my book lending record. Sign, please."

Cyril signed and put the book into his bag, tucked it to the back where it wouldn't get scuffed. He sat taller, knowing that he could accomplish this big thing he had chosen to do. That he had his teacher's respect, and that the book in his bag was proof of that. His prof, John, was a white man whose Irish accent had until now been a novelty but had somehow become warm. He had children, because their pictures were on the cabinet behind him, a wife and two small kids, and they weren't white. She was brown, his wife. Maybe she was Indigenous. The teacher really cared about the First Nations people, that was clear when he talked about them in class.

Cyril intended to follow his prof's instructions. "Most of the stuff is digitized now," John said. "Which makes it easy for you. But don't do it the simple way, sitting at home in front of your computer with one hand in the refrigerator to feed your face! Get out of the house and see where it happened. Go to the University of Toronto. That's history right there. Have you been?"

Cyril shook his head.

"Then go. Don't let them tell you otherwise when you get there. Have a look at the building where the story you're following started, and while you're there, find a computer and check their archives. Show them the stamp on the back of the photo."

"Okay."

"Tell a good story, like you told me. That's how you'll get in."

Cyril saw that the prof's faith in him was subsiding and knew that he must be looking skeptical.

"I'm okay with that, sir." Cyril smiled.

"John."

"Thanks for your help. Very much."

Cyril turned to leave, fumbled awkwardly with the doorknob.

"Cyril."

He turned. The prof handed Cyril the photograph. "Your man."

"Thanks."

Outside, he was furious with himself. For not having been clearer. For not being able to turn the fucking doorknob. For forgetting the photograph and being called back. But the prof hadn't seemed to notice. Just smiled and called the next guy waiting to come in.

And then Cyril soared clear of his anxieties. As he walked back through the halls with the kids swirling around on all sides because lunchtime was over, he knew that he was changed, a different man than he'd been just an hour before. He was proud of himself. He had met with a teacher and had a conversation about a piece of Canadian history that he had discovered for himself, that had relevance to him and would be a story he could tell. He was grown-up and capable. He already looked forward to seeing John again to report on what he had learned and to ask, because he really was interested, about the man's family and where his wife came from.

Cyril looked for Randall, Leon, and Paul – the big guys. They were not at the table in the back of the cafeteria where they often hung out when they were not in class. He might not have told them about his mystery and John, but he would have liked to sit with them and share his mood.

AT AROUND 2:00 A.M., CYRIL gave up on sleep. He'd finished the night's homework, spent half an hour in front of the little television with its rabbit ears and five channels that spattered in and out on the screen. Then climbed into bed so tired that he was asleep in moments. But it didn't last. He was wide awake and wanted someone to talk to. At home, when they'd been a family, he would often wake to find his mother busy with something under the electric light. Then he'd make tea, and she'd talk while he listened. And if she spent too much time on God and his good works, he'd steer her back to her stories about Rio Bueno, where she'd grown up over her father's dry goods store.

When she was eighteen, she'd met Cyril's father, who'd come

in on a ship, a sailor from Britain. A romantic who'd escaped from Northern England, where life was damp and dark and cold, come to the islands to collect sugar to take back for tea and puddings. He'd found Mavis with her sweet smile and full breasts, who fell in love with him within three days. He married her because he was far enough away from home, because life was an adventure and his nineteenth birthday was yet to come. They'd stood in the church aisle, and the congregation had blessed them, though the ladies muttered their doubts and the men looked askance at the white man who assumed his privilege with one of their daughters. But the church embraced him because that was what their God insisted on. When Cyril was born, they celebrated. His father left two years later with the big duffel bag on his shoulder that he'd kept sealed in a box under the house to keep it safe from rats. He climbed the ramp to a bauxite ship and said he'd be back. The congregation sorrowed.

When Cyril was nine, his Aunty Vi told him that his father had run from her sister, a woman whose life he found frighteningly small. Who had whimpered at the very idea of travelling with him back to England, of making a life in a cold place where nobody knew her. Who was committed to working and waiting for God's Final Reward. Aunty Vi told him that his father's leaving hadn't been easy. That he'd loved Cyril but could not have taken the little boy with him, away from his mother. Once he'd gone, she said, he must have found it easier to forget he had a son.

Some days after his father left, the pastor paid a visit to their little house and said the congregation would always hold them safe. They were children of the church, the mother and her boy. Cyril's mother had a photograph of her husband in a sailor's uniform with the duffel bag over his shoulder. A pink face with light brown hair and a smile that looked as though he loved the world. They said Cyril had his father's eyes and hands. Cyril couldn't see himself in that face at all.

CYRIL SET TO HIS RESEARCH armed with a fabricated confidence and the firm push from behind that was Nelson, steady, encouraging, faithful. Cyril practiced an expression of self-assurance in the basement shaving mirror tacked up above the sink. It said, *Don't challenge me.* It was always like that with new things. He was excited by them, made sleepless the night before, painstakingly imagining how it should be, what people might say. How he would seem to have done it all before or say the thing that was just right or impress with his knowledge.

One day, in class, a kid had called him arrogant. She had misinterpreted his fear of rejection as presumption and entitlement. He hadn't known what to say. He preferred being called arrogant to the truth and let them believe it.

His first intended stop was the *Varsity* office. He had not been there before, to the part of town with Toronto's most expensive stores: Bloor Street and Yorkville. The imposing Royal Ontario Museum that presided over the sidewalk. He didn't dare to go in, or even to look in from the entrance, which was a demoralizing beginning. And then he walked onto the University of Toronto campus, which he'd thought would be like UWI, but it wasn't. It was grander in every way. As he walked along the sidewalks, he read the banners hung from the light standards with their photographs of important graduates and felt increasingly less able, so that by the time he got to the *Varsity* office he just could not fucking go in.

A few nights later, Cyril walked the convenience store aisles with a feather duster in hand. Defending the store from the dust and grime of the road and sidewalks was Cyril's job. Thirty minutes of work a night, in between customers. It was a productive procrastination, a necessary occupation for which he was paid. Also, he liked the activity. It made a difference, the daily dusting. The store looked good, felt good, which was why it did better business than most. Cyril shared a corner piece of the pride that Mr. Lee clearly felt as he surveyed his domain before leaving Cyril for the evening. *At least*, thought Cyril, *I am good at this small thing.*

He was working the third shelf, canned vegetables and beans, closing in on tomato sauces and condiments, when the door chime sounded. It was a girl his age, what the guys at home called fluffy, wearing a waist-length jacket that hugged tight to her big curves, set off her woman-rounded hips and bottom in stretch jeans. She watched him as he moved behind the counter, stowed the duster underneath.

"Hello. Good evening," she said.

"Can I help you?"

She handed him a five-dollar bill. "Give me a 6/49 with the extra number. The Encore."

Everything about her was fresh Jamaican: her double greeting, soft voice, brusque command. Demure demeanour coupled with uncompromising attitude. He'd missed that complexity of messages and wanted her to feel welcome in Mr. Lee's store.

"You're Jamaican?"

She looked at him with round, dark eyes, the yellow fluff of her scarf wrapped up to her chin.

"How do you know that?" She didn't trust him.

"I'm Jamaican."

"Why are you working here? Jamaicans don't do this job."

Jamaicans don't equivocate either, thought Cyril. "Do you work?" he asked.

"This is my night off."

"You work shifts, like I do?"

"Noooo." She drew out the word, lingered with it. Let the pause that followed extend to silence. She was deciding whether to talk, judging Cyril's intentions.

Then she said, "I work in Scarborough. In a factory. It's a ten-hour shift four nights a week."

"Ten hours, that's good."

"I have to get the night buses home. More than two hours each way."

"Fourteen hours a day!"

"Minimum wage," she offered. "There's lots of us there." By this he knew she meant new immigrants. "It took me three months to find my job."

"Not so bad," Cyril said. "I go to school downtown, but I live here. In Mount Dennis." She would have a good reason for living here, not in Scarborough. He didn't ask.

"You're lucky. I was at school too. I finished in May. I have a Human Resources Management Certificate from Seneca College. I'm a nurse," she added, as though the certificate needed explanation. "Trained in Jamaica." He was to understand that her current occupation was temporary. She had a future.

"You want to stay here?"

"Of course. That's why I came."

"It's tough."

"Everyone says just stick it out and it will be okay."

"Don't you miss home?"

She didn't answer. And Cyril understood that the question,

and how she felt about it, were irrelevant. She was doing what was expected and giving it what she had.

"Why can't you get a nursing job?"

"I have to pass the Canadian exams. I took them last May, but I failed the cultural competency practicals. So now I'm saving money to pay for the upgrade courses. Anyway," she said abruptly, "I have to go." She tucked the lottery ticket into her wallet and pulled her scarf tighter. "Safe travels," she said, apropos of nothing. Cyril watched her go, clothed in black like everybody else; she crossed the street and disappeared. Stick it out and it will be okay.

THE REFERENCE LIBRARY WAS MUCH easier than the archives. Cyril visited both on his first day of research. He didn't make contact but strode into each building as though he had every reason to be there and familiarized himself with the space, the faces, the open hours and restrictions. Looked about as though he were a man who belonged but was short on time and so must come back later. He'd have visited the *Varsity* office too, but it was so small that he knew he'd be questioned if he walked inside. It could wait. He knew libraries now, the building near his house in Mount Dennis, which he'd once thought of as palatial, with its extraordinary inventory of books. But then came Ryerson's library and now this, the Toronto Reference Library, which as far as he could tell had no books at all on the first floor, just a sea of computers and people at work. Cyril walked across the floor and circled back. He followed the directions for the newspaper room and stood in the doorway, took it all in, the desks and machines and big study tables.

Edward was in there somewhere, waiting to be pulled from the potential stored in all the reams of microfilm, stacks of bound paper, and computer databases. His teacher had said to look at the popular papers of the day. To search for orphanages and stories of abandoned children. To look for clues. He had a mystery to solve. And, along the way, he'd discover the context for his search, for Edward's life — if he'd lived. Cyril was going to start in the year that Edward was born and move on from there. He looked for the indexes and found rows of them shelved in order of newspaper and date. It wasn't going to be easy. He'd need some luck; then he remembered that he had better than that. He had Edward.

ELEVEN

CYRIL WAS ON HIS WAY to work. Slowly, because he was early. A red helicopter moved swiftly across the sky, and he tracked its progress. He still enjoyed the novelty of those things. One day, there had been five of them, not red but noise-heavy black, hovering above Yonge Street. Someone said it must be serious. Like a police chase. But now he was the only one looking up. Around him, people moved steadily on, forward in their lives — toward that career they all talked about, a family, a house of their own.

Pat was rolling toward him in a motorized wheelchair, straight down the middle of the sidewalk. It was too late to pretend he hadn't seen her when she shrieked, "Cyril!" She grinned wide with the pleasure of finding him, and he was ashamed of his ambivalence. She was excited.

"I've been looking for you for days. You've been in hiding."

"Just busy at school." He hadn't told her he was working at the store. He didn't want her to show up there. "What's with the wheelchair?"

"I ordered it from the authorities. Look at my legs." She peeled back her long coat and tugged her pant leg up her calf. It was swollen, red, a nasty, painful mess. "See what they did to me?" She winced as she rolled her pants back down. "It's abuse, and I'm fighting them in the courts."

She turned her attention back to Cyril. "I've got some impor- tant things for you. I found them in bags behind the charity shop. They shouldn't do that." Food crumbs were scattered over her copious chest, caught in the footrests of her wheelchair. Her aviator ears looked even more ragged.

"There is evidence in here of how it started," she said. "I knew the editor. He and I had lots of disagreements, but I always liked the pictures. We were lovers once. Here." She twisted in her chair, reached for the grocery bags hung from the handles behind her. They were stuffed full. Two of them.

He took them from her. "These are heavy," he said, feigning physical effort. "What do you want me to do with them?"

"They are for your university research."

He opened one of the bags and pulled out a handful of mag- azines. Old ones from the twenties. *The Beaver*. A whole five years' worth. It was a Canadian history magazine that was on his research list, but he hadn't yet discovered how to access the archive. Some of them were stained and torn, but others, probably because they came from the middle of a pile, looked as though they were in pretty good shape.

"Thanks for your help, Pat. I go all the way downtown and spend hours in the libraries and then I come home and you hand me a bag with exactly what I've been looking for. You're awesome."

"You're welcome. Now you'll find what you need."

"I'll take a look."

"Have you got two dollars? I can't eat there tonight. It's shepherd's pie, which would be good if they made it properly, but they spit poison in it. Look what it's done to my legs."

Cyril didn't have two dollars. "I can give you fifty cents."

"It's a start. I'll have to beg. Give me more when you make tenure."

Now he had heavy grocery bags full of old magazines. But he was not unhappy. They looked interesting, and it seemed likely that he'd find something of relevance. More context. He'd have more time with them in the store than he would have had in the library. And they somehow seemed more authentic than microfilm.

"Isn't it too cold to stay outside?"

"I'm fine. I've got this." She patted the large faux fur hat that covered her aviator cap and its dangling ears.

Cyril carried the bags into the store.

"You're early," said Mr. Lee.

"It's okay. I don't mind starting now, if you're ready to go?"

"All right."

"Is it busy?"

"It was a good day."

Mr. Lee emptied the till, leaving Cyril with the usual float.

"I'll see you tomorrow."

"Goodnight, Mr. Lee."

It was always busy between five and seven, when people came home from work and needed their cigarettes and milk. On lottery nights, hope and desperation sometimes triggered a lineup, especially if the prize was big. But lots of the business was chips and chocolate bars and cans of soup. Cat food. He was getting to know some of the customers. The lottery people for sure, who emptied their change beside the cash register and added it up in front of him. They'd already counted two or three times before — he could see how they were familiar with every coin.

It was very quiet after 9:30. Cyril started to work through the magazines. One of the bags was damp and smelled sour, like something had spilled. He was conscious of the face he made — screwed nose, pursed mouth — and stopped himself. It was just dirt. There was a sink in the back with hot water and lots of soap. A clean towel — Mr. Lee insisted on cleanliness. Dirt was an old familiar — they'd been without running water at home sometimes. Besides, he, Cyril, was a man, and Pat had been hauling these things around, just for him, for three days she'd said. One day it had rained, and she'd had to duck for cover at No Frills. To keep his bags dry. He did appreciate that.

As he began to flip through the magazines, the thinnest vibration ran through his arms and fingers.

His skin was tingling.

At about five minutes to eleven, Cyril opened a magazine from 1921 that promised photo illustrations of Canada's New Immigrants. He stopped to savour the anticipation that pressed at his chest. He looked up at the entrance door and around the store at the shelves of canned food and boxes of cereal. Bottles of cleaning stuff and garbage bags. Coolers full of milk and yogurt. Pop and juice. He took stock of where he was in the moment: a new immigrant — same as them. This was about Edward for sure.

He turned the pages, tugging at the places where the paper stuck. It was on page twenty-three, near the middle of a page with portraits of people from different ethnicities: small black-and-white portraits of The Irish Catholic, The Italian, The Greek, The Northern European, and The West Indian — his high eyebrows and cheekbones. Thin moustache. And that expression, the defiant mix of assurance and confrontation – the same portrait of Edward's father. The caption underneath read: *The West Indian students at the University of Toronto will return home with skills that benefit their island homes.* None of the men had names. Just an ethnic origin along with the role they played in Canadian society. The Italian who builds our houses and repairs our shoes. The Greeks, long recovered from the riots of 1918, bring traditional cooking and thriving restaurants. The Northern European farmer, the sturdiest of all immigrants.

I found your dad, man, Cyril whispered urgently to Edward. *I've got him! He was a student like me. From the West Indies. Which could be Jamaica. I'm sure he is; he's got to be Jamaican. We're almost brothers, Ed.* Cyril looked quickly through the remaining magazines then returned to the photo essay. Upon second reading, he realized that all of the other immigrants made a contribution to Canadian society. But the transient West Indian student returned home, and the article didn't question that. It was what they were supposed to do.

Cyril closed shop: cleared the cash, checked the coolers, turned down the thermostat, set the alarm, and stepped out into the cold, dark night with Edward's father tucked into his bookbag. He would go to the *Varsity* in the morning because there had to be a name to go with the photograph. They could help him with student records. He knew where to go next and what to do.

GETTING THERE WAS EASY. HE'D walked by it before and knew his way. He passed the Robarts Library, whose looming concrete presence again reminded him of how tremendously relieved he was not to have to go inside, and walked to the much smaller buildings behind it, the home of the student *Varsity* paper.

Cyril climbed to the second floor. The dark, narrow stairs and warren of small offices were disappointing. Someone should paint the walls, he thought. Wasn't this an important place? The rooms were empty, but he could hear people talking at the end of the hall. The door to a meeting room was open, with six or seven kids inside. Cyril quickly scanned the colour spectrum: two of them were brown. The others were Asian and white. All were gathered around a big computer monitor. No one looked up. The slim white girl in the middle was pointing to something that mattered. The others watched and listened. "What the fuck! Right there!" She stabbed her finger at the screen, and they all laughed, the Asian guy particularly, bent-forward, belly-clutching laughter. Cyril was about to leave; he wouldn't understand the joke, he'd be intruding. One of the women looked up and saw him.

"What's up?"

Push yourself to this, Nelson urged.

"I would like to talk to someone about a little historical research I'm working on."

"What is it?"

Cyril pulled the photo from his bag.

"Let's see then."

He slipped it from its envelope and gave it to the girl, who turned it over, then looked again at the portrait.

"I need to find his name," Cyril said.

"He's cute," she said, handing it to her colleague, who also checked the back.

"Well, it's from here for sure. But finding out who he is could be work. There are photo archives at Robarts, and you could check the newspaper archive to see if it ran. But you won't know until you see it. Not without a name."

The white girl, who looked puzzled, said, "So what's your interest in this guy if you don't know his name?"

"It's a small mystery someone shared with me," said Cyril. He liked saying "mystery." It gave his project an air of importance. "It's about a little Black kid who went missing back in the twenties. This guy's son, I think." They nodded, the three who were listening. They took him seriously.

"Cool," said the slim girl.

"I can't find anything about the father. If I could just get his name or at least find out where he was from ... ?"

"Worth a try. Like we said, check the paper. It's online."

"I don't have a computer."

"Really?"

Cyril nodded.

"Are you an undergrad?"

"Yeah."

The Asian guy wasn't so friendly. He took Cyril into one of the little offices and made a point of moving everything to the back corner of the desk so that when Cyril sat in front of the computer he was surrounded by empty space. On the other hand, Cyril told himself, he was here in the offices of the *Varsity* newspaper, which had been publishing since 1880. And the man in the photograph he was holding might have stood in this very room.

He began in 1921, the year before Edward was born, and ploughed through to 1924. He tried all the search words: *foreign student, Jamaica, Negro, Caribbean, West Indies*. Nothing. Nothing for *Jamaica* in a whole year's worth of millions of words. He widened his search to sports: *cricket* and *soccer*. Nothing. There were very few photographs, and none of them were anything like the one he searched for.

After about an hour, Cyril sighed and pushed back from the desk. Edward's father had never appeared here.

"You could go and ask Jim," said one of the women, who must have seen his frustration.

"Yeah?"

"He's been around forever. Looks after the photo archives. He might be able to date what you have."

"I'm pretty sure I'm close on the date," said Cyril.

"But not certain?"

"Within a few years."

"That's a long stretch of time. I'll make a photocopy and give it to Jim when I see him. He likes a challenge."

With some reluctance – it was his mystery, after all – Cyril handed her the photo.

"Try these," she offered, leaning over him to select another database. "We have access to the mainstream newspaper archives from that time."

"Okay. One last go for today," said Cyril. He began again: *Jamaica, pimento, sugar, banana, Caribbean.* This time there were photographs. Not a lot. But some, and once all the other searches had again come up empty, he clicked through the papers page by page, taking care not to skip because he had said that he was on a professional search, and that meant looking at everything. Not one picture of a Black person. Even though they had been here. In Toronto. Not so many of them, but a number of important businessmen who should show up at least once in a whole year. *I'm not here,* Cyril thought, then corrected himself. *He's not here.* The handsome, elusive father of Edward.

Cyril had ten more minutes and then he'd need to leave for work. Back to the little corner of Toronto that was more real to him than where he sat now, with the mouse in his hand, looking through an old newspaper — and he wasn't there. Cyril knew that he'd have to come back again. Someone had taken that photograph for a reason, and he needed to know what that was.

"No luck?"

"I guess not."

CYRIL'S LANDLADY HANDED HIM A letter from his aunt and brother and sister. "Where's your daddy?" she asked. Just like that, as though she were entitled to the answer.

"I don't know. In England, maybe."

"England. Now that's a good place. Why'd you come here if your daddy is there?"

"I don't know if he is there. Like I said."

"You don't know him, then?"

"No. He left when I was small."

"All those horny Jamaican men are bastards," she said. "I tell my daughter to stay clear of them."

"I'm a Jamaican man."

"I know, honey. But you're much too young for her. She a grown woman." She snorted her noisy laugh, which had a cruel sharpness.

"Whatever," said Cyril.

"I thought that's who you were searching for? This man you talk about and do your research on? Which is why you want me to put Wi-Fi in the house when you get your laptop?"

"It's okay."

"So that's not your daddy you look for?"

"No. Another guy."

"Well, darling, you puzzle me."

Cyril left her in the kitchen, where she turned up the radio so that the loud entreaty of the evangelist followed him downstairs through the closed door and streamed down the vents until Cyril stopped hearing it, inured by now to the sound.

"Fuck my daddy," Cyril said and dropped his bag on the bed. He opened the letter.

> We love you. We miss you. Daren got an A for his essay and teacher said that was just like Cyril. When are you coming home. Can you get us good toys in Canada. We had eggs for breakfast.

Cyril thought of his mother patiently guiding his baby sister's hands as she whacked a hard-boiled egg on the table to crack the shell. While his mother cupped the egg in her palm, the little girl peeled, pudgy baby fingers tugging at the shell that came off in fragments; his mother helped by teasing it from the firm, white flesh with her thumbnail, then steadying the girl's hand as she cut it with a fork.

From time to time, they had chickens in the yard — until a dog took them or they were snatched for a stranger's dinner plate. When they did have hens, it had always been Cyril's job to search out the eggs. By the time they disappeared into his sister's little, round mouth, they represented a satisfying return on the investment of Cyril's time and commitment to his family. He'd been caring for chickens and collecting eggs since he was five.

How could his mother have loved that man whose commitment had been so lacking? Cyril's birth certificate carried his father's name: Sidney Rowntree. He was probably on Facebook like everyone else. Cyril had looked for Edward Davina on Facebook right at the start, in the Mount Dennis library. He could look for his father's name there, and it wouldn't be nearly so hard as finding a kid who'd been born in Canada ninety years ago. But he wasn't going to do that.

TWELVE

YELLOW POLICE TAPE STRETCHED TAUT across the road that fed into the Ryerson campus. Streetcars, nose to tail, squealing grinding metal, crawled around the corner, diverted north.

"The front of B Building's closed," said one of the kids.

"A gunfight," someone else said.

"They think it's a gang thing. Black guys fighting over turf or a girl or some fucking shit."

At the back of the courtyard, on the other side of the street, a girl was wailing. A couple of girls stood by her, but she continued to howl into the empty air. A Black girl. Her grief sounded like fear and fury. But, like everyone else, whether still standing about or long gone, she knew nothing. Had seen nothing. Because reporters said that the police were calling for witnesses, and, so far, not a single person had come forward. On an early morning on a downtown street where people walked to work or rushed to early classes, nobody had seen a thing.

"There was a guy lying right there," someone said, pointing to the place on the sidewalk where a couple of cops stood off to the side and a woman recorded distances with a measuring tape.

It was jarring, this aftermath of violence in a place where people were supposed to be safe. Cyril had twice seen the mess that came from violence at home; it happened. A sad fact. But it wasn't supposed to happen here.

Cyril walked into the cafeteria, scanned it quickly for Randall, Leon, and Paul. They'd be just out of class and usually hooked up with him to eat. They invited him out to party with them, too, though he knew they didn't really expect him to join. He didn't share their interests — clubs, building music tracks on their computers — though he did sympathize with their pursuit of girls. They were kids. Not a whole lot younger than him, though sometimes it felt like years of difference. They didn't have his responsibilities. He needed to keep his head down and work. But they respected him. And they sought him out, as the kids at home used to do.

The cafeteria was teeming with people. Everyone pouring in from morning classes, buzzing about the shooting. "Starving hungry," groaned a guy who pushed up behind him in the line-up. The front half of the room was a row of fast-food stalls: Cultures, McDonald's, Pizza Hut.

"Hey, Daddy." Leon and Paul appeared, freed from the dreaded statistics class. "Where were you last night, brother?" asked Leon.

"I had to work," said Cyril.

"Sad."

"Leave him, Lo," Paul said. "He's got career issues. Got to increase profit margins on the milk and butter inventory." The guys laughed, the stress of making a passing mark in statistics released into the noise of the school cafeteria. Leon smacked Cyril's shoulder. Like the other two, he was half a foot taller than Cyril, who rocked slightly forward, keeping his balance.

"Where you been last night, Daddy?" The third of the trio,

Randall, jostled in between them. "Getting your beauty sleep? Didn't do you no good." Randall walked through women; his coiffed dreads and too-cool clothes had them lining up for him. The guys envied how he tease-talked with girls. Cyril couldn't flirt.

"Oh, man, look at all these people," said Paul.

"You do the lineup," Leon said. "I'll find a table." He shoved a bill into Paul's hand. "Chicken wrap or a cheeseburger. I don't care." He headed toward the back of the room, threading through the crowd.

"That guy who got shot. You know him?" asked Cyril.

"Not from here, man. But he got some friends who were," said Randall. "Someone said his name's Odel."

"My mom was calling me about two seconds after it happened," said Paul. "She's like, if it's a Black guy it must be me who's dead. Man, news travels fast."

"Yeah, mine's scared all the time," said Randall. "I'm telling her she should keep me safe in the house till I'm sixty-five."

"And she's gonna be a hundred and three," laughed Paul, miming a bent back and shaky cane.

"Seriously, dude. This is bad that it happened down here," said Randall. "It's gonna start all that security shit again. And you know who they'll lean on the hardest." The crowd swarmed around them as they picked up their trays and headed back to find Leon. Cyril was glad he had friends to sit with.

All three of them were Jamaica-connected. Leon's family had come to Canada when he was a baby. Paul had been six when his mother sent for him to join her. Randall had been born in Canada. Jamaican-Canadians were all across the city. Some of them concentrated in neighbourhoods where bad news too often came from. Bad guys in gangs shooting at bad guys in gangs.

Cyril had seen them around at home too. Canadian-raised guys, deported to Jamaica, nursing bad attitudes with big ideas about survival.

"All of them that come back from Foreign, they jump like trapped rats. Don't poke him, he'll bite you," his mother had invariably warned.

"Come out with us tonight? Friday night," said Randall. His eyes followed a girl who'd squeezed in between her friends at the table beside them.

"Yeah. It's just a school dance, but the DJ is good," said Leon.

"I have to work," Cyril said.

"Afterward," said Randall. "Oh, I forgot," he added, shaking his head, "that's when you have to study."

"You're right," said Cyril. "Then I'll probably go for a stroll. That's what I do."

The men laughed. "You stroll alone. We'll dance with the ladies."

Cyril smiled and pictured himself dancing with the girl at the next table, her breasts pressed against his chest. So close and tight that he could touch. "No women for me," he said as he walked away.

He had twice been downtown late at night. Begged the night off from Mr. Lee to come in for a school talk. It was a different world, the city in the dark. Yonge Street was as busy as morning. He avoided the drunks. Edgy excitement sparked through the crowds of people who gathered outside bars and restaurants. The girls were scary — so sexy in their heels and dress-up clothes.

Cyril was sometimes keenly aware of a peripheral threat of violence, a parallel possibility that was with him all of the time. They'd drummed this into him at Mount Dennis. Everyone living there brandished the warning like a weapon. "Your black skin's a target," said a cousin. Uncle Junior said, "If you find trouble, walk away from it. I haven't got time to deal with any of that." Cyril always walked with care, as he had back home. Except that downtown, it wasn't just to avoid confrontation but also to be sure that *he* didn't frighten anyone. And once he got off the busy main streets at night, to walk with businesslike purpose. "Don't move too fast, never run," Evan told him. "Running While Black can be cause for arrest."

What he watched for — on any night, anyplace — what he refused to let intimidate him into staying at home, was the police. A cruiser driving slowly by on the other side of the road would quicken his heart, and he'd fist his hands before forcing his fingers to relax. He'd been stopped twice already. Some of the guys who lived in the gun-plagued neighbourhoods got stopped all the time. Mount Dennis was definitely not the worst.

The second time it happened to Cyril, he'd been ready. One of the officers said, "Where are you going this evening? To a dancehall party? Seeing a lady friend?" and looked him up and down while the other leaned over him and stared, challenging him to drop his gaze. He did. His stomach soured, buttocks tightened. "Answer only what they ask you, and keep it brief." He'd heard that instruction many times and stood stock-still until they told him to go. A couple of people glanced over as they walked by, but Cyril and the police were barely a distraction on the busy street.

Cyril weighed the humiliation and the risk of being stopped against the pleasure of walking in the night. He kept walking because he loved it just a skip or two less than running. Because it was the most relaxing thing he knew how to do. It taught him about his new life and opened up memories that reconnected him to the one he'd left behind. Because after walking for an hour, he'd get home body-tired, brain-tired, fall into bed, and be quickly asleep.

SINCE THE SHOOTING, THE UNIVERSITY had posted security guards at the main doors. They regularly checked bags, rifling through them with their latex-gloved hands, which Cyril deeply resented – all the more because he was sure that the level of tense interaction that he and the other Black guys experienced with the security guards was exactly because they were Black. Guys like Leon were wound tight with it. It was a game now – testing the guards' cool. Most of them were just young guys. The school's mood had changed since the shooting. There was a self-consciousness that hadn't been there before.

A group of kids that included the girlfriend of the mur-dered man were the permanent hosts of a table inside the main entrance that was piled with pamphlets and all the parapher-nalia of a busily occupied space: coffee cups and food containers, someone busy with an open textbook or a laptop. A handful of them hung out there every day asking people to sign a petition that demanded justice for Odel and all the other Black victims of crime. It took courage to do that. He could see how the girl-friend, whom nobody had noticed before, must be changed forever. Randall often sat with them.

Cyril avoided them if he could. Walked an extra minute to use another exit because ever since the cop who'd killed Michael Eligon had been cleared of responsibility, people had started to gather outside the main entrance. Michael had walked out of his hospital on a cold day in February wearing only a hospital gown and without his shoes. What the video showed was a street full of cops, twelve of them, spread out across the road, and the single cop who had shot at Michael three times; in fear of his life, the cop said. Because Michael held a pair of corner-store scissors in each hand. Two fucking pairs of scissors. The anger of the protesters was so charged that Cyril felt the fresh shock of it every time, and that image – Michael walking on the road in his socks – was trapped in his mind forever. But he would not let either the murder or the protesters' anger overwhelm him. He did not want the politics of it. He didn't want the issue to be any bigger in his life than it already was.

Cyril and the guys, Paul and Randall, were closer now, though Leon wasn't around as much. "School sickens me," he said, though when he did come he stuck with them. All that height and muscle made an impression; people skirted them when they were together, and Cyril liked to be the guy in front when they walked through the halls. But these days he was glad to get out of school after class; the pleasure of working in the study rooms or the library was gone.

He spent more time in a corner of the Mount Dennis library where he had discovered that the building's white noise helped his focus. And he could book ahead for computer time. Good public space, Cyril thought, for people like himself who needed someplace to go outside of where they slept. Some of them needed it much more than he did, and, though he was ashamed to know it, that cheered him because at the very least he was better than them: he wasn't crazy yet.

Then there were times when the dreary reality of a difficult and lonely day was as ugly as stained cardboard spread on the ground with a sleeping bag on top and a human shape in between. The unthinkable hard press of bone on damp concrete, chillingly cold in the outside air. Cyril had seen people curled over subway grates, warmed by hot blasts from underground – unimaginably hard-won comfort. Noisy, stinking, industrial heat.

There were more Black people on the streets downtown than there should have been, disproportionate numbers – shaking empty drink cups, begging change, or shouting at the passersby. Fighting their personal demons. White people too. Brown people. Old ones, some with walking canes; young ones, defiantly dirty, white kids with dreadlocks and silver jewellery in their noses, through their cheeks and their tongues. He was fascinated but afraid to stare, afraid to stop. And he would not share his money with any of them.

When Cyril saw the Black ones, he crossed the road, afraid that they would know how tenuous he was and think him one of them. But he had money in a bank that was saved for school, and what little he earned from a day's work was more than they would collect in their pathetic and sad rattling cups in a whole week of shaking and asking. If he met their eyes by accident, when they were close, a rush of panic set his heart racing. Because homeless mad people in their solitary spaces on the far-too-public sidewalk battled to be seen – to be acknowledged. Acknowledgement and respect. Street people got none. And Cyril could be one of them if he made a misstep in this new place. Because he still could not fit in. And when he tried, he could not sustain the person he made himself become. He preferred to go for a walk, and maybe that was a first sign of mental illness. There was no one to ask whether this might be so.

Cyril was afraid of many things: that he would never have a girlfriend or a wife – a woman like Black History Girl would never want him; that his work would always be mundane and poorly paid; that no one would look him straight in the eye and say "Well done" and mean it. As he listed all these fears, he felt the disappointment of Nelson, who had taught him, over and again, you will be as good as you wish to be so long as you work hard. Then Cyril was angry because Nelson had thrived inside his own country, born into the middle-class privilege that served those Jamaicans so well. Cyril had stacks of odds against him. He could count them up, name each one of them, and fan them out to show them off. It was one thing to know how hard it would be and quite another — he said to Nelson, whose heavenly presence was bearing down on him hard — quite another to experience it. "I don't belong here," was what Cyril said out loud, in the muttered voice he'd learned from Pat. And when he heard himself, that was frightening too. Because Patricia certainly was mad, and she could go from sweet to threatening in seconds.

He had once seen her yelling at a man who obviously didn't know who she was, calling him a fucking pervert and a rapist. "I'm getting the police," she'd screamed, her whole body shaking with anger. But as soon as she saw Cyril, she lowered her voice and was almost coy. "I'm in a little bit of trouble."

"What's going on?"

"Oh, not him." She barely glanced at the man as he hurried across the road. "It's the mice." And then she giggled. "My landlord found out that I'm feeding them. I said I wasn't, but he'll evict me if he finds out that I still am." She sighed happily. "I love the mice. They're so busy and cheerful. But they're always hungry."

THIRTEEN

❧

EDWARD CAN'T THINK WHERE SHE finds those shoe sizes. The new woman who has moved in lives a couple of rooms down. They come and go. This one is young, maybe early forties with scrappy hair that sticks out everywhere. She's a short Black lady, but her boots are too big for her feet. She is always talking about her boyfriend who is coming to get her and then they'll live in a house with a "kitchen shiny as a spaceship with sparkles on the cabinet handles." He likes those sparkles, thinks he could use some of those himself.

She gets mean too. Probably when she's off her meds. Then she's yelling at everyone to stop harassing her and how she'll get a gun because you don't fuck with her. She's got a mouth when she's in her episodes. But when she's quiet, he likes her. Nice short Black lady. Got a warm way of talking like she just came from the islands.

A boy comes to see her, hanging off his grandmother's hand. That's unusual, having visitors in here, especially a child. But this is the short lady's son. She calls him "Likkle Ting." The boy reminds Edward of someone, standing there in his oversize jacket with two big eyes staring. He doesn't smile, except when Edward gives him a candy, which he's taken to doing, keeping an eye and ear out for these visitors on weekends. The kid has a big blue knapsack with a picture of cartoon dinosaurs. He's about three feet high, the likkle ting. Around the same age Edward had been when he was sent to scrabble for scrap wood in his baggy pants, sizes too big, that he tied up with string. They were always coming undone because he wasn't good at knots. Never had any underwear till he was seven. Bare feet half the time in the summer, and then waiting for boots to get handed out in the fall. The cook was always telling him, "Remember you're a lucky boy. Lots never had anyone to feed them. They're gone to heaven, and you're still here." She'd turn her face upward and open her arms wide. "Praise the Lord." Edward rarely got sad. Not happy either. What he remembers is the hard work of it. Every day after day.

Likkle Ting has a nice smile when he lets it out, worth waiting for. But this morning, when the grandmother comes with the boy, the short lady's mind is sick. Her eyes are yellow and full of fear. She's wild in her dressing gown and boots. Her back is pressed to the wall, as far as she can get from her child. She starts to scream, "Mi always hab crosses. Wa yuh dweet fah? Yuh is a likkle devil, yuh wah stress mi?" The boy must be stricken. Must be. Though his face doesn't show a thing. Just his wide eyes staring the way they do. The grandmother pulls at him hard, pushes him behind her, says, "He is your son. You are wicked to say these things."

Edward watches from his doorway as Security Sam — Thank the Powers for Sam — comes out of his office and talks to the lady, calm and gentle. Edward would pull the other two into his room and leave the mother outside. He wants the grandmother to hold his hand, too. What he wants to tell the boy is that when he's grown it won't be so bad. But Edward closes his door. After a while, it's quiet, and he's pretty sure he won't see Likkle Ting again.

FOURTEEN

SCHOOL HAD BEEN TOUGH. LEON was pulling low marks and was pissed at everyone. He didn't study. Didn't show up for class. His parents whaled on him when he got home, so he went out, and then the women he was sleeping with gave him trouble. He was a mess, and that contamination leaked into the rest of them. There'd been more problems at school. Not guns. But a campus stabbing had put everyone on edge all over again. Cyril was struggling with his accounting class. Not the material but the prof, who smirked and patronized through the whole three hours and filled too much time talking about how well his investments were performing and how he'd retire early and not have to teach anymore. Mr. Lee's store had become a welcome haven.

"Hello. Good evening."

Cyril looked up from his homework, rubbed at his tired eyes. It was the Jamaican nurse, who looked at him as though she thought he should be pleased to see her.

"Your night off?" Cyril said. "Or did that lottery ticket win you the big prize?"

She giggled. "Not really, I guess."

"What have you been up to?"

"Not much. I stay home. Or I study. Go to work."

"You don't go out? I walk. Doesn't cost anything."

"Why would you do that?"

"To see things. The neighbourhood. Downtown. All sorts of places. I've walked all the way to the lake."

"Where's the lake?"

"South of here," said Cyril. "Straight south."

"I wouldn't do that. It must be far."

"Don't you want to know about the city?"

"I have a friend in Scarborough. I go to her house."

He knew he'd disappointed her. "Okay, so long as you're getting through."

"I'll have lots of time to see things," she said. "After I'm done. When I've got my permanent resident card. Right now, I keep my head down and work." She looked as though she felt sorry for him. "Give me another lottery ticket. One of the instant winnings."

She took time to weigh the pros and cons of the scratch and wins. Then gave him her five dollars. As she left, she said, "Safe travels."

He did get it. Of course, he knew how international student fees were so much higher than home fees. And how important that PR card was. It meant possibilities, a real future. It got you knowledgeable counsel from all the people working in settlement services who needed to see your PR card before they could help you with work-skill upgrades and professional mentorship. It meant that you could stay.

TWO DAYS OF RAIN SIGNALLED the end of winter. Not its real finish, because forecasts called for snow later in the week. It was Sunday night, and Mr. Lee's daughter was visiting, filling in at

the store — "For old times' sake," she'd said. "Take the night off."
But Cyril felt tight as a drum, his rising anxieties uncontain-
able. He was painfully homesick and missed his mother with a
longing that made him hollow. She was unreclaimable, passed
on forever, and Cyril had never been able to satisfy himself as
to where. But if he could be home right now, in the Jamaican
sunshine, on his way to Brown's Town, walking by fields of yam
and cabbage or under a moon with the tree frogs singing, then a
heaven might seem a possibility.

He wanted to belong to someone. He wanted to hold Black
History Girl. And maybe, if he could find the courage, to work at
fitting in. Then life would be better. But he wasn't bold enough,
he told himself, and so he used Edward as a distraction. And then
he was ashamed of himself for blaming Edward.

Cyril had a spring coat with a big rain hood, rain pants, and
rubber galoshes from the Value Village bargain bin. He put
them on and opened the door to the backyard. Wind shook
the branches, whipped shadows through the light thrown by the
motion detector: crude duppy shadows to frighten children,
though they didn't scare Cyril. The night sounded of metal gutters rattling under the eaves of the house, a car alarm on an
endless loop across the street, and the constant pounding rain.
He pulled his hood over his head as he stepped onto the path.
He had ID in his pocket and a twenty-dollar bill — safeguards. He
needed only to walk off his restlessness. To make himself tired
enough to forget how bad he felt so that he could get some sleep.
He pushed into a fast walk, and a part of his mind had to focus
on that, so it was harder to tell the difference between loneliness and anger. Anger was better for walking. Physical, sharp, it
pumped energy. Loneliness was just sad and depleted.

Back home in Jamaica, Cyril had taught himself to find his way by holding on to the night, eyes closed. Now his eyes strained to see through the pouring rain; he would never trust Toronto well enough to close them. The rain was loud, and his boots slapped through water. Now and then he pulled his hand from his pocket and tightened his hood. He walked in and out of pools of light falling from windows or streetlamps. Car headlights made the sidewalks glow a dark, wet sheen. Silver bullets of rain burst on the ground. Red tail lights snaked by. Two guys swaddled in rain gear and riding hard on bicycles with little lights flashing appeared and were immediately swallowed again into the teeming liquid dark. A dog pulled a woman by its leash while she struggled along behind with a broken umbrella.

In the inner suburbs of the northwest and across town in the east, Randall and Paul would be in front of computers multitasking. Doing schoolwork, Skyping, and texting friends. They'd been collaborating with musicians from the U.K. and Germany, laying down tracks online for weeks. They said that staying at home was okay because making music was the best. Evan wasn't even in town. He'd won a university prize that came with money and had gone to Halifax to see what was left of Africville for a planned writing project.

Cyril walked and walked. Pounded out a rhythm that scrubbed his anger loose and into the rain. Night in a city of 2.5 million people where it's raining so hard that even those usually undeterred by weather — snow, wind, freezing rain — stayed home. Cyril pushed his legs faster, almost to a trot, and his body warmed with the effort. His mood began to turn. He was dry, though his feet worked double hard as they fought for stability inside his rubber boots. It was time to turn back. He had got the comfort he'd known would come from walking. He always did. He pulled at the cuff of his coat to read his watch. Late enough already.

Cyril hadn't seen the cop car before it slid alongside him. He always watched out for them, but his hood was drawn and his eyes focused straight ahead. He felt for the ID in his pocket then pulled his hand quickly free and stood still, facing the car with his arms extended and his open palms facing front. Now he remembered the headlights in his face a minute or so ago.

"Pull the hood down, buddy." The voice came from behind the car window, only partially opened. Shouted, because of the rain.

Cyril tugged his hood back from his head, which immediately streamed with water, filling his eyes and falling from his chin.

One cop got out of the car, ordered Cyril's hands to the roof and his legs apart as he patted him down. Cyril felt like filth. He was glad of the storm, the dark, and no one around to see him. Anger was back, gathering deep in his stomach, filling his chest.

Cyril said "Yes, sir" and "No, sir" and "Yes, I do" as he handed over his ID and showed his money.

"Where have you been tonight?"

"Just walking," said Cyril.

"On a night like this?"

"Yes, sir. I like to walk, regardless of the weather."

"Regardless," repeated the second cop from inside the car.

"Where are you from?" asked the first.

"Down at Weston and ..."

"I mean your accent, buddy. Where do you come from?"

"I'm originally from Jamaica," said Cyril.

The first cop made a sound like a laugh that had caught in his throat, then mimicked — "originally"— made it sound pretentious and stupid. The second cop said to his partner, "Have you heard what they say about guns?"

"What's that?" said the first.

"It's not guns that kill people. It's Jamaicans."

Cyril's anger punched into his gut. The words he'd never spoken out loud spilled from his mouth. "You fucking racist assholes," he heard his own voice say and didn't care because he was so angry.

"Dirty nigger mouth needs cleaning," one said.

"We've been looking for a Black boy who looks like you," said the other. "Hands back on the roof!" Cyril fought for balance with the rain pouring down the back of his neck and the repulsive hands again searching his legs. "Your boots," The cop said. "Take them off." Cyril turned to lean with his back against the car, struggled while the cop watched and then his socks sucked water while the hand that had searched through his boots pulled his wrists back into handcuffs. Then the hands turned to fists, and it didn't hurt, but the shock of it at his ribs made him cry out, and he groaned as the kick at his shins took him down to the ground, shoulder spearing the sidewalk before the boot smashed his chest. *Don't break my bones.* He prayed for his mother and heard her shrill scream, *Stop now,* and the cop who'd stayed in the car said, "Fucking stop it. Now!" And the cop who was beating him stopped.

When he gathered Cyril from the ground, he was almost gentle, one hand under his elbow, the other across his shoulders guiding him to the back seat of the car. "You were acting out, brother," the cop said. "I had to do that for your own good. Be glad we caught you before you did some damage. We're taking care of you."

Cyril faced the steel mesh and the bulletproof glass that was between him and the cops as water puddled along the seat and at his feet. His confusion, the pain and shame, was as heavy on his chest as the knuckled fist. Cyril had walked by police stations many times. He had never stopped to wonder which door they took the bad people to or where they put them once they got there. The car pulled into a big, wide, brightly lit garage at the back of the station. When Cyril put his foot to the ground, the pain buckled his knee. He stumbled, and the cop who'd stopped the beating grabbed his arm to steer him through a short, narrow hallway and into a room with a number of cells. Another cop appeared and opened the cell door. "We'll be discussing your case," said the cop who'd hit him. "You'd better pray my supervisor's in a good mood."

Cyril stood until the door was closed and then sat on the bench. He was damp and cold. The hard surfaces and bright light made the night seem very late and very empty. He could still hear the distant rain. Any other sounds – footsteps, a ringing phone – had a hollow echo. The cell was narrow, like the ones on TV, with a barred door. But he hadn't known about the stale stench of fear under the wash of disinfectant. He wanted some Aspirin. Water to drink. He hurt all over. He'd left his house angry, pissed at the world, but proud of himself also. Because really, he'd been doing okay. He'd been getting through. He heard a snatch of song, a hymn, a woman's voice passing in the hall, and was momentarily back home in church surrounded by his mother's people. Her congregation. But it was disappointment that they showed him.

He couldn't fight the disdain, the scorn the cops threw at him. He was ashamed of how they made him feel. He pushed his face into his hands, glad his mother was dead because this would kill her. When he heard her whisper, *Mi alreadi wid di laawd, darlin, so nu worry yuh self*, his mouth shaped a smile. Man, he longed for her. He hated this place. Then his nostalgia and anger were lost to the hurt under his ribs, the pain in his shoulder and his foot. He was aching-tired, longed to lie down but refused to give them the satisfaction of seeing him sleep. He waited.

He asked for a lawyer, and they said he hadn't been arrested. "Why am I here then?'" he asked.

"Go if you want," they said. "But, hey, it's still raining." Cyril made a short list of options. The first, to leave now. The second, to stay. Because what they'd done to him once, they could do again. Because he wasn't sure that he could walk very far, didn't know if his twenty dollars was enough for a cab. Because he needed help. And he was frightened.

"I want to call a friend," he said.

"Who do you know here, buddy?"

"I have a friend with a car."

"Maybe he doesn't like to visit police stations." The cop smiled.

"He'll come," Cyril said.

"We're not obliged to give you a phone call," said the desk sergeant. "But I'm going to let you have it anyway because you need looking after."

They brought him into a room with a chair and a phone and a list of lawyers' telephone numbers on the wall. He'd have called Evan, but he was in Nova Scotia. Calling his Uncle Junior would be one of the hardest things he'd ever done; he would be sure to tell him that he'd brought it upon himself, he'd been warned about walking at night. And he might wake him up. Also, he thought, with real trepidation, what if Junior thought that if the police had picked him up, he must deserve it? What if he said no? He pressed the numbers and breathed deep while he waited for Junior to answer. After that, Cyril went back to his cell until another cop came to unlock the door and said, without explanation, "You can go."

Junior arrived filled with righteous frustration, which he directed liberally at Cyril; he waited with characteristic impatience as Cyril collected his belt and ID and twenty-dollar bill from a plastic tray.

"We have a tough job to do, sir," the sergeant said to Junior. "And we do it every day. My officers are top-notch."

Junior glared.

The sergeant said, "Take it easy now, kid. Don't get into any more trouble."

THE RAIN OUTSIDE WAS EVEN worse. The car was noisy from the din of rain on the roof, the tires on the wet road, and the grind and swish of the wipers. To make himself heard, Junior bellowed: "How long did you say you were there?"

"Since eight," said Cyril.

"And they never said they'd charge you with anything?"

"No," said Cyril. "I didn't know who else to call."

"They mistook you for another Black guy," said Junior with disgust.

"It's racial profiling."

"So what?" said Junior. "What difference does it make? It's always been this way. Doesn't matter what you call it. I told you to keep your head down."

Cyril looked through the bleared passenger-side window into the night, at the empty sidewalks and the indistinguishable profiles of passing buildings. He imagined his mother here with him. Her dark, round face. Skin soft like powder. Sunday hat on her head for formal. Endlessly polite, her small body shivering in a big coat. Her girl-voice patois would have been a soft song they'd never have listened to in that ugly police station waiting room. She'd have waited for him all night on the uncomfortable bench under that fluorescent light and been frightened all the while.

Cyril leaned back hard into his seat and didn't exclaim when the pain jabbed at his shoulder. He forced a smile to his face instead. "Thanks for coming to get me. I didn't know what else to do."

Junior grunted. "I've been in this damned country a long, long time."

They turned left through the rain-blur of green traffic light onto Weston Road, and Junior pulled up at the corner of Cyril's street.

"Don't let it happen again."

"No, sir."

Cyril's greatest shame was having to concede that he had met Junior's lowest expectations. In his basement, Cyril slept for twenty-eight hours. He woke too tired to eat and watched the promised snow fall through the little window over his desk — waited for the ghosts to gather. After a while, he slept again, and then he heard the breathing, ragged, raw — for life itself.

EDWARD RUNS LIKE AN ANIMAL runs for its life, heart beating dangerously fast, blood pounding in his ears, feet slipping over the rough stones of the back laneways. Desperate to get to the fence, hands and arms pumping furiously, frantically. Under his jacket, the little purse of money burns into his chest. Now the fence: hands tearing at the wooden boards, searching for a grip then pushing up with his feet that slip and slip again, but then something cracks and he has a toehold to push himself up so that he can grab at its top. He knows that he has cut his palms on jagged splinters, but it doesn't matter. In a moment he is over and falls to the ground on the other side. Now he crawls along the bottom of the fence, over the muck and garbage. Not to be seen. Stay in the shadows. He's moving slowly, but his heart hasn't slowed at all. Then the door to the shed that looks closed but isn't. He pulls hard at the door with hands that slip with blood but don't hurt yet. His fingers still work. That's what matters.

The door cracks open, and he pushes it further with his shoulder, still crawling, and slides into the pitch dark that's inside. Breathes in the reek of slaughtered poultry. Now he pulls the door closed behind him, back those few inches. This is not a place anyone will come to until morning. There is a pile of sacks in the corner and a can of water. Those are what he's here for. His breathing slows enough that he can hold his breath for a moment, test the air with his ears, his nose, until he's sure that he's alone. His eyes adjust to the dark. The walls are built from slats of wood, some crooked and gapped. Dim light seeps in. He holds the can of water to his mouth with his torn and burning hands until the cold liquid fills him. As he lies back on the sacks, the hurt comes. The pain in his legs. His foot starting to scream where he landed so hard. His arms aching from effort. He is exhausted. He is thrilled. He has made more money this night than he has made in the last four months.

CYRIL JOLTED AWAKE INTO THE dark room. His heart was racing, he knew his limbs had been jerking in sleep paralysis — that's what had woken him — and he was breathing so hard that his throat was sore. He wondered if he had called out in his sleep. He could feel Edward's presence, hear his snores.

Cyril held his breath. Edward must have been about twelve.

He was still skinny, small but wiry. His hands looked strong, big for his size. One lay at his side, seemingly relaxed, palm up, wrapped in a bloody rag. The other was curled against his chest. Edward was wearing a cloth cap that looked too big for him. It was grimy and darkened with sweat where it circled his head. His pants were the sort that stopped at mid-calf. He was still a boy, though his face was angular. Even in sleep it was tense, forehead drawn into a frown. If Cyril could have, he'd have washed Edward's face. Bandaged his hands. Covered him with a blanket. Comforted him.

EDWARD ROLLS FROM HIS SIDE onto his back. Slow, stiff, awkward, old. He turns his head and opens his eyes to check the time. First light of day, 7:00 a.m. Early yet. Spring snow on the roof outside.

What Edward remembers is the thrill of it. Robbing them of what they didn't deserve. Those who looked at him and his friends and saw scum not worth the pennies they begged. Out on the sidewalks downtown where the people came to restaurants, to the theatre, wearing their bags of money. Climbing down from their taxicabs. Laughing their shiny, soap-scrubbed laughs. Ladies stinking of flowers and fruit and jewels. All with their noses turned up and away from the boys in their ragged clothes, reeking of sweat and dirt and grease: dark things clustered in shadows, counting out their pennies, dreaming of food. They'd approach a man, hold out their hands, and reach forward, noisy, busy, begging. And while the man's friends, distracted, looked on, one of the boys – on that night, Edward – would creep up behind the target and slide the purse from his pocket. After that, the only business was to run as fast as you could to a safe place. Snow was a problem, unless it was falling real hard. You could never risk them following the tracks, being found out in the precious secret hiding places.

Snow is a problem now. Because his cheque comes today, and he has to get to the bank that is only four blocks away, easy enough on a clear day. But he's terrified of the drifts and skids of snow or ice on the stretches of sidewalk that don't get cleared, of breaking his bones in a fall that he can't stop. Makes him laugh because back then they'd shoot like bullets over the ice, piling into each other at ferocious speeds, screaming with plea-sure to see themselves tumble and roll. And then they'd scramble upright to do it again. Last man standing won! If they'd ever had skates, they would have been the fastest men on the rink.

The thrill, to open a purse and feel the coins with your fingers. To see if what you'd imagined from the size and the heft of it was really there. All that money for a minute's work, though the race afterward could bust your heart. The risk was huge. But then came all the food you wanted.

There is a can of beans in the cupboard. He'll sleep till noon. Make tea with used bags. Eat the beans around four. Go back to bed.

FIFTEEN

SOMETIMES, WHEN CYRIL WOKE IN the morning, he thought of Edward; on some days, Edward stayed with him, close as a friend. He appreciated his company, especially now, when things were not going well. When a teacher's lecture failed where he stood, the lessons spoiled by the monotony of his voice: the energy suck, the sorry excuse for taking Cyril's precious money. It was harder when things went smoothly. Even when Randall was around. Absence constantly nagged at him: he missed his mother and Nelson, his culture – all of it. Jamaica, where people lived their lives so differently from those he was among now. Sure, eating, sleeping, working, if you were lucky, those things were the same, but he missed the joyful hoots of laughter, the vibrant image-charged patois. The sheer creativity of life in so many of its aspects. And the sun-saturated colours with plants that grew so fast you could watch it happen.

Toronto sometimes surprised with fleeting moments of joy. His moments. Not to be trivialized by sharing. He found them when he was walking – he could never explain it to the guys or the Jamaican nurse. About a low bush in an ordinary front yard stuffed with the sound of a hundred birds chirping. A dense brown leafless bush stuffed with little brown sparrows shouting at each other, and at first he couldn't see them in their camouflage colours. Then his eye found their flitting and twitching. When he stopped, they froze and quieted, and as he began to move away the volume turned up full again. If he was not supposed to feel that jolt of pleasure because he was a man, and young, and they were just birds, he didn't care. He loved those small things in the world. Like the three little birds on Bob's doorstep that sang sweet songs about how everything would be all right. Birds made him feel that way: if they were still in the world, he was going to be okay. Cyril knew exactly what Bob's lyric meant.

Edward lived on shelves and in cubicles, hidden away in the buildings that collected and preserved Toronto's history. Cyril had begun to look forward to his time in those places. Despite the endless repetition the search demanded. Regardless of the days upon days without any success. The unexpected learning along the way was a gift of sorts. *This is how you know yourself*, said Nelson in his stern schoolmaster voice. *Through history and language — this is theirs, but take what you need, make it your own.*

He'd seen a picture of a big street protest in a photographic history of Toronto. Below the photograph, he'd read that the men were marching to protect their livelihoods, their families, their children's futures. Fascism had spread from Italy and Germany to Canadian cities, nurtured and propagated by immigrants whose home countries were recovering their national pride. So in Canada, where the Depression was spreading and the economies they'd left behind were beginning to thrive, small numbers of Italian and German immigrants had led a spread of hatred. They loathed Jews and homosexuals and communists and all sorts of other minorities including Blacks. It was people like Edward who'd been protesting.

The next visit to the research library was after a morning class – the last of the day – and Cyril planned to work until four, when he'd need to head back in time to take over from Mr. Lee. What he now thought of as his private cubicle was free, a good sign, and he sat back with the index, paged through it, looking for keywords: *racism, communism, anarchist, protest, fascists*. At the microfilm reader, he threaded the film and cranked the handle, scanned the date and page numbers. He liked the sound it made, how once he had the feel of it he could control what he saw.

People at nearby machines came and went. When Cyril caught himself dozing, he left the building, walked its circumference, ignoring the panhandlers and the crazy woman at the corner. If Pat had joined him here, she'd have liked it. But she couldn't travel, not in her wheelchair.

What he finally found was a newspaper article from 1933 with the headline "Police Prevent Anarchist Bloodshed" and a photograph of an anti-fascist demonstration that filled Spadina Avenue. There were masses of men in dark coats and fedoras, some carrying banners. The policemen were obviously there to contain them, not to support them, despite the cheerful tone of the article:

By 3:45 P.M. when the first section of the parade moved off, the park was a sea of humanity – a host of workers taking up battle against a common enemy. Ten thousand workers, three hundred banners, all raising the voice of proletarian struggle against the murderous regime of Fascism.

As the revolutionary organizations left Wellington Park, the strains of the "Internationale" rose above the throng — sung with a spirit that is characteristic only of proletarians on parade.

The people were angry, and the war that had ended fifteen years before still festered in their hearts and minds. Cyril was looking for Edward, as he always did. And Edward's father. Then his eye found the darker face toward the front of the crowd in the bottom right of the photograph. The rest was a blur. "How do you know?" Cyril challenged himself, demanding. Because this felt right, that boy standing still while the men marched. Cyril squeezed his eyes shut, rubbed at them hard with the heel of his hand, and looked again. He'd make the Toronto Archives his first stop tomorrow, right after his business class.

THE ARCHIVES BUILDING WAS VIRTUALLY empty. Everyone was out in the fine spring weather. The staff were nice. He filled out forms and waited while they fetched him a small box with photographs of the same demonstration, many from similar angles to the one he'd seen in the newspaper but closer, which was exactly what he needed. He borrowed a magnifying glass and searched again for the dark face.

The boy was standing at the edge of the crowd, watching, not participating. Not yet, anyway. At his side — and it might be that he stood back to protect them — was a pile of stacked newspapers in a little wagon with tall sides. *He's the right age*, thought Cyril. It was the shape of his head. Of his forehead. Cyril stared, felt for the second sight that had introduced him to Edward; he shook his head, sharp, to wake it. Because there was something about the slope of bone. For a moment, the air around him clouded, dense with Edward's presence, the reality of his life, his history. *I can't believe I found him in this crowd!* Cyril was thrilled because now he knew without a doubt that this was Edward. He rubbed his fingertips against his palms to soothe their tingling. Cyril nodded, tamping down his excitement, but couldn't stop the smile on his face.

Now he would get serious. He laughed at himself. Back at the library, he started to search with new keywords: *newspaper boy*. Moved from the *Globe* to the *Star* to the *Telegram* and back and forth. And then some few days later, thoroughly triumphant, he found something else. In the last frames of another roll of microfilm was a photograph of a gang of newspaper boys who'd been arrested for smashing the windows of a fascist meeting hall. The five boys were lined up for the camera. Miserable, shoulder to shoulder, grubby boys with old faces. And there, second from the right, was the same dark face and his name: Davina. It was Edward Davina.

It was incredible to see the definitive evidence of the boy he'd been dreaming of for the last few months. The editorial that accompanied the report commented:

> Boys who are an unmanageable nuisance, who are not going to school, must be taken in hand by the authorities. This newspaper condemns Communism. These miscreants should be punished with the full force of the law.

The very fact that the newspaper had published the photograph underscored its disapproval. All of the paper's other pictures were of important people. Or important people's weddings.

Edward's was the darkest face in the photograph. A kid surviving on his wits who'd got caught up in politics and landed in some serious trouble. Cyril steered clear of politics, had an aversion to organized partisan groups. The Black Students' Association had asked him to join, but he'd sensed unstated expectations that reinforced his reluctance.

Edward was real. He couldn't leave him buried there in the library. Cyril learned how to scan the image. He printed four copies. One to pin on his wall.

CYRIL HAD A PHONE CALL and ran quickly upstairs before his landlady lost patience and told his caller that he was indisposed. It was Evan, to say that he was back from Africville and wanted to meet up.

He could feel Miss Beale listening to him. She was pretending to clean the counters, but he knew her ears were flapping. *You've got to get a cellphone*, he told himself, even if it meant giving up school lunches. Cyril turned to the wall, twisted the telephone cord as far as it would go, and found himself looking at a calendar with a picture of Rocky Mountain scenery. Two days of the week were marked by an X in red with a note that said "Clinic." He didn't want to think about that, about her. When he put the phone down, he was ready to glare at her, determined to show his displeasure, but she had her back to him and was furiously chopping onions.

Cyril walked back downstairs with an unexpected surge of relief because he was going to tell Evan about the police beating. It had been three weeks. He hadn't told anyone else. He hadn't wanted pity or someone else's self-righteous anger. It was his to come to terms with. Racism that had been directed at him, that had hurt him. And they'd have loved it at school: the Black activist crowd and Randall. He particularly didn't want to become anyone's political pawn. It was okay; he was fit now, bruises and pain gone, body repaired, no longer had to keep his arm steady against his side by holding his hand in his pocket. He was back to walking at night, though he kept to busy places, made loops near home where he was just one dark face among many. Hearing Evan's voice had brought it all back.

Evan had said to come by after school: "I'm home tomorrow afternoon, but I might not be so available later in the week." Cyril hadn't been to Evan's house before, but it was easy to find. Take the Bathurst streetcar to Dundas and it was a couple of houses up. A great big house, mansion size. A Black woman opened the door. She was maybe Cyril's age. Serious, glasses, with hair tied up in little knots. She barely glanced at him as she held the door open and he stepped inside. "Evan," she shouted up the stairs. After a moment, she called again, "Evan. Visitor," then left Cyril where he stood and headed toward what must have been the kitchen at the end of a long hallway. It was a communal house. Grad students, mostly, though Evan said a couple of them worked full-time. Cyril stood alone, uncomfortable in the dark hallway with its piles of coats on hooks and tumble of shoes and bags on the floor beneath them. A couple of bikes leaned on the opposite wall, and another hung on a hook from the ceiling above. It sounded as though there were at least three people in the kitchen.

A minute later, he heard the stamp of feet above him, and Evan appeared with a slim, pretty woman following close behind. At the bottom of the stairs, she stood to shake his hand. "Hi, I'm Penelope, and I know that you're Cyril. Pleasure to meet you."

Cyril grinned. "Me too. Glad to meet you."

"Evan's told me lots about you and his freshy piece, 'International Students' First Year.' You're doing well, I hear. You must be proud of yourself?"

Cyril said "Thanks" and "Good" and felt like an asshole because he couldn't think of anything else to add.

"Nice to see you, brother," said Evan. "How you been?"

"Pretty good," said Cyril. "How was Africville?"

"I'm writing about it now," said Evan, patting the laptop under his arm. "The Black Loyalist communities. You know Black people have been in Nova Scotia since the seventeen hundreds? Here, too, of course. But where I really want to go now is British Columbia. Black folk actually got a genuine welcome out there when they got out of California in the 1850s." Evan smiled. "Now all I have to do is find someone to buy my plane ticket."

"And one for me too," said Penelope, who had been searching through the coats. She found hers in the tangle, pulled on a pair of tall boots, zipped her coat, and put on a striped hat that suited her, Cyril thought, perfectly.

"Bye, Cyril," she said. "Bye, sweetie," to Evan, and she disappeared through the front door.

Evan looked appreciatively after her. "It's all been good," he said. "Good visit with the folks when I got back. Now school's full-on. I've missed a bunch, so I have to catch up. And I've got this freelance work on Africville."

"That's busy."

"You too, I guess?" said Evan. "Come on in." Evan steered Cyril into a big living room that contained three couches and a couple of oversize chairs. It was shabby, but big colour posters hung on the walls, interspersed with black-and-white photographs. Books and newspapers covered a couple of coffee tables and had begun to collect on the floor.

"This is cool," said Cyril.

"I share it with six other people," laughed Evan. "But it's good, yeah."

Cyril sank into the sagging centre of one of the couches.

"So, how's the freshy experience going?"

"A little rough."

"Tell me."

"It's hard."

"Do it, man," urged Evan. "Talk."

Cyril swallowed a couple of times because his mouth was dry, then started in, pushed himself to speak. "So I got into a thing with the cops. I was walking. Early evening, a few weeks ago. It was dark, raining real hard." Cyril could hear how his voice sounded angry, heard how the words that had played through his head for weeks told the whole thing like it was yesterday. And he could see how closely Evan was listening, like he'd known he would. Was listening and was angry along with him.

"Did you see a doctor?"

"No, man. It wasn't so bad. Just bruises around my ribs. My arm was kind of a mess, though. I guess I twisted something in my shoulder. But I knew I'd heal up."

"Not *you* twisted something," snapped Evan. "*They* twisted it!"

"Okay," said Cyril.

"If you'd seen a doctor, we'd have some evidence."

"Evidence?"

"You could make a formal complaint."

"Oh, no, man. I don't want to do anything like that." Cyril shook his head, shocked.

Usually, Evan asked good questions. Didn't make judgments. Cyril had once asked him about that, and Evan had said, "I'm a journalist. I'm not here to put words in people's mouths. I want to hear theirs." Talking to Evan had always been good, and his insights, when they were offered, were often as helpful as Nelson's.

Cyril lifted his hand to his chest, involuntarily, to cover the place the bruises had been, caught his breath because it was as though he'd been hit again. He couldn't imagine standing up against those cops, angry though he was. He wouldn't have a chance. He was a foreign student with work privileges. People thought it was simple — you hired a lawyer and fixed things. What they didn't get — though he'd thought that Evan would — was that they, the cops and the courts, had the power. There were plenty of young Black men in prison to prove it. So what if Evan was ready to back him up? He wasn't even a real journalist yet. He was a student. Younger than Cyril.

"Looks like it still hurts?" said Evan. Cyril dropped his hand to his lap.

"No, not anymore. I'm just remembering how it was." Now Cyril felt worse than he had when it happened. The shame was back; he wasn't tough enough. He'd let Evan down.

"Hey, man, it happens," said Evan. "Some people here are treated like shit, and most people don't care." Evan breathed out a long, sad sigh that made him seem suddenly old.

"You okay?" he asked.

"Yeah," said Cyril.

"So you suck it up or you fight it. Fighting takes courage and lots and lots of patience."

"I already sucked it up," said Cyril.

"Whatever," said Evan. "I want to write about this in the piece. It's important. We'll talk about it again later, okay? You've got to share this experience."

"I don't know, man ..."

"Later," said Evan. "Let's get some tea." He stood up. "Come meet some of my roommates."

Cyril pulled himself up from the sunken cushions. Winced

at the body memory of those bruises. Talking to Evan was meant to be cathartic. But now Evan wanted to write about it, and Cyril was going to have to fight him on that. He followed Evan into the kitchen. He didn't need telling that racism was meant to humiliate. He knew that. He wanted to get some sleep. He wanted to go home.

CYRIL WAS LEARNING HIS PLACE in the structure. Bumping just above the concrete and cardboard-bed bottom. The bottom he'd known before, at home, had a different profile. The beggars were the mentally ill. The community cared for them – to some extent. They didn't starve. It mattered less where they slept when it was nearly always warm. Sometimes they got messed up, and if they got really sick, they disappeared to the mental hospitals or into the jails. Those places swallowed people whole, and when they came out they were often worse than before, kneaded, pummelled, and person-shaped into someone who babbled instead of threatened. No longer knew how to do constructive harm – deemed safe.

But here, in Toronto, so many seemed not so much mad as fallen. The big net of their world had been worn so thin that it opened a hole. Then the weight that they put to that place, the burden they carried, the great and growing bundle of it ripped the hole open – and they fell. Cyril's net-world was a little scuffed. He tried to keep his burden light.

He and his college friends back in Jamaica had been determined to make professional lives. No petrol stations, supermarkets, or retail stores. No hotel jobs, management or otherwise. Nothing whatsoever in the tourist industry. They were going to become a Professor, a Businessman who also made smart investments and had his pilot's license, a Human Rights Lawyer.

Cyril had dreamed of teaching, like Grandpa Nelson. His mother had told her friends that her son would teach their grand-babies when they got to primary school. She couldn't imagine him as a university professor. But that was what Cyril had wanted. He'd been to the University of the West Indies three times with Grandpa Nelson. Once to pick up some documents. Twice to parties for Kingston College Old Boys and their families. Nelson had said that all things were possible. He had said that academia was a great life. He had said he'd help Cyril when he got to UWI. Then he was gone, before the help was organized, arrangements were made, and Cyril had been safely delivered into the new life he'd longed for.

When his mother died, Cyril's personal convictions died with her. He'd fallen into Canada; it was what everyone else thought was best. The two dead people couldn't speak for him. Nelson to say, "Do your academic work at UWI, know your own culture." And his mother's plea, "Never leave me."

It had been easier for most of Cyril's high school friends. Their parents were professionals from generations of profes-sionals whose ancestors had owned land planted with sugar cane, pimento, and bananas. Cyril's mother's people were market-garden farmers, parish curates. Churchgoers, small people. For Cyril, in a country where unemployment was high and the popu-lation bulged with young men like him, work didn't come with options. Too many faced a life of frequent unemployment and begging for help when times were hard. Walking for miles with a machete to clear someone's land for a few dollars. Heavy work on construction sites for as many hours or days as they were needed. Gathering with friends on street corners to make a dent in the day. Staying clear of the gangsters who could make you rich or make you dead. It was harder for some than for others.

Downtown, on his way home from Ryerson, two young men his age walked toward him, laughing with each other. They stopped suddenly to look briefly in a window, then another burst of laugher as one pointed and said something Cyril didn't understand. They held hands. One was dark, head shaved close and earrings flashing gold. The other was white, red-haired and bearded. Their smiling teeth were the same even white. They were full of pleasure, and nobody looked. No hissed or spoken condemnation, and it really did seem to be okay because Cyril knew how to read the silent disapproval that Canadians were so good at – expressed only to each other through brief eye contact, and only as they walked away. It was not happening now. Really, nobody cared that these two men held hands.

Did this prove Toronto was an open society? And that was a revelation. Because he felt unfree in a way he never had in the past. Was it okay to be homosexual but not Black? But Black was also everywhere, and lots of it busy and attractive, well-dressed, driving good cars and headed home to houses where children were going to become lawyers and doctors. He knew that as well as he knew anything else about this country. So where was the divide: Black History Girl's racism; the Juniors' warnings not to run in the street, to always carry money and ID? How did prejudice know who to smack down? Was it only for poor dark people?

He'd been eleven when they beat a boy at school who was too gentle and too pretty; the kids moved in on him, mostly boys but girls too. They'd started with taunts – snarls and shouts in loud, scary snaps of sound. But then someone threw a juice box – an ordinary orange juice box with the straw still inside. No juice. It hit the kid's cheek, and he screamed. It couldn't have hurt too much, but the kid was frightened. And then a couple of boys started to kick him, and the girls jumped up and down and shrieked their approval. Cyril had watched with horror that first time, but the second time, remembering the bruised and bleeding boy from before, he ran to a teacher. Got there so fast he didn't remember running. Demanded intervention. After that, the kids turned on him. Not for long, but for a while, long enough for him to question his actions. Because their indifference, their contempt, was almost a physical threat, and he was very afraid of taking his own beating. The ostracism almost wasn't worth it until Nelson said, "Well done, Cyril." And then the kids were back to speaking anyway because they needed help with a project, and the respect they'd had for him before pulled them beyond just looking to talking, and then it was okay.

The boy's name was Jamal Williams, and he disappeared. They said that he dropped out of school. Went somewhere else. Nobody looked for him. Cyril never heard where he had gone.

CYRIL HAD CRAWLED INTO BED at about four, studies for his history exam finished. He draped a coat over his blankets because, despite the warmer spring temperatures, the basement was cold. One of the guys at school said England was worse. Damp cold that went straight through you. It had occurred to Cyril that his white English blood should help him fend off the chill. He'd thought more about his father in the last few months than he had in years. It was seeing the people who sometimes reminded him of the man in the photographs and his sighting dreams: red face and thin hands. A man on the streetcar had looked that way, in the seat across the aisle. He was reading a paper but must have felt Cyril's stare because, for just a moment, their eyes met, and it was as though they had physically touched. That night, Cyril dreamed of his father. And his grandfather too, who was indistinct but very real. He had a line of ancestors from a country he'd never even seen.

The clock read 6:00 a.m. when a truck rattled at the corner of the street. It was a weekly sound, one that often woke Cyril from sleep thirty minutes before his alarm. The heave and hiss of diesel engine and air brakes, then the crash of steel on metal as the truck's forklifts engaged with the ten-foot-by-ten-foot disposal bin that was a permanent fixture at the back of the community centre. Noisy as hell. Cyril pulled a pillow over his head. Finally it slammed, wheezed, and drove slowly off. And he fell asleep.

THE RACKET OF SOUND IS the rattle and clang of a passing trolley. Edward is on a street corner. It is a cold day, and his hands are wrapped in strips of cloth. He's wearing an oversize pair of shoes, insulated with more fabric. He has a cart with him. A small thing with wheels that is piled high with newspapers. Edward must be thirteen now, grown a couple of inches. His skin seems darker, though his eyes reveal the same contradiction, apprehension and defiance.

He is holding a newspaper and shouting, "*Telegram*. Evening Edition. Bennett's New Deal." There is urgency in his voice. Now that he is his own man, newspaper sales are the difference between food or not. He's run from the children's home. They say he still owes them money for keep that was never paid. He sells his papers on a corner that is across town, where they're unlikely to find him. If they do, he'll take the beating and move on.

But right now, he has a decent place to sleep, and that's worth a lot. Not in the Ward, where he moved from the boarding house with the beds packed so tight you had to step on them to get to yours, the one you shared with the guy who worked a night shift.

Not in the lean-to where he spent the last three months, built with slats from broken packing boxes and angled against the back of a house. It got wet when it rained and came apart in big winds, twice with him inside it. Now he has a room with two other boys in a flophouse on Spadina near Dundas where the rats are generally outside and the stink of sewers is not so bad most of the time. They're not boys, really. Men, fifteen and sixteen, old enough not to have to go to school. They didn't want him at first, but he introduced them to men who ran booze cans, and the prospect of money made them friendly.

The house he lives in is owned by a Jewish man. He rents to Blacks. The older Black couple who lived in one of the upstairs rooms were a fascination for Edward. He stared at them, and they stared back at him. The woman always smiled. He didn't dare talk to her, though, and he could tell that her husband didn't like him. Didn't want her talking to any of the men in the house. They were gone within a week of Edward moving in. The two boys he shares with are Jewish. And there are some Irish men in the rooms on their floor. All of them are dark people. One day, they wake up to find graffiti on the front of the house that reads *Dirty Foreign Coloured Communists Go Home*.

Despite the intimidation, Edward wants to stay in this house. In some ways, it is comforting to be identified and categorized as part of a group — the group that lives in this house. They are all sorts, transient and unwelcome elsewhere. What Edward has never felt with conviction is a sense of belonging. He was abandoned. He understands anger and that formalized anger is a political thing. He thinks he might become a communist so long as they don't tell him what to do. He hates the fascists. But Edward's personal hurt is his own private business. He nurses it. And most of the time, he controls it.

CYRIL WATCHED AS THE NIGHT cast grey and black shadows in his room. Grey on black. No stars in Toronto, never from his basement window. Only the abbreviated glimpse of the yard. Only moonlight, never the moon. It was a long time till dawn, and not the first time that Edward had left him sleepless.

Fascism came out of poverty and marginalization. Same as communism; both promised pride and hope. Cyril's last school reading had shown how the conditions that followed the First World War caused the second. Jamaicans were in that second war for sure. His mother had kept his great-grandfather's medals in a little leather case, fighting the rainy-season mildew with cleaning stuff. Cyril had left the medals behind for his brother and sister. Both his mother's grandfather and the former prime minister, Michael Manley, had fought for Britain in the Royal Canadian Air Force, though Manley had been a pilot while Cyril's great-grandfather had pumped fuel. His mother said, "My family collected money to buy bombers for Britain. Every likkle penny sent to the *Gleaner*, and they sent it on for the fighters. That is a landmark." She said, "We were a crown colony. If Britain went to war, we went too."

War created jobs. Being poor in Jamaica was like living in a permanent economic depression, Cyril thought. The difference was that the Depression in Canada had cut down the middle classes too. There was a letter reproduced in one of his books.

Well Mr. R.B. Bennett, arnt you a man or are you? To be the cause of all this starvation and privation. You call us derelicts, then if we are derelicts what else are you but one too. only a darn sight worse. You said if you was elected, you would give us all work and wages, well you have been in the Prime Ministers shoes, now, for 4 years and we are still looking for work and wages. You took all our jobs away from us. We can't earn any money. You say a relief camp is good enough for us, but it's too good for you Mr. Bennett, you are on relief your own self. You put away your big govt salary, then ask the gov't to pay for your big feasts, while we poor fellows starve.

The unsigned letter was in a history book that topped a thick pile of books on the floor by his bed. It was dark, but he could just make out the depth of his pile. He'd been so impressed by Evan's house, its bohemian style. He'd told himself to loosen up, let his house breathe. Not to be so damned tidy. Make piles! And while living alone was good for his work, it would have been nice to share a place with people he admired. Evan's lifestyle was pretty compelling. His roommates were interesting and involved. The best thing about having people around, and about school, thought Cyril, was the way it opened up all these other worlds. Those guys helped give context for what was learned, helped to see things differently. Though sometimes it might have been easier not to know. To be oblivious to things like systemic racism. Not to know or to care about the big picture. His mother had been innocent and relatively happy, he was fairly sure. But if she'd been educated, socially and politically aware, demanding and angry, she might still be alive. Cyril turned onto his back, closed his eyes, and sank into deep sleep.

He dreamed that he walked across a limestone field that ended at a lover's leap, a long fall into breaking waves that would smash a fallen body onto rock, lost to the insatiable appetite of the Caribbean Sea. He knew that above him the sun continued to shine and the sky was a translucent blue with drifts of white cloud scudding east, blown by a tropical breeze. Just as the travel brochures said. Though all he saw was black, and the roar in his ears was the weight of water pressing down upon him.

SIXTEEN

EDWARD INSPECTS THE DAY THROUGH the little frame of his high-on-the-wall window. It is a real spring sky, the bluest kind that fills your lungs with air even when you're inside. Puffy white cloud and a sun that reminds you of summer. He shifts his weight on the bed, tests his muscles, flexing, stretching. Legs, feet, arms, back. He's excited by the day's promise, though he has to leave his room and look from the front door to confirm it. Freedom to move. And months of it to come. Winter's sidewalk treachery gone. It takes ninety minutes to wash and dress. Interminably long when he looks at his watch. And then he's another ten minutes because his damned wallet isn't where it should be. But when he walks out into the crisp new air and breathes the clean of it, turns his face up to the warmth, it is astonishing and glorious.

Another hour, and the social part of the day is done. The bank. He got the nice teller. The shop next door to the bank. Edward climbs the path into the parkette and settles onto the bench across from his building. A woman walks by. She's in her thirties. Brown and pretty. Wearing a blue hat, she's like a bright bird. A blue scarf too. She looks straight at him and smiles. Her face lights up like she's shining, and the sun makes a halo behind her head. He stares back, shocked by the contact. He wants her to stop, but she's long gone, slim hips swaying neatly in a checked coat that falls just below her knees and grazes the tops of her tall, narrow-heeled boots. He's staring after her, the way the hem of her coat swings as she goes — the blue hat — and then she blurs. He's crying, and he can't stop. Wipes at his eyes with his gloved hand. Stop! Pathetic. Old. But the tears wash down. He closes his eyes and lets them come. Because his head is full of Celia like that was her who walked by and didn't stop.

It doesn't matter that they were just teenagers when they first explored each other's bodies in that hidden place on Toronto Island. It doesn't matter that the last time he saw her was in Nova Scotia more than sixty years ago. The way his heart breaks, it's like it was yesterday.

CYRIL WALKED INTO THE MOUNT Dennis library for the one hundredth time. He had hoped to run into Pat, who hadn't been around for a while. The last time he'd seen her, he'd asked if she was losing weight. Time spent in the wheelchair was compressing her body, her big front tilting slightly to the left. But her face and neck were thin, and the wheelchair hadn't done that. "No," she'd said. She wouldn't eat the food where she lived because they poisoned it, and they wouldn't give her the antidote. And then she told him that her U.S. accounts were frozen and asked him for a dollar. Very occasionally, Cyril fantasized that Pat really did have money and would one day offer to pay all of his tuition. But she was losing weight. That was obvious.

Cyril strode toward the checkout desk, and there was Black History Girl. Right in front of him. Wound so tight she was bouncing on the spot in her high-grade sneakers. She was arguing with the librarian. He heard her say, "Revolution!" The librarian turned sideways and banged down on her computer keys, refusing to look up again. Cyril was afraid of all that loquacity, but he wanted her. Had been thinking about her for months. And now she was here. She did have dreadlocks, and not only that, she had shed her winter clothes. Maybe it was not yet warm enough for the shorts and top that put her skin on display, but that was okay by him. She wasn't the only one, either, because most of the young people had ditched their coats. Coats, jackets, and sweaters peeled away, bodies on show. His was still hidden inside his long raincoat. He opened the zipper.

He couldn't imagine why she was here, in Mount Dennis. And it was likely that she hadn't been in before because the librarian, who was generally pleasant enough, though never chatty, was definitely very annoyed.

But Cyril had imagined this conversation, their second meeting, numerous times over, and having her appear was a major gift. She'd moved over to the new release books, and just like he'd rehearsed in his head, he said, "Hey! We met out on the street a few months ago. Remember me? Jamaica? All that stuff?"

She pulled the headphones from her ears.

"Yeah, I do remember you. This is where you live?" She swung her arm to indicate the streets of Mount Dennis.

Her body, the in-the-flesh presence of it, was even more than he'd imagined. "I do," he said. "What are you doing up here? You live downtown, right?"

"I'm putting these posters in all of the libraries that serve our communities. But," she sneered, "they have rules. Rules that the smart and engaged librarians disregard in order to do what's best for the folk in their neighbourhood, while the others stick their heads up their asses and fail to do the right thing." She looked directly at the checkout desk as she spoke and did not speak quietly.

"Okay," said Cyril in a voice several decibels lower than hers. "I wanted to ask you something? About your Black History."

"Our Black History."

"Marcus Garvey. You know him? A famous Jamaican activist?"

"I know him, of course. But do you know Donald Willard Moore?"

"Okay?"

"Must have been a sweet guy because they called him 'Uncle Don.' He started a chapter of the Universal Negro Improvement Association right here in Canada. And in the nineteen-fifties, Uncle Don led the fight to allow Blacks to immigrate to Canada. But that's not what you want." Her tone softened. "I think ..." Then she spoke slowly, stretching out the vowels. "I think that you ... want ... me." She smiled sweetly and brushed the top of his hand with her fingertip. "What's your name?"

"Cyril."

"Oh, that's unusual." She smiled. "So if you want to see me, show up on Saturday. Remember? I told you, Moon Moves?"

"Yes."

"Ten o'clock. I'll be there."

"Wait! What's yours? Your name?"

"Jaycee."

As she left the library, he panicked. The earliest he could get to Moon Moves on a Saturday night was midnight, and even then he'd have to close the store thirty minutes early, which was a little like lying to Mr. Lee. But he could still feel the heat on his skin where she'd touched him, and the rest of him was warming to the same temperature. He found a free computer and keyed in *Donald Willard Moore*. Which took him straight to the Heritage Toronto site. Uncle Don had started the Canadian branch of the UNIA in Toronto, right around the corner from Evan's house near Kensington Market. Garvey had been to Toronto a couple of times and would have spoken there. Edward must have heard about the visits. It was as likely as not that he would have gone to see Garvey. Who better to have inspired Edward's interest in politics?

There were some records of the UNIA meetings, and they were online. It was as easy as clicking through a list of titles, and when he used his browser's search function to look for Davina, it came up on the fifth try. This was the easiest search he had ever done. Edward was there. He'd been present and raised his hand in support of a protest that would demand better jobs. He'd been required to state his name for reasons of politics, pride, and solidarity. Edward had stood up twice. Right there, in 1937, at the downtown Toronto UNIA. There was even a photograph, just the VIPs, though, definitely no Edward. Lined up in rows with the ladies in front. Taken in what was probably a community hall. All Black faces. All well-dressed. According to the minutes, many of them were visiting Americans. Businessmen and entrepreneurs whose families had moved to Canada during the Civil War but weren't so welcome to stay. Eventually, many had gone back home.

Jaycee was amazing. She had made him lucky. From now on, it would all be easy, just like this. But the new shape of possibilities for Edward was chased from his mind by the lingering feel of Jaycee's fingertip on his hand. Because what she could give him was suddenly one thousand times more exciting than figuring out Edward's life. He headed out of the library.

And then Pat was right there in front of him. In her wheelchair.

Which somehow seemed bigger than before, with her bags and plastic bottle and the ears of her aviator helmet looking ragged as ever. But over that was a purple wool hat that looked brand new with bobbles of white fur on top. It was pretty.

"Nice hat," said Cyril.

"My companion gave it to me." She was flattered.

Cyril didn't want to talk. Didn't want anyone interfering with his mood; he was buzzing with it. Jaycee. Sweet, and more to come.

"I've been to see my guardian," Pat said. "They won't increase my payments, even though the money is legally mine. I've filed a lawsuit against the government. But my husband is coming soon, and then they'll have to give it to me."

"Okay, Pat, I'm glad to hear that," he said. "Well. I'm kind of in a hurry."

"Have you presented your doctoral dissertation at the Munk School of Global Affairs yet?"

"Edward? Wow, you know what? I found him." Cyril recovered his excitement. "I found a picture of him when he was a kid. He was busted for smashing windows." He held out his palm for a high five. Pat swung back hard and laughed.

"In a newspaper," said Cyril. "Hey, he was an anarchist. Like you, Pat!"

As he spoke, Cyril realized that he hadn't discussed his research with anyone. A conversation with his prof, a brief exchange with Randall, who really wasn't interested, but that was all. It was only out here on the sidewalk with Pat that he got to talk about Edward, to share hope or disappointment, and right now he did have something. A triumph that ought to be celebrated.

"I knew he was brave," said Pat. "Can I see him?"

"Yes. I'm gonna carry it with me so the next time I run into you

I'll have it, okay? I'll be around the library a lot now. It's getting near exam time."

She was disappointed for a moment but then resigned.

"I'll look for you," she said. "Have you got any money, Cyril? I need special kitten food for the new babies, and I have to buy it at the criminal's store because my battery's low. I can't go far."

Cyril had a five-dollar bill in his pocket earmarked for a box of ginger cookies. Study food. He handed it to Pat, who was visibly surprised and pleased.

As she steered her wheelchair down the curb and onto the road, headed west – and he wished she wouldn't because the road was so dangerous – thin sunlight spun off the chrome basket behind her seat and shimmered in the air for a long moment, nothing more. But it left him unsettled.

THE GUYS NEEDED TO TALK. On Saturday. They had issues that needed strategizing, and Cyril was their man. Not at my house, said Cyril. No friends allowed. But the library's on the corner. And when they said too far, come to us, he insisted, because Jaycee might be there, though he didn't tell them that. He felt important when they said they'd come.

He found an empty table in the corner. His friends were a delegation of six-foot-plus with footballer shoulders and size thirteen running shoes who made the library small when they swung through the doors. "They don't get it, man," Paul said. "We did this great pitch, but they're saying, 'You have to give us context.'"

Leon twisted his voice into a shrill whine as he mimicked the school's theatre director. "Without context, we have to ask the question, What Does It Mean?"

"Shhhh," said Cyril.

"What we need is someone who's good with formalities, who really gets what the administrators need to hear, who can write up the context of the piece so's they get to say yes before we run out of time," said Randall.

"And that someone is you, Mr. Cyril. Sir," said Leon.

Cyril was flattered by the guys' trust in his ability. It was a play performed in dub poetry. Cyril was not at all inclined to stand on a stage. But he was very interested in the idea of Black kids acting as colonials and white kids as the colonized. Also, the dub — rhythmic poetry over reggae beats — sounded smart and funny. And he loved the call-and-response parts, where the audience had to shout back.

"You got to get in there that Black history isn't just twenty-eight days of February," said Randall. "They were totally into this two months ago. But now that we've got it worked out, they're saying they're all booked."

Cyril asked many questions and made three pages of notes. Once they'd worked out an approach and were packing up to go, Cyril said, "You could do something on Black history in Toronto next. You know, how it all started?"

"What the fuck is that?" said Leon. "You've been reading your big books, Cyril, sir." He and Paul smirked.

Randall said, "Yeah, there's lots to know, but don't no one really give a fuck. What do you want to tell, Cee?"

"The Invisible History of Canadian Black People?"

"Not invisible," said Randall. "Hidden, right? Because it's there if you look. You're just not going to find it in the way our history's told. Canadian history is white people's history, and they don't get that because they don't even know that white is a colour. They think they are invisible. Know what I mean? We see them clearly because we have to. And we see that they definitely control the story."

"What difference does knowing this shit make," muttered Leon, who picked up his phone and leaned back in his chair. Paul did the same. They'd heard it all before.

"See, some of it is a history of slaves, and they don't tell that," said Randall. "It wasn't just the romance of freed people who came north from America to fight with the Loyalists. Not just the people running north for freedom along the Underground Railroad. Not just men like the first African to stand on Canadian soil in 1608. A free man. Mr. Mathieu da Costa, speaker of many languages, interpreter and translator." Randall kept talking, reciting the history that was rarely told except by people like Randall in the month of February, at schools and colleges, in community centres and public libraries.

"We had it here too." He looked directly at Cyril. "Mr. Let's-all-just-try-to-get-along. The colonials brought slaves with them. The first recorded was only six years old, sold to a Frenchman nearly four hundred years ago, Cee." Cyril saw his baby brother's face — a little child. "They kidnapped free Black people and took them south to sell to American buyers. And the people of the First Nations were also enslaved, sometimes by each other and in even bigger numbers — and some of those had Black slaves. But it's not a numbers game. It's about living souls." Randall glared at Cyril. "Canada never was all good and white and free."

Cyril nodded. Randall sometimes made him feel less than capable, like now, as though he were not enough of anything: not activist enough, not Black enough, not cool enough. So then there was nothing more to say. Whenever he was ready to share what he was learning about Edward, it turned into this.

As they stood to leave, Randall asked Cyril to join them at a house party that night.

"Not this time, man," said Cyril, and the guys spoke it out along with him in synchronized chorus, "Not This Time," followed by hooting laughter, some vigorous backslapping, and a loud high five. The librarian stood up and glared. Cyril urged them all to the door.

Cyril didn't need them. He wanted a girl to share his time with, a girl who knew how to talk to him, to give him space so that he could say who he was. He knew how to open that welcome space for others. If they wanted. "It's your feminine side," Randall had said once. "Use it well, Cee, women love it!" Cyril wanted Jaycee, whom he had fantasized about, but not so innocently. Not with his feminine side. It was all male, what he dreamed about with her.

MOON MOVES WAS A LARGE basement cavern at the bottom of a wide set of stairs. Cyril had put a lot of time into dressing and settled on blue jeans and a black sweater, Evan-style. The best he could do. Inside was dark and loud. A DJ in the front corner, head wrapped in giant headphones, bopped up and down, territorial over her turntables. It was midnight, but only a few people sat about in the room's gloom, against the walls and at the long bar that ran down its far side. Cyril didn't know the music. Didn't know the fashion signals the kids displayed. He sat down at the bar, ordered a beer, and kept his eyes on the DJ — much too conscious of how awkward he must look — watching the way her headphones flashed as she moved. And the door.

By 12:35, the place was filling up. The music was good, he'd found his way into its rhythms, and it pumped up a need that sparked sharp alternating lashes of anxiety and hope. When

Jaycee finally came in, she smiled but stayed with her friends. Cyril was trapped, locked to the stool. He couldn't cross that distance, the thousand miles down the bar to where she leaned in on one elbow with her face close to the woman beside her. And when she reached to caress that woman's face, the same way she'd touched his arm but with so much more intent, he understood. She looked his way then, to make sure he'd seen, then turned her attention back to her girlfriend's cheek.

Cyril's disappointment was bigger than anger or jealousy. All she'd had to do was tell him. Her cruelty was more unfair than all the crap she preached about. She was the worst of hypocrites. Months of his best energy wasted on her. But in the next moment, there was a girl beside him who smelled good, who stood close enough to shout in his ear, "Hey, I've been watching you. Why don't you buy me a drink?" She sat on the stool beside him, edged it closer, and her naked arm took the drink, her shoulder bumping his. Her red spangled nails danced with her fingers, tapped at her glass, grazed the cuff of his sweater. Her skirt was so short. She moved her legs so that her thighs angled in toward him, knees almost touched his. He did have money to buy a girl a drink. And because he was so ready, it was more than okay. She wanted, and so did he. When they walked to the door, he knew that Black History Girl watched them leave.

Her name was Lucy, and she took him home in a taxi, upstairs to a place she shared with two other people who would not be home for hours, she said. They sat on the couch and swallowed their drinks. Then his mouth was on hers, and in moments he was made utterly compliant by her tongue and her lips and her teeth. She wouldn't let him inside her, she said, but she gave him her mouth — the mouth that he'd watched obsessively as she talked, and it hadn't mattered what she said. She sucked and licked him from himself until he was only that – her wet, pulling heat, his hardness. And then later, he learned how to use his mouth on her. Discovered how versatile his tongue could be, how to listen to her breathing and the sound that came from her throat. He was enthralled by the power of his mouth. And delighted with her body. As he watched her drift into sleep with her head on his arm, he thought how much better this was than the two guilt-ridden experiences he'd had at home.

But Lucy was strange. Unfamiliar. With ideas that made him wary. She liked to cause alarm, switched in an instant from affection to disdain. He watched her with people she called her friends, but all of them seemed steered by self-interest. "Cyr," she said, "come with me," to places he didn't want to go. Clubs where people came to confront and conquer – like Black History Girl. Where the women proved their sexual power by the heads they turned, the men whose gazes they pulled from another girl's hold. And the men were equally narcissistic. Lucy didn't want to know about Edward or any of the things that Cyril was learning. She wasn't interested in his process, his Canadian experience. He would never tell her what he valued. And when he didn't care for what *she* wanted, he kept silent because he found it so hard to say so. If he did, her voice cracked brittle with frustration, and her soft edges turned knife sharp. She was razor-blade mean. Within three weeks, he watched as she slid her body up against another man, pulled his pelvis into her groin with her spangled fingers. In front of Cyril and everyone else on the dance floor. His humiliation was a whole-body experience. He would never go back to any of those places.

Cyril spent two days in bed. Longer than after the police beating. He skipped classes and begged off work, forcing Mr. Lee to work double shifts. Finally, the relentless tug and pull from his mother and Grandpa Nelson rolled him from his mattress and into his shower stall. As he ate cornflakes with milk from his emergency carton in the corner of Miss Beale's fridge, he remembered Edward, his co-traveller, his inspiration. "I need you Eddie," Cyril said. "I can't believe I dropped you so completely."

Cyril called the girl at the *Varsity* who'd sent an email two days earlier to say they had Edward's father. Jim, the man in charge of the photo archive, had found him. "Always up for a challenge," he'd said, and he had discovered an exact match for the photocopied image and a name and interview to go with it. No part of the interview or anything related to it had ever been published. But it had stayed on file in the dusty basement storage of paper archives. "You're really lucky," the girl said. It had probably been saved from the shredder because it was part of a major immigration research collaboration with several of the university's senior sociology and history professors. They'd worked with someone in the fine arts department to photo-document their subjects, and there was a box full of black-and-white negatives. Which must have been how the photograph ended up in *The Beaver*. Jim suspected that the research had never been completed. He'd checked, she said, and there was no one more thorough than Jim. She had attached a scan of the interview and written, "Sorry it's not longer, but at least you have a name and some history."

His name was Vincent Watson, and he was twenty-five years old when he sailed to Canada in 1919.

INTERVIEWER: How did you come to Canada, Mr. Watson? Why did you choose Toronto?

MR. WATSON: I was inspired to travel upon hearing the story of Mr. Robert Sutherland, who was born in the same parish as me in Jamaica. Mr. Sutherland graduated from Queen's University in the year eighteen-fifty-two: the first Black man to graduate from a Canadian university. And you should know that upon his death, he bequeathed a large sum of money to the same university, which saved it from annexation by the University of Toronto. Queen's was my first choice, sir. But the U of T Faculty of Law made me the first offer. I will complete my studies at Osgoode Hall Law School, as did Mr. Sutherland. An additional advantage to Toronto is the home where I now board with the fine family of a man recruited from Jamaica by your Canadian Pacific Rail.

When asked about his own family, Mr. Watson had demurred.

MR. WATSON: My father was a cow man. So was his father before him, and his father the same. That, sir, takes us back to the first free generation to follow slavery. My name is Watson. That is not an African name. It is not a Jamaican name. It is, assuredly, an English name. My birth in Jamaica did not come about through the free will and movement of my ancestors but was the consequence of a slave ship's arrival. Our own names were stolen from us. Our families cleaved in two. Man separated from woman, parents from children, brothers and sisters scattered at the whim of men whose perverse and obscene conceit presumed their entitlement as the owners of other human beings. The great many of us who fought back were murdered. I will not engage in an interview about my family without this true and proper context.

The interviewer changed the subject then and asked if there were plans to build a university in Jamaica since so many nationals seemed to travel abroad to attend school: in America, in England, in Canada. Mr. Watson's answer — "Ask the Jamaican government that question" — suggested that he was tired of the interview, and so it ended.

They established the University of the West Indies in the 1940s, thought Cyril. Vincent had probably heard about that Jamaican Toronto lawyer in high school. A Black lawyer with Vincent's politics would have belonged to the UNIA chapter, would have known people there. The following morning, Cyril was back at the library searching for Vincent Watson's name in the UNIA records. Scouring through the history of Black protest in Toronto. He didn't find him. But he was sure that Vincent's son would have protested alongside the Black men and the communists.

EDWARD IS SKINNY AS A rake, though his shoulders and chest are starting to fill. The physical labour in the relief camps made him fit and strong. He looks older than sixteen. This night he's all cleaned up, wearing clothes he's borrowed from one of the guys at the rooming house. The room is hot and filled with people, mostly older Black men. It is raining outside, and coats steam over the radiators. Lots of the men are in suits, and a good number of them are Americans. The man on the makeshift stage is speaking into a microphone. When the tall man he has introduced walks on, the crowd hushes. Edward is standing against the wall. He has helped put out chairs for the ladies among them, and he and some of the other young people have put plates of food on the tables outside the room for after the speeches. He likes being useful, on his terms. He doesn't have to do this. He's here by choice.

He and a girl carry one of the tables out from the storage room. She is strong and capable. She also has a very pretty smile. They exchange amused glances when the bossy Communist Party lady tells them to move the table left by one foot, then right by six inches. When the lady leaves to finish putting out the cutlery, the girl makes a face at her back, thumbs hooked around her ears while she wiggles her fingers and points her tongue, which, Edward sees, is a perfect, moist pink. He laughs with her.

She has been in domestic service for years, though she is only eighteen. She came to the UNIA meeting because of the visiting communist speaker. The communists are fighting for workers' rights, she says. She is shy and reserved. Not brave. But she's sharp as a tack. He understands her completely.

She has a day off, and Edward makes himself free. They ride on the ferry to Centre Island. They walk through the little town and imagine that they are staying in the hotel and will eat dinner there later, tapping at their lips with linen napkins and sipping champagne from crystal glasses. They ride on the carousel and pay for a second turn. They walk across the grand park, and, as the sun begins to colour the western sky, they find a dense planting of shrubs and trees. The last ferry has gone. They heard the horn sound.

She opens her arms to him, and he learns, for the first time, what it is to touch and stroke and feel another person. When she opens her legs, he is startled and anxious, but she gentles him and makes a promise. When he enters her, he is amazed.

She knows how to have loving and not become pregnant, she says, and teaches him to pull from her before his climax. Her name is Celia. Wrapped in her arms, he revels in her strength.

In just a few weeks — they have only one afternoon a week to see each other — he has learned every inch of her. The muscle in her bicep, the iron hardness there and in her calves. The shocking softness of her breasts and stomach. The lean, firm curve of her buttocks. All of her covered in the dark silk of skin that seems sometimes to glow. He loves her hands, long fingers curled in his. Her eyes, her nose, and her brush of hair, cut short, that she keeps under a hat. He walks his fingers through her tight, soft curls.

CYRIL'S BASEMENT WINDOW WAS OPEN, and the air smelled good. Not warm yet, but it reminded him of what warm felt like. He'd only ever had one real conversation with his mother about his father. "I loved him," she'd said. "I never felt anything like that before. I was who I was because of who he was. Who we were." She'd stumbled over that. Cyril had been only twelve, but he'd known she was trying to tell him the whole truth of it. "It's not like knowing God, baby. It is like being a complete human person. And then you came and made it perfect."

"I hate him," Cyril had said.

"God forgives. So must we." She'd hugged him pretty hard then.

When he had a family, he'd never leave them.

PAT HAD SAID THAT HER mother had left her father. By choice. But Pat's mother had taken Pat and her sister with her to England. It was a story that Cyril believed must be true because he'd heard it repeated many times. Pat's Ojibwe father had stayed home on Bear Island. He'd never left. Pat had visited sometimes, though that must have been long ago because the only place she visited now was the library.

Mr. Addo had said Pat was sick and for sure her leg was a mess. He'd said, "Go see her, she'd like that. You know the place, Central Care? My ninety-two-year-old aunt lives there."

Cyril had said he would. When he had some time.

He curled back into the bed and pulled the pillow under his cheek. He'd go soon. Probably next week.

SEVENTEEN

❦

NOON ON A FRIDAY WAS like a holiday. Especially this one, as the temperature promised to climb past nineteen degrees. The students were piled into a long lineup that extended out of the cafeteria and into the hallway. The campus pub would already be half-full as DJs all over town took one last snooze before waking up for Friday night. Cyril had pulled himself from bed without too much struggle. Had even looked forward to handing in an assignment and the extra money that would come with his double weekend shift. He needed a better job, though. Every week, his bank balance dropped like the village well in a drought. Cyril shuffled along with his tray in front of the buffet servers in their white hairnets. It was much busier than he'd expected spring classes to be. Seemed as though everyone had stayed in school.

"Here's the flyer, man." Randall appeared at his side, waving a paper in Cyril's face. "Looks good, huh?"

It was an explosion of purple and black. "*Shout*," read Cyril. "Good name. Except, what exactly does it mean?"

"It's about the art form. The audience calling their responses," said Randall.

"Yes. Okay," said Cyril. "But maybe you should add 'participation poetry' under 'Poetical/Political.'"

"Yeah, sure," said Randall. "Listen, man, I'll do the marketing, you stick to management."

"You saying I'm business, not creative?"

"So true." Randall rested his oversize hand on Cyril's shoulder. "We're not doing any of this if we don't have a venue."

"Okay, okay. You're buying, right?"

"Surely, brother."

The men found a table littered with dishes at the back of the hall. Randall scooped them all onto a tray and carried them off. Cyril watched him thread through the thick of people and tables. His walk was graceful, a gentle swagger. He was all confidence, and so tall that Cyril could still see him above the crowd at the far end of the room. When all three of the guys, Leon, Paul, and Randall, were together, they were unmistakable from a hundred metres. Cyril liked being around them. Their respect for him was genuine, despite his diminutive size and lack of street cred.

Randall came back after a few minutes with patties and a bottle of ginger beer in each hand. "Jamaica-style," he said, "to get us in the groove."

"So the theatre director is backing off again?" said Cyril.

"First he finally says yes to staging *Shout*. Which is down to you, Cyril, your letter."

"Our letter."

"He made a commitment, but now that we've started rehearsals, he's saying it won't find an audience, and he's having second thoughts. He wants big changes. He's a wuss, man. Talks like an activist, but then he's kissing ass all the way to his pension."

"But what did he think he was saying yes to before?"

"Yeah, exactly. And when he read the play back in the winter, he loved it. Said it was exactly the sort of work he wanted to develop. He called it *Roots*, like he knew what that meant."

"So we have to pin him back to that," said Cyril.

"Yeah, man. But don't let him wriggle, 'cause that's what he's best at. Know what I'm saying?"

"What are you thinking?"

"Use your language, man. Write another letter. But this time, a copy of it goes to everyone, including the school papers. Use an anti-oppressive perspective."

"What's that mean?"

Randall shook his head, "Like Marxist, you know? Like starting with us understanding that he's got the power, and then we get to show him how to use it by shaping his with ours."

"Where's that from?"

"Sociology class." Randall gave him a pitying look. "The dude's Black. You only take classes wid dem highty-tighty white professors."

Cyril met Randall's gaze, then smiled. "Whatever. Who's going to teach me how to use that kind of language?"

"You're looking at the best, brother."

The details of the play's script had become a battle, both sides generally unwilling to budge. Randall insisted that the white characters, the colonized, would speak a simple patois without any sort of translation, while the Black characters, the colonials, would speak an archaic English. The theatre's director argued that they'd lose the audience. Not because of the archaic English but because of the patois. "And don't fool yourselves," he'd said, "it's the white audience that buys the tickets."

"He feeds on these stereotypes," said Randall. "It's making me old." He was going ahead with planned rehearsals even though they were once again far from sure about securing the venue.

Randall and Cyril had learned how to work together. Randall was always quick to react, Cyril might have said, quick to judge, but he chose not to and listened instead. They were both pleased with the first draft of the letter, formatted and spell-checked on Randall's laptop. Addressed to the theatre director, it was also copied to a short list of important school officials, including the university president, the senior editors of the student papers, and the head of United Black Students. "Jump over the director's head," Randall said as he dashed off to get it printed. They'd wait for feedback from Leon and Paul before sending it out.

This was Cyril's first political act, and he felt a mixture of pride and anxiety. The signature on the letter was Randall's, as *Shout*'s producer and director. But Cyril was part of it. And the first letter, much more conciliatory but with a firm tone, had worked. This one was controlled but angry, and it was going to be read by many more people.

When Randall returned, Cyril said, "You know that history stuff I'm working on, about the Black kid who was born in Toronto in 1922? I think he could have been into Marcus Garvey, though I don't know for sure. See, Garvey was here in Toronto to speak at the UNIA, they were downtown, same area this kid lived in? So that's where he, Edward, that's where he would have found other Black people."

"Sure."

"What do you know about Garvey?" Cyril asked.

"Jamaican activist who started the Universal Negro Improvement Association." Randall pushed himself back from the table, metal chair legs scraping the floor, and stood up. He lifted his right hand and placed his palm over his heart. With a dramatic flourish, he took a deep breath and then, from all of his six-foot-three-inch height, looked down at Cyril and spoke.

"Look for me in the whirlwind or the storm, look for me all
around you, for, with God's grace, I shall come and bring
with me countless millions of Black slaves who have died
in America and the West Indies and the millions in Africa
to aid you in the fight for Liberty, Freedom, and Life."

Randall had a deep, powerful, engaging voice. He was trained,
and he could project. The big cafeteria was already filled with
the noise of a few hundred kids, but Randall made himself
heard, so the kids at the tables nearest to them had stopped talking in time to catch his last few words: "Liberteee, Freeeedom,
and Liifffe."

A few girls clapped. Someone whistled. Randall bowed from
his waist, turning to take in the room.

"That's Garvey. He was an activist. Yes, he was." Randall
laughed as he pulled at his chair and sat back down. "What's your
interest?"

"I don't know how much of an activist Edward was, but
he was definitely anti-fascist. Got into lots of trouble in the
nineteen-thirties."

"Makes some sense," said Randall. "Though Garvey didn't like
communists. I'd probably have signed up to work for him. Not
you, though."

"Why not?"

"You had to be all Black. The Real Black McCoy. He wasn't into
mixing up. It was about back to Africa for the true Africans."

"Edward was mixed-race too."

"So maybe he wasn't working for Garvey. Maybe he was working for the communists?"

Cyril pushed his plate away and rubbed hard at his forehead.
"Why is it all so complicated, man?"

"Everybody gotta carve out their niche. Always gonna be someone left out." Randall looked pleased with himself.

"Could we meet up?" said Cyril. "Talk about this some more?"

"Could do. Maybe."

Randall's cellphone burst into dancehall beats. When he hung
up, he said, "Paul wants to meet out at the wall. Can you do that,
man? 'Cause I can't. I have to go."

"I've got a little time," said Cyril. "I'll head over there now."

The walk was long enough for him to shake his disquiet.
There were people back in Jamaica who'd never quite trusted
him because he was lighter. But, man, it was like being squeezed
between two extremes. Crazy stuff when all it took to mix up
colour for every future generation was one conception. Garvey
couldn't have been Edward's hero.

It was four minutes from the cafeteria to the stretch of wall
where people had been meeting up for decades: universally seductive, located where just about everyone on campus had to pass
by at least once a day. Cyril walked along the busy street, taking
in the energy that spun through the fine spring air. Sexual
energy, kids and hormones; he had it too, though he pushed it
down. She'd fucked him, and then she'd fucked him over. That
girl Lucy. He scanned the street for her big hair and a low-cut
tee busting out into the sun. If he saw her, he'd run. Fast as he
could, through the campus up to Bloor and all the way home
to Mount Dennis.

The wall fronted a pocket-sized park. To its left was a planting
of wild rosebushes just starting to bud. Trapped inside the thick
of thorns fluttered scraps of paper and fragments of plastic bags.
Behind the wall, a dog arched its back and deposited its scoop-
requisite leavings while its owner talked into a cellphone. The
city was ugly just before the pop and sparkle of spring.

Much of what he kept hidden, the press of emotion that surfaced when he felt boxed in, was heightened now. He was angrier and increasingly sad. These were not feelings he allowed himself to consider too often, but they had always been there. Not undermining his efforts but keeping him focused on his work, his studies, a future. He had to make good decisions about what to include in his life, what to ignore. No more women.

Worst was that despite all his efforts, it looked as though he would probably be at least $350 short for a trip home in the summer. An almost impossible amount to find in the next few months, even though he'd scored a job at the school bookstore, early mornings stocking shelves. Considered a very generous benefit for students like him. The money was good, but it was just an hour a day, and the morning ride into town was painful.

All around him, kids spent their student loans on toys and holidays while the salaried people, college employees, strategized their investments. Students and staff alike consumed new fashion as if it were life-proving, buying up shoes and bags and gear that would be replaced as the seasonal cycle came back around. Once in a while, he'd walk through the mall and look at price tags that made his stomach ache. So unfair, because Aunty Vi worked so fucking hard. He knew she'd cry if she saw how much people had here. How easily it came. Clothes and gear mattered to most of the kids at home too. But it was on such a reduced scale that it made him laugh. They had two consumer choices in Brown's Town market: buy it or leave it.

He glanced at his watch. Paul needed to show up soon because Cyril was due at work in less than two hours.

"Sorry, man."

He hadn't heard Paul coming. Paul was like that. A tall, quiet guy who kept his head down and worked hard. Randall loved to play to a crowd. Leon could charm and offend, back to back, but Paul was much harder to know. He'd shaved his head this term. It didn't make him look tough, just studious. His face was long, like his body. Nose, brows, cheekbones; all his features seemed somehow to curve upward. Almond eyes. Sometimes he didn't look at you when he talked. Girls checked him out. He liked them, was respectful, but kept himself to himself: an independent operator. *A bit like me*, Cyril thought.

"Here's the letter." Cyril handed Paul the paper.

"Looks good," said Paul, who barely glanced at it. "Randall ain't coming?"

Cyril shook his head. "You okay?"

"I'm sick of riding down here on the fucking bus and subway. It's three fucking hours out of a day. Then I've got to study and do my own shit, but my whole family's in meltdown right now, so I get nothing done except talking with them."

"Whoa, man. You never said any of that before."

"Because I don't need everyone to know my shit." Paul folded his long body down onto the wall beside Cyril. His face was a tense mask. Behind it, Cyril could see what he must have looked like at ten, the child's mouth squeezed tight, eyes fierce with anxiety.

"What happened?"

"Oh, man. It is such a mess," said Paul, pushing his head into his hands.

Cyril looked up as a couple of guys rollerbladed by, shouting back and forth.

"I don't want people to know, okay?" said Paul. "Including Randall."

"Sure."

"I've got this cousin. He's just turned thirteen. A good kid. Really. I've known him three years, since he got here from

Jamaica, right? So I know who he is. He hung out at our house a lot in the first year when my sister was still home. She watched out for him."

"Yeah?"

"So he's got caught in a gang." Paul spoke quietly, almost whispered. "YBK."

Cyril knew the name. That and several others. You couldn't avoid it.

"Shit."

"It happened so fast. We knew something was going on about four months ago, when he started to act kind of stupid, you know? Like he knew better than us. And I really noticed because he used to come to me for advice, and he stopped. He never said a thing about gangs."

"What are his parents doing?"

"Oh, man. His dad is saying, 'Something must have happened to him on the plane over to Canada 'cause he was a good kid in Jamaica.' His dad lives there."

"In Jamaica?"

"Yeah, and his mom is freaked. Because it's serious. Do you understand how so?"

Paul glared at Cyril, who stopped himself from replying, struggled to put himself where Paul was. Pictured his brother, grown to thirteen years old and fallen into the same trap. A nightmare.

"They kill them if they walk away." Paul's voice was raw. "He's just a little boy."

"What are you going to do?"

"What can I do? You think I can walk up to them and say give him back?"

They sat in silence for a while.

"They really do that?" said Cyril. "To a kid?"

"That's how it works, man. The kids get pulled in. They think they're tough enough because they don't know the beginning of what they're doing. And then who's there? On the other side? Kids like themselves but grown older inside of it. Mean as hell, totally lost their souls to the bullshit."

"Shit."

"It was high school, man. He made it through grade school, and that was hard. It was a big change. He never spoke much standard English before, right? It was patois. But you know how they assume the kids are fluent in both?"

"Yeah."

"So he worked hard, and he did do good. Had decent grades. Then he gets into high school, and it's all about the right attitude and potential and shit that Black kids are *not* supposed to have. They want him to be good at sports, and you know what? He's not."

"I get that."

"It's a fucking mess."

"Listen," said Cyril. "I've got a friend, his name's Evan. He's cool, really. He knows a lot of stuff, a lot of people."

"Does he know YBK?"

"I don't think so, but ..."

"Then he don't know no one. 'Cause that's the only way to reach them. There's no intermediary. They don't give a fuck about anybody else. Their life is cheap."

EVAN WAS AWAY AND DIDN'T answer his phone. He sent Cyril an email describing his work obligations, writing assignments, and romantic complications — Penelope was in a demanding phase – all the very many reasons why he couldn't meet up. Cyril didn't know how to put his concern for Paul's cousin in an email, didn't know the kid. He had his own preoccupations. His own life at school and at work. He'd follow up with Evan later, when he was less distracted. But he didn't have any other inspirations; Evan was the only person he knew who might be able to help.

CYRIL HAD HOMEWORK, BUT THE store had been busy. He'd had to unpack and inventory twelve cases of food cans and stack them on the shelves. One of the regular customers wouldn't leave and had Cyril trapped while he talked about his dog, who was outside yapping, and the mess of recycling bins in front of his apartment building. Cyril had heard it all before but had never learned how to get the guy out faster so that he could count the night's take and lock up. He wondered for the thousandth time how Mr. Lee had done it, mostly alone, for all those years.

Now that he was home, he still needed to study for at least another hour. He sat down in front of a pile of books, let his head rest on top of the desk, and, for just a minute, allowed his eyes to close. He was tired. He heard his mother's whisper, *Bone-tired, baby*. At the back of his neck, a tight, sore muscle protested his bent back, the angle of his head. He felt the cold air against his legs and urged himself to get up and close the window, but he didn't stir. His mind played with the smell that grew stronger as he lay there. The smell of tar.

IT IS COLD. HIS SHOULDER hurts. Edward opens his eyes to the chill damp of the dirty stone steps he's lying on. Light seeps through the seams of the heavy fabric that covers him head to toe. He is under a tarpaulin. He remembers dragging it down from a truck parked around the corner. His head hurts like hell, rings to the sound of the waking city. A clang of trolley. A newspaper caller. He pulls the tarp up and looks out at the shoes of two men passing by who don't see him. They are talking earnestly about money. He smells the tobacco smoke that drifts behind them. Then the seductive scent of bacon frying somewhere close. That wakes him up all right. Hungry as hell now, as well as hurting. He touches his head, rubs at a sore place. His hair is messed up, stiff, matted, and something is sharp; he pulls at it, flinches with pain. Glass. He remembers now. The guy was a greaseball, walked into the bar and started up right away. "I don't like to drink with coloured boys," he said as he shouldered into the bar, pushing with his arm at Edward's side. Edward held on to his glass, too precious to lose. The guy didn't stop. "I don't like to drink beside a nigger." Edward pulled away from him and walked over to a table where some guys he knew from a communist meeting were sitting. They found a chair and moved him in with them, between the two big guys at the end of the table who slapped his back with huge hands, palms like paddles. All of them were union guys, out on a Saturday night, and none of them had wives to go home to.

It was a doozy, he remembers that. They were laughing, the union men, when the greaseball suddenly stood over the table, several friends at his side, and then all hell broke loose and somebody threw him at a wall and then somebody hit him on the head. He didn't know it was a bottle. Not till now. He grimaces, which also hurts, pulls at the bruises around his mouth, stretching his swollen lip. But they were good men, that union lot. They were going to call a meeting where they'd ask why coloured men couldn't work at the factory. They were going to make demands. Edward imagines a job where you go every day at the same time with Sunday off. Plus a holiday. And it would last forever so that you could buy a house if you wanted to.

When Celia smiles, he feels like that: lasting forever in a room that will always be there with food and heat and light. It has been fifteen days since he's seen her. She is trapped at work. The family is moving, and they have everyone on extra time, sorting and packing and cleaning. Celia has big decisions to make because they say she's going with them. She wants to stay with Edward.

Edward pulls himself out from under the tarpaulin. His legs are damp, and the cloth of his pants clings tight. His torso is sore, bruised but dry. He will go back to the flophouse and get cleaned up before he sets up the newspapers. Some people say that the best thing for the country would be a war, jobs for everybody. In the last war, Blacks couldn't fight in the same units with whites — "I don't want to fight with coloured boys. I don't like to fight beside a nigger." But the Black guys formed their own battalions and went to war anyway. Edward can't see why you'd fight at all if they didn't let you have what they had. Isn't this country as much his as theirs? He carries that question back to the flophouse along with his bruised body, matted hair, torn jacket, and damp pants. The union guys thought he should have what they have. But they are the organizers, the idealists, the communists. The regular guys don't feel so strongly. They protect their jobs.

Edward is seventeen years old, and he's had worse beatings than last night's. He is a target because he is poor, a street hustler, a cheap opportunist by virtue of circumstance. He is a target because his dark skin and tightly curled hair set him apart.

At the house, he finds a change of clothes. Not clean, but not torn. It takes a while to peel the old ones off. He wishes he could get a bath over in the steam house. But he needs money to do that and so has to get out on the street and sell newspapers. He has nothing but those.

Then he remembers with a visceral thrill that he has Celia. But how would they live? She could never stay with him in this rooming house. Will she curl under a tarpaulin with him? Once again, he is filled with the dread of losing her. Celia is the first person in his entire life who has loved him, and she has made him whole. Gathered up the pieces of him that were once a baby without a mother, an unloved child, a boy alone, and made him into Edward, who is ageless and who will always survive.

EIGHTEEN

THE MAN ACROSS FROM CYRIL in the subway car held that morning's newspaper. The page facing Cyril was headlined, "Arrest following scuffle at citizens' town hall on gang crime." He had read the same piece forty-five minutes earlier in a newspaper he'd found stuffed to the side of his seat on the bus. In the news again, he'd thought as he scanned the page. They were a public concern. Brown and Black people, Indigenous included, were too often in trouble. They were arrested and went to jail, got out, then reoffended. They abused drugs and alcohol and were inclined to be violent. Out of control – control of themselves – they lacked stable family structure and squandered their opportunities. Toronto's mainstream cultural convictions poured in at a steady rate and were Cyril's growing burden. He hadn't known about this on arrival. He had known it wouldn't be easy. That jobs were hard to get and that he'd have to work even harder to make a career. That it took time. He'd known all of that. But he hadn't known how Canada would count him out.

From his fourth-floor history classroom, Cyril watched a slip of blue appear through an opened seam in a grey blanket of sky.

Alongside it, a billow of steam rose up from a chimney somewhere, a chimney he'd never seen. People did make it. Lots of
them. He just had to figure out how to be one of those.

In the library after class, instead of studying for accounting,
Cyril walked through the stacks, following a compelling urge to
know more about something the teacher had mentioned. About
Canada's immigrant gateway, Pier 21, back when Europeans came
by ship to Halifax on the east coast of the country. As he walked,
the library's carpeted floor rocked ever so slightly, not so anyone
else would notice. Edward was there somewhere. The sound in
the library, the dense presence of people working, thinned to a
distant murmur, surf on sand. The finest of mists moved over
his eyes, shifted the light. And he knew which book to take from
the shelf. He turned the pages and saw warships, naval des-
troyers, found the section on corvettes, the little ships that sailed
in convoys to protect the freighters on their perilous journey
across the Atlantic.

Edward had been there. Cyril was as sure as he could ever be
when these through-sights came. Edward, in that frightening
place where the men – most of them really just boys – slept in
hammocks or on tabletops, wherever there was space. More
than eighty of them in those little ships as the water bounced and
churned them seasick, and what food they could keep down was
over and again corned beef and potato made from powder. The
foul stench of stale bodies and cooking grease; oily, suffocating
clouds of cigarette smoke; no water to wash; and toilets that
sent a flush of dirtied ocean all the way back up again when the
seas rolled. Mostly nothing happened for days, and the grinding
monotony made them tired and anxious. Then the U-boats
sounded on radar, and the boys either killed or were killed.

Cyril went to the archives. Stood outside on the opposite

sidewalk mustering confidence, calling it up like a flank of soldiers. But they were perfectly nice inside. Listened to what he
needed, said they could help, though he'd set himself a big task.
Some of the records were digitized and would be easy to search,
but most were not. It would probably take weeks. A needle in a
haystack endeavour, they said. Good luck.

Edward was war-age in the 1940s and twenty when conscrip-
tion was introduced. He might have been sent overseas then. Or
joined of his own accord before that, like so many young guys
had. Cyril asked to look at fleet lists, and to his astonishment, the
archive arranged a reference loan from Ottawa's naval archives.
For the personal convenience of Cyril Rowntree. His work was
important, and Edward mattered. It would take time, the process
was slow, but they would arrive before too long.

CYRIL WAS READY TO SHOW Professor John how well his research
had paid off. There were fifteen minutes left in office hours, and
no one was waiting. He stood in the doorway, and John looked up.

"Come in, Cyril."

"I've got a picture of Edward — the kid I told you about — and a
name for his father. The guy in the photograph? And the Toronto
Archives has asked for naval records to be sent from Ottawa. For
me." He couldn't stop the smile that took over his face.

"Well done," said John, looking at the pictures. "And I have
something for you. It's long before your man's time, but I was
just reading about this. Interesting in so many ways." John pulled
a notebook from his bag. "Toronto was the political centre for
anti-slavery, as you know." He glanced up at Cyril for confir-
mation. "The period of time that the Underground Railroad ran
was, what? Fifty years? But that's pretty much all the Black
history that Canadians know."

Cyril nodded. "Yes."

"So freedom runners and freed people came up from the States. Especially after the Fugitive Slave Act gave slave catchers leeway to kidnap freed people in the north and sell them in the south."

"In the mid-eighteen-hundreds, right?"

"Yes. Eighteen-fifty and earlier." John opened his notebook. "This man, James Mink, who owned one of Toronto's fancy hotels — and by the way, there were lots of successful Black businessman in Toronto back then. Like Wilson Abbott, who owned property all the way up to Georgian Bay."

"He was a city councillor too?"

"Yes. Good." John was impressed. "So Mink — and this story was made into a movie — Mink is supposed to have offered a big marriage dowry for his beautiful daughter, Mary. A white man responded to that offer then kidnapped her, took her south, and sold her into slavery."

"That's evil," said Cyril.

"But here's the thing. I just met a researcher who is writing an academic paper that proves this story is not true. Despite all of their successes, because the political work Black people did back then was really effective. Despite all that, this is the story that lasts. It makes me think that if you're Black, you're bound to lose. Mary actually married a Black guy right here in Toronto, and they lived a quiet, uneventful life. But the movie story makes her father the villain and Mary a loser."

"Wow. That was also eighteen-fifties?"

"Yes. The best known story. And it's a fairy tale." John pushed back in his chair and swivelled toward his bookshelf.

"Hey, Cyril."

"Yes?"

"Mary Ann Shadd?"

"A Black newspaper publisher in Toronto. An abolitionist. Also from the eighteen-fifties. Another success story?"

"You really do know your stuff!" said John. "And she was also the very first woman publisher in Canada. It was a force, the Black community back then. Still is, of course, though I guess the enemy now is systemic racism. Back then it was slavery, which would have been easier to fight somehow. Not so slippery."

Cyril left John's office with two more books and a head full of ideas. Edward's father must have gained something positive from his time in Toronto. But it was probably harder then. By the 1900s, the Black community's force seemed to have faded. Tucked into Cyril's bag was the story of Dr. Alexander Augusta and his wife. She had owned a big downtown store that sold high fashion, and he was a surgeon who'd graduated from the University of Toronto. Another important Black couple. Would it have been easier for Edward if he'd been born in Toronto in the 1850s?

THE DAYS WARMED, THOUGH THE basement stayed cold. Cyril, wrapped in a big cardigan, sat at his desk with a pen and a lined pad. He listed the bills he needed to pay alongside his monthly income. He'd just hung up from an expensive telephone call with his Aunty Vi, who wanted more money for the babies. Times were harder than the usual hard, she'd said. She's selling vegetables in the market: yam and callaloo and Irish potatoes. But it's not enough. All the prices are high, and people buy less, so she sells low. She doesn't make enough to shop for anything other than staples at the supermarket. No extras. She's scrubbing floors with a cleaning crew at the bank when they need another body even though her knees are sore, her arthritis screaming, but it's not enough. They are eating breadfruit, but there is no money for chicken. What about paying for school lunches? Because she can't keep that up. She has spent the money on shoes and uniforms for the children. Her best friend used to work at a Free Zone factory, but those jobs are nearly all gone, moved to Foreign where workers are cheaper. Her cousins couldn't get work anywhere. "Every likkle ting, Cyr. It add up to small, small, small. Mi mus have more or mi kean keep those chil'n."

Cyril pictured her talking into her cellphone, standing in front of the three-bedroom house in Philadelphia that was home to two families. Her urgent insistence put him on edge. He had a tiny bit of money saved toward his trip home in the summer. But how could he use that on a flight for himself if he couldn't give his aunty what she needed? He felt the trip collapse under him.

Now he got it: all those mothers who left to go to Canada or the U.S. or the U.K. to make enough money to raise their families back home, like Paul's aunt. Why they left their children for years. Didn't come home to visit. Now he understood. He was trapped. Stuck in the same cycle. Poorly paid work. A school program that was costing him a fortune. It was a fantasy, leaving the country for a better life. He needed the right education to make it work. Or to be full of ideas with connections to money so that he could start a business. He had none of those things.

Cyril pushed back at the all too familiar mix of frustration, anxiety, and sorrow and made himself compare what he had to what Edward had lacked. When he did that, his own deficits seemed like riches. God's Gifts, his mother would have said. He let himself conjure Edward's life. Let Edward lift him from his own. Cyril closed his eyes.

EDWARD IS LYING PARALLEL WITH the steel rods that make up the undercarriage of a boxcar. They've laid narrow boards across the rods to support their bodies. He lies on his stomach, cheek pressed to his knuckles where his fingers hold tight to a plank of wood. His feet dangle, toes pointed to the rails. Another man lies alongside him, and another man beyond that. They are, each of them, head to toe. Edward is looking outward, away from the train. When he turns his head, his view is of the other man's shoes. The man has good shoes, real boots that look as though they might have been new not so long ago. His pants are soiled with the dust from the tracks and soot and grease from the engines and couplings. He appears to be sleeping. They are waiting for the engine to start. The train is going east, and Edward thinks he'll get off in Halifax. He has never ridden rails before and imagined a drafty corner in a freight car. But now he's what the men call a trapeze artist, squeezed into this place where all he'll see are the tracks that will soon roar by below him. When the train starts, he'll have to close his eyes so as not to panic, and when it reaches its full speed, he will wish that the bulls had found him and pulled him off the train.

The Depression battered Toronto and finished him off. He fought to keep his newspaper pitch, and succeeded for a long time, but watched with increasing despair the tide of men that seemed to grow larger every day, pressing into the corners that Edward and his sort previously held for themselves. These new men took what jobs there were. They flaunted their connections and their education and were articulate about their need. Lots of them had children who needed to eat. It was simple. There wasn't enough for all of them. Some of the older men who'd fought in the Great War and suffered through the crop failures that preceded it said that they needed another war — for the wages and decent food. He'd heard talk of that before.

Edward got in with the crowd that was going to the relief

camp in Trenton. That was a few years back. Before Celia. They took them there on a train, clearing them out of Toronto like a plague of rats. Paid them a dollar a day to pick and carry rocks. Those were make-work projects dreamed up by government men who kept their good salaries and summer holidays and could spend like kings because people with money were rich with it now. And if it wasn't make-work, it was doing a job that other men got paid ten times as much for.

The camp deducted room and board from Edward's dollar, and that left him with twenty cents a day. A guy said that there were more than half a million of them, men on relief. Young, unmarried, and unemployed men. We're an army, some of them said. And when you looked around at the faces that were all male and all hungry, you felt the possibility of power. But it never came to anything, and really, they were all of them just dirt poor. For some of the Royal Twenty Centers, the camp was the whole of life. Year after year.

But they closed the camps, and then Toronto was worse. Edward has been hungry all his life, but now he knows what starving is. When he could, he ate at the soup kitchens. You heard where the food was in all its details, the measures of salt and fat, how thick the slice of bread. Sometimes the sense of hearing it was as rich as the smell of it, and it stuck in your dreams.

He marched with men from the labour unions in protest and solidarity. That was in 1938, when he still believed they could save themselves. He slept outside with a hundred men all huddled together for warmth, breathing the stink of each other's piss and filth. But the march down Spadina Avenue that next morning, their faces bathed by a wind that was warm despite the cold night, was grand. He'd walked with the communists, who had the best chants. He knew all the words to "Bread and Roses."

They marched behind a banner that stretched the width of the road. It took ten men to hold it. The words waved in the air, letters big enough for everyone to read: WE ARE CITIZENS NOT TRANSIENTS.

They wanted respect. Respect and work and wages and food. He was marching, and then the word spread that the communists were outlawed — banned by the government. They'd be deported or locked up. He hid out in the dark corners of the city. He knew how to disappear. How to show up just in time for the food at the Black churches or the labour halls. And then there was Celia. Celia, who changed everything. After Celia, the only day that mattered was her day off. Not the Depression or the war or the constant hunger. Then she was gone.

Families on relief in Halifax made eighteen dollars a month. In Toronto, they got ten. It didn't matter where single men were, they got nothing. Edward knows a man who moved his family to Halifax, and that's where Edward's going. He won't stay in Toronto where the Negroes look at him with suspicion because he's been in prison and has no family. They don't want him around because they have ambitions for their daughters that don't include a rounder. He hasn't heard from Celia in sixteen months.

NINETEEN

❧

"WHEN YOU GET TO AFRICVILLE, jump off. You'll see how the train slows when it goes through town, and that's when you hop quick. There's no passenger station. See, this train has supplies for the diseases hospital, the big prison, and the glue factory. Africville's in the middle of all of them! Oh, man, and there's also the place for Halifax people's shit, and I mean what comes out their assholes. Night soil." He chuckled. "They got disposal pits for that, right next to Africville! But I'll tell you what's pretty. It's the houses, all painted different colours. And the girls." The coloured fellow riding the freight car with Edward was full of talk and stories that kept coming for miles. "It's astonishing," he said. "You'll see when you get there."

As Edward walks, he rolls the word *astonishing* around in his mouth. He loves that word, and he is prepared for everything. He jumped a little too soon, before Africville, on the outskirts. He knows it is up toward the top of the hill, so that's where he goes when his legs find their balance and he's searched out some water to drink. His muscles are so used to clinging tight, balancing with the moving train, on top, down below, wherever, that he has to force them to relearn walking uphill along the paved road. He can see the buildings at the top, just like he was told. And then the pavement ends, stops right there at his feet where a decision was made to finish it. So he follows the worn dirt path that takes him straight into the town of little houses scattered higgledy-piggledy around the hill. He can see how the train tracks go straight through, cutting the town in two, but he stays away from the tracks. Wants the feel of grass and dirt and solid ground, doesn't need reminding of the rails for a while.

The very first astonishing thing he sees is that everyone is coloured. A couple of old ladies, holding hands for balance, negotiating a low wall. A man in blue jeans planting a garden. Six men who stroll by, assorted sizes, wearing overalls, talking, carrying tools. A lady walking toward him with a couple of little kids grabs the hand of the smallest when she sees Edward. Behind her is a young woman with a baby in her arms.

The path forks off at a little yellow house. A group of kids sit outside, at least twelve of them, chewing on gum, sharing a bottle of soda. Edward stands and stares, and they stare back. His body is all sore bones and muscle aches, and he longs for one of those sodas. And food. Real food, like chicken. He has ten dollars in his pocket; it's everything he has for the rest of his life, but right now a soda is the best thing that a fellow could buy. He says, "You boys buy that soda here?"

"I'm not a boy," says one of the littlest kids.

"She's a girl," they all say at once. "Her name's Gillian."

"You're dressed like a boy," says Edward, though now he can see the female in her face.

"I'm a tomboy. My mommy says so." She's proud of that and sits up straight when she says it, then slumps back to chewing along with the rest of them.

What Edward is trying to remember is the last time he talked to little Black kids. It would have been in Toronto at the UNIA Christmas party. If he'd ever gone to church, he'd have known more children, but he never did. Wouldn't go, although a couple of ladies pressed him to come.

"You kids all live here?" he asks.

They laugh. "Yes, sir. This is a coloured town." The oldest boy is talking. "What colour are you?"

"I'm coloured like you are," says Edward. "Now show me where to buy a soda."

"The Penny Shop," says the biggest kid, jerking his head back to indicate the yellow house behind. "She's got seven left. Two root beer, four cherry, and one cola like we just had."

"After they're gone, there's no more coming," says the girl.

"We had this for Mat's birthday," says another, pointing to the kid now holding the empty bottle.

"All my birthday pennies went for sharing soda," says Mat, grinning wide.

"That's a nice thing," says Edward, who knows that he won't share a drop of his.

Inside the Penny Shop, the woman looks him up and down. Says she'll take ten cents for the root beer, but keeps looking at him like she doesn't think he'll buy.

"I need a place to stay," says Edward. "I need a job and a bed to lie down on at night. I'm good at work. But right now, I'm real tired because I just got in."

"Just blew in to Africville," she says. Then smiles like he's probably turned up in the right place. "Sit down," she says. He sits in the chair in the corner of the shop that is really just her front room with some shelves and a counter, a woodstove, and a couple more chairs. The kids wandered off when they realized that no one was going to yell or buy them candy.

"There are no jobs here," she says. "It's the Depression. Could be that it's better in the rest of the country now that we're at war, but not much changes here. There are jobs in Halifax. I'd never go there." Then she laughs, a giggle that rises up through her throat and lands like a gift in between them.

Edward smiles. "I came in on the rails," he says. "The other fellows got off in Halifax."

"That's where you'll go," she says. "Soon as you've had some rest."

One man comes in. Then a couple more. They've come for tobacco and rolling papers, to share the reading of a newspaper. They stand around and talk. When a fourth man arrives, the shop is full, so they all move outside, tell Edward to bring his chair with him and sit with them on the porch.

"This really is all coloured, this town?" says Edward, looking up at the Black faces standing around him.

"Some of us is descended from the Maroons of Jamaica," says the tallest of them. "My family's been around here for more than two hundred years. We built the Citadel, the fortress on the hill. And we defended it."

A couple of the men groan like they've heard the story so many times before and would not choose to hear it again.

"Some been here even longer," says the tall man. "The French brought slaves into Louisbourg three hundred years ago. Louisbourg wouldn't be there without them. Then came the Loyalists, though they never got what they were promised and most went off to Sierra Leone. For a better life than they got here." He stops to survey his audience. "Hope they got it," he says. Then he lights a cigarette, tossing the spent match into a wide-mouthed can in the corner of the porch. "Maroons followed them out a few years later. But enough stayed. There's coloured settlements all over Nova Scotia."

"Let him rest," says the shop lady with her smile. "Sleep first, history of the world from you fellas later."

"How old are you?" asks one of the men. Not like it really matters.

"Nearly nineteen," said Edward, who knows he is as grown as he'll ever be.

"If you're staying around, you'll be going to the church. Someone there will find you something useful to do. We don't need any more rounders here."

"Maybe you're headed for Halifax?" asks another.

"Not for a while. I like it here. It's like no place I was ever at before."

"Where've you been? You're a travelling man?"

"Only here," says Edward. "Toronto is where I came from."

AFTER A FEW DAYS, IT'S as though he's been there for years. One of the fellas who works the night-soil truck let him have a cot in his house. It's pretty good. A straw mattress. Pump outside for water. He gets to use the kitchen. He's met a bunch of people who call him by his name, and he's learned theirs. When it comes to Sunday, he knows better than to upset folk by staying away from God, so he scrubs up good, borrows a suit from a lady's dead husband's cupboard, and walks to the Seaview African United Baptist Church.

And that is the second astonishing wonder of Africville. The view of the sea. The Bedford Basin spread out below with its changing colours and feelings, the constant sound of it. A living thing. The ocean is something else he never could have imagined, but to see it now feels as though it has always belonged to him.

Like a mother who got lost but was found. He could stare at that ocean for hours, and on the first day he did. Sat all through the afternoon looking at how the water moved under the shifting clouds, sparkled like glass when the sunlight hit it right, then gloomed under the gathering dusk as the sun fell flaming pink into the horizon.

In church, he sits near the back, where a couple of fellows make way for him, shuffling their behinds along the wooden pew. When he settles, and the talking starts — priest mumbling on about things Edward doesn't want to know, won't ever believe — he looks at the backs of heads. Everyone cleaned up, suit jackets and straight backs. All the ladies wearing hats. Some men with their hair pomaded and combed, others with their heads bowed. One old fellow already snoring in the second pew. The tops of children's heads bobbing about, a bow, a pigtail; one of them turns to look at him, but her mother pulls her attention back to the front.

Off to the right, about four pews down, there is one little hat, bright blue with a slip of lace hanging down behind. And below the lace a navy collar, then shapely shoulders compact in a royal blue dress. The back of her neck above the navy and below the lace is straight and attentive. Her long neck. If he could see her from the front he knows that her throat would be as long and as delicate as the ballerinas he once saw in a newspaper picture.

For a moment, he panics at the violence of his question. What if it's not her? And the time when a bird hit off the train comes into his head. He cradled it in his hand, stroked its breast, soft down over fragile bone, till it opened its beak, pushed out with its wings, and he straightened his palm. Some seconds later — he held his breath — it flew. And the panic is gone because he knows now without a doubt that it is her. He knows her throat so well that the taste of her skin now tickles salty over his tongue. Celia sits there with her back to him, just four rows down. She is the third, unequaled and astounding, astonishing wonder of Africville.

Edward watches her back so hard that he can almost feel her up against him. He slides the Bible over his lap to cover the need that's growing in his trousers. He swallows as his muscles tighten up along his arms, across his back, rigid like he's back under the train, clinging on for life. It's been sixteen months since he last saw her, and she never did say goodbye. She'll be twenty-one in a couple of months, he remembers.

When the service is finally over, he gets up quick, moves fast to find a place outside where he can catch her. He is sweating, even though the air is cool. He fumbles with his collar to undo the button. He wishes the borrowed suit fit him better, but he thanks the God back there in the church that he is at least clean. Not the same man who fell from the train stinking and muck-covered just days before. As she steps into the sunlight, he stops breathing, then, in a moment that happens outside of himself, moves forward to touch her arm. She is so shocked that she doesn't speak for a minute. Then she says, "Edward."

When they are beyond the view of all the eyes that watch them walk downhill and away from the church, he takes her hand, and she clings to his as though she is falling and only he can keep her upright. Down near the seawall, they sit facing each other so that all the remembering that's to be done happens fast, gleaned from each other's faces. They don't touch but talk instead in a tumble of explanations and sorrows, the time they've lost compressed into just the few days that he's been here in Africville, only a few hundred feet from the house where she lives.

Celia has run away. She calls it next-to-slavery, the life she lived before, working for people whose decisions ruled hers. Who assumed that when they moved, she would come too. And she did. But then her unhappiness overwhelmed her, and when they sent her to help set up an aunt's new house in Halifax, she ran. She never thought to get back to Toronto. How would she do that? She doesn't know about trains like he does. She couldn't manage on her own. Here in Africville is a lady who was help in the house of her mistress's aunt. And that's how she came to be here, because she knew someone. Edward had no address, was a street boy. A teenager living on his own devices, and she is a young lady.

She lives in one of the pretty painted houses, rose coloured, with flowers out front and more tucked in behind. She has a room of her own. The house catches the best view of the sea from the front porch. Its back is blind to the top of the hill and the sad industry that goes on up there. She has day work at the hospital, where she cleans up the mess that sick bodies leave behind. She's paid as a Learner, even though she's worked for years in domestic service, since she was a girl. It's thirteen cents an hour for a fifty-hour week. Edward worries that she could get sick herself. "What else can I do?" she asks. She's lucky to have work, and he can't argue with that. But her house is a beauty, and the room she sleeps in is fit for a princess. She lets him have a glimpse of it that first Sunday afternoon.

He lies awake at night and pictures her there, head on a pillow cased in white cloth, slender body under the patchwork quilt that covers the bed, framed picture of the ocean on the wall. She says that's when she was always happiest, lying on that bed, ready for sleep. But now she is happiest when she's with him. Edward feels as though he has reached the solid middle of his life.

He is completely adult now. They want to marry and make a life for children who will always know that their parents love them. They want them educated, to read and write and learn their sums so that the work they get when they're grown will be decent and safe. But first, Edward has to get a job.

He finds a place to stay where the rent is cheaper. Mabel Marvel is a friend of Celia's. Her mother has a house full of children but needs the extra, and so he is invited to sleep in the back shed where the tools for the garden are kept. Her granddaughter Gillian, the proud cola-drinking tomboy, is Mabel's little girl. Edward is entirely happy for the first time in his life. He is a moving part of a growing family, and he learns how to help out. He's good with the little ones, and he can do small repairs that Mrs. Marvel is grateful for. He knows enough to clear out when the place is too crowded, and he has good places he can go. There's always a reason to head down to the church. He helps with the youth club. They meet in the same room as the ladies' auxiliary. Same place the Bible classes are taught. The church is where funerals see off the old folk and infants are welcomed. One day it will be he and Celia who stand in the aisle to be married.

Best of all is Celia. She is his future. And the time he spends with her is an astonishing gift. Some Sundays, when he's sitting beside her in the pew at church, he thinks that this God they all seem to love might exist after all. Even if only in Africville.

THEY ARE LISTENING TO YODELLING Hank Snow. The radio is turned as loud it will go, and a few of the young folk are standing around, tapping their feet. Mabel and Billy are there with a couple of other friends. Mabel's mom is babysitting little Gillian. This is as close as they get to dancing. He can put his arm around Celia's waist and sway side to side, but there is no room for a romp. Edward would love to take Celia to a real dance, but they'd have to go to Halifax, and that seems as far away as Paris. He wouldn't risk her to all of that, anyway. He's heard it's a rough town where lots don't like coloured folk. The war's made it tougher. Halifax is the convoy assembly port. It is full of soldiers waiting to be shipped overseas and sailors who come in on leave. In Africville, they joke that the Halifax Home Guard Platoon, made up entirely of Black folk, protects the soldiers from the German U-boats that lurk outside Halifax Harbour.

They stay in Africville on Saturday nights and stand around the radio with the rest of the young people. Everyone in Africville knows that he loves Celia. Not everyone understands how a woman like her could love a scrappy boy like him.

He can hear how Yodelling Hank must have really loved that woman he's singing to. The violin plays on the sadness, and the guitar picks out the longing. The yodel is as true and as sorrowful as any he's heard. Edward squeezes Celia's hand hard, and when he turns to look at her, she is looking up at him, full-on, all bright and glowing and open. He knows that it's love she's shining. He knows his face is showing it back at her. This is the best time there is.

But then it gets harder to make a life without a decent job. To make promises without believing in a future, because they can't marry without money to live on. And then the war is what's on offer because the longer it lasts, the more people they need. They take all sorts now. It's their chance. War wages. Money to send home. In 1943, he gets on a bus to Halifax and joins the navy. Celia stands with him at the bus stop and holds him tight.

EDWARD WRITES TO CELIA THAT it is a great adventure, a real laugh. But really, it is as grim and as hard as riding under that train. The first time that the ship sails is a thrill with wind in your face and all the men in crisp uniforms full of excitement and bravado. But then it is just hard work and foul living, waiting around in the muck of the ship for the German boats to blow them to bits. He chose the navy because the Africville people told him about their William Hall, a Crimean War veteran who'd saved a whole fleet of naval officers. "The first Canadian sailor to get the Victoria Cross," he told Celia, impressed and pleased. "The Queen gave it to him herself. A coloured man!" Before long, he wishes he never heard of William Hall.

There are jobs at home now that the men are gone. The women have to work them. Celia writes that she is trying for one of those, but the jobs are slow in coming to Africville, and she doesn't want to leave for Halifax. Not yet. He would have gone to Halifax. They don't like the coloured guys in the navy anyway; he could have hidden out at home. Hidden out and held on to Celia.

CYRIL SHIFTED IN SLEEP. HE was hot and pushed his feet out from under the bedclothes to cool them. The radio station on his alarm clock was playing some crazy old-time music. It crackled and spit its thin, resolute sound into the room. As the words came clear, he smiled, still sleepy, because it was so corny: a man singing about how he gave his woman all his love, and she only gave him the blues. But something in it stirred a sense of longing. Maybe it was how the man really meant what he sang. Cyril opened his eyes. His desk was lit by a stream of morning sunlight bounced from the window of the house next door. It was Saturday. He had the morning off. But his melancholy, roused by the song, lingered. He wanted a mug of tea and some breakfast. He wanted to take the morning off.

Cyril's milk carton had disappeared, which had happened once before, and when he tried the kitchen door it was locked, which really pissed him off. He had to put shoes on to walk around to the front and ring the bell. His landlady answered almost immediately.

"I needed it to make a pudding for my friends." She was accusing, as though that justified taking it from his fridge. "You were out."

He tamped down his annoyance but heard himself huff it out in frustration.

"You'll have to get more," she said as she handed him a five-dollar bill. "You owe me the milk from last time, remember, and get OJ for me while you're there. Bring back the change."

While she talked, a man — definitely male — in an open and flapping bathrobe crossed the hall behind her, bare feet moving fast. Cyril looked to see if she realized what he now knew. Was it the same man from the kitchen that time, he wondered, because it could have been. His landlady hadn't noticed. In fact, despite her usual abrupt manner, she was pretty relaxed, and now that he looked again, she very definitely had a glow. Her face was shining.

"Was it a good pudding?"

She was startled. "What?"

"The pudding?"

"Oh. One of my best." She was suddenly a happy girl. Turned away with a smile, though her voice was as sharp as ever. "Don't forget." Then she added, "Just leave them inside the front door because I'm going to be cooking, and I cannot have you in the kitchen."

It was a bright summer morning, the street not yet busy. It was nice to be outside, and Cyril's frustration evaporated into the day. Walking toward him on the sidewalk was Mr. Addo with a young woman and two small children alongside. The little boy wore a dark suit, like Mr. Addo's.

"Cyril. This is my daughter, and these are my grandkids." He turned to his family. "This is Cyril, the boy who is looking for the mystery man in my display case."

"Edward," said Cyril. "That's his name." The boy slid behind his mother's leg and looked at Cyril, open-mouthed.

"You heard?" asked Mr. Addo. "About Patricia?"

"How is she?"

"She passed. A couple of weeks ago."

His breath stopped. He saw her standing there behind Mr. Addo, heard her shrieking call, *Cyril!*

"I didn't know."

"Did you get to see her?"

"I was going to. I meant to."

"I miss her," Mr. Addo said. "She made me crazy, but I always thought I'd see her. At least once a week."

Cyril had never looked for her. Had never been to see her where she lived. Just around the corner from his house. Why, he wondered, had he not concerned himself with a person who had considered him a friend, a person he'd really liked? He'd spent months searching for Edward. He had never once looked for Pat.

"Wow. I'm so sorry that I didn't go."

Mr. Addo touched Cyril's shoulder. "God forgives you," he said, then chuckled, "Though I don't know if Patricia would." Seeing Cyril's distress, he said, "She didn't do so well at the end. They told me she got some terminal dementia on top of her everyday crazy stuff. She probably wouldn't have known you anyhow."

The kids were bored, fidgeting to go. The care home was just a few streets away. Pat had told him that she looked at the photocopied picture of Edward every day and thought of Cyril. He needed to see where she had died, although his heartbreak about coming too late made him more miserable than curious.

It was a long brick building, four storeys high, with a revolving door and a side entrance with a sign that warned not to let any of the residents out. He found the doorbell and was buzzed in, where a man behind the reception desk asked how he could help.

"I just came to see where my friend lived. She died two weeks ago. She was a little bit crazy. She usually said she was a either a nuclear physicist or a painter. Her name was Patricia."

"Oh, yeah." He smiled. "You upset her and she would say, 'I'm going to show you my knife.' Would not let us touch her. Smart lady. She did have a knife, you know? They kept it locked in a cupboard for her. I liked her. Yes, she passed away." He shrugged. "That was on my day off, so I didn't see her."

Cyril felt a familiar grief building just below his ribs.

"Did she leave anything? Not the knife. I mean, she had a picture I gave her?" He wanted something of hers to hold.

"What was it?"

"Just a paper copy of a photograph."

"I'll ask."

Cyril waited in the visitors' lounge, which was big, with two couches, a few chairs, and a TV on the wall. A little old lady sat in the corner slumped forward on her wheelchair with her face pointed down to her knees; a seatbelt kept her from falling out. A man with a walker shuffled endlessly up and down the hall.

The receptionist returned holding a postcard. "Only this, from a lady in England. We kept it for the address to send a notification. That's all they had. They'll throw it away. You can have it if you want."

"Was there a funeral service?"

"Always. In the chapel. But she didn't have friends or family, right? We didn't know about you."

"Yeah, okay. Thanks."

Later, when Cyril looked for a death notice online, he found her name and dates. There was only one message, a nurse who said that she missed seeing Patricia feeding the birds under the trees. Cyril didn't know what to write.

TWENTY

CYRIL SPENT AN HOUR ON the back steps of his house making a budget that took him all the way to graduation — just as they'd been taught in the school's financial planning seminars, which were endlessly cheerful and painted rosy pictures of their futures, despite the size of their student loans and the latest youth employment reports. What Cyril planned had nothing to do with sensible finances but was all about satisfying an emotional need. Exactly what the finance people warned against. Pat's death had made his trip home even more urgent. Because, really, anything could happen. Cyril needed to see his brother and sister. And more than that, he had to know that he'd been right to come to Canada. His move had been precipitated by the good intentions of others. In the turmoil that had followed his mother's death, he'd been unable to think. Now he wanted to put himself back there, to find the perspective he'd lost.

His aunties, kids from college, teachers, business leaders, newspapers, all framed the trip to Canada or the U.K. or the U.S. as a natural part of Jamaican life — if you were lucky enough to get a visa. His legacy from Nelson had got him a head start on his tuition. And that, plus Junior's sponsorship, had got him his visa. A Canadian education was worth so much more than the temporary work visas others racked up as domestics and personal care workers, picking grapes and apples, caring for other people's children.

Cyril was not going to spend Nelson's money on the trip home, but he was prepared to gamble it, which would not make Nelson happy. *Never pay interest.* Nelson's voice was sharp at his ear. *And if you must, then know how to manage it!* Cyril stood his ground. The answer to his trip home was so simple — the credit card they'd offered to students in their first weeks at school. He had a bonus job now, the five hours a week in the school's bookstore. He'd never get more hours, but that, plus the convenience store, was probably enough.

He completed the credit application in front of a man almost Nelson's age who wore a sleek grey suit and banker's tie. He leaned back in his chair and said, "We're all over the world, Cyril. You know that? Every likkle nook and cranny have a Jamaican ex-pat."

Cyril couldn't smile. He was waiting for an answer.

The man looked over Cyril's form, picked up his pen, and made the signature that assured Cyril's credit, interest-free for six months, then payable at a gambler's rate of 22.5 percent per annum.

"When are you going?"

"August. The only month when I don't have any classes."

"Hurricane season."

"It's going to be hot," said Cyril and shared his first smile of the day.

"MR. LEE'S BACK IS VERY bad today," said Mrs. Lee, whom Cyril rarely saw because she was an artist who split her time between painting very early in the morning, helping her sister with grand-children, keeping the accounts for the store, and teaching three classes a week at the local art school. When Mr. Lee talked, which wasn't often, it was about his wife or his daughter. He was very proud of both of them.

"He's getting it checked." She was elegant and pretty. Cyril felt clumsy when she was around.

"I'm sorry."

"How are you getting along, Cyril?"

"I'm okay." He hesitated. Then, in a tumble of words, "I wanted to ask Mr. Lee if I could have ten days off because I have to go and see my family in Jamaica. I really am sorry, it's just that I need to know now because I have to buy the plane ticket."

"When?"

"In August, I hope."

"Well, I guess that's lots of notice."

"I know. It won't happen again. It's just that I need to do this, and I've figured out how to manage it. Financially, I mean."

She looked suddenly old and very tired. "Okay. I know he likes your work. We'll figure it out."

Now the thrill of the trip was spoiled with guilt. Going home to kids he should probably never have left. And leaving Mr. Lee, who had always only been kind. But it was just for ten days; the ticket was as good as in his pocket, and he really was going home.

EARLY-SUMMER HEAT WAS A MAGNET that pulled people to the streets and produced spontaneous smiles from those who were usually too busy for pleasantries. Downtown, in Trinity-Bell-woods, big trees in full leaf made green canopies of shade. Babies in carriages and carriers slept or flapped their way into the first summer of their lives. Friends met up, window-shopped, trailed in and out of storefront art galleries. Someone had ice cream. Shopkeepers put dog bowls with water and biscuits outside their doors to please the locals who walked with dogs of all sizes. Downtown was fresh and gleaming on both sides of its shop windows, and everybody on the sidewalks looked good.

Evan was leaning back on a bench outside the coffee shop. His dark glasses made a discreet pleasure of watching the passing girls, legs and cleavage, acres of skin. Cyril squeezed in beside him as everyone on the bench edged down a few inches.

"It doesn't get any better, hey, Cee?" said Evan. The women saw Evan. Didn't matter what colour they were, their radar found him, and even though they kept walking, talking into their phones or at each other, their eyes swivelled over to scope him out. Mostly they slid right over Cyril, though one or two gave him a moment's hesitation.

"Man, the ladies like you," said Cyril despite himself; he hadn't wanted to sound envious.

"Hey," said Evan. "My mommy and daddy are good-looking people. Nothing to do with me."

A tall girl with red hair and incredibly long legs in white shorts slowed her stroll as she passed, half turned her face toward Evan, big sunglasses making eyes at his. *It's a secret code*, Cyril thought. The hair, the clothes. The glasses.

"What's up?" asked Evan.

"I've got this friend at school whose cousin is in big trouble."

"Black guy?" asked Evan.

"Yeah. The cousin's been here a few years. From Jamaica. He's only just turned thirteen."

"What's happened?"

"He's with a gang."

"Which one?"

"YBK," said Cyril, conscious of the shift in Evan's tone.

"Listen to me, Cyril." Evan turned his mouth toward Cyril's ear, voice pitched low and earnest. "Those guys are very definitely unreasonable. I mean, you cannot reason with them, understand me?'

"Sure."

"You're not getting involved in this? Because if you are, you're in way over your head."

"No, man. Of course not. That's why I wanted to talk to you."

"Look," said Evan. "There are blocks in this town where kids have to fight their way to growing up. You know the discipline from home those moms lay on them? Those expectations? The way it used to work in the islands where the kids say 'No, sir' and 'Yes, ma'am'? It doesn't work here. The guys get the discipline on the street, and it's harsh."

"Yeah, I know," said Cyril, "I just —"

"I don't think you do," Evan interrupted. "I know you've been beaten up by the cops. That's not the same as being watched by everyone, cops, teachers, shopkeepers, neighbours, pastor included — and did I say cops — since you're four years old, with all of them waiting for you to make your first mistake. Frightened for you, but also bracing for it." Evan stopped for a moment and eased his shoulders. "Sorry, but it makes me crazy. People talking about a four-year-old going bad. So what happens? Like they're pushed into it."

"Okay," said Cyril, who thought of his brother, wanted to hold him tight.

"This whole thing about respect?" said Evan. "Don't underestimate it. When did those kids ever get respect? Their moms try, but they're so frightened of what could happen to their babies that they end up disciplining them right out of the door."

"What's going to happen to his cousin?"

"He wants to get out?"

"I think so. That's what his family wants."

"Then he should get clear out of town. Not back to Jamaica though, because our courts keep bouncing the kids who grow up here back over there. You know those guys? They take Canadian trouble with them."

"But isn't there someone he could talk to who knows about this stuff?"

"If he was my cousin, I'd get him out before he hurts someone or they hurt him. I would not be hoping that he ends up in juvie so that I could negotiate some kind of help."

Cyril leaned back into the bench, his shoulder pressed against Evan's. Evan's intensity had shocked him. How did a kid get himself into a mess that could kill him? Because he was Black, and that made him stupid? That was ridiculous.

Cyril knew he took lots for granted. Made assumptions and left them unquestioned. He knew the cops were potential trouble and so he took precautions: stayed polite, carried cash and ID. He looked down at his hands. Brown. Evan's too. There was an Asian guy toward the end of the bench, and a white couple squeezed in next to him. There were no race issues here. No one was going to challenge him and Evan. In fact, Evan was perfect in this place, with his imminent journalism degree and good looks. You could put his photo on a magazine page and call him anything: journalist, actor, businessman, doctor, designer. He fit in. But, man, he'd never seen Evan so angry, and it shook him. Cyril breathed deep. His chest felt tight, and he put his face into his palms to ease the tension, rubbed hard at his eyes with the heels of his hands. He was startled by swelling tears and kept his hands there while he swallowed hard, willing them to stop. He stood suddenly. "I've got to go. Thanks for your advice."

"Okay?" Evan said and waited for more but then nodded behind his glasses while the people on the bench spread out to fill the extra space.

Cyril walked rapidly along the sidewalk, straight to the park. His eyes were still wet, and from time to time he swept at them with his fist. The street was thick with happy people. He had to weave his way through them. The park was full too: people with picnics and coffees, dogs and kids. He cast about, looking for Black faces. Three of them. Not together. One of them leaned on his bike, talking to two older white women. Cyril found his way to the chestnut tree and sat down abruptly at its foot, leaned against its trunk. For a moment, he imagined the guys, Randall, Leon, and Paul, with him here, and he knew that certainly Leon and Paul, without purpose other than pleasure, would feel like outsiders in this place. And that in spite of the vibrant variety all around them. Because despite the multitude of eclectic youth with a good assortment of browns, the park's diversity was mostly middle class, gentrified, and fashionable. Randall was an artist, but like the other two men his background was hardscrabble. Cyril was clean-cut. Polite. His clothes were tidy and conservative; not this neighbourhood's culture, but he knew he seemed appropriately conventional. That was what he intended. Nobody looked at him here.

CYRIL WOKE IN THE COLD of his basement. It was three in the morning. He was frightened, not by anything in his present but by the future, which seemed suddenly as bleak and as dark as the ocean floor. He pulled his knees to his chest, pressed his back to the basement wall, so alarmed by what he'd done, coming here to Canada. For a full few minutes, it was hard to breathe. Equally frightening was the idea that he might go back to Jamaica and never return. He opened his mouth and sucked in air as deep as his lungs could take it. Calm came eventually, but in minutes, not right away. He had dreamed he was alone on the street with bundles of grocery bags stuffed with old photographs and magazines and nowhere to go. As he regulated his breathing, listened for his mother's soothing whisper, closed his eyes, let the tension ease from his body, he found Edward.

EDWARD LAUGHS LIKE A LOON. Sits splay-legged on the beach on a perfect summer day with the sun high and hot and the sea a shimmer of baby blue. Beside him, his best friend, Harry, wears a smile as broad as the slick of sand they sit upon. This is the best moment in both of their lives.

They have been walking. A trail of footsteps marks the way they have come, from beyond the rocks where the beach curves out of sight. They have lost their shoes and hats and their uniforms are a mess of tears and dark stains. But they are laughing. They are alive. Harry's arm, alongside Edward's — because now they are lying side by side, becoming quiet — is dark and smooth and gleams with youth and health. Beside his, Edward's arm is smaller, and while his brown skin is darker than it was, painted with a palette of sun and wind, it is still lighter than Harry's. His bicep does not roll in his arm like Harry's, but he is muscular and strong.

Harry's other arm is broken and loose. The pain has started, and now he moans rather than laughs.

"We'll be all right," says Edward, gripping his friend's good hand. "Hold on."

Beyond the rocks, where the coastline curves from view, the beach is strewn with the battered and torn bodies of boys and men. They lie among the detritus of their smashed ship. All of them, ship and boys and men, were blown high into a smoke-filled sky.

The noise of the blast still rings in their ears, and the shriek and scrape of tearing metal, the horror of the screams of men, are the cacophony of nightmare. They were sorting supplies together, Harry and Edward, readying for the deployment of troops to the shore. In a box container, side by side as they are now. The ship seemed to rise from the water. They never let go of each other, holding wrist and hand like children because each knew his survival depended on the other.

Harry and Edward clung to each other and to the ineffable wonder of floating wreckage that was caught in the miracle of a rising tide. All the while, the awful dark water roiled and heaved in the stinking air as the screams of dying men mercifully, tragically diminished. "This is a miracle of God," said Harry when they knew how alone and alive they were.

They lie side by side upon the sand. Edward's face is turned to Harry, and he holds Harry's good hand, whose palm and fingers swamp his own. Harry's face is turned to the blue sky, though his eyes are squeezed shut. Tears run down his cheeks, and he moans his pain. Edward makes soft sounds of comfort, like a mother. He hears Celia in his soothing murmur.

He signed up for the duration, but nobody thought it would keep going like this. He hopes Celia still gets her share of his wages. He hopes she is safe. He prays that she still loves him. "When I come back, I'll be a man that can get a job," he told her. "The government will look after us because of all the sacrifice." That was what he believed.

It seems a lifetime ago. It was a few lives he lived on that ship that is now in pieces, scattered from here to Timbuktu. He doesn't let go of Harry's hand, even though he's stopped moaning. "No vc for us, Harry," Edward whispers. The sea is calm now, waves rolling smoothly up onto the beach and washing back. It is good to be on land.

Edward's legs are damaged, but he won't know that until he tries to stand up, when the first state of shock has passed. They've lain on the sand for more than an hour since making their way from the wreckage, but they won't rest for many more hours yet.

CYRIL PUSHED HIMSELF UP FROM sleep and into grey confusion, lost for a moment with his leg caught in a tangle of sheet that he pulled at with his hands. His breathing was heavy and his body slick with sweat. His mother's gift made hard demands, this sight into people's lives. Sometimes Edward was as real to him as Randall.

When he put his foot on the floor and tried his weight, the pain shot through to his hip. *Edward, man, your life is wicked*, thought Cyril. *You've got nine lives like a cat. You did more in the first twenty years of your life than I'll probably ever do.* Cyril eased himself to his feet, held on to the top of his dresser for a moment or two until the pain disappeared. He made his way to the toilet and then, blessedly, back to bed.

THREE LARGE BOXES OF FLEET records were waiting for Cyril on the archives' big table. He prepared himself for a search that could take a week. The lists were long and dull, and his eyes glazed from struggling with writing that was not always easy to read. The navy was small at the start of the war, massive by the time it finished, nearly one hundred thousand men and women.

But Cyril counted on Edward having signed up early, in Halifax, because it was navy. Although in reality he had nothing concrete to go on. Cyril focused on his task, didn't want to come back for a second week and needed to score a win for the lady who'd begged this special consideration for his request.

On a Thursday morning that he'd stolen from class, he found Edward's name on an infirmary register. A set of entries that included a list of the injured in the month of August 1943. A, B, C, Davina. He had found his needle in a haystack. His friend Edward. He'd turned the page without any presentient tingling or misted sight, nothing to suggest that he was about to see the name he'd been seeking for days, as though this were an ordinary school task. He doubted himself for a minute, but this was certainly Edward Davina. Twenty-one years old. Reservist. Ordinary Seaman FR577. Sailed on a corvette, HMCS *Colborne*, for six months – destroyed by German submarine. One of two survivors.

That first entry was followed by the details of traumatic injury: acute compartment syndrome in legs, five broken ribs, fractures to right shoulder, multiple severe lacerations, and more. Then a repetitive list of doctor's visits, nine weeks of records detailing vital signs along with medical jargon.

Nothing described how Edward was, his state of mind or the degree of healing in his legs, though he was released back into service in October. Cyril knew that they'd sent them back to fight patched and bandaged but not necessarily mended. Now that he had a service number, a search through the names of war dead shouldn't take long. Though he worried that the reason his find had come unheralded by his sight was because Edward had not lived through the war.

When Cyril was eight, a girl in the grade below him had been

hit and killed by a car. He'd watched her from across the road as
she lay on the ground. He'd been holding a box drink, sipping at
the purple juice through a straw. She wore a pink and white dress
that lifted a little in the breeze. He thought she was sleeping and
wondered why her mother didn't carry her home but instead
knelt over her and screamed. Her mother screamed on and on.

Three years ago, on a Saturday afternoon, there'd been a dead
man in Brown's Town. Everybody stood around him as he lay on
the sidewalk in front of Crazy P's while they waited for the police
to come. A church lady said to take him to the undertaker, to
any of the three funeral homes in town. But someone else who
seemed well informed said the coroner would need to see him at
the hospital forty minutes away. The ambulance was busy somewhere, and nobody wanted to be responsible. All that paperwork,
they said, and you wouldn't be able to answer the questions
they'd ask anyway. None of the people standing over him knew
who he was, though just about everyone claimed to have seen
him somewhere before. Cyril had been with his mother when
she suffocated in an asthma attack. But he didn't allow himself to
think about that.

Edward might have died. Was that fate? God? Luck? Circumstance? Grandpa Nelson would have said that the sacrifice of
young life to war was wrong. Let the old men fight. Those who
make the decisions should be put on the front line, and then war
would stop. He would have said that the man who hit the girl
should not have been speeding and that the government should
provide safe roads with sidewalks for people to walk on. He
would have said that Cyril's mother should have had the money
to buy the medicine she needed – and when Nelson was alive
he made sure that she did – or that the government should have
subsidized her prescriptions.

But he'd never really convinced Cyril that what was wicked in the world was anything more than random. *Wicked* was a word Cyril's mother had used a lot. The excitement with which he'd begun the records search calmed. He had managed through the hardest part. The death records would answer the remaining question. Cyril leaned back in his chair and closed his eyes. He couldn't conjure it, this sight of his; it just happened. But he needed to know.

TWENTY-ONE

❧

THE LIGHT FROM THE WINDOW teases his eyes open. Edward follows the trace of its shimmer across his white bedsheets. But then everything blurs; the trolley, the blinds, the bucket and mop, the cot next to his, each dissolves into the other.

With the light comes a smell of illness and disinfectant that sours his belly. The pillow, scoured rough, scrapes his cheek. He turns his head from the window, away from the sickly bright light.

He is afraid. That's what comes next, same as every morning. The fear sails through his night dreams in picture-book colours. He's never seen anything like the places he goes when he dreams. Or perhaps he has, and that's where the dread comes from: he doesn't know who he is or where he has been.

"It says here that you're twenty-one years old?"

He makes a sound that growls up from his throat.

"Are you?"

He has nothing more to give her.

Every day, the nurse's lips move around the same words, the same calm-crafted sounds.

"How did your legs get hurt?"

This question is so enormous that the air spills from him and anxiety burns a scoring line across his forehead. He closes his eyes.

He can read the time. Sometimes it shoots him a memory sharp as a needle jab. This morning, when the small arm of the clock touches eight, he remembers a field of cows with their heads bent down to green grass.

The days slide by through the ever-present fog of sleep and disinfectant. He doesn't know what his life was before he was hurt, but he knows that he is now in a convalescent hospital. His legs don't work, so they're fixing him. And the men in the other beds too. Though some of them were certainly not fixable because they are dead when the orderlies take them out.

YESTERDAY THEY TOOK AWAY A lad they said he knew. They arrived together, they said, both of them badly injured and lucky to be alive. The other's name was Harry, not so lucky now because he's checked out. Harry was a dark-skinned man, and the interrogator-nurse gave him a package that Harry had left behind. "That's for his family," she said. "He told us you'd promised to take it to them. But you don't remember, do you?"

He reached up to move his palm across his head, stroked the rough, dry stubble, grown from when he was last shaved here in the hospital.

"Your friend," she said, "you survived together."

From the sea. Hot grinding sand under the soles of his feet. Swallowed salt water. Is it better to be fixed and sent back or to die and never again know the worst of it?

ANOTHER DAY, HE SUPPOSES, BECAUSE the nurse is back again.

"What year is it?"

This is a better question, and he should know the answer. His frustration forces his fist to lift from the bed then strike the mattress.

"Don't be too angry," she says. "It will come back."

He looks at her whole face this time, not just her mouth. Her eyes seem almost kind today.

"Nineteen-forty-three," she says.

That seems right. "Thank you." He can sound the words now.

"What nationality are you?"

"Canadian."

"Well done!"

The answer came easy, so there must be more where it came from. Squeezing out from where it's buried. He runs a palm across the top of his prickled skull. Canada. The word sits fixed in his head, and he sounds it out to the room, pushed through his dry throat. It's a big country, Canada.

"We're fighting Nazis." He knows he must have done because everyone else in here has been doing much the same thing. They are at war. He remembers his question: "When can I walk?"

"What will you do when you can walk?"

Go over there, he thinks, and motions to the end of the dorm, the open door to the room where chairs line the walls and normal people, soldiers and others, sit, chat, laugh, and smoke. Walk there, like a regular human being.

"Smoke a cigarette," he says.

"That's good, Edward."

Soon after that, he can name the days with confidence. A week later, he is in the chat room. Hurt like rotting hell to get there, but his legs make the moves so long as he keeps his weight off them, gives it to his crutches.

"All these lovely young men," says an old lady with a red cross on her sleeve, "with all their broken limbs." She moves in close to help him.

"And broken heads," says Edward, pleased to be freed from his bed. "I've lost my memory. Wiped clean!" He smiles down at her grey hair.

"Oh, you'll be all right."

"I know."

He lets her hold his elbow to support him as he sits. He's careful not to topple. She's so little she'd never hold his weight.

"I'm English," she says. "Do you know where you come from?"

"Canada."

"No, dear. You can't be. You must be from the islands. You'll be a West Indian fellow with your dark skin. Your little curls are sprouting on your head."

"No."

"I don't think you'd be fighting with the white men, dear. They wouldn't have it."

He eases himself into a new position in his chair. He hasn't thought of that before. But now he thinks of Harry who is gone into the ground and can't help him with the answers. Edward opens his mouth and grins at the lady.

"I guess I was there," he says. He wishes that Harry were still alive to tell him the truth and wonders what is in the unopened package that Harry has left in his care.

"There's another one of you here," she says. "Maybe he knows where you're from."

A sadness sinks him, streams over his head, washes misery down his chest to his thighs and puddles at his feet. His head is heavy when she speaks again and he doesn't want to lift it to look at her. But because he is a polite man, he makes himself match his face to hers.

"I'll search him out for you," she says.

The length of his memory stops there. He is a man who knows sadness. He's a little guy, he can see that. But his head and his limbs are too heavy to move. He sits until they get lighter.

NOW THAT HE'S A LITTLE stronger every day, he's ready for the nurse when she comes.

"What day is it?

"Wednesday," says Edward. "I checked before you came."

She smiles. Today her eyes hug his. They lift him up and pull him close. She is sweet as cream cakes. Cool as iced soda. He hopes for things in his life that are yet to come. It's the same fluttering, tentative optimism that came before, when he woke from the last surgery.

ON SUNDAY, HE PUTS BOTH feet full flat to the floor, and they hold him upright. So long as he's scaffolded on both sides with his crutches. Both feet full to the floor, but he's still holding back with his weight.

"Coming better," he boasts to the Jamaican fellow who's waiting with tobacco and papers.

"Why you hurry so?" he says. "Dem sen' you back."

"Doc says I'll remember who I am. And now my memory's good. See how I remember you every day!"

"I will never get my sight back," says the Jamaican fellow. "I cannot tell my wife. Blind, and I have a baby boy I've never held. I am twenty-three years old and I will live forever in the dark."

Edward watches his new friend's chest empty and fill. His

sighs are cavernous, echoing, and he heaves up another one. Then he says, "Do you know what Jamaica looks like?"

"No," says Edward, who is still amazed by this man who pours out his sorrow in torrents of words. It is a looseness in him. The injury has closed his eyes and opened his mouth. Edward has never watched an unguarded face before. Never spent time with a blind man. Never known anyone so primed to spill. Unable to stop.

"Jamaica is a place that's green and yellow and black," he says. "The green is every green in creation, from the smallest blade of grass to the greatest banana leaf. And I must tell you that the yellow sun warms your back and is sometimes so hot you must swim in the turquoise sea. Yellow is also the sand, and the black is who we are, our strength. Our crea-tiv-ity. The sun shineth. And the green land is our everlasting resource."

"I only know I come from Canada."

"You can see it for yourself. It's painted into the Jamaican flag. Black with yellow and green."

"I don't even know for sure that my name is Edward. They could have made it up."

BY SUNDAY AFTERNOON, THE CHAPLAIN has been and gone. They sat in the chat room that morning with the chairs drawn into neat rows, and God spoke to them in the chaplain's voice. He loves them all, they were told, and He will save them all too. Their sins will be cleansed from them.

All the men in the room have sinned. They have all killed or tried to kill or wanted to kill. All of them need to be cleansed. That would be far better than hospital-clean. God-cleansed is fresh open air and waterfall-washed. Edward thinks it might be like Jamaica. The Jamaican man must think so too because afterward he says, "I am cleansed by my blindness. All men are the same to me now. I can't tell an enemy from a friend. And I can't see a coloured skin. You don't sound like a Black man, but I know that you are. Like me."

"You have brown skin. It's my colour."

"Mixed white and Black?"

"I don't know," says Edward. "I can't tell from the colour how it's made."

"I'm no colour now," says the Jamaican. "I'm colourless. Like everyone else around me." He smiles. It is the first time Edward has seen him happy.

On Monday, the Jamaican man is dead. Edward watches them carry him from the bathroom where he bled so fast from the cuts he made to his arms that he was gone before they found him. He'd have felt the warm rush of it. Edward puts his palm to the top of his head and pulls it across his curls. It would have been a good thing to say goodbye, but Edward didn't know about the decision to go. He didn't understand the need. One of them is gone because they couldn't fix him. One has chosen to check himself out. That leaves Edward.

The old English lady is beside herself with shock and tears. She went looking for him. She found him. "I didn't know," she keeps saying. "He was going to be with his family soon. They were going to send him home." There is a rusty brown stain on the cuff of her blouse and another along the hem of her skirt, at the back.

The next day, the nurse who asks the questions gives him a postcard with the Jamaican flag printed on the front. A yellow cross like a big X with green cradled above and below. At its sides are the black triangles that represent his friend's people. It is from the Jamaican fellow's mother. He reads it slowly, but it's not hard. They are all words he's spelled out before.

*We love you Darling. Your Mother, your Father, your Wife
and your Dear Little Boy. Your Sisters and your Brother. We
all miss you and we are only waiting for the day when you
come home safe to us.*
    God bless you.

The nurse leaves the card with him and goes to the next bed,
taking her eyes and mouth with her, and her bob of chestnut-
brown hair, stirring a sweet draft of air as she moves away. He
watches her go, crossing the divide between his bed and that
of the man next to him, whose leg is wrapped in a cast that's
tied to a bar above his bed. Once the very last particle of her is
gone to someone else, Edward considers the postcard of black,
yellow, and green. And then the package that Harry has left
behind for Edward to take to his parents. Edward knows the
order and the importance of these things. A mother and a father.
Brothers and sisters. Then comes a wife and child. No children
for Harry. He pulls Harry's package from underneath the pillow. As he unwraps it, he fills again with sadness. Holds the
locket with the photograph of Harry's parents in his hand. A gold
locket. A family.

The struggle for memories makes his mind ache, but he can't
stop it, like a tongue working to free a loose tooth. A memory
would be a relief because the fear of never remembering is constant. How has he come here? Who is he? He won't take Harry's
package to his family. There is no address. Unless it comes back
with his memories.

On the first day that he can really walk, he makes his way
outside. Down the hallway, along to the front door, and through
to the open air. He knows it was once a school, now kitted out as a
hospital. And the buildings that surround it, filled with military

people, are parts of the same big complex. He doesn't care what country he is in, and he cannot speak the language anyway. It doesn't matter. In fact, it helps. He is utterly lost, and a man without a history doesn't need to understand what people say, can't join a conversation. No need to know where he is because the question of who he is overwhelms all else.

Edward sits in a patch of warm sunshine and looks at the tree in the corner of the yard. Its leaves are turning orange and gold. Occasionally, one drifts to the ground. There are men on the other benches. Smoking. Waiting. His memory loss is also a sort of blindness, he thinks. Because he wouldn't know an enemy from a friend either. He will have to fumble through and hope for the best.

IT IS EARLY MORNING WHEN they leave. Dark — before the birds start. Edward is single-file with the other men along the narrow path that hugs the sides of the buildings, the way out of the complex. He saw it from where he sat with others in front of the schoolhouse hospital to smoke, to talk, to wait. But he never bothered to consider where it might lead. Now he'll find out. In one place, the buildings are so close together that the men's shoulders touch both sides as they push through. Just for a few seconds, but long enough for a rush of panic, to be caught in a place so small that the air is hard to breathe. He's felt it before. It happens on ships, where he's headed now.

They come out onto the main road, and, when he glances around, he sees the four shapes of the men behind him picked out by the officer's watch light, and those of the two men in front. The truck is waiting for them. It's cold out in the street. For a moment he thinks he can remember when he last felt air so crisp, a winter warning. But it's a moment that slips by and is gone.

He's dressed in full kit for the first time in weeks. The uniform is heavy, and it's work to move. His belt was too big when he first put it on, and one of the boys made a new hole. Now it feels too tight, as constricting as the uncomfortable weight of his jacket and boots. *I'm straitjacketed*, he thinks, *and I'm supposed to be sane*. Though there's nothing sane about a man who has lost himself but still obeys the orders when they come. Barked in the morning dark.

They clamber up, over the sides, and into the back of the truck. Edward can't get his right leg that high, and a couple of the guys haul him in, pulling at his arms. Once the truck starts to move, the men bounce with it. Sacks of potatoes, Edward thinks.

At the waterfront, the men walk across the sand to the boat that's waiting for them. It rocks with the surf. The men wade into the water and push their way onto the boat, their feet already cold and wet. Men line the sides, and the ones in the middle are kept upright by the crush of bodies. There are boys from the hospital and others who have been on leave or are fresh to the war.

Now they're a party, and the boat heads for the ship that's anchored offshore. The grey bulk of it sits in the first morning light that's creeping in over the horizon. They bang over waves that bounce them worse than the truck as the boat goes nose up, suspends in air, then smashes down. Hits hard, shooting spray from the bow that showers them all, then lifts and crashes again to the water, a regular beating. And every time it hits, a fierce pain shoots through his legs, and he clamps his teeth closed, jammed tight to keep his yelling in.

When he looks back, a coastline has come in with the dawn, and there is a church spire and tall, thin trees. It's already growing distant, and soon enough he won't remember that either. He's been away from the war for nine weeks.

Edward hears the screams of seagulls, feels the splash of seawater on his face, the wind, the sun coming up. Bumping over a choppy sea. It's more movement than he's had in weeks. His legs battle to keep their balance. He holds so tight to the gunwale that his hands cramp, and he shakes them out, one at a time.

The man beside him coughs sick into his own hat so as not to dirty the other guys, while someone else holds the back of his belt as he bends to the water. All the men rock with the boat and keep silent. Only the retreads shout to each other, to be heard above the noise of the motors and the batter of waves.

And then a big one breaks the bow with a pounding crash, smacks his face hard with spray that soaks his whole head wet, and in that moment he knows who he is. He is Edward! Skinny boy. Hustler. Lost, but now found. A boy without a family. No family at all. But that is Celia in the blue of the sky that's coming in beyond the ship. Celia. She is waiting for him in Canada. Oh, my Lord.

He doesn't know the ship they're headed for, but he does know what it means. He's twenty-one years old and going back to the war. And now he knows why. Celia. She's a song inside him. Everything he looks at is brighter, and soon the sea will mirror the blue of the sky, and it's not so threatening anymore. He's alive, and the thing to do is to get it done, fast as he can, so that he can go home to Celia. Tears mix with the spray that coats his face.

"How are your legs, Eddie?" shouts the lad from the hospital whose side he leans on as they sway and bounce.

"Yes," says Edward, good and loud. "They're all right."

"You're ready for it?" There is fear in the sailor's voice.

"I think I am," says Edward. "It's astonishing!"

TWENTY-TWO

֎

TORONTO ROLLED HEAVILY INTO SUMMER, languid and hot. Late July heat steamed down through the tree canopy, burned the sidewalks, and dampened thirsty skin. Summer exams were gruelling. In the few hours that Cyril did manage to sleep, he dreamed of his mother. Did the crazy part of his brain imagine that she'd be there when he got back? His life in Jamaica without her, after she'd died, had been so brief.

By the time Cyril's alarm rang at 4:30 a.m. and he'd bumped two big suitcases up the back steps and trundled awkwardly up the street toward the bus stop, he was strung like a wire. The result of two sleepless nights and overwhelming excitement, all coupled with an unrelenting anxiety that he would never get there. The plane would fall from the sky. Or, if he landed safely, he'd be smashed in a car crash before he made it to the house. As he boarded the plane, he said an ambivalent farewell to Toronto.

His anxiety melted when he saw the Caribbean Sea from the plane window. His well-being grew as the plane banked over the edge of the island, cut across the green hills, and then skated so low over the water and the buildings lining the roadside that he could almost see the faces of the people sitting along the seawall. He was completely immersed in his return. It was so much more than he'd remembered. When the immigration officer looked up from his passport and said, "Welcome back to Jamaica," Cyril almost skipped with excitement.

An hour later, bags inspected, duty paid, he walked out of the airport and into brilliant sunshine. The waiting crowd, ten deep, formed a boisterous horseshoe around the exit doors. Then two children cut from the crowd and raced to meet him. Daren jumped straight up into his arms, thumping against his chest, and Keesha flung herself against his leg. As they moved through the crowd, the children stuck to him like limpets. Keesha cried, sudden, noisy sobs that shook her overexcited five-year-old body. Cyril pulled her up into his arms, and she clung to him, monkey-like, arms and legs wrapped tight around him, her face wet against his neck. Daren, all grown up at seven, walked alongside, hauling one of the wheeled suitcases that was nearly as tall as he was. When Cyril's cousin appeared, they relinquished both cases, and Cyril took Daren's hand.

As they crossed the wide, tree-lined parking lot, Cyril tasted the air, revelling in the forgotten tropical smells and marvelling at the intense heat. They pulled the suitcases into the back of his cousin's pickup truck, then Cyril and the children climbed in to join the two women who'd come in on the same plane and whose bags and cases were already on the flat bed of the truck. A big pink plastic rocking horse, red bows around its neck, leaned up against the back of the cab. Keesha climbed over bags to sit wedged between Cyril and the horse. She gripped the leg of Cyril's pants in a tight knot of cloth and stroked the long, blond tail of the horse with her free hand. Daren settled in Cyril's lap. The two ladies chatted enthusiastically about their children and homecoming parties, about the price of rice and their mothers' health and making it through customs without too much duty to pay. The truck turned out of the parking lot and joined the thick traffic winding through the roundabout; it headed east, following road signs for Savana La Mar and Negril. Cyril held Daren tight, his arms wrapped firmly around his brother's middle.

About ninety minutes later, they started the climb to Brown's Town. Big trucks blared warning horns, belching smoke as they entered the tight blind curves. A mile outside of town, and instead of the clean air of the foothills that Cyril had anticipated for weeks, he breathed the stench of gasoline and diesel fuels. Alongside the curbs, collected in ditches and washed up against the lush greens of the roadside bush, were discarded packaging and containers from boxed drinks and candy wrappers and masses of plastic bags. He'd been walking or driving past those all his life. Probably the very same things were pressed into archeological layers below the last year's leavings. Filth and mangy dogs. A dead cat driven over a hundred times. Schoolchildren and old folk walked along the roadside, sometimes within inches of their truck. Cyril tightened his hold on Daren.

Brown's Town traffic crawled along the narrow main street that led through town. One of Cyril's fellow passengers jumped up as the truck passed the market building, waving madly to a friend: "Woooie, mi fren, me ova yah so!" She hung on to her girlfriend's hand to stop from toppling over. "Cum quick cause me hab tory fi gi yuh." The truck was slow enough that conversation for a minute or so was possible. When she sat back down on her suitcase, she pulled out her sequinned blue phone and began texting furiously. They crept slowly toward the CIBC bank, where a long line of people waited for the ATM. The truck idled in front of it as a man steered a wobbling cart piled with sugar cane across the road. The CIBC was Cyril's bank in both Toronto and Jamaica. The words from the dub poem Randall had played for him many times ran through his head.

ITT, ALCAN, KAISER,
Canadian Imperial Bank of Commerce,
These are privileged names in my Country
But I am illegal here

"Lillian Allen," Randall would say. "She telling about our Canadian condition." When Cyril had told Evan about the Jamaican-Canadian dub poet, eager to share what he'd thought was a new discovery, Evan had recited lines from the same poem:

I came to Canada
And Found the Doors
Of Opportunities Well Guarded

Now Cyril drummed his hands on Daren's chest and chanted:

"Why did you Leave There
Why on Earth did you Come?"

Daren giggled and took up the refrain, "Why did you leave there, why did you come?" banging his hands on Cyril's thighs. Keesha joined in, "Why did you leave, why did you leave, why did you leave?" Cyril bent down, cupped a head in each hand, and kissed both their faces.

His cousin stopped the pickup outside Super Plus, the biggest supermarket in town, and the ladies climbed out. Cyril passed their bags and the pink horse down to them, and Keesha waved goodbye, blowing kisses to the horse she'd named Happy. Cyril understood that the relief he felt as the women left the truck had nothing to do with them and everything to do with being in a busy, noisy town where everyone was Black: the drivers of the cars and trucks that nose-to-tailed their way through the narrow streets, the higglers on the sidewalks, men and women in business suits, security guards, children, old folk and beggars, police officers. Not a white face in sight. Even the dogs were quintessential Jamaican: beige, medium height, foraging for food or lying flat in the sun.

Fifteen minutes later, the truck slowed as it turned onto the road to Philadelphia. "Worse than ever, man," said his cousin, making his voice heard through the cab's back window and over the rattle and squeak of the bouncing vehicle. They'd picked up an old couple in town who sat squeezed into the cab along with a little boy who was on his way home from school. "Potholes so big they could swallow this pickup," his cousin called.

"Need to have an election," Cyril shouted back. "That's the only time they get fixed, huh?"

"Yeah, man."

It was as slow on the Philadelphia road as it had been through Brown's Town, even though they saw just a handful of vehicles, and the only car headed in the same direction, crammed with kids on their regular taxi ride home from school, overtook them at about thirty kilometres per hour.

The truck finally pulled up at the foot of a steep climb to a little house perched on the hill. Big-leaved red and black crotons marked the path. As good as a street address, thought Cyril, who couldn't stop smiling. His cousin pulled down the tailgate, and the kids spilled onto the road, dashed up to the house screaming, "CeeCee's here, CeeCee's here." His aunty appeared at the door, and his two small cousins darted around her and raced down the hill. She walked toward Cyril and hugged him tight. She was thinner than he remembered and looked as though she didn't smile very often, though she was smiling now. "Hey, darlin'," she said. "You looking good."

"You too, aunty."

"Oh, you look like your mommy when you say so."

It was jarring to hear someone refer to his mother. It had been so long.

"Baby, I do miss her," said Vi. "But these children are doin' good, no? Look at how them grown. And they so excited for you coming." She stroked his cheek.

"I can't believe how big they are," he said.

"You filled out like a man," said Vi. "I think you eat good."

"I do. I'm really okay."

"Mommy would be very proud. She always was."

Within a couple of hours, the children had unpacked the suitcases, and their toys were scattered across the grass at the front of the house. Cyril sat with Vi and watched them play. He was exhausted, but the magic of the place kept his eyes open. A flock of kling-kling swooped in with squabbling shrieks and noisy demands. Aunty Vi had a big stone with a shallow depression that filled with water when it rained, and the shiny black birds with their busy yellow eyes bathed there with customary enthusiasm. Dipped and flapped in the water and dried themselves in the sun.

"No running water yet?" said Cyril.

"They say it's coming, baby. But I don't see no sign in the next year." She laughed. "No water, but we got electrics and Digicel."

Cyril looked up at the hydro wire strung through the tree beside the house. "There's a bunch of billboards coming out of Montego Bay about stealing electricity."

"What else can we do? No money to pay it. Children got to have light." She left him while she went into the house to fetch food.

Cyril felt his body relax, and the ground cradled his weight. He stroked the stubbles of grass and dug his fingertips into the red earth. His aunt brought him a sweet fruit drink and a slab of hard dough bread topped with corned beef. Soon he was full of food and very sleepy. He let his body fall backward. Lay looking up at the brilliant blue sky where the John Crows circled high and wide beyond the leafy shade of the rough lemon tree.

THAT NIGHT, CYRIL READ A promised bedtime story to the four children, all of whom slept tucked into two twin beds in the corner. Vi's cot was on the other side of the room. The family that shared the house was quiet, the door between the two rooms firmly closed. Cyril was to sleep on the porch. He'd bought a mosquito net that he would leave behind when he returned to Canada. Cyril read to the children from a book he'd brought with him. Anansi the Spider Man − African folktales. His mother had never read to him, but she'd told lots of stories in her soft, singsong voice.

Once the quiet settled, Cyril and Vi talked as though they hadn't spoken on the phone at least once a week since he'd left. Now she talked to him like an adult. This was new. No longer her sister's cherished first-born but a grown man who shared the burden of her marginal life. Fair, thought Cyril. He sent her a good chunk of his income every month.

"I do what best I can. Truth is that one, two times a week I don't eat, and there's not enough for the children. They walk to school, and you know we have to pay for their lunches. And they need shoes or they can't go."

"I know all this. I lived here too."

"Yeah, baby, but I'm still living in it every day."

Cyril sighed. "Maybe I should be here to help? You've already got two kids; you didn't ask for two more."

"I did ask, sweetheart. Remember? Was my idea to have them. The thing that's changed is the cost of living. When you left, a pound of rice was maybe one hundred dollars. Now it's one-forty. We need a government that stops the inflation."

"It's changed so fast," said Cyril, shocked.

"It's what I've told you before."

"Cousin told me he's getting a bit more than seven thousand a week driving truck for Nam's Hardware."

"He's lucky. And it is steady work. I know I'm lucky too. I get about five thousand in exchange for the hundred-eighty you send me every month," said Vi. "It is good what you send. It's just not enough for every little thing."

"I know."

"My friend is living in Calgary, Canada," said Vi. "She says she can get me work in the hotel there."

"You can't leave the kids."

"I don't want to. And yours lost their mommy, they need me as much as mine do."

"We'll figure something out," said Cyril. "I promise. I can make extra. One more year, okay?" The need for money overwhelmed him. He looked at her thin brown face. She was young, really. Just past forty. Her hair was deep, dark brown, pulled into cornrows. He remembered how pretty she'd been before her kids came. She would bustle into their house wearing red lipstick. Going to a party and trailing little puffs of perfume. Her eyes were the same as his mother's, hazel with specks of gold.

He couldn't make more money yet. He — they — were at the

low end. Disposable people. The kind of jobs he had, anyone could do. He had to make money to get out of the trap. Education was supposed to be the answer. He was trying. He wanted to shout, "I'm only twenty-one years old." But that was the same age as lots of daddies, lots of mommies. His little family slept, innocent in the corner.

In the following days, he made a couple of trips to Brown's Town and one afternoon took the children to the beach in a packed bus that raced downhill at breakneck speed. He'd forgotten the thrill of those rides. But, for the most part, he walked around Philadelphia and Sturge Town and saw the beauty alongside the poverty. The few friends who were about were glad to see him but spoke to him like someone from away – he'd be gone in a few days. There were mothers who gathered him up in warm embraces and talked about their own children who'd gone to other countries. Or shared their worries about the ones who'd stayed, or fallen out of school, relegated to the realm of temporary employment.

Under a hand-painted sign, Santy Drinks and Snacks was Sturge Town's only rum shack. A twelve-by-twelve-foot wooden building with a corrugated iron roof. The walls were painted baby blue with letters in red, green, yellow, and purple that shouted *BIGGA* to the street. Santy's was the only place to buy a Red Stripe or a soda. The small cooler on the left side of the room didn't always work, so cold wasn't guaranteed. If you had money, someone might go and find a patty for you from the lady at the corner who worked at the Spicy Nice in Brown's Town and brought them in to sell from home.

Cyril sat on the doorsill and ate plantain chips, drank a Coke. Reggae played on the boom box, and he could smell the roasting chicken from the BBQ barrel next door. He watched the sway of thirty-foot-tall bamboo moving in the breeze across the road as a flock of bright green parakeets landed in the ackee tree beside him. After a while, a boy he didn't know appeared in front of the shack and stopped to stare. He was about seventeen, sullen and closed.

"Hey, brother," Cyril said, "what's up?"

"You from Canada?"

"How'd you know?"

"I heard."

"Toronto."

"Me too, I'm from there."

On the road, a troop of goats moved at a trot. Babies in the middle. Follow the leader. It was the hottest part of the day, but the shade from the overhanging roof of the shack was cool enough. Inside, the shop lady, Miss Wood, sang at mid-volume, a church song strung around a gospel beat. Her voice was pretty.

The boy didn't move, stayed stuck and staring at Cyril.

"I'm going back in a couple of days. What about you?' asked Cyril. "We on the same plane?"

"I can't go," the boy said.

"Why not?"

The boy was silent, his face a blank mask. He had a long scar on his chin, no beard stubble yet. He looked fragile.

"How long you live there, man?" Cyril asked.

"Since five years old," the boy said, mouth tight like talking was what he didn't ordinarily do.

"So what are you doing now?"

The boy went back to silence.

Miss Wood stopped her singing and called out to the boy to take himself home. "You got jobs to do for your grandmother? Go do them." The boy stood for a while longer then walked away.

Slowly. He stopped a distance off and leaned against a tree while he bent to fiddle with his shoe.

"He's a bad boy," she said. "So hard for him granny. She have to look on him now, and his mommy just keep working hard."

"Where's she?" said Cyril.

"Ajax. Near Toronto. Where you are."

"Yeah," said Cyril. "What happened to him?" He looked over to where the boy still leaned on the tree, staring off into his own distance.

"They sent him back here. After all the years it took to get him there, and then he make himself a pile of trouble." Miss Wood swiped hard at the counter with a wet cloth. "His mommy worry for him since he was born."

That's shit, Cyril thought. This boy wedged between two cultures. Growing up in a place that threw him out. Kids have to know where they belong. Cyril was still working on that, a constant and serious occupation. But he had no doubt that he belonged to Daren and Keesha.

Daren and Keesha, who'd been so thrilled to see him, had retreated somewhat, reassured that he loved them. In between the clinging, they made it clear that his life was separate from theirs. Aunty was the boss, not their big brother.

A visit to Brown's Town had turned into a battle — their sense of entitlement to all of the things that Cyril and his money represented expressed in a furious refusal to budge from their demands. In front of the vendors' chain-link fence opposite the market, where multiples of similar toys were hung or displayed on the ground, Daren had stopped, rooted to the spot, fists clenched and utterly defiant. "Mi waan it," Daren had demanded. "You a nuh mi mada."

"Calm down," Cyril snapped. "You don't behave like this."

"Mi nuh kya," Daren shouted, louder than before. Beside him, Keesha wailed tears that shocked Cyril because good Jamaican kids didn't have tantrums. The vendor looked at Cyril as though he were pathetic. "Is only five hundred," he said holding the helicopter just short of Daren's grasp. In the end, Cyril bought them what they wanted. A little plastic doll with long blonde hair wearing a bright pink tank top. And the shiny plastic helicopter that Cyril knew would break the first time it flew. They were cheap, ugly things. He hated them. But the children were thrilled. He took them to Spicy Nice for patties, and they sat on the bench at the table, Cyril sandwiched tightly between them, playing with their new toys, sweet as the coconut pastries they all had for dessert.

They didn't want him to go back. He understood, after some personal struggle, that, in the inarticulate manner of children, they were angry with him for leaving. Sending money, filling a barrel with food and clothes and toys for Christmas, the stuffed suitcase on his visit home, all that was not enough. They would never understand the work he had to do to make it happen. And he did work hard. Because this, his holiday, was the first time he'd stopped racing since he'd started school, and his body was soaking up the sleep and free time. How could they understand any of it? Their mother was dead. Aunty loved them, but Cyril had once been entirely theirs. Now they shared him with places and people they'd never seen, never met. How could they forgive him for abandoning them?

Cyril was distressed at the idea of returning to Toronto. He felt an overwhelming need to stay. To make sure that his kids read books and thrived at school. To keep them safe. Daren particularly. But after seven days, he also found himself looking forward to his Toronto rhythms and his academic and professional responsibilities, his future. When he'd planned the trip home, he'd hoped to find time to visit UWI. He'd had some notion that he might work at a degree there. That perhaps he could get a scholarship. That it might be easier in some ways to be closer to where he'd thought he belonged. But belonging had turned out to be elusive. Nobody asked when he'd return. They all wanted to know what sort of a job he would get when he graduated.

Cyril gave himself up to the heat and sat shirtless with the children out in the rain when it made its daily afternoon appearance, warm raindrops shimmering in the sun. The pleasure of being cooled by a shower under a hot blue sky was extraordinary. It was one of those things he'd almost forgotten.

He talked to the children about trains, had even brought a toy train for Daren. He told them how big the real ones were, as long as the road into Sturge Town. "They go on forever, the noise, horns like trucks. Think about how heavy they are, rolling along on iron rails," he said. "When you come to stay with me, I'll take you on a train to the Rocky Mountains. We'll ride in the carriages and look from the windows. It will be like a movie, only what we see will be real."

"We'll eat chips and drink pop," said Daren.

"Chocolate ice cream," said Keesha. Cyril thought about the train at the bottom of his street. And Edward, whom he now realized he was missing.

TWENTY-THREE

THE DAY EDWARD LEAVES, SHE cries like she has oceans of tears in her. Breaks his heart ten times over. But it's what she wants too. They've both decided. He is going to Halifax to sign on as a railway porter. You can raise a family with that job. You have to work double-hard for the tips, but they are what make up the wage. That was as much as they'd got out of fighting and dying in the same war, and you could Take It Or Leave It. It is the only job for coloured men that pays a decent dollar. Celia wants to feel safe. She wants a little house with plenty of room for their children. She waited for him all through the war and said prayers for him every day. That's how much she loves him.

What Edward wants is Celia. It's as simple as that. And they don't want her working at the hospital any longer; it's not a safe place. Mrs. Marvel has a friend who's been working as a sleeping car porter for ten years. He says he can fix it. He doesn't say much more. He sometimes works for three weeks at a time. When he comes home, he's worn-through tired. His house is one of the nicest in Africville. His family wears new clothes, and his children are going to go to college. They are good people.

Edward walks to downtown Halifax. He applies at the office and writes the names of the men who recommend him along with the record of his navy service. He downplays the leg injury because they don't want cripples, and it's never so bad that it stops him from working.

The Canadian Pacific Railway takes him on! This is a triumph because in Halifax he sees for himself how many coloured men want this job. Some of them have big university degrees in science and medicine. He takes the training, which isn't much: straightaway onto the train with a hundred details to learn about his impending duties. It is all easy after the navy. Same sorts of things — working in a tight space that's always moving. Keeping it shipshape and properly stowed. Polishing the buttons and chrome and shoes. Obeying orders without question. At sea, lives depended on that. It is a piece of cake. He writes to Celia that the fellows are decent and he'll see her in a couple of weeks.

HE LEARNS HOW THERE ARE two ways to look at the job. One is out the window. The other is inside the train. A senior porter, though not so old, explains this to him on the third day.

"You tired, brother?"

Edward chuckles. "I'm making adjustments to the night hours."

"You get used to it. Three hours' sleep a night starts to feel like a big package of rest." He shakes his head slowly, side to side. "When you get home, though, you'll hit your bed like you've been awake for a year. Takes a day or two to catch up to it."

"It'll be good to get home."

"You have a wife?"

"We're going to get married."

"Tell her to wait a day or so before she gives you the chores."

He grins. "The other business comes naturally. Don't matter how tired you are."

Edward smiles. Celia in his arms is what all this being away from her is about.

"You're a young man. But you know how to work. I've been watching you. You'll be okay so long as you remember one thing."

"What's that?"

"You're going to see the wonders of this country outside these windows. On the long runs that take us through the prairies, hundreds of miles of flatland, and then into the Rocky Mountains and out to the sea on the other side. You'll go east to west. West to east, and it's never going to be the same thing twice in all of the seasons and changing weather."

Edward looks out. They are passing through the small towns of Ontario on their way to Ottawa. He does love it. That is the difference between the navy and the train. On a ship, you look at the sea, and it has two moods. Quiet or mean. This train is a whole different story.

"You hold on to that, you see? That's the beauty of the job."

"It is astonishing," says Edward.

"But inside here," the man says with a gesture that takes in the whole of the train, "there ain't no wonders in here. This is where you keep your eyes closed. Figuratively speaking. You know what I mean?"

"I'm not so sure."

"They told you every passenger who rides on this train is your boss. Man, woman, or child?"

"Yes."

"That is the truth, and don't forget it. If anyone says jump, you jump. Understand?"

"I think so," Edward says. "I served in the navy."

"That was about courage and acceptance," says the man. "In here is about fortitude and endurance. Every damn day of it."

Edward can hear how the man is angry, but it doesn't show on his face in any way. He has a small smile the whole time, and his voice is calm and quiet like he is talking to an old friend about fishing.

"I heard about some of the things they say."

"You never get used to it," the man says. "I been called 'slave' and 'boy' and 'nigger' so many times, and I still have to stop myself. But I always do." The man splays his hands on his thighs. "Worst is the bar car when the men have been drinking. But it is unavoidable," he says. "Hear me?"

"Yes."

"We sit behind that green curtain, that's a shameful thing to humiliate us, and on the other side you hear what they say about you. As though you're less than a human."

"I've heard it before," Edward says.

"THE DAYS GO LIKE THIS," Edward explains to Celia. He is holding her hand while they lie side by side in their cave on top of a sheet and blanket. "Morning is for cleaning up behind them all when they leave their berths and head to the dining car for breakfast. We're to change the sheets and pick up the mess. Fold all the beds back into benches for them to sit on during the day. Then we clean up after they've eaten, and all the time you've got to be listening for an order from anyone who needs something. A little child needs a glass of water. Or a man's lost his paper and needs another. Then you've got to find an old one and iron it out so it doesn't look too beat up. That's how the day goes. Clean and serve. Smile and always say, 'Yes, sir,' 'Yes, ma'am,' or they start to look at you like something's wrong. Then, last thing at night, when they're all in their berths, you polish their shoes. They put them out every night. It is their bonus for riding the train."

Celia squeezes his hand. "You work so hard, baby doll."

"Then you get your three hours in the berth. Three hours only, that's if you're lucky, and then you're back to it. We got lots more sleep time than that in the navy. But it's going to get better because we've got a union and we're fighting for change. Me too. I'm working with the fellas that are doing that." Edward puts his arm around Celia's shoulders, moves her closer. "The Chinese who built that railroad? They could have used a union. Hundreds of them died building it, and the ones who survived were never treated fairly. But we've got a union. Change is going to happen. Then they'll have to treat us right."

THE WAY HE REMEMBERS IT is this: she was a nice little lady with light brown hair and pink on her cheeks. She might have been around thirty. She carried a big case in one hand and struggled with a couple of smaller ones in the other. He moved to help her, just like he would have helped anyone. That was his job. She was grateful, gave him a big smile, and he followed as she made her way to her berth. He can still picture the dress she wore. Kind of greenish-blue with a light yellow stripe. He remembers thinking that it would have looked good on Celia. She was sweet. Gave him a tip and wanted to know had he been working at the job long? It was a fair question, and he answered that. Then she asked about his family, and because he was missing Celia in a big way that day he started to tell. How good she was, how pretty, how hard she worked. The lady asked more questions, and he kept talking. So maybe he was leaning in the doorway. Maybe he shouldn't have held her elbow to steady her when the train rocked as it travelled a bend. Certainly he had stayed too long, because the captain snapped up behind him and told him he was needed at the front. "You must not be overfamiliar with the white women."

He was put on notice. That was forty demerit points, cause for dismissal. But he was a good worker, and it hadn't happened before, so they let it go. Four months later, on a winter run through the mountains, the worst thing happened: a senior porter — same fellow who told him to look out the windows for the good part of the job — had a sick child at home and was worried sick himself, got into a major pickle. Late night, dog-tired, and one of the male passengers calls out, "George. Here, George!" snapping his fingers like he's calling the hound. Porter said he just ignored it: he thought, my name's not George, I will not. That and the passenger had drunk too much gin so was unlikely to remember. But he did. First thing the next morning. They summoned the porters and stood them out in a row while the man looked them over and pointed a finger. Edward could see how he wasn't sure, how he was thinking, "They all look the same," so he stepped forward and said, "It was me, sir. My name is Edward Davina." And That Was The End Of That.

Forty demerit points plus the forty he's already racked up. Deduct those from the sixty maximum they are allowed and it is simple math. They let him off the train in Halifax, and he goes home to Celia.

It isn't simple for Celia. She loves him, but she wants a home. She was ready to marry, but she needs stability. He is young and foolish. That is the best job there is, and he's thrown it away. Edward thought she'd understand about the sick child and the need that the father had. But she says, "I see sick every day. I see death every day." Her voice gets loud. "I want a good life and children. I want the respect of my neighbours. I want to be treated like a human being."

She has her hair done. Takes her good dress from its wrappings, puts on her new blue hat, and is gone.

WHEN EDWARD THINKS ABOUT CELIA, he imagines her an old lady. She is still everything she was: sexy, slim, clever, adorable, heartbreaking. He hopes she has plenty of grandchildren, maybe even a great-grandchild or two. She should have what she always wanted. He is sorry that they couldn't have it together, but he doesn't blame her. Not in any way. She had her fears, and he had his. Not many of those matter anymore. His life is moving on to the Home Run. Hers will be too.

He does have some friends. And he likes Security Sam a lot. Even misses him when he's not on shift. But Sam's work puts him in Edward's life, otherwise he would not be around at all. That's okay. People have their personal situations, and Edward is the last to imagine that he should be anyone's priority. He knows that's why people like him. He's a nice guy who makes very few demands. And he doesn't judge, either, wouldn't know how. So there's that. Plus he's clean. And he likes to make jokes, to see people laugh. That gets him invited. To the Legion with the boys. And for the last five years to the retirement home. "Loony bin," the residents call it. A number of blocks away on the King streetcar line. He goes to the birthday parties. Events no one claims to want, but they celebrate all of them anyhow. Except for the handful who fiercely object on the grounds that they do not accept their situation and are waiting for a husband or a daughter to take them home. But for most of them, including those who are so far gone that they've forgotten they ever had husbands or children, it's all okay. The same cake and ice cream, which he loves. A couple of balloons and a sing-along with the visiting service-support ladies who come by nearly every birthday.

It is a struggle to get there on the streetcar, like getting any-where now. But once he's in, through the security doors, they're on him and he's welcomed. Dee's yelling, "Eddie, honey, right over here." Taking a few steps toward him, swinging her thick, stiff-boned legs, rocking like a barge on an ocean, side to side. She shouts, "What took you? The weather's not so bad?" And Rena, who always waits for him, wheeling along in her walker, morose face as always, with her usual list of woes. About her blood pres-sure and falling down and how they'll have to do more tests. She comes up close, walker taking the weight of her ungainly, slumping self, and gloms on to him from her round, pink face with her mournful blue eyes. Her hair is thin and blonde, and she says it smells like cherries. It's natural, her hair. That's her one lucky thing. She is sixty-six in a home for the old because she nearly can't walk, but she doesn't have to dye her hair like the other ladies do. "Lucky Rena" he calls her; she doesn't smile, but if a woman could purr that would be it. She's happy when he's around. Everyone says so. And Rena is always there, pretty much right beside him, as soon as he takes a look.

Loopy Ida is saying that she didn't feel so well this morning, but they don't let them sleep in. "Two thousand dollars a month I pay for this, and I can't sleep in some morning when I don't feel so good." She is outraged. Edward is outraged on her behalf.

"That's appalling," he says. "If Sam tried to get me out of bed when I didn't want to, I'd kick him down the hall."

Ida likes that and giggles. "Good swift kick to the backside takes care of that!" She's delighted. Ida wants Edward to do some ass-kicking. He says he's working up to do it.

"Barb," shouts Dee, "you came!" and teeter-totters over to the community room doors where Barb climbs down from her scooter and walks in swinging a bag with the extra plastic cups and sugar for tea.

Edward is one of a very few men left standing, and that adds to his popularity. He can still walk, he has a deeper voice and a penis. Sex is a favourite subject.

"Eddie," says Hollis, who is hunkered down in his wheelchair. "We men got to stick together. Protect ourselves against these ladies."

Then Barb says, as usual, "We're the dum-dums and the wackos and the crazies."

That's how it goes. Most birthdays are the same. Although from time to time the birthday's family shows up, and then it's usually better because there are new things to say, and they always bring food from outside. The families take photographs, and all the ladies jostle to get in them. They tell each other how to pose and shout for Edward to join them: "Tilt your head to your best profile and stick out your chin." Then they laugh and hold each other upright while someone takes the pictures. Most of the time, if they come, the families are nice, and Edward's glad he made the trip.

But lately, without outside distractions, the parties turn into work real fast, and he has to fight his anxieties. Then he's ready to go home, a good hour before it's polite to leave. And sometimes going home seems truly urgent because he feels like if he doesn't he could be stuck there. That something could happen to keep him from leaving, a physical thing like they all have hung on them so that they need help to do the simple things. Trapped in a place like this one, and he'd wind up on the third, the dying floor — and hopefully in double-quick time. Edward

understands this about himself very well. He is afraid of what
will finally stop him, that it won't be quick but will keep him
trapped inside a place like this. And in that case, it's the dementia
ward for sure. Behind the locked doors on the fourth floor. You
hear it. Screaming protests, repeated looping, wailing cries:
"Hellpp meeeee, hellpp meeee." They all know that's their fate
if they don't keep themselves sane with social pleasantries like
birthday parties. Edward blesses his ninety years because the
more they add up, the faster it will come. And he'll still have his
sanity when the time comes to get done.

EDWARD SLEEPS IN. IT CONTINUES to amaze him, the energy
it takes to travel a few short blocks on a streetcar. When he
clambers out of bed, it's already mid-morning. He has the fans
going full blast. Both of them point at the bed. Last year, he had
only the one, but after the heat wave the volunteer people came
by with a trolley full of fans, and he figured he had room for
another. If he didn't live on the first floor, he'd be in trouble when
the temperature was on the climb, like today and for the rest of
the week. The radio said to keep cool. Hah! The little window at
the top of his room was as far open as Sam could get it. He could
leave the door to the hallway open, and he did sometimes. But
that ran the risk of unwelcome visitors. Also, he prefers that
people not see him in his underwear, which is how it has to be
in this heat. Every time he turns the tap on at the sink, to get a
drink or to cool his wrists, he is forever and eternally grateful
that he has this room – Room With Sink. Ground Floor To Boot.

It appalls him some, the sight of his near-naked body that
he rarely looks at anymore. But lying around all day in his
underwear means he gets a glimpse whenever he looks down.
Earlier in the week, he pulled out the mirror he kept behind the

wardrobe and had a real look to confirm what he'd been seeing. Wrinkled old man. Sagging folds of skin, everything pulling down at the sides, drooping from his breastbone like an upside-down horseshoe. All the good luck falling out. The red scars on his legs from the war. Belly like a skin sack. He ran his hands over his chest. Big hands strung with lumpy veins and spattered in brown spots. Then what was left of his rear end falling into skinny chicken thighs. Endless trails of veins on his legs. He could weep, but he chuckled instead because being old was not a Walk In The Park, and kids won't know that till they get there.

He pulls on the cotton pants of his pyjamas and puts a T-shirt over top. It takes ten minutes and has him dripping sweat by the time he's finished. It's the standing and bending and sitting that does it. He wets his facecloth again and wipes his forehead and neck. A few more steps, and he picks up the cane that he keeps hung over a chair beside the door. Edward makes his way down the hallway, screwing up his nose at the smell of cigarette smoke. Shouldn't be that in here. Not allowed for years now. He knows who it was, too — that rounder would be gone within a week or two. He'd put a bet on it. Scabby guy with a bad attitude and a bruised-up face that he must not have had when he checked in here, because they wouldn't put up with it. Zero tolerance on the fighting. It says so on the sign at the front office. Front office at the end of the hallway is where he is headed now. Mail. Whatever. Security Sam always has a funny on the go: "Eddie, dude! Postie had a sackful, but it was all envelopes with cheques for you, so he took it home with him." Something like that is what Security Sam always says. Same basic stupid joke every day, but he is a nice guy. Worth a laugh. "Gets me out of the house." That is Edward's standard reply. "The exercise is good for me."

This morning's walk is real exercise because his legs aren't working so good, so he is giving too much weight to his cane, which strains his arm and cramps his hand. It seems a very long way to the end of the hall. He opens the door to the office. Sam's there, same as always. Sitting at his desk doing his sudoku. Desk's just a tabletop, really, room's only eight feet square. A filing cabinet, telephone, trash can, fan spinning the fastest speed. First aid cabinet locked up behind him on the wall.

"Eddie, dude!" Sam looks up at him, smiling. "Postie's been. Had a big load today."

"Any money?" asks Edward, easing himself into the visitor's chair.

"Something for you. Maybe a cheque?" Sam stands up and crosses over to Edward, an envelope in his hand.

"Holy heck!"

"That's not what I said." Sam laughs. "Mail from a real person. I'm betting this is not a bill."

It is a letter. Tidy handwriting with a curly "Mr." in front of his name. Postmarked Halifax, which gives him butterflies. Can't remember the last time he felt those. His mind blanks for a minute on the name in the top corner. Gillian Marvel. He shakes his head to wake it up. "Who's this, then?" he says out loud.

"Same question I asked," says Sam. "Maybe you should open it?"

"The daughter!" says Edward. "That's who it is. I knew her mother and grandmother. Her grandma was my landlady for a few years. During the war. Mabel Marvel is her mother. We were good friends."

"Could be sad news, then?" says Sam.

"Mabel would be my age," Edward says. "Probably is." He looks up at Sam. "How'd she find me here?"

"It's probably pretty easy these days, Eddie. Internet and all of that."

"What a thing," says Edward, pulling himself upright on his cane. "Well, thanks, Sam."

It is a lot easier going back to his room. He doesn't notice the pain. Inside, he closes the door and sits on the bed. Takes a deep breath before opening the letter.

August 4, 2012

Dear Edward,

I am so glad this letter has found you. Sid Joyce told me you still send money for the children, and he gave us this address. I wanted you to know that we lost Mom last year. She always did talk about you. She wanted to have a big reunion and get you to come back and see us. She always meant to write.

You should come. I'd like to see you too. Remember how I was such a tomboy when I was a little girl? Well, I've got two little grand-children now. They made Mom real happy.

You'll remember Africville, I bet? Life's never been the same since they bulldozed it down. That's a long time ago now, but I remember all the details. Seeing our house we lived in with my grandmother smashed to the ground. They wanted us out, like exterminating roaches.

But that was back in the sixties. Sorry for going on. I've been working with the anti-racism people here in Halifax, and I'm real sorry I didn't know them when I was younger. It's an evil thing, racism. It ruins people's lives.

But you were always a strong fellow. How are you now? I hope you've got your health because that's the main thing.

Please write me back and tell me you're all right. If you're on the internet here's my email, gillianbmarvel@hotmail.com.

My Warmest Regards,
Gillian

Edward reads the letter a couple of times. Then he folds it back into its shape and slips it into the envelope. He sits for a while, looking at it in his lap. It has a big blue-and-white stamp. Pretty. He'll read it again later.

Mabel Marvel. Gone. All the things he'd have asked her. A reunion would have been a great thing. They'd been so good, the Marvels. Sharing their house with him. Mrs. Marvel fitting the teenage boy into a family that already had a teenage mother, Mabel, and her little girl, Gillian. There'd been four other kids, Mabel's brothers and sisters.

He never could stay in Celia's room. That was understood between the two of them. Her landlady would have thrown her out, and it was much too good a place to risk. He worked when he could. A few dollars here and there. Celia kept her work up steady. Every day. Even if she got sick with a cold, like the rest of the human race, she'd get herself up the hill, put in the full day, and when she got home hit the bed like a dead thing, she said, and sometimes not even eat more than a bite till morning. Then she'd go back up the hill for more. She got every other Wednesday off.

They lived for those Wednesdays. In the summer, he'd make up a basket for them. They'd hike down to the sea and lay out the picnic things. They ate like royalty because he always, no matter what, found something to add to the rations. The place they went to had a little cave that no one came to, and after they'd eaten, when they were almost perfectly satisfied, they turned their attention to each other's bodies. They waited because they had all the time in the world, and the anticipation was so desperately sweet. He couldn't bear to think about that now. Even all these miles and years later.

Mabel was a friend. Tried to teach him about girls and families. Not that she knew a whole lot about the male side of things. The last time he talked to her, she was on the telephone telling him about the tragedy at the dump. First of all, he couldn't believe the dump. That they put it right there, practically in Africville. And that they burned it off, regular, so the smoke and stench was all over town. Mabel said it got into your clothes and sheets, you lived with it for weeks, and then, when you finally couldn't smell it anymore, they lit the fires again. Of course the kids played there. And lots of folk scavenged. Why wouldn't they? They're poor. The thing is right there.

Edward had been living up in the Sault for about three years when he heard news that men had been poisoned in Africville. He telephoned Mabel, got a number to reach her through the post office. She said that her friend Billy, friend of Edward's too, was one of those who'd died after picking up alcohol from the dump. That was more than forty years ago, but Edward's stomach churns bile like it was last week. The truck brought in the barrels and left them there: they told the men there was alcohol inside then drove away. They must have been having a laugh because they knew what would happen next. The Africville fellows broke into the barrels. Drank the poisoned alcohol. And died. They died of it by the next day. Even now, Edward wants to plow someone for it. Wants to smash the faces of the men who drove away. Because Billy died in terrible pain, and it never had to happen. He was just going for the lark. No one was ever punished for those killings. They would still be laughing down in hell for that. Anyone could have drunk that liquor.

Edward stands up. He has a newspaper clipping. It was after they bulldozed most of the place. It's up there in a box on the shelf at the top of his wardrobe. There's an envelope with photographs there too. The most precious thing he has. He never looks at it. Last time was probably three Christmases ago. He stretches up to pull it down and brushes the dust from the box with his hand. He puts it on his bed and eases down beside it. He is wet from sweat and lets the fans cool him for a few minutes before he pulls off the lid. The envelope is on top of the clippings. He hesitates before opening it. The picture of him and Celia, Mabel and Billy is on top. There they are, the four of them. Holy heck, it was a long time ago. They were so young. All smiling, all beautiful. It was taken at a wedding. He and Celia planned their own after that. It's time he framed that picture, he thinks, and puts it beside him on the bed.

Edward reaches for the clipping. *Halifax Herald,* 1969. The story had been in the papers before that, starting in 1963, but this one told it closest to how he'd heard it from the people who were there. He and Celia had been gone for years, and Billy was dead before it happened. The story was about Mabel and Gillian and all the others who were run out of their homes. Mabel held out until 1969. Her mother died before all the bulldozing started, which was a good thing. Mabel was one of the last to leave. After they smashed down the church in the middle of the night, she said her heart was broken, and she lost her fight. Halifax people called Africville a slum. But they had forced it into a slum. Never gave it what a town needed to have: no sewers, no running water, no roads, no electricity. Mabel was always fighting for those before the church went. Taking all her dignity with her into the city, carrying official papers, wearing good shoes, and making her formal complaints.

They sent the garbage trucks to move the people out! Edward's stomach twists the way it always does whenever he thinks of it. Moving Mabel's nice things out on a garbage truck. Her cushions and quilts and big rocking chair. The rest was lies: the compensation, the relocation programs. It was filthy, lying crap.

The picture in the newspaper clipping is Mabel's house with a bulldozer out front. Just before it happened. The bastards moved everyone who didn't have money into social housing in Halifax. Edward loved Mabel's mother's home. He loved the town. When he finally got back there, after they let him out of the navy, he felt like he'd come home. To Celia and to Mrs. Marvel and Mabel. To the blessed Seaview African United Baptist Church. And to Africville.

TWENTY-FOUR

❧

CYRIL TOOK SOME SATISFACTION FROM looking at books that he could actually afford to buy. The bottom shelf of the bookstore's used and discount shelves included the last-stop books direct from the sales table. Fire-sale prices. Back in his early-morning routine at the university bookstore, Cyril's holiday in Jamaica now seemed surreal, as though he had seen it through the same gauzy mists that had transported him home in the past.

On the discount shelf was a thin paperback, *My Name's Not George: The Story of the Brotherhood of Sleeping Car Porters: Personal Reminiscences of Stanley G. Grizzle*. The photograph on the front was of Mr. Grizzle in his porter's uniform. Cyril had read about the Brotherhood of Sleeping Car Porters, an American Black-led union. But this man was Canadian, a leader with the Canadian BSCP. This new information immediately propelled Cyril into Edward-search mode. He checked the acknowledgements, flipped through the pages looking for familiar references and dates. This guy would be close to Edward's age. Cyril knew about Edward and trains. Felt his presence sometimes in the tons of steel and iron rumbling over the tracks at the end of his street.

He squatted down on the floor in front of the shelf and looked for names, Edward or Davina. He could speed-scan printed pages now. And he trusted his pace, didn't miss things. Edward's name was not there, but these were certainly Edward's contemporaries. And trains. Cyril paid for the book and took it home.

The porters' job was to serve and obey. People bought tickets to experience being waited on by someone in uniform, someone who would prove their superiority every time they snapped their fingers. It was all about status, thought Cyril. Somehow, human beings found validation in being better than someone else. In this case, better than a Black man. It was a simple concept that ensured the success of the sleeping car. Mr. Grizzle had been a fierce labour activist, like so many of the other Black porters.

Two weeks later, Cyril was back in the archives. His search through the Canadian BSCP records and minutes was painstaking, demanded patience. He'd included a request for any notes from early meetings, 1925 on. It had taken twelve years of unwavering effort to finally establish the Canadian branch. The minutes of the meetings were not in the least bit dull because of Cyril's new relationship with Mr. Grizzle and all of the men whose names were not George, whose pride and determination had established an organization that was about so much more than railroads. They made the records rich with relevance: sustaining pride through economic security. There were endless records, and Cyril quickly learned what to skip and where to linger. In meeting minutes, he always started with the names of the attendees.

On his fourth visit, during his first half hour in the chair at the big table with five years' worth of papers stacked beside him, came the very welcome and familiar tingling, the gauzy funnel of sound and shifting light. There it was. He looked again. Then up to the back of the room to refocus his eyes. It was Edward Davina. At the end of a long list of signatures near the bottom of the page was Edward's. Large, round, looping letters with an ink point at the end. Dated October 21, 1946, Halifax, Nova Scotia, Canada.

Cyril read quickly through the minutes. There was nothing more from Edward, but that in no way dampened his excitement. He worked eagerly through the rest of the stack, checked the signature pages on all of the documents. Skipped lunch, despite his growing hunger. Sucked instead at the neck of his empty orange juice bottle. Edward didn't turn up again. Not in all of the five years, and the search felt colder as he moved through the pile. There wouldn't be anything else. But what he'd found was triumph enough.

Edward and the trains were inextricably linked, and Cyril heard them differently now. Before, they'd borne Edward's presence. Now, they carried another man whose name was not George. Maybe the proudest of all the porters who'd worked hard and took shit but joined with the other men to turn adversity into a powerful force: a union. Cyril knew exactly what sort of work Edward would have done. The duties that added up to a day and night on the sleeping cars. Polite as an English TV butler, smiling all the while. Deferential but never obsequious; consciously respectful, which no doubt gave the passengers what they sought. And if the passengers were pleased with the service, they'd leave a tip, which made up a large part of the meagre pay.

The rumble of a night train travelled smoothly through Cyril's sleep. Edward balanced easily with the movement of the carriage, white linen napkin over his forearm, accepted a tip with a nod and a quick smile. Cyril smiled too, quick as Edward, who had much yet to do in a job with a thousand tasks.

THIS TIME, EDWARD BUYS A ticket and rides the train as a passenger. Second class. The year he devoted to waiting for Celia weighs heavily on him. He didn't want to miss her if she ever came back. Then knew she wouldn't and could not be there without her. Edward packs his honourable discharge – he exercises his legs every day with the stretches they showed him – and follows the rails across the country. He's done it so many times before, but it is a significant pleasure to sit in his own seat and watch from the window without disturbance. He does a lot of landscape watching, doesn't think too much about how it was when he worked the sleeping cars. He eats the food he packed himself and drinks hot tea served from the trolley. His carriage is full of European immigrants headed to the prairies.

In Toronto, he gets off and finds a room near what is left of the Ward. There is nothing to miss about the place except the rooming house he lived in with the other boys, and that was torn down long ago. Edward walks to the water and looks at the lake. There are jobs unloading freighters, and he does that for a while, but really there is nothing here for him. He misses the ocean, which makes him laugh because he lived and worked and slept on top of it and hated that. But it's in him now, seeped in and saturated so that he wants the smell of salt water. Or maybe it's just that he thinks she might be there. The first time he saw her in Africville, the ocean was spread out below them.

When he gets off in Vancouver, they say, Can you swing an axe? Do you know trees? And then they show him because he is always there and ready to give it his best. People like him, anyhow. Most of the time. Unless they want to fight him. But he knows how to deal with that too. The ocean he looks at from his rooming house is bigger and wilder. That's a comfort; that's a difference he's thankful for. It's not the Bedford Basin. They tell him that the trees extend for hundreds of miles. When they go into the forest, it will be weeks or months before they can go home to see their families. Doesn't matter to Edward, who has no people.

Despite the difficult ride out to the site on the crummies, seated on rows of wooden benches with all the guys smoking and no proper ventilation and sometimes the men's faces turning black with bugs, little no-see-ums that eat you alive, and the relentless drizzle that makes mud so thick that you wade through it — despite all of that, he likes the work. It's hard and skilled. You can't be there and not know your business. He has to learn how to do it well, and that's a pleasure for Edward. He's always ready for more. It has a season too, which he also likes because when it ends he is free again to travel some more and find a place for the winter where there is other work. For two years, that's in Campbell River at whatever is going. Winter maintenance on the logging machinery, mostly. He always has enough money, with a bit to put by — which he does — to send to the little school in Africville.

One day, an old Scottish logger bums a cigarette and tells a story. "The first governor of this province?" he says.

Edward nods, sucking smoke into his lungs.

"First governor of British Columbia? His mother was a free Creole. Coloured, like you." The logger grins. "Father was white. A Scotsman like me!"

"Imagine that," Edward replies, though he can't really. The governor's name was James Douglas. Edward thinks they should teach that name to the kids in Africville. Edward gets along with the Finns and the Germans, the native Coast Salish people and other assorted Canadians. He is good in hard, lonely places like ships and logging camps.

One season, there is a woman assisting in the camp kitchen. That is a first. She speaks in an accent so thick that he sometimes asks her to say it again. And he works to understand her because she is a decent person. She's hard as nails, a woman in camp has to be, and doesn't spend her spare time with anyone. Rachel is buried somewhere deep inside herself, and when the work is done she goes to her bed and sleeps.

Edward is there in the moment when she trips over something on the floor in the doorway she passes through dozens of times a day, carrying trays full of food or tubs of dishes. He is right behind her when she stumbles, and he catches her by the waist even as the tray she carried crashes to the floor. She stays upright in his arms. That's how they know each other, from the press of their bodies. When he lets her go, she turns to see who's caught her — really looks. Truly sees him. And it's not just because neither of them has touched another person, man to woman, woman to man, in a very long time.

She says she likes him because he listens and doesn't repeat what he hears. They sit together, but not often, because when he is done working, she is cooking or serving or cleaning up. But they do find some time. He understands pretty quickly that she is like him. Rachel is alone and strong with it. She doesn't need another person. One day, when he should be working but says he's sick, they take a walk. When he caresses her face, she's ready enough, and they love each other for a while. She's not whole. He knew the damage the first time he touched her. Saw the fight in her eyes, how she wanted but didn't want. It is good, though, and they don't stop making love. They take their opportunities when they come. And then afterward she sleeps, but never soundly, slips in and out of it, twisting over the sheets, calling out sometimes in her own language. If he speaks to her, says her name, she wakes instantly, like a part of her never slept at all. And then she looks at him like he is a stranger. He is afraid for her. She is pretty, even though she never smiles, but strange, so that the other men don't try to woo her. Also, Edward is fierce, so that if they do make an attempt, he sees them off.

She lives with shadows all around her. She's got a foot in somewhere else, and it's made her unbalanced. You can't be in two places, living two lives, and not be broken in half. Edward thought he was damaged like that, but he learns from her that he was wrong. What he loves is with him all the time in the good parts of himself. He doesn't forget what he has had. This is the first time in his life he has known this about himself, and he cherishes her for showing him who he really is. She never cries, but he knows the water's dammed up inside. When they're alone together, he strokes her like he'd pet a cat, and she responds, pressing into his hand. They never speak about love – just need. "I need touching," she says. "I need to touch," says Edward.

One night, after the men have eaten and the kitchen is scrubbed down for the morning, she finds him outside, under his mosquito net, back to the ground, face to the stars.

"I want to tell you about something," she says. She kneels, then shifts to sitting with her arms wrapped around her knees, holding herself in place.

"Why I cannot ..." she says. "What I see ..." Her voice trails out, drifts into that other place she goes and reaches him from there. "If I say it to you, it can help me?"

"Yes." He reaches for her hand, and she lets him hold it. He studies the numbers on her forearm, the brutality of the black ink scratched in there. He strokes it with his fingertip. It burns through his hand to his heart.

"When we were freed, we hadn't eaten real food for weeks. Just broth and scraps."

Edward stops breathing.

"They fed us stew. Which I cooked here today. The same I cook every Thursday." She stops again. He can see how hard it is; anguish twists her face. "I helped to feed the first of them because I was stronger. I helped them to eat. To fill their stomachs. And then two days later, they started to die. Their bodies could not process the good food, and they died." Her voice, already so quiet that he leans in to hear, becomes a whisper. "When it should have been so good." Edward is stopped with the shock of what she says. He plays it over again in his head as they sit in silence until he finally grasps what happened.

"The things you've seen," he says.

She nods as she relaxes. Her face, which was screwed up so tight, falls back into place. "You're a good man. Strong and good in here." She taps his chest.

"You're a good woman," says Edward. "I admire you very much."

"Admire?"

"You are a very special person. A special woman. I look up to you. I think you are truly astonishing."

"Astonishing!" she says and laughs. A rusty bell of a laugh, deeper than her voice, bigger than her rare smile. It's the first time he's heard her laugh in all the months they've known each other. He laughs too, surprised and utterly delighted. They shake with it, together, his right arm pressed against her left as she leans in sideways, unbalanced by laughter, and he keeps them both from toppling over though he is joggling with laughter too.

CYRIL WALKED ALONG EGLINTON AS far as the Flats, then cut off on the path to Topham Pond, where he looked through the tall cattails and grasses at the still, dark water. The signs said there were snakes, and he always stopped to look. He had never seen a snake in Jamaica. When he got to the river, he followed it north, up through the park. He walked all the way to Lawrence, where he caught a Weston bus that took him back down south. He had plenty of time and an abundance of good spirits. He didn't want tarmac and traffic. Cyril swiped at his forehead, squeegeed sweat with the back of his hand, and untucked his shirt. It was hot and very humid. The greens of the park seemed deepest now, toward the end of summer. Bushes of wild roses in pinks and reds were a hedge of colour. A pair of mourning doves, just like the ones from home, stepped delicately across the path, heads bobbing for seed. At the playing field, he came too close to a flock of pigeons gorging on broken loaves of bread scattered over the grass. They rose into the air and circled above him, moving in a sweeping rush of wind and wings.

Cyril was on his way to meet a sociologist at the University of Toronto, an introduction made by his history prof. And that, Cyril recognized, was the real source of his elevated mood. The professional acknowledgement that his research, and Edward, had value. Evan knew the sociologist's work, had attended a talk by her once. He was impressed, and said so, a highly regarded scholar. The little bundle of newfound energy that danced just above Cyril's diaphragm was excitement. "I'm back in my office now," she'd said. "Come before I get busy with the start of term."

She was tall and imposing. Stern. But her long, grey dread-locks had little button bursts of colour at their tips. Cyril watched their gentle motion as she moved her head, gesticulated with her hands, explained how things worked.

"There are protocols that I have been known to dismiss," she said. "But you must be very careful not to look beyond your brief. Don't take unfair advantage of what I am proposing, and we'll all keep our jobs. You are serious, and that is why I'm willing to help you."

"I won't let you down," Cyril said and hoped that he sounded as sincere as he felt.

"I find the hoops and hurdles of ethics review boards tiresome. They discourage public engagement. These days, I work on crowdsourcing. Keep that in mind, Cyril," she said. "You are probably not the only one looking for men whose experience was similar to your Edward's."

She took a paper from her filing cabinet.

"We have to learn for ourselves the history that is *not* taught to us. I work with a project that searches out the erased history of Black settlements across Canada. The abandoned cemeteries and broken, scattered gravestones."

Cyril could see how sad she was as she told the story. "The demolished churches and the obliterated record of anything to show that Black people once were there. It is in the enduring interest of white history to keep it hidden. But we *will* reclaim our history."

It was evening and getting dark when he left with the keys to the professor's castle in his pocket. Her signed permission giving him access to precious data, entrée to the sociological records that generally only graduate students, by virtue of their thesis work, got to see. Cyril walked through the hallways of the old campus buildings with a rarely felt confidence. Despite its grandeur, despite the many white faces.

The place announced its privilege all around him. The paintings along the walls and in the lounges with their red leather couches. A man, stretched across one of them with his legs dangling, watched Cyril as he passed. Cyril met his gaze and nodded briefly; the man dipped his head in return. A small orchestra rehearsed in one of the larger rooms. He could see the musicians through the polished wood and glass doors and stopped for a moment. He'd been to one Jamaican Symphony Orchestra concert with Nelson and knew the strings and percussion and brass. The woman closest to him, with her back to the glass door, held a shimmering trumpet. In the middle of the room, the conductor made a sudden, forceful signal, and as Cyril watched they played a burst of music that was beautiful to hear and to see. It was so cool, thought Cyril, what kids could do at this school.

As he neared the exit, ladies and gentlemen walked slowly along the corridor toward him on their way from what was probably a ballroom. Cyril could see only the uniformed staff who stood at either side of its doors and a glimpse of the chandeliers beyond. Most of the guests were white and old, dressed in suits and dresses and jewels, talking to each other while exchanging farewell hugs and kisses. Several of the women, graceful in their tall heels, carried vases of big flowers. They'd been celebrating, and now they were on their way home. Only a few of them glanced at Cyril.

When he left the building and walked alongside the playing field back to the road, the sky was a dark wrap of indigo blue, and the crescent moon in the middle was a child's perfect cutout. The paper-lined sky arched over the grass, lit from below by towering poles of lights as bright as daytime. Underneath them, women played soccer on emerald-green turf.

TWENTY-FIVE

❧

CYRIL HAD PROMISED TO JOIN the protest of Black killings that was happening at City Hall. A bunch of the guys had made costumes, and they'd booked a ska band that played activist songs. The event had started at 2:00 p.m.

"Just bring your body, brother," said Randall. "We need more than the usual forty people that always show up. You know the crew: there's the Black Action Defence Committee and OCAP. Then there's the anarchists, communists, animal rights, and some Greenpeace people. A few from the New Democratic Party sometimes show up, plus a guy from Quaker Jails and Justice. And environmentalists. The usual sussspectsss." Randall played the sssssses with his tongue. He was responsible for getting the press out. That meant doing something unusual because Toronto was full of organized protests – even in the fall.

Cyril walked east along Queen Street West. Past the bead shops and Korean fusion restaurants. Beyond the shoe boutiques, across University Avenue, and alongside the wrought iron fence of the Osgoode Hall law courts. The clock on the Old City Hall tower struck 3:00 p.m. Cyril knew that the whole area had once been a slum called St. John's Ward. A Black businessman, Thornton Blackburn, had bought some of the houses in the 1840s and rented them out to newcomers and freedom runners at affordable rents. Stuff people who'd lived there forever didn't know, thought Cyril, who was sure that Edward would have known the Ward. Now it was all glass towers, restaurants, banks, and government.

In Nathan Phillips Square, the band's instruments were already assembled on the stage, and costumed characters marched at its foot. They'd been joined by some people from Shadowland, the group of puppeteers and stilt walkers from Toronto Island that Randall had invited especially for the cause. The stilt walkers had drawn a small audience of tourists from the big buses parked along Queen on the south side of the square.

Two of the protestors were dressed as parodies of police officers, big bellies with large, dark sunglasses and oversize guns holstered at their sides. Another guy was in black and bling with a do-rag covering his hair. A giant gold chain dangled from his bound wrists, which he held, prayer-like, near his chest. One of the stilt walkers wore a grinning Mayor Ford mask and swayed above the crowd, waving a hand in greeting like the Queen. It was all pretty funny. Cyril smiled as he walked toward the hot dog stand.

While Cyril squeezed ketchup onto his hot dog, a Black man in his thirties wearing an African caftan strode onto the stage and, once the screech of feedback stopped, began to introduce the main speaker. He told the crowd that they had come together to protest yet another murder of a young Black man in Toronto. The man on the stage said, "What better way to solve the problem of Black people making demands and fighting back than to marginalize the kids so they learn to mistrust themselves and each other. Have you ever heard of white-on-white violence? No! Because the term 'Black on Black violence' is a white convenience. A concept created by racists and perpetuated by Canadian society." He stopped and glared at the crowd. "They want you isolated and weak!" he shouted. "They want you kept in chains." He pointed to a group of women who stood at the bottom of the steps to the side of the stage. "They keep our families in chains."

The handful of older Black women looked out of place among the hip urban kids with placards who were clearly having a good time. They were a small, cheerless group, the women, with children hanging from their hands or chasing wild into the square while a sister or cousin ran to catch them and bring them safely back. Somehow, the women made the man's words a truth. Cyril had heard the conspiracy rhetoric before and dismissed it as political posturing. But the mothers were real. What they had in common was the colour of their skin and their sons, who had grown to boyhood full of promise then lost themselves to frustration and anger and the belligerence they nurtured before they became men. Or who had simply been in the wrong place at very much the wrong time – and sometimes that place was their neighbourhood.

The lady who was going to speak next was short and thin and dressed in a neat coat and hat. The three women who accompanied her hovered like chaperones. They might be a daughter and the woman's sisters, perhaps, or friends. They pushed her gently toward the steps, gave her tissue and a sheet of paper. Cyril could see that she was frightened by the crowd. She clutched a purse that got in the way, and she shifted it from wrist to wrist. When it dropped to the ground, her women pounced. The first to reach it lifted it up in triumph and slid it back onto the mother's arm. She stood frozen at the side of the stage as the MC introduced her, the mother of a young Black man murdered in Toronto in 2012. "She is here to tell us who he was," he said, "a man with a future, not an invisible statistic."

The mother walked toward the MC as he stepped back, allowing her to take centre stage. Her voice fell short of the microphone, which was too high, and she fumbled ineffectually at the stand. Her companions hung back, reluctant to bring their helping roles onto the stage when they too had never handled a microphone. He finally stepped forward, the negligent MC, and corrected what should already have been done.

Now they could hear her, and in the moments it took her to say, "My name is Mrs. Boyne, and I am the mother of Lester, who was taken from me three months ago," Cyril heard his own mother's voice and the fear for him that she had carried with her all the time, despite the fact that he was a good boy. "He was a good boy," said Mrs. Boyne. "He loved his family, he made us laugh." *And you make us laugh*, Cyril's mother was saying. *Please keep away from the Rude Boys.*

"He wasn't a gangster," said Mrs. Boyne. "He loved to draw. He is a boy who loves his family, and he would always call around suppertime to say he loved me. Why did they do this? Why do our children have to die? Why won't they stop the killings?"

There was a murmur from the crowd, a sympathy that extended beyond the woman on the stage and gathered each of the watchers into a unity of grieving that was for much more than the loss of Lester — it embodied all of the lost opportunities of so many young people.

These were not ideas that Cyril had contemplated, though he knew how they were framed and had seen firsthand how they played out. *I have not been touched by this*, he thought, then a moment later knew that he had.

Cyril looked about him now with a sense of trepidation. He saw the men at the periphery of the crowd, men who didn't look as though they belonged. A group of young white men under the curving arch of the building's elevated walkway who laughed too loudly as they talked to each other. Randall was standing still as a tree, which was not like him at all, as he gave all of his attention to Mrs. Boyne, whose paper fluttered in her hand while she carried on despite the tears that now trickled from her eyes.

"I am a mother," she said and looked out at the small crowd with a defiance that could slow even the riot police who were standing by, around the corner, out of sight. The MC walked slowly across the stage and put his arm around her. She'd said all she was able to say, and he helped her to the side, where her women gathered her up and led her away. The crowd steadied itself in the following moments of silence that bore witness to the mother's grief.

Once Mrs. Boyne was gone, borne off by the women, a band took the stage. The six men found their instruments and started to play. The drummer was white and blond and wore a black, gold, and green cap, Jamaica colours, over his dreadlocks. They started into a ska arrangement of "No Woman, No Cry," having a good time. Three white girls who looked like sixties flower children in bright Indian cotton dresses danced and twirled in front of the stage. Some Black kids formed a line and moved in a synchronized ska slide, forward and back with the beat. "Everything's gonna be all right," sang the band. It was a party, just like Randall had promised. The tourists, who'd disappeared once the talking started, were drifting back to watch. An older white couple danced together, his hand on the small of her back, hers on his shoulder. They wore smiles like professional dancers. They were really good, Cyril thought.

Somebody shouted, and Cyril turned to see the costumed police officers chase across the square while two black-and-bling-costumed men ran in front of them. All of the characters, police and bling alike, produced oversize guns, cutouts that they waved in the air, and then came the racket of firecrackers. Mayor Ford and the other stilt walkers moved toward the action, surprisingly fast for people on stilts, and one of the bling characters fell to the ground in a mimicry of death. A girl screamed, and the riot police appeared from around the corner, where they had been stationed. They were grim-faced, not entertained at all, and with their arrival the mood in the square completely changed. Cyril fought the urge to leave.

Randall approached the riot police with his hands in the air, which seemed to Cyril a superfluous and overly dramatic gesture until one of them shouted at Randall to stand still. Three of them walked toward him and began an obvious interrogation. Randall was joined by a couple of fellow organizers, and the band started up again – a love song – while the anarchists and communists, Black kids and hippies all milled about. Mrs. Boyne left the square in tears, flanked by her entourage of women, who threw angry glances over their shoulders at the organizers and the costumed characters and the riot police.

Cyril made his way toward Randall, who, ordinarily so controlled, had begun to get agitated. Alongside the police was a white man in blue jeans and a T-shirt who seemed to know the police very well. He looked arrogant and aggressive, and as Cyril came closer, he could hear the man saying that the act of representing police officers in a shooting along with the intentional and frightening effect of the firecrackers was a terrorist act. Cyril's jaw froze as the muscles across his shoulders tightened and his fingers curled to fists. He stood and watched until one of the officers turned to him and said, "Step over here." Cyril moved to where he pointed, afraid that when they asked a question he wouldn't be able to answer, the way his jaw was tight and his mouth dried to sawdust when he was distressed. But he would not let them see his fear.

Randall's voice was getting louder, and Cyril saw that Randall could not quiet himself. He knew that the cops weren't listening to Randall, they were laughing at him. Cyril was sure of that because their faces were ugly with it. Nelson's whisper was urgent, forceful: *You are in the right, here. You are in the right place for the right reasons. Look to your friend.* Cyril stepped forward, five long steps that put him between Randall and the officers. "We are here with a permit to demonstrate," said Cyril. "Our police costumes are parodies. These are two-foot-long cardboard pistols. Even a five-year-old would know the difference." He heard how his voice shook, but it was still clear and calm. Now the officers' attention had turned to him, and he fought for the strength to stay still, rooted to the ground. He stared back into their faces. And for the second time, Cyril found himself in a police station's holding cell. This time, though, the lawyers, and Evan, were on their way.

When they walked out of the police station three hours later, into the early evening dusk, Cyril wore a smile that he didn't try to hide. As they turned the corner, out of sight of the station, Randall let out a whoop and thrust a fist in the air. Cyril laughed with him as they linked arms and skipped along the sidewalk, Randall, Evan, and Cyril. They were a small crowd of young Black men and women, nine of them, including the other organizers and two lawyers who'd evidently convinced the cops that the best course was to let their clients go. Especially since an article sympathetic to the protest organizers would probably appear in the following day's *Toronto Star*. The lawyers had demanded an apology, and word had come from the police chief's office that this was under consideration. Cyril walked tall and light like he could fly. He had never been so proud. He wished that Grandpa Nelson and Mommy could see him now, then knew that they were right there beside him, same place they had always been.

The young people piled into two cars and drove back to City Hall, where they checked to see that the volunteer cleaning crew had done its job. It had. Randall, with one of the lawyers at his side, led them west along Queen Street, then north on University Avenue. Nine young Black people, strolling up the ceremonial boulevard with its landscaped median and the statues that celebrated Canadian triumphs. They walked up along the wide thoroughfare that housed the courthouses, the U.S. Consulate, the major hospitals, and other important institutions. The power-boulevard that led directly to the provincial seat of government, Queen's Park. This was the avenue that ruled the city, and the chattering, laughing, noisy group of young people owned it.

EDWARD HAS ANOTHER SEASON AT the logging camp. His fifth, like a full-time job. He's in the city, on his week off, and he's supposed to spend his money on drink and girls, maybe buy himself something special. There's nothing he wants except, perhaps, a camera. One of the guys has a Kodak, and Edward has seen the photographs. He would like to have a photo of the ocean. And pictures from the window of a train. He frames them in his mind. He'd like to have those images to keep. Rachel has moved on, but he has her Winnipeg address and could send her photographs of the mountains and the sea. He doesn't frame mind-pictures of Celia. He has only one photograph of himself. From Africville, standing with Celia and their two best friends.

He would not take photographs of people, but he does like to look at faces. He is in a diner getting breakfast, pancakes with bacon and plenty of syrup. Coffee made light with cream and thickened with sugar. Down at the end of the counter is a Black man. There are not so many of those around here. He is a Rare Thing, which is when Edward remembers that he himself is also a rarity, his skin the colour of the warm, sweet liquid in his mug. But that man is dark, coal dark. And he's talking like he comes here all the time. He's laughing with the waitress, and she's pleased to serve him.

There was once a man who was maybe as Black as that. Who had sex with a woman as white as the waitress, and what came out was a kid the colour of Edward. That's what they always told him. White mother, Black father. It made him a three-times-over bastard. That night, Edward pushes his way between two white men at a bar. Makes himself comfortable like he has a right to be there, even though it's one of the places you stay away from on a Saturday night. But it is Saturday night, and Edward doesn't have a date. No other business to get to, and he has already visited a whisky bottle at the bar down the street.

When it's over, and even though not too much got broken — glasses and a bottle that he'd have paid for, maybe some damage to the bar, and the car outside has just a few dents — it is Edward who is handcuffed and taken to the judge. You don't fuck with people's property.

You can piece a life together. He has. You're alive, so you stay that way. It's a matter of Keep Going Forward, Don't Look Back. Edward has all of that in hand. He's done it for decades, and that's what he tells them. "I don't know for sure how old I am, but I've been around for decades. So maybe I'm thirty-one? Or thirty-two? It's a mystery."

"Your mystery, sir?"

"It's the truth. I lost my papers. There. I'm truly sorry about that. I get paid, and if I need a bank account, I get one. When I'm sick, I find a clinic. Still got most of my teeth." He grins. "Just missing the one or two."

"You'll do jail time."

"I've been there before. It's okay." And so the gates close behind him, and he's back inside where he knows the routine, which is Dull as Ditchwater. It was hardest when he was a boy, those two short stays. But he learned how to do it. It was easier when he did the longer stretch, after Celia, when he had nothing to lose but time. If he keeps his nose clean, which he knows how to do, he'll get out soon enough.

TWENTY-SIX

THREE WEEKS AFTER THE CITY Hall protest, in a borrowed suit to match Penelope's party shimmer, Cyril sat beside her at a table in the ballroom of a fancy downtown hotel. Penelope Pong was being honoured at the annual dinner of the Black Community Achievement Awards for her work with kids. She'd started a dance club that had prospered and multiplied across the city so that kids all over town had put together their own chapters to meet after school and dance. It was an ABC to Z alphabet thing. You had to learn a dance that started with every letter. She had produced YouTube videos that showed the steps for dances that came from all around the world, with music — a whole mix of crazy stuff. It took the kids out of themselves, said Penelope. They didn't have to think about how sexy or how talented they were. They just had to make their way through the alphabet.

Penelope was the recipient of the award for a woman under twenty-five youth leader. Cyril was her date because Evan was busy covering the dinner for a couple of community papers. "We want you there, Cyril," Penelope had said. "Because you should see how this political stuff works."

"I told her," said Evan. "About the cops beating you and how you felt." Cyril's embarrassment must have been evident because Evan was quick to add, "She's my girlfriend. I share my shit with her. We figure stuff out together."

"Don't be ashamed of it, Cyril," said Penelope. "I do know something about this stuff, and you need to be productive with the anger. That's critical because otherwise it will mess you up."

"That's what I feel," said Cyril. "Exactly that. The anger's useless unless I know how to use it."

"Well, I think that's actually pretty wise," said Penelope.

"So, I said let's take Cyril to the dinner so he can hear from some people who do use their anger in a creative and forceful way," Evan said.

The mass of people made a bright, luxurious noise of talk and laughter. They all seemed to know each other, excited to be together. These were not people Cyril knew. They weren't students or corner-store customers. They didn't come from Mount Dennis. But he felt an unfamiliar sense of affinity, and not just because the greatest number of them were Black. Penelope called it community. But Nelson was grinning at his side. These were Nelson's people!

Evan was plush and handsome in a dusky grey suit with a deep-pink tie. His glasses matched the tie, and none of the guys would have laughed because Evan looked very good indeed, like he was in a short line to take his turn as an important person in the community. He knew lots of people in the room and took Cyril's arm to make introductions. When he delivered him back to Penelope, he told her that Cyril had made a good impression.

Even the speeches were good. Words and ideas for a room full of businesspeople, entrepreneurs, academics, scientists, artists, philanthropists, athletes, teachers and doctors, nurses and social workers, civil servants, and leaders from the charitable sector. What they had in common was the spectrum of colours of their skin. But most significantly — because they by no means represented the entire variety of Canada's professional Black population — they were communitarians. The awards were a celebration of everyone present but also included those who were not. All of the families who stumbled through poverty. The kids who'd lost sight of themselves, misled and muddled by chaos spun from the false promise of Canadian opportunity: that you could become whatever you chose to be.

"Life ain't no lottery," said the handsome Black man at the microphone. "You don't just keep on buying the ticket. You gotta make your own plans."

Grandpa Nelson used to ask, "What are you going to give the world?" Cyril had never found an answer. He'd played for time, said he'd get an education, figure it out later. "What makes your heart sing?" That was the other question Nelson had asked. Cyril hadn't known how to answer that either. His mother had tried: "It all about your family, darlin'. Your church and your family. They the ones does matter. Love is what God gives you to do." At seven, Cyril had accepted this without question.

"Don't lose sight of this," said the man. "We are most of us here living comfortable, middle-class, professional lives. But we have not come together tonight just to give lip service. These awards matter because they are the community's support for those among us who continue to work hard for social justice." He stopped to scan the room. "This is what we have yet to change," he said. "Our kids who mash up each other because they don't know how to believe in themselves. The people who say affirmative action works against them because it gives us opportunities we don't deserve.

"But here's what the research tells us. Even when our Canadian kids earn a university degree, it still doesn't get them any better employment than the white kids with their high school diplomas. Let me repeat that," he said. "Because this is a fact of Canadian life for our young Black folk." His voice rose until he almost shouted, "Our children, born and raised here, earn the same university degrees as their white counterparts — and it takes them only as far as the white student who has only his high school diploma." His voice turned from insistent exhortation to a punch of syllables. "How does that happen in our ce-le-bra-ted, mul-ti-cul-tu-ral, cos-mo-pol-i-tan, aff-lu-ent, soph-is-ti-ca-ted so-ci-ety? How does Canada still manage to exclude us when so many of us have contributed for generations? And those of us who have not, who have come here more recently, from Haiti, from Africa, from other lands — many with postgraduate degrees and years of experience — and who, years after arrival, are still working three jobs that still don't add up to a decent day's wage?"

His voice softened, implored. "We are all part of the weave and fabric of this land. How does Canada justify the exclusion of so many, and how can we continue to challenge this and make ourselves heard?"

Cyril listened, fully absorbed. He heard the echoes of Randall's activism and Leon's angry complaints. He felt the whisper-breath of his mother's fears and the sharp inhale of Nelson's caution. For the first time, he really understood them.

As the audience applauded, Cyril was transfixed, immobile in the force of revelation. When Penelope's fingertips brushed his arm, he leaned back, felt a smile open his face.

"Okay?" she asked.

"Yeah. I feel good."

When Penelope accepted her award, Cyril clapped furiously. Afterward, people surrounded her. He didn't mind standing outside her circle. People introduced themselves to him as he stood waiting. He shook their hands and told them he was as proud of her as they were. When they asked what he did for the community, he shook his head and said, "Nothing, yet."

After the dinner, Cyril, Penelope, and Evan went to a nearby café. To wind down, they said, because they were hours away from being able to sleep. They talked about how much they'd enjoyed the awards, though Evan said the politics of the dinner were complicated. Because there were lots of folk who didn't get recognized. And a couple of those who did receive awards got them because they worked as hard at getting them as they'd worked for the community. Sometimes even more so. "That's the way it is, though," said Evan. "That's how people are."

They were the only ones in the café, just the three of them at a table in the window. Cyril said, "I want to ask something."

Penelope had her head on Evan's shoulder, but she sat up, sensed the seriousness of what was about to come.

"Remember I talked to you about my friend Paul's cousin, the one who got into YBK?"

Evan nodded. "Yes."

"They sent him back to Jamaica to live with his daddy. Before he got any kind of a criminal record. Because they want him to be able to come here again. To live with his mom and his aunt. When he's ready."

"How's he doing?"

"Pretty good, I think. Paul says he's back at school and talks about studying criminology and immigration stuff."

"That's great."

"So, I just wondered," said Cyril, "who to connect him to if and when he gets back? Like a mentor or something. Like you two. Because I know his mom is saving hard to get him here again, and she needs some help, to see him through college."

"I think we can do that," said Penelope. "In fact, I'm thinking of that guy, you know, the one you met tonight, who's a counsellor at the university? I think he'd be a great place to start."

CYRIL WALKED HOME. THERE WAS a cold, crisp edge to the air, and he felt for the scarf in his pocket, wrapped it around his neck. The dinner had been awesome, Cyril thought. In so many ways. Penelope sitting beside him. The community in all its finery. The work that they celebrated. But it was that speech that kept running through his head. He felt that he was finally about to figure out who he was and what was expected of him. And it was going to be very different from the expectations of him at his job, at his school, from Aunty Vi.

He knew he had something to give. Something important. He was smart — he understood the work of listening — he could build bridges between folk. Like the dub play thing — both sides of that debate had needed his perspective. They hadn't entirely won, but they'd prevailed. *Shout* was scheduled to run in February 2013, Black History Month. All Cyril needed now was a plan, and Evan and Penelope could help him with that. He was, all at once, proud and satisfied, and the rest of it — money, jobs, grades — seemed remarkably insignificant up against a real purpose.

Cyril thought about the two boys in Jamaica. The kid at Santy Drinks and Snacks. Paul's cousin, who was hopefully on the right path to college. It was all so accidental. Kids didn't understand consequences, and the trap was so easy to trip. He didn't know what could make a difference, but he was suddenly struck with the thought that he might well have just made a difference himself.

Because when Paul's cousin got back to Canada, he was going to have help, a chance at getting through.

Cyril didn't mind another winter so much. As long as he could walk or run, pump the life energy through his limbs. The mournful night whistle of a train sounded somewhere far off. Edward had worked the rails as a porter and probably walked the length of those carriages for years. All that walking, and chances were good that he'd never reached anywhere that the train was going. Walking for miles while the train travelled from east to west and back again. How much had Edward wanted something different, he wondered. It would have been clearer back then — options were so limited. Edward would have liked tonight.

Cyril felt for the motion of the train, its steady travel along steel rails. He pictured the passengers, all of them white, snoozing in their seats or reading. Maybe talking. One snaps a finger and calls for George. Edward must have hated that. Cyril's leg began to ache, and he slowed his walk, just a touch. It wasn't his pain. It was Edward's.

EDWARD IS AT A VETERANS' dinner. It is in a Legion Hall with many tables set about the room. Each of them is decorated with a central feature vase of plastic daisies. A Canadian flag hangs above an upright piano alongside a framed photograph of Queen Elizabeth II. There is a small bar with Export beer for sale at $3.25 a bottle. Edward remembers when beer was fifty cents, and he says this to the big woman with the thin, pink lips behind the bar. She gestures with the back of her hand, a dismissal. She says she has heard this complaint so often that she hears it in her sleep. That he should spend his money in the fancy restaurants where they sell microbrews for eight dollars a glass. Edward has three beers, which help to soothe his aching leg. There are a couple of East Coast Blacks here. Guys who worked the trains. Both of them were army. They have what Edward thinks of as Their Conversation: about the sergeants and the train conductors and the good old union days. The women they all remember so fondly, in such intimate detail, who have never aged.

These days, Edward is visited sometimes by flashbacks of sound and smell from that awful time on the beach. It happens to him this evening, and he panics. Somebody drops a bottle, and he starts up from his chair, much too quickly; his cane falls to the floor, and, as he swings around to grab at it, he hits the knee of one of the volunteers. Things are spilled – a tray of cheese and crackers, red-tipped toothpicks pinned to squares of yellow scattered all across the floor. Edward has to leave. He leans on his cane, a little unsteadily now because he is drunk. One of the women is very kind. "Be careful on your way home now, Mr. Davina. You don't have far to go, do you, dear?"

Edward needs to get into the air, away from the clatter of noise in the room and the grating music that seems to peak sometimes in shots of piercing sound. He nods at her, grunts a response. He wants to say, "Help me home, please." He wants to say, "When I'm struck with this thing, I want some comforting." But he's learned, really quite effectively, how to manage it on his own.

The air is clear. The rain that nearly stopped him from coming this evening is long past, dried by a chill breeze that forecasts winter. His room is just a few blocks from the hall. He has only to focus his walk and not let go of his cane. To remind himself that he is walking along King Street in Toronto, heading home on a beautiful late-fall night. A streetcar passes, and he braces himself, mutters, "Streetcar, streetcar, streetcar." He names it, and it cannot frighten him. He battles against the noise.

He has been going to this Legion for ten years. Ever since he moved in to the King's Arms. His home. He won't be moving house again unless it's into a casket. He pushes at the door with his good arm. It is stiff, and Edward has complained; he has said, "We are the old and infirm in this place, but that door could stop a baseball team." Security Sam appears, pulling the door fully open. "Hey, Eddie, you remembered to come home. I'll bet those girls at the club were disappointed."

"Leave them wanting more," said Edward. "Thanks."

This evening's beers mean there'll be nothing for tomorrow. A whole day's budget gone to a night on the town that's been spoiled by a panic attack. Still, it was nice to see the boys. They are good people. He has known lots of good people. In all the years of scraping by, he's always said he's never been lonely. Didn't need more money — he loved the freedom of Pickup-and-Leave. You could do that when you worked temporary. He'd got to know the country that way. Caught the travel bug from the rails. There was so much to see, and he was a guy with the time to do it.

Not so good being old, though. His time as a porter was far too short to get him a pension. He doesn't even have the CPP; nearly all of his work was under the table. Not that it would make that much difference. Lots of the guys in here have it along with their Old Age Security, and it doesn't buy them any better than this. He's always known how to work hard. He did some logging. Worked one of the big freighters for a while. One of the best was on a Parks Canada crew, where he booked in for months at a time. Hard physical work. Lots of good men.

He swore off women, although one or two made it through. And Rachel. He sends her cards, sometimes. Celia left him red-sore underneath. Women didn't like that when they found it. He lost a couple of them after Celia, but he never, ever loved anyone else the same way. Never again considered marriage and children. That would have been a thing: children.

He still sends money to help the little kids with school. Has kept it up since he left Africville, how many decades ago? Something to be proud of, that. First it went straight to the school, sent from wherever he was — unless he was inside, then they had to wait until he got out and found a job. Nova Scotia stopped segregating its schools in 1953. They closed the school in Africville, and Black kids had to be bussed to the white schools. The Black students were put into special classes — they had a really hard time, those kids. Edward didn't stop sending the money. It went to the church for a while, to tutor the children, and now there is a little charity that does its best to help. He likes to think that's what happens with his monthlies — helping a whole parcel of children, year after year, learn how to live right in the world. That is the cycle that never ends.

TWENTY-SEVEN

❧

CYRIL WAITED FOR THE WALK light at a busy intersection on the downtown's west side. Parkdale's southern border was the lake, and he'd walked down to look at it. He'd seen it before from a number of places, but the lake had been unexpected this day. When he'd caught his first glimpse of it, before the King streetcar began its curve north toward Roncesvalles, he'd been surprised. He often forgot that Toronto was a city on a lake.

He stomped his feet. Someone on the streetcar had said it was cold enough to snow. It was a ten-minute walk up to Queen Street and the office of the important sociologist's generous colleague, the research consultant who would show him the data. He felt for signs, any indication of how close he might be to finding definitive answers on Edward. But his senses were overwhelmed by a persistent apprehension that had troubled him all week.

Four days earlier, he'd dreamed of a hospital room, lit bright and scrubbed clean. A TV-show scene with sounds that bothered his ears, hissing white noise, beeping machines. As he'd pushed his head deeper into his pillow, he had found Edward, lying on his back in a hospital gown, shrunken and old, hooked up to tubes and wires. His eyes were closed, but he was conscious, and Cyril could feel his fear.

He'd know soon enough, thought Cyril, who was impatient to move. Five main roads met at the intersection, and the traffic light was interminably long. He watched as a man drove a motorized wheelchair along the sidewalk toward him. He looked about fifty, though alcoholics like that could be any age. A few long strings of grey hair hung down from under his hat and lay flat against his black leather jacket. The hat was a big, dark cowboy thing that looked as though it had been around since the sixties. The woman behind him, whose age was equally uncertain, had extended her arms to hold on to the back of his chair by the push handles. Hers was an ordinary, non-motorized wheelchair on which she sat with a big case of empty beer bottles balanced and belted onto her lap. She was also dressed in black – leather jacket, sweatpants, and runners. Her ball cap was a faded and stained blue, topping long, lank brown hair. The pair stopped beside Cyril and waited for the light to change.

The woman being pulled didn't move her eyes from her partner's back. She looked numbed, not a part of the street or the crowd. It was just the two of them in their exacting world with their single purpose: getting to the Beer Store and getting home again. Cyril wondered what their house looked like. No images came to mind. As the light changed, the man turned his head to the woman behind him and said, "Are you ready, baby?" in a voice so caring and gentle that it shook Cyril from his thoughts. "Yes, darling," the woman said and grimaced with effort as her chair followed his, pulling at her arms, rattling the bottles, bumping down into the road and then picking up speed as he motored them both to the other side. Cyril blessed his legs and his health.

Cyril was excited about meeting the researcher, whose work looked at the historical and contemporary inequalities of economic opportunity for Black people in Canada. She had studied several major Canadian employers, including the Canadian Pacific Railway. She had a data table that recorded lifetime earnings and compared the entitlements of the Black Brotherhood members to those in the white union. Everyone who'd been employed by CP Rail since the Brotherhood was formed, cross-referenced to their Canada pensions and income tax returns.

She met him in the lobby: short, round-faced and smiling, tight black curls. She was totally unlike the tall, austere sociologist. "So nice to meet you, Cyril," she said. "Let's get you down to business right away?" She led him to an elevator that took them to the fourth floor and stopped at a big glass door where she swiped her security card and pushed it open. Inside were offices ranged along a square of corridors, rows of closed doors, many pinned with posters and signs. "The offices have all the windows," she said. "That's why it's so dark in here when the doors are shut." She flipped a switch that turned on a second row of lights and stepped toward the end of the hallway. "This is mine." Inside was a desk, filing cabinets, bookshelves. A computer. "The deal is that I can only log on from here," she said, "and I have requested access for just two days, right?"

"Yes. I understand."

"If you don't find it today, you can try again tomorrow. I'll be here all morning. But after that, I'd have to ask them to extend the privilege, and I'd rather not. On the other hand, if the name you have is really what your man went by, it won't take any time at all."

She sat at her desk and started her computer, motioning Cyril to pull up a chair. He slid in beside her as she entered the security code for the database along with her name and authorization. When the reams of data scrolled up onto the screen, she rolled sideways in her chair so that Cyril could sit in front of the monitor. What he saw were dozens of columns and countless numbers.

"Looks like a spreadsheet," said Cyril.

"These," she said, "are the social insurance numbers. And those columns are government benefits. Here are the union benefits." She moved a finger down the screen. "Look how many of them were Americans, or from the West Indies. Lots of Jamaicans."

"They were supposed to be less demanding workers, right?"

"Yes." She leaned across Cyril and moved the cursor over to the left. "And these are the lifetime earnings."

Cyril looked where she pointed as he began to make sense of the data.

"Go on then," said the researcher. "Put his name here in the search field. This is the first five years after the Brotherhood was formed."

Cyril keyed in Edward's name. In seconds the screen changed, and Edward's name was at the top. Edward Davina's social insurance number. He got Old Age Security and the Guaranteed Income Supplement. The union benefits column was blank. In the column beside it was a special note explaining that Edward Davina had been removed from his job, and the union, before entitlements became due.

"There's an address category," said the sociologist, obviously pleased and excited for Cyril, who remained silent. "Just move the arrow to the right."

"This is too weird," said Cyril as the columns rolled out across the screen.

"Double-check that you're still in Edward's data row."

Cyril scrolled quickly to the left and back again to the city column.

"He lives in Toronto!" They both said it at the same time.

"And here," said the researcher, pointing at one of the pink-coded columns. "The deceased box is empty."

"He's alive?"

"Here's his address. Though he might not be living there anymore. This data is more than two years old. He could be in a nursing home by now. Or might have died, I guess. He would be ninety." She watched while Cyril copied the address down into his book, which was hugely unethical and legitimate grounds for firing. But she didn't hesitate for a minute.

"Oh man!" Cyril's smile collapsed, and his lips trembled. The office seemed suddenly huge and the world a very strange place. He felt as though he'd stepped off its edge. The researcher patted his back, her bangle-encircled wrist jingling along with her firm touch, a reassurance that all of this was real. She closed the record, then encouraged Cyril to search the address on a map, right there on her computer. Edward was less than a kilometre from where they sat. "Oh, man," said Cyril.

It was already dark when Cyril walked the short block from the Weston bus stop to his basement room. A couple of the houses had Christmas lights up. Cyril had loved those fairy lights as a kid. His mother once had four strings of them that she said his father had bought. They'd managed to keep them going for years, stripping them one by one for replacement bulbs until the last one was gone. About four years before Cyril's mother died, Grandpa Nelson had given Cyril money to buy her new ones. Nelson had died a few months after that. He only saw those lights up once.

The air was biting cold, snapped at Cyril's face and neck. He pulled his scarf tighter. Here comes the real winter, he thought. His second Christmas in Canada. A number of weeks back, he'd packed a box full of toys for his brother and sister. Each item wrapped in bright paper, with extra sheets in case the customs people tore them apart and his aunt had to rewrap. He could imagine the litter of colour and squeals of delight on Christmas morning. Both of them were already taller than they'd been in the summer. Lately, when he talked to Daren on the phone, it was like a real person on the other end. More grown-up than he'd been in person a just a few short months back, he had things to say about school, football, his friends. The kid had a life. And his sister wasn't far behind, though she still rambled on in her funny little overexcited voice, and Cyril often didn't really understand what she was telling him. He always understood the last bits, though, when she said, "I love you, Cyril. I miss you lots and lots." He was very glad that he'd seen them in the summer. And now he was ready to risk seeing Edward.

EDWARD IS GOING TO THE community hall for Christmas. He's been there every Christmas for twelve years. This year, he will deliver one of the after-dinner speeches. They are short, the only sort he is interested in. He will give sincere words of thanks for the efforts the volunteers put in all year long on behalf of those less fortunate. Most of the time, Edward doesn't mind being less fortunate. He is never sorry for himself. Only sometimes wishes that he fought harder, got involved with the activists, so that today's kids could have a better shot at life. But he stayed away from politics after the trains.

Edward searches for his big, brown sweater. It is damned cold out there, and he has to bundle up to get to the shop. He needs wrapping paper for the shot glass, the Token Gift that he's bought for Security Sam. Inside his room it is as hot as Hades. The boilers bang away on their own schedule. The people nearer the front of the building walk around in their T-shirts in the winter — it's that hot. The guys at the back of the building have to keep their jackets on inside. The way the heat works is stupid and wasteful, but the management says it would cost too much to fix. Edward isn't allowed to open his little window in the winter because that would waste heat, so he suffocates in the stuffy room. Today his door is open to let in some air. As he digs through the clothes in his drawer, he hears Timmy and Marg rattling along the hall in their wheelchairs. Timmy's wheelchair makes long, dark stripes along the length of the corridor wall all the way down to the room he and Marg share at the cold end. Management charges the social services extra for the regular paint jobs. A motorized wheelchair. Edward thinks he could maybe use one of those himself. Not yet, though. He isn't decrepit yet.

He spots the brown sweater under the laundry that's piled on his armchair. Tomorrow is washing day, with the long trek down to the basement where an unreliable machine bangs and shakes through the cycles. It is much better than the old days, though, when he had to haul everything to the laundromat a couple of blocks away. As he leans down to pull the sweater from the pile, a Dizzy hits him so hard that he tips off-balance, has to hold on to the chair to find his feet, and then he can't hold anymore as pain grabs at his chest and squeezes like it won't let go, will bust right through. The fear, the outright scare of it, is worse than the pain, and his voice doesn't work, so he lies with his face to the open door, and his mouth gasps for breath.

TWENTY-EIGHT

❧

ON THE SEAT BESIDE CYRIL was a big, green bag that he'd found at the Goodwill store. It contained the child's blue suitcase, the sailor doll, and the children's home book of records. The photograph album and the letters were inside the suitcase. The doilies too, though Cyril had never understood their place in the mystery. He clung to the handle of the bag as though his cargo were potentially life changing.

Mr. Addo had been most reluctant to let his treasures go. He'd only relented when Cyril presented him with the binder of research that included the precious newspaper photograph of Edward in the lineup of bad boys. Mr. Addo had put a framed copy of that in the display case. He hadn't seen Edward's signature before, the large, round, looping letters with an ink point at the end. "This is really him?" He shook his head, slow, side to side. "His handwriting. Good lord. I never dreamed you'd find these things." He handed the binder back to Cyril. "If he really is there, please take a photograph for me? I'll give you my camera. We can get it printed big and frame it. I'll put it in the display case. And if the gentleman is able to travel, perhaps he would come and see it for himself."

"If he really is there," said Cyril, who was as nervous as the first time he'd left Jamaica — flying into the unknown. "But I've just thought of something. I can tell him about Pat. Because it was Pat who made this happen, right? I mean, you found his things and put them on display. And I did the looking. But if Pat hadn't brought us together, it would never have happened. So, yeah. I get to tell him about her. I think he'll like that."

Mr. Addo looked a little skeptical but nodded agreement. He opened the display case and watched as Cyril took the pieces from it and packed them into his bag.

"I know you'll keep them safe, Cyril. I'll go and get my camera."

CYRIL WATCHED THE PASSING CITYSCAPE from the King streetcar as he travelled west. Tried to see it through Edward's eyes in the 1940s. There were streetcars then. Thornton Blackburn — a self-emancipated Black man — had started the city's first taxi business in the 1830s, and Toronto's new streetcars had used his taxi colours, maroon and cream. Cyril's head was full of names and dates now, memorized like the poems he'd once recited for Grandpa Nelson.

Cyril looked around at the other passengers. A very pretty Asian girl and some old Chinese people near the front. A South Asian family, a bunch of Somali-looking guys. A couple of probably Middle Eastern women. There were a few white people and some Latinos. The two men in front of him were speaking what Cyril guessed was Russian. All of this was new knowledge, learned in the past year. When he'd first arrived, he could identify only Chinese, and he had since learned about all the other Asian nationalities living in Toronto.

It wouldn't have looked like this when Edward was growing up. They'd all have been pretty much white because people who looked different weren't allowed in. Not until 1967, when they changed the immigration law. Before that, Blacks were kept out because they wouldn't be able to handle the cold, which was such a lame excuse for discrimination, thought Cyril. Especially since some were allowed in to look after people's children and clean their houses. They couldn't bring their families; they were supposed to leave when the work was finished. Those women sent money home to help someone else raise their kids. Cyril shivered with disgust; it was so unfair. That kid in Jamaica outside Santy's, Paul's cousin: something happened to people when they got here, especially kids, and it had to do with never being allowed to properly belong. Could it happen to him? Even William Hubbard had felt it. A city councillor in the early 1900s who was acting mayor more than once, which was amazing. He fought to get energy out of private control and helped start Toronto Hydro – People's Power! Cyril had copied out what Hubbard had said back then

> I have always felt that I am a representative of a race
> hitherto despised, but if given a fair opportunity would
> be able to command esteem.

Hubbard was born in Toronto; his parents had been escaped slaves who'd made it up to Canada in the 1840s.

Cyril had found very little about Blacks in Edward's time. Like Randall said, they had been unwelcome. Most of the successful Americans moved back south after abolition, frustrated by Canada's ostracism. Canada was not the promised land. It could have tried to keep them, but it didn't. Cyril wondered if Edward had known about the Black VIPs who'd preceded him. If they really were about to meet, he'd be able to ask him.

Across the aisle from Cyril was a little blonde girl his sister's age, curled into her mother's side and playing with a pink toy cellphone that made different ringtones when she punched the numbers. Her mom looked tired and bored. Edward's mom had given him to a children's home. Cyril knew that children as young as four had been sent out to work back then. Cyril's own mother had seemed quietly, sweetly, eternally tired. Or he'd assumed that was how she felt. She'd never said. She would have been forty-three next year. He wished he could show her all this. Take her on a streetcar ride. She'd have said, "Oh, Cyril, oh lawd!" overwhelmed and so impressed by what she'd see and his place in it all.

The King's Arms was a long, brown brick hotel whose ground-floor windows, once handsome, were scarred with grime and rusted iron bars. Cyril pushed at the big industrial front door, but it was locked. There was a faint smell of urine in the cold, damp air. He pressed the doorbell and, when the buzzer sounded, pushed again and walked inside. A young guy wearing a green T-shirt sat in a little square room to the left of the door. He had an open lunch box in front of him and was reading a music magazine. It was very warm inside, and it smelled of cleaning stuff. A small plastic Christmas tree stood in the corner of the room. He looked up, curious.

"I'm looking for Edward Davina," said Cyril.

"Why do you want him?"

"I've got some things." Cyril held up the bag to prove his good intentions. "A gift, and some family items that he should have. That I believe he would be pleased to see."

"I didn't know he had any family," said the guy. "Are you his grandson or something?"

"I'm not family," said Cyril. "But I've got his stuff." Edward really did live here then. This was real.

The guy's expression softened. "Okay. Look, he's not here. I don't know when he'll be back."

"Later on today?"

"I don't know when. Not today, for sure."

"Is he okay?" Cyril asked.

The guy made a decision. "I'm going to give you a cell number for his social worker, okay? See if she can help you. I'm not supposed to talk about the residents, and honest, I don't know much." He tore a sheet of paper from a pad and copied the information from a card pinned to his bulletin board. "Tell her you got the number from Sam," he said, handing the paper to Cyril.

"Is there a pay phone near here?"

"At the Coffee Time, last I looked. So long as it's working."

Cyril crossed the street to the restaurant. It smelled like sugar. He ordered a tea and a donut and found a table by the front window that ran the length of the café.

The anxiety that had crept across his chest as he stood in the lobby of the King's Arms returned. He couldn't shake the image of Edward in the hospital. He sipped slowly at his tea. Let the donut melt in his mouth. Cyril closed his eyes – didn't care what the people around him thought – let time stand still as he sought Edward's hospital bed, rested his hand on the mattress, felt the life that was still there.

He'd made a small stack of quarters on the table, pushed it around with his fingers as he finished his tea. The pay phone was next to the washrooms. The handset was sticky. He pressed the number keys and waited, watching the dreary street. An empty and grime-covered out-of-service streetcar lumbered along the tracks, made the window tremble.

Then a woman said, "Hello?" He repeated Edward's name a couple of times until she understood what he was asking. "Unless you are next of kin, I can't tell you anything," she said. "Those are my instructions."

"It is true that I'm not related to him. But I have things he'll want to see."

"Can't help you. As I've said, those are the instructions unless you are a relative."

"Is there one?" asked Cyril. "A relative I could talk to?"

"I can't help you with that unless you are next of kin."

"I have photographs of his mother and father for him. I don't think he's ever seen them."

He could hear her thinking in the silence.

"Please," said Cyril. "I'm a university student. That's how I found him."

"He's a sweet man, Edward."

"Is he?"

She must have heard how much he wanted this because she said, "He's in hospital. He had a heart attack, and I guess he'll pull through. But if you really have photos of his parents, then maybe he should see them before ... He told me he grew up without a family."

"I think he did."

"Look. He's been disoriented, and you shouldn't confuse him even more. He definitely won't be out before Christmas, and even then ... you should be aware that he is a very sick and elderly man. But I will let you know when he is released. Or if something else happens."

Cyril said goodbye, grateful for the little information he'd been able to extract from her. Edward had failed to keep the date he'd known nothing about. Cyril wished he'd asked to see Edward's room at the King's Arms. If Edward didn't return, he'd never know what his home looked like. Cyril pushed his hands into his pockets. He felt so close to Edward now and still didn't really know what he looked like. If his own father was sick, would anyone try to contact him? He could be dead already, and Cyril wouldn't know. He'd been six when he'd had the last communication from his father. A birthday card had arrived by mail. Three weeks late.

THE NURSE SAYS IT'S FRIDAY, January Fourth, of Two Thousand and Thirteen. If you say so, Edward replies. He can't believe he's been here since before Christmas. Since last year. A tube runs the distance to his arm from a bag upended on a stand. He is in a regular room now and feels as though he might actually stay alive. Before, in the ICU, he wasn't so sure. It was surreal, like a dream that kept going on and on whether he was awake or not. He was completely lost in the sound and smell of it, inside a body that didn't work anymore. He understood that it was the buzzing and pumping and beeping machines that were making him go. Beyond that, there were just blurred images, faces, shining steel, medical gowns. Hands everywhere. Except that once he saw God float through the room in his white robes with a halo over his head and a beatific smile that beamed out love and comfort. He thought, *I never knew he was real.* Later on, he described his experience to one of the nurses, forcing his stubborn, dry mouth to shape the words. She smiled at him like a benevolent angel. Much later, he realized that God had probably been the young blond man who pushed the trolley full of cleaning supplies. A sweet young fellow who teased the nurses in a gentle, quiet, respectful way. Everyone seemed to feel a little better when he was around.

Another tube runs from his penis to a bag beside the bed. If he could make his mouth work to smile, he'd smile about that. He can lie in bed all day if he wants – except they won't let him. They say he should be up and about as soon as possible. They've already made him sit up in bed to eat lunch, and he felt like a sack of stones. Nothing worked, no muscle, like his spine had worn out. He told that to the nurse, and she said, "It'll get better, you'll see. Faster than you think."

Everything hurts. But he can handle that. He's used to aches and pains that make him slow. Sore. They have him on a bunch of drugs, and that's okay for now. *I am an old man*, he thinks. Well, it comes to everyone; but he's not ready yet. The day before, there were some carol singers. A bit late for Christmas, he told them, but just in time for me! They were better than the singers at the Legion.

EDWARD COMES OUT OF THE hospital into a dull, grey early morning. He wears a big coat that the social worker has brought for him. The damp cold seeps through the sleeves, and he pulls the cuffs down over his hands. He feels as old as heck and vulnerable, stuck in a wheelchair. They've decided that they don't want him walking on his own yet after all. They say he might have to think about the chair becoming a permanent thing. He isn't ready for that. He feels okay. Very sore, but not so bad. They say he has to go home because they need the bed, and he'll be better off in his own place. But he can't be at home alone, so once he gets back to his room someone, probably the security, is going to have to check on him a few times a day. That's fine by him. He likes Sam. The guys on the other shifts are okay too. He hopes they won't mind the extra work. Because if they complain, he'll end up in the loony bin with Barb and Dee and mopey Rena.

Once they get him inside the ambulance, he feels better. Safe. He can't remember the trip to the hospital except that the colour bled out of everything. It was all black and white and slowed down, like that thing they did in cinema films. The fear is still there now, in the ambulance, but separate from him. That first trip he thought he was dying, and he didn't want to go. That was a bit of surprise because he'd always thought that he was ready for the exit. They always joked about it in the war. They were all kids then, of course. They didn't know what a lifetime was. What it had in it, except for girls and mothers. Not his. And you had the guys to share a good time with – or bad. It was all the same; they'd have a few beers and tell the same jokes. Laugh the same no matter what, as though the big, life-changing mo ments didn't really matter.

This is one of the big moments. As he waits for them to leave, a slice of sunlight comes through the open back door of the ambulance and straddles his knees. He can't think why this makes him smile, but it does. Edward sits in the ambulance and rests his eyes on the place the sun has found, illuminating the patch of brown and blue on the blanket that one of the volunteers has draped over his legs, tucked around his waist.

CYRIL WATCHED LEON, RANDALL, AND another man from school pull up in a car across the road. Two very pretty Black women Cyril had never met before climbed out from the back seat. Penelope P. arrived moments later on a pink bicycle, and Evan was on his way. At Penelope's urging, they'd picked up expensive wraps and smoothies from the restaurant next door to the park. "Health food is good for freedom fighters," said Randall, who seemed an older, wiser version of the man he'd been before what they'd come to call The Firecracker T Incident. *T* stood for *terrorist*, a word they'd pledged to neither speak nor write ever again since they were pretty sure they were now on some sort of list.

They stood at the edge of the park and looked south across Queen Street where the last of the Boxing Day sales were winding down. The cold circled, licked at their hands and faces, a reminder that movement was the best way to stay warm. The two girls wore puffy jackets that stopped at their waists. And while he appreciated what was on show beneath, Cyril thought that they must be as cold as he was. He wished he'd worn his parka, not his fall jacket.

Penelope tucked her gloved hand into the crook of Cyril's arm. "Take a back seat on this one," she said. "You don't want to get pulled in a third time."

"Isn't it just dancing?"

"On a public roadway without a permit. We'll all be very nice, but they may not regard it as entirely harmless. Also, it's protesting racism, and they will definitely not like that."

"They won't," said Randall. "That's why we'll do it right here, alongside the park. When the cops arrive, the kids can dance up across the grass and then circle back along the path. They won't stop them doing that. Not in Trinity-Bellwoods."

"You hope," said Leon. "We gotta have the lawyers on hand in case it goes wrong. This is white Toronto."

"We will," said Penelope, whose skin glowed from the exertion of her bicycle ride. Brown skin and eyes, black hair that fell in curls below her shoulders. Her scarf matched her bike in pink and white. Cyril, who'd caught himself staring, pulled his gaze away and looked at the others, pretended an interest in what was being said. It was Penelope's idea that had them excited. "And that's the point," she said. "This is where we'll get the most press. This is where what we do will get talked about on the following day. And this is where we'll get political support."

"You are right," said Randall.

"Get the kids to come in bright colours, flowing things, scarves and skirts, and bandanas for the men," said Penelope. "We'll choose a theme colour, maybe orange or yellow-gold. They should all have something with that colour. A hat maybe, or shoes, or a painted placard."

"How many people can we get out?" asked Leon.

"Lots for something like this," said Randall. "It's a real party. We'll book a hall somewhere to give them a place to celebrate afterward."

"We should connect with music and dance students at the schools," said one of the girls.

"Not too many white kids," warned Randall. "This thing is about racism."

"Racism is complicated," said Evan, who had just arrived, smiling broadly at all of them as he bent to kiss Penelope's mouth.

"You're right," said Penelope. "And this is also about inclusivity. But, yeah, we want lots and lots of dark skin out there. They are going to dance right down the middle of the road. Twirl and jive and move their arms like they're flying." She held her hands high above her head and turned her body in a series of skipping steps. When she stopped, she was breathing hard, and her smile was fierce and lovely.

"It's the best multi-culti mix on the planet," said Randall.

"What is?" she asked.

"Jamaican and Chinese. You are so hot you melt the tarmac."

Penelope laughed. The other two women rolled their eyes and sucked at their smoothies through their straws.

"I like the silent dancing," said Cyril. "It's so strange and interesting. People will want to know what the kids are listening to."

"Let them ask what's on the iPods," said Evan. "Get the passersby involved. Hand out some literature."

"We are all Canadian," said one of the girls. "That's what it should say. That's what we should call the demonstration."

"That is so weak," said Randall. "Sounds like a beer commercial."

"But it's about belonging. We want consensus, not confrontation," said Penelope. "I like it."

"Gotta agree," said Evan. "It's gentle enough that people might actually be able to hear it. Too confrontational and they dismiss you."

"You let them off way too easy," said Randall. "Nothing changes without confrontation. Racism kills. Don't forget that."

They agreed to meet again to talk about the name, the slogans, and the music choices. The song titles should have real significance. There was a lot of research to do. But lots of time. Cyril sensed that all of the men very definitely looked forward to the winter meetings. This dance wouldn't launch until the first bright days of spring.

The girls were going to window-shop the fashion stores and walked off arm in arm, Evan alongside them. A few feet on they stopped and, in unison, Evan included, bent forward and wriggled their bums to a soaring accompaniment of giggles, certain that they were being watched. They were.

Cyril said goodbye to the guys, who were headed to a rehearsal, and crossed the road that would become the stage for next spring's demonstration. He was immediately transported by an image of Penelope dancing, her legs, her arms, her wild dark hair. He skipped onto the grass, which was dry, free of snow and ice, then started to run, a sprint that would take him all the way to Christie subway station. It was a long time since he'd run in his street clothes. He only ran in running gear so as not to draw attention, cause alarm, attract the cops, frighten little old ladies – or anyone else.

He turned off the path and ran across the playing field at full tilt and into light that was suddenly brighter, spun through a gauzy mist that made him fully alert. Suddenly, beside him, running in tandem, was a thin white man with a red face, mouth puffing furiously at the air, legs a twinkle of madly pumping pink knobbly knees, fully kitted out in football shoes and knee socks, red shorts and a number seven shirt. They were so close that if one of them tripped they'd both have tumbled. Cyril could hear his grunting breaths. They raced all the way to the end of the park, where they slowed and grinned at each other in recognition – pure appreciation of the shared joy of running. Cyril didn't look back to see if his father followed. He knew he'd be gone.

Cyril ran so fast that his feet must have seemed a blur across the winter-browned grass. Cyril ran because this was his city too, ran until he felt foolish and the air was sucked from him. He slowed to a stop and ducked his head, hands on his thighs, chest heaving ragged breaths. He grinned, then laughed out loud, not caring who might be watching.

TWENTY-NINE

EDWARD WAS EXPECTING ANOTHER VISITOR. One more in the stream of people since he'd got home, so that the days began with the Business As Usual social worker at 9:00 a.m. and stayed busy all day long. Security Sam was in and out, often with another hockey funny: "Hey, Eddie, what do the Toronto Maple Leafs and the *Titanic* have in common?"

He'd roll his eyes and say, "I know you're going to tell me."

"They both look good till they hit the ice ..."

An old Chinese guy came every day with Meals on Wheels. He didn't say much, just, "How ya doin'? I'm doin' great."

The new visitor was a mystery, though. Sam thought it was pretty entertaining. He kept saying it was family, which was a really big joke because for sure Edward didn't have any of that. He was coming at 2:00 p.m. After lunch. Edward had dressed in a fresh pair of jeans and a white T-shirt. His room was clean because they had a lady come in and give it the once-over every week. She was another subsidy from the disability. He sat down to wait in his armchair across from the bed. The visitor would have to sit on the stool.

He could hear him out in the hallway. The uncertain scuffle of a stranger. The boy looked uncomfortable, hung back a bit. A skinny kid. Dark. Maybe an inch or two taller than Edward. Who looked at him like he was a ghost he'd been afraid to see.

"Hello. Good afternoon, Mr. Davina," he said from the doorway. "I'm Cyril Rowntree. I'm a university student, and I've been working on some history research that has a great deal to do with you, sir." Then he seemed to run out of things to say. He was dressed in a black parka that was a little too big for him. A good one though, thought Edward.

"I've been looking for you for a long time," said Cyril.

"Why?" Edward could smell the kid's soap and shampoo — couldn't see so good anymore, or walk very far, or dress himself without a lot of effort, but his sniffer worked well enough to impress the doctors. "Better come in," said Edward. "Now that you're here." Cyril was hesitant, stayed where he was. Edward motioned to the stool. "You've found me," he said, "job done," to help the boy feel at ease.

"I've got some things that belong to you, things I think you'll want to see." Cyril rushed the words, then remembered to deliver a smile and held out his hand along with it. Edward gave it his best squeeze, to show he had the strength.

"You're cold," said Edward. "I haven't been outside in a while. I guess it's still winter? Hot as Hades in here, though, eh?"

"Yes, sir."

"You haven't told me why you're here," said Edward. "Maybe now's as good a time as any?"

The boy lowered his bag to the floor, crouched over it, and pulled out a couple of kid's things. Handled them like they were treasures. "I think these are yours," he said.

Edward felt like his head must still be drug-fuzzy because this didn't make sense. But the kid was so sure of himself.

Cyril put them in Edward's lap. A suitcase made of blue cardboard — an old thing with scuffed corners and a tear down its side. A doll with a sailor's hat that fell from its head when Edward touched it.

"What are these?"

"I think they were yours. When you were a child." The boy was nervous.

"Why?"

"I found them in a church. A display case. The gentleman, the one who looks after the place, he's an amateur historian. He'd been given them by one of the church people."

"I'm not much for religion," said Edward. "Are you a proselytizer?"

"No, I'm not," said Cyril. "My mother was a church lady, but I never could believe in it." Cyril flushed red in the heat and removed his coat. He could be a Church of God the way he was dressed. All tidied up in a yellow cardigan and crisp, creased trousers.

"We're agreed on that then," said Edward.

"It's just a storefront church," said Cyril. "They're nice people. The man's name is Mr. Addo, that's an African name. But it was the historical context of your things that interested him. Nothing to do with religion."

Edward looked at the suitcase in his lap.

"There are some letters inside it," said Cyril. "I think they were written by your mother." He couldn't think of an easier way to say it.

Edward's mouth was open, but he didn't speak. He looked steadily at Cyril, whose face seemed honest, eyes begging for trust.

Edward nodded finally, then turned his attention to the blue case on his lap. He pulled gingerly at the leather straps and opened it. Picked up the photograph album first, turned the empty pages till he found the small snapshot of the child. Then the pretty fair-haired woman.

Cyril sat down hard on the stool, fingers fisted into his palms, thumbs scrubbing hard over his knuckles. His face was damp from the heat in the room, but, unsure of his welcome, he kept his cardigan on. Edward adjusted his glasses over his nose and looked again at the pictures. The larger photograph of Vincent Watson was tucked inside the back cover of the book. "Who are these people?"

"I think that the child is you. I mean, I'm sure it is you." Cyril stood, took the book gently from Edward's hands, and turned the pages back to the photograph of the small boy seated on a chair. "This one." He turned more pages and pointed to the two pictures with the woman. "And this is your mother. I think, though I can't be sure. But it must be."

He was earnest as all get-out, thought Edward; he watched Cyril's face as he talked. Selling it hard.

"And this big one, here at the back, that's your father. I am absolutely certain of that." He put the book back in Edward's lap.

Edward studied his old man's hands as they held the book. Flexed his fingers. Gave himself time. Think it through, he counselled himself. He was an old man. He could be confused, the same way he had been in the hospital. Be wary of scams, he told himself.

"I don't know why you think so?"

"I'm sorry. This is a lot to take in all at once," said Cyril. "But it's the letters. You should read them."

Edward fumbled at an envelope. "These are old ones," he said, touching the stamp with his forefinger. He pulled out the letter. "Nineteen-twenty-three," he read. He pushed at his glasses. "I have to take my time. It's a bit of work for me, reading."

January 1923

Maggie,

I've done what I had to do. He's gone to someone who will look after him. He'll have to work hard as he grows, but he'll be safe. I've cried for six straight days. My milk stopped coming over a week ago, so I couldn't even feed him anymore. I don't know if it was the right thing. But it was all I could do. I can't protect him with his dark skin, and he would ruin me.

Please forgive me, Maggie. God forgive me.

Davina

"You think this was my mother?"

Cyril thought he might be angry. Edward's hands were trembling, and they hadn't been when they'd first sat down.

Edward read slowly through each of the letters without further comment. The room was very quiet, just the bang and hiss of hot water running through old pipes, cycling through the radiator, and the occasional raised voice from someone passing by in the hall. Cyril took stock of the patch of counter space that served as a kitchen. Of the microwave and array of pill bottles alongside a box of tea bags, a jar of instant coffee. The simple treats he'd brought as gifts, chocolate-covered cookies and mixed nuts, seemed luxurious.

After a long while, Edward put the last letter back into its envelope and dropped it into the suitcase. "They say I'm buried in a pauper's grave!"

He opened the photo album again and looked, long, at each of the photographs. The kid was telling the truth, he told himself. Images raced through his mind and collected there like piled pebbles. The Black lady and her husband in that boarding house so long ago, when he was still a kid. The tiny picture of a mother and a father inside Harry's locket, the only jewellery Edward had ever owned, now hidden at the back of a drawer. Then Mrs. Marvel, with the children about her on a Sunday afternoon when they'd all laughed for more than an hour as her granddaughter, dressed in a tissue tutu, had danced her very best for them. They'd shared her joy. How often had that come? There was no joy in the photographs or in the letters the boy had brought him. But this was who he was. He had a mother and a father. He'd never belonged to them, but they are who he is. How he was made. And they'd given him up.

Edward felt the familiar balled fist behind his ribs, below his diaphragm, the anger that made his breathing shallow. It was the same he'd had all his life, but now his life was almost lived through. And she, that woman with the fawn-coloured hair — and somehow he was sure of the colour and the smooth feel of it — she'd had pain, she'd felt it for him. For a short time. And he didn't care what had happened to her after that. Or to him, the smirking man he held in his hand.

The heat in his chest swarmed to his face, sending a prickle of sweat across his forehead. He was dizzy in his chair, his heart racing. But he would not scare the boy who was so earnest and so clearly needed something from him. He must not die now. Edward did his deep breaths, the way he'd learned in the hospital. He looked at the damned white face of the fawn-haired woman whose whining words filled those awful letters and at the arrogant smirk of that damned black-faced man whose eyes shone with miserable pride that counted for nothing when you had left your baby with a stranger.

Cyril watched as Edward looked again at the photograph of the little boy. Himself. He closed the book and put it back in the case. He didn't look at the doilies or the records book. His fingers fumbled with the small buckles of the suitcase as he put the leather straps back in place.

"Can I keep this?"

"It's for you."

Edward put the suitcase down on the floor beside his chair. He picked up the sailor doll and fitted its hat back to its head. Pressed it in place with his fingers. He studied its face. They sat quietly for another few minutes. Then Edward spoke into the silence. "I don't need much. So long as the security looks in on me once in a while. Truth be told, with that Meals on Wheels, I'm better off than I was before."

"Okay," Cyril said.

"Why did you look for me?"

"I've been trying to think of an answer because I knew you'd ask." Cyril looked down at his knees. "I think I have it now."

"Well?"

"I came to Canada because everyone thought that was the best thing for me to do, after my mom died." He rushed to add, "Back home in Jamaica." He drew a deep breath. "There are crocheted doilies with your suitcase, they're in there now, for you. They made me look, because my mother used to make them. And then when I saw the picture of your ..." He stopped suddenly. "Sorry. I'm not telling it very well."

"You're doing okay," said Edward. "What were you going to say? My what?"

"Your father," Cyril said, almost apologetic.

"Yes?"

"My father is white. Yours was Black. I wondered where he'd come from and why he came here."

"And did you. Find out?"

"To go to the University of Toronto. He was a law student."

"You are sure of that?"

"Yes. That wasn't in the display case, though. I have more things to show you if you want to see them."

But Edward was clearly overwhelmed, and Cyril knew it was time to pull back. To give Edward space and time.

After a while, Edward said, "Why would this African man put these things on display?" He was thoroughly bewildered; the images of the two people the kid called his parents were swimming around in his head. He couldn't piece it together, could not make sense of the story.

"He just likes to do that sort of thing," said Cyril. "It's to start conversations about compassion and justice, to get people thinking. But they don't pay much attention. He gets really frustrated. When my friend Pat took me to see them — you would have liked her — and I said I was interested, he invited me to read the letters."

Edward patted the sailor doll. "You've got a much longer story to tell than that," Edward said. "I believe that the letters are about me. But the rest of it? The photographs and the children's things. What makes you so sure of those? You're a good kid, I can see that. But I'm not convinced."

"I guess I thought that you were so interesting because you'd been through what I was going through." Cyril stopped for a moment then plunged on, encouraged by Edward's nod. "My father left me too. I loved my mother, she was always there, but then she died, and I was on my own. When I got here, to Canada,

I had to make my own way. As a mixed-race man. Like you. And you'd already been through it."

"They used to call us mulatto," said Edward quietly.

"Because you were alone like me," said Cyril. "Only it was so much harder for you."

"Was it?"

"Yeah, for sure. I mean, I've got an okay place to live and two jobs. And when I finish school, I'll have a chance at a real career. Oh, and the best thing is I've got a half-brother and sister at home in Jamaica."

"That's good, then."

"But you had to fight for it all. And now I can see that I have to fight for it too."

"I didn't do any fighting," said Edward. "Not that kind, anyway. Why do you think that?"

"Being sent out to work when you were just a little boy. The protests that you did. Like when you broke that window with those other guys. After that demonstration on Spadina Avenue?"

"What a thing ... you know that too."

"Going to Halifax. Fighting in the war, in the navy. Which amazed me because I didn't think you'd know anything about ships."

"Couldn't swim," said Edward and lifted his hand to stroke the top of his head. "Still can't. But lots of the fellas were the same. It was the war. Your old life went on hold, you Back-Burnered it and did what they told you."

"Like being a sleeping car porter, right? You did what you had to do?"

"I didn't do my life that well," Edward said. "I messed up a lot of it." He put the sailor doll down on the bed beside him. "You know a lot. You're right. I was in the navy. I was a porter. There's a lot more though. What else do you know?"

"Not much," said Cyril. "You were injured in the war."

"That's true. I lost my mind that time. For a while. Maybe it's gone again now ..."

"I really want to thank you for talking to me," said Cyril. "Because I've been ... I've been thinking about you for a long time. You didn't know anything about me. You could have just told me to go away."

"Oh no," said Edward. "You're a fascination, that's for sure. Astonishing." He pulled himself out of his seat and made his way to the kettle, fingers knuckling for balance along the back of the chair, the corner of the bed, the kitchen cupboard. "I'll make us some coffee. Where's those cookies you bought me?"

Cyril stopped an impulse to help. Waited while the little kettle boiled. Over the dresser was a small framed black-and-white picture of four young people standing in front of a church. Two couples. He thought that the man on the right might be Edward. A calendar picture of flowers hung beside the microwave. There were some boxes on top of the wardrobe, a pile of clothes on a wheelchair in the corner, a cane. A shopping bag.

"You think I'm a hero," said Edward. "I do that myself — believe that ordinary people do amazing things. Like you. You're quite a young man."

"I'm trying to figure out how to make things work."

"You will. But don't romanticize me. You'll be better off." Edward put a small plate of Cyril's cookies on the corner of the bed. Cyril circled around him to fetch the coffee mugs. They sat down again.

"Sorry about the heat," said Edward. "I can't open the window. Management rules." They both looked up to the little framed piece of sky at the top of the wall.

Edward bit into his cookie, chewed slowly through the whole thing. "What more do you know?"

"Nothing much really. I thought you were probably on the trains for a long time, but then I found out that you were let go. I hoped that you got married. I really didn't know if you'd still be here. I mean, I know how old you are." Cyril trailed off, embarrassed by his suggestion that Edward might have been dead.

"I nearly wasn't here. Could have gone any time in that ICU."

"Do you mind telling me more, sir? About your life?"

"I think you'd better call me Eddie like everyone else does." He chuckled. "Sir makes me feel old." He stopped smiling then. "Okay, I'll tell you. I did lots of things after the George Pullman rail. Logging, machine maintenance, short-order cook, national parks. And a few stretches inside."

"Inside prison? When you were a kid? I knew about that."

"You do? Well, there was a lot more than the one. So that's what I mean about not romanticizing me. You should know."

"I never thought to look there."

"I guess you'd have found me in a few of our finer institutions. Provincial. I never did federal time. I've got some anger in me that most people don't know about." He shook his head. "See, and now I'm telling you. My heart attack must have made me soft." He looked across at Cyril, who saw his frailty. "I'm sorry," said Edward. "You don't need to hear about that."

The skin on Edward's big hands was thin, bruised in parts, blue veins standing out from the brown. He really did have a sloped forehead; his face was all angles. Kind eyes. His hair was old man's silver fuzz.

"I don't mind," said Cyril. "I want to know about you."

When Edward looked at Cyril, he saw a decent-looking boy who wouldn't have made it in the places he'd been. But he'd never need to, a well-spoken kid like him. He liked the honesty in his eyes. He was quiet, might even be a little shy. But he wasn't afraid to hear about an old man's anger, and that was impressive.

"I never hurt anyone who wasn't a scrapper like me. Just broke up a few places here and there in the process. Nothing more sacred than private property. That's what put me inside."

"What's it like?"

"Prison? Life away from life. It's easy enough if you keep your nose out of other people's business. Stay out of other men's rackets."

Security Sam appeared at the door, pushed it open to put his head in. "You okay here, Eddie? I told you it was family." He was looking at the sailor doll in Edward's lap.

"Family," said Edward and smiled. "Could be something like that I guess."

"Okay. Don't let him cause any trouble," said Sam to Cyril.

When he'd gone, Edward said, "He looks after me, does Sam."

"What do they say about your health now? Will you be okay?"

"I'm on the Wait And See. I'll live, though. For now."

"Oh."

"What about you? You spent all that time looking for me? You're a kid, you should be hanging out with friends. Chasing girls. If girls are your thing – I'm easy. Whoever you like."

"I have some friends, just spend a lot of time alone, I guess. I haven't been in Canada very long."

"Oh? That's an interesting thing. Where did you say you were from?"

"Jamaica."

"I knew some fellows from there. Good people."

"You never went?"

"The only travelling I did was across this country, and I did lots of that. Except when I was in the navy. And that was no holiday."

"Me neither. I've never been anywhere else." Cyril wanted to tell Edward that his father was from Jamaica. That he, Edward, was half-Jamaican. But it would have to wait. Edward had heard enough for now.

Silence drifted back. After some time, Edward said, "I could never have read those letters if my fiancée hadn't taught me how to read. I was in my twenties already. She made me go over and over the alphabet, spell out all those kid's words. Dee Oh Gee, Dog, Cat, Hat. It was the best time in my life."

"You were married?"

"No. We never made it that far." He pointed to the framed photograph. "That's her, standing next to me. Her name is Celia."

Cyril stood and bent to look at the photograph. Her face was tiny in the frame, a little faded. "She's beautiful," he said. "And you, this is you? You were a handsome man."

"Celia," said Edward, and started to sing, "I gave you all my love, and you only gave me the blues." His voice was old and thin, but the words were clear. "Never trust a woman," he said.

"What happened?"

"She went to find a better man than me. I couldn't blame her. She knew what she needed. I was never so clear on life's purpose."

"I'm sorry," said Cyril, then after a moment, "Where did she go?"

"I never heard."

The way they sat together, in intimate silence, was exactly as Cyril had imagined it might be. Though a small part of him worried that Edward could still decide that what Cyril had done in searching him out was unwanted.

"I get these visions," Cyril said, "of people and places. Events. It's called second sight. My mother had it. Sometimes I think I might be a little crazy. I'm not, though," he hurried to reassure. "Really."

"Crazy is lots of things," said Edward. "And lots of people. Nothing to be ashamed of, even if you are. What do you see in your visions?"

"I saw you in the hospital."

"Did you?"

"And in other places. You came into my room once, but you were just a kid. The first time I saw you."

"Astonishing."

"I've never told anyone here in Canada that," said Cyril. "About my visions I mean."

"We've all got something in us that's askew," said Edward. "Good and bad. I can read people pretty well. You're fine. What you have is probably a gift."

"That's what my mother used to say."

The sky from the little window was almost lost to night, and the room had grown dark. The only light came from the hallway; the door wasn't quite closed.

"What about your father?" said Edward. "You say your mother died, but what happened to your dad?"

"He left us when I was two."

"Have you looked for him?"

"No."

"Why not?"

"I hate him."

"Oh, that's a hard word. Hate. There's probably things you don't know."

"He's in England, I think. That's where he was from."

"Keep a little bit of yourself open for him, maybe? I met lots of guys who loved their families very much, just didn't know how to do their lives in ways that showed it."

The faucet over the sink dripped. Louder, somehow, now that the room was in shadows.

"I've just thought of something," said Cyril, suddenly struck with inspiration. "I could look for Celia for you. I know how to do it now, how to search. Would you like me to try?"

The mug of coffee in Edward's hand jiggled, and he spilled a little on his knee. "Damn," he said and patted his hand about for something to wipe it with, picked up a corner of the throw rug beside him and dabbed at the spill. When he spoke again, Cyril could hear a small, tight ring of fear in his voice.

"I don't want that. I have her in my head. In my heart. She's been there for a very long time. I've made up a nice life for her. That's good enough for me."

"Sorry."

"Don't be."

They finished their coffees in silence. Eventually, Cyril stood up, took the mug from Edward's hand, and put both mugs back on the counter.

"So I had a mother and a father, what a thing!" Edward's eyes were wet, but it was too dark for Cyril to see that. "My mother loved me. Think of that? Maybe my father did too. But both of them left me anyhow."

"Like mine left me," said Cyril.

"I guess we do have a couple of things in common." Edward smiled.

"I wonder ..." said Cyril, then stopped.

"Tell me."

"Mr. Addo. He gave me a camera. Would it be all right if I took your picture? Not if you don't want to."

Edward pushed himself to an awkward stand and looked toward the door. "I don't know."

"You don't have to."

"Well. That's okay," he decided. "I'm so old, and that's not going to change." Edward chuckled. "Is he going to put it in his display case?"

"Yes."

Edward's smile dissolved. He shook his head. "I don't understand why he would do that."

"You really are important to him. He wants me to take a few, and he'll make a big print of the best photograph. Then he wants you to come and see it."

Makes no sense, thought Edward. "We'll have to turn the light on," he said as he sat back down in his chair and smoothed his clothes. "I used to have a camera. I don't know much about those new ones."

Edward sat under the light in his chair at the foot of the bed. He brushed his palm slowly across the top of his head and turned his face just a little to the right. Tilted his chin up.

"Have you got all of me in," asked Edward, "top of my head and my shoulders?"

"Yes."

"Go on then."

Edward's forehead really did slope. His hair was mostly gone, but he still looked defiant.

Cyril took ten pictures.

ACKNOWLEDGEMENTS

Nearly ten years ago, when I wrote the first draft of this novel, a central theme was that nothing changes. Canadian Black activists have always been extraordinarily brave and determined, but the events and activism of recent years really do seem to be changing the system. I am deeply indebted to the writers, historians, artists, and others, who have searched out and reclaimed Canadian Black histories. Some of that history is included in this book. Enormous thanks to Karen Mulhallen who introduced this book to my editor Marc Côté; I am so grateful to Marc for his belief in it. More thanks to Diaspora Dialogues and my terrific mentor, Cynthia Holz. Lesley Krueger, Susan Mockler, Katherine Bruce and the late Martin Mordecai were valued readers. Janice Zawerbny encouraged a rewrite that made an essential difference. Jim Van Waggoner has been my second set of eyes. Much gratitude to my two young Jamaican friends, Daren Johnson, who is now in the US, and Kimoney Gabbidon, now in Canada. Their struggles and triumphs helped to shape my character, Cyril. Thank you to my copy editor, Andrea Waters, for her skilled attention, and to Sarah Cooper at Cormorant Books. The support of the Toronto Arts Council, the Canada Council for the Arts and the Ontario Arts Council is very much appreciated. Early stages of the manuscript were reviewed and generously discussed by our Maitland Street writers' group: Anthony De Sa, the late Bernie Grzyb, James Papoutsis, Rekha Lakra, Susan Mockler and Susan Shuter. My parents' courage to marry in 1950s England humbles me. I will always miss Michael Mitchell, who loved good writing.

PERMISSIONS

Lines from the poem "I Fight Back" [page 237] are taken from the collection *Make the World New: The Poetry of Lillian Allen*, by Lillian Allen, selected and introduced by Ronald Cummings, published by Wilfrid Laurier University Press, 2021. Copyright 2021 © Lillian Allen. Used with the permission of the publisher.

[pages 137-138] Angus, Ian. "The Toronto Anti-Fascist Strike, 1933. A Hidden Chapter in Labour History." *Socialist History Project*. www.socialisthistory.ca/Essays/Angus/TorontoStrike_33.htm.

[pages 176] Garvey, Amy Jacques, ed. *The Philosophy and Opinions of Marcus Garvey: Africa for the Africans*. Centennial Edition. Baltimore: The Majority Press, 1986. Print.

[pages 151-152] Greyson, Linda M., and Michael Bliss. *The Wretched of Canada, Letters to R. B. Bennett, 1930–1935*. Toronto and Buffalo: University of Toronto Press, 1971.

[page 18] Shelley, Percy Bysshe. *The Complete Poems of Percy Bysshe Shelley*. New York: Random House, Inc., 1994.

We acknowledge the sacred land on which Cormorant Books operates. It has been a site of human activity for 15,000 years. This land is the territory of the Huron-Wendat and Petun First Nations, the Seneca, and most recently, the Mississaugas of the Credit River. The territory was the subject of the Dish With One Spoon Wampum Belt Covenant, an agreement between the Iroquois Confederacy and Confederacy of the Anishinaabe and allied nations to peaceably share and steward the resources around the Great Lakes. Today, the meeting place of Toronto is still home to many Indigenous people from across Turtle Island. We are grateful to have the opportunity to work in the community, on this territory.

We are also mindful of broken covenants and the need to strive to make right with all our relations.